Doubleback
The Hunt

G S Lester

G S Lester currently resides in Perth, Western Australia and was born in Wakefield, a Cathedral City in West Yorkshire, England. Doubleback, The Hunt is the sequel to Doubleback which was released on 15-04-2021.

G S Lester has a several projects on the go, watch this space.

If you would like to order Doubleback from Amazon,
Paperback: ISBN 978-16641-0199-9

A quick thanks to everyone that has helped me with this book ☺

Chapter 1

A gagging sound emanated from his mouth, caused by the gun barrel. Saliva started to fill it, to the point that a slight dribble ran down the right side of his lip.

This had not gone to plan. After all, the man holding the gun in his mouth was supposedly The Prey, not The Predator.

"Can we talk for a moment?" the man with the gun in his mouth tried to say. He had to accept that he didn't sound like he should, because of the gun barrel impeding his tongue and lip movement. The barrel was now starting to warm up as his body heat was beginning to transfer to the gun. Second, by second, he prayed that the finger on the trigger stayed still. After all, he didn't want a bullet through his head today!

The taste of the barrel was not what he expected! It had a slightly salty, metallic taste which he imagined contained all sorts of chemicals, with unknown tangs to add to that elaborate flavour.

1

The Predator thought, *mmmm what's that?* That subdued mystery taste came to him like a light bulb coming on – the taste was fear itself. The question is, who in general knows what a used gun barrel tastes of? Maybe it tastes like apples, bananas... or even chicken?

Focus, focus, The Predator thought, as the situation was starting to take its toll on the man in question's nerves.

"Can we talk for a moment?" The Predator asked again with a mumble as the gun barrel slowly started to move out of his mouth. Now he was looking down the barrel of the Glock17 Gen 7.

Is this a better situation or not? he thought. *Well, I may have a chance of dodging the bullet, as it would only be travelling at 2,735 kph. Yes, I should be able to move out of the way of that, even though it will leave the barrel of the gun before I hear it fire. Stop it, brain! You need to think of a way out of this,* The Predator thought.

"What do you want to talk about, you piece of shit?" was the response he got from the man holding the gun. He then pushed his black-framed glasses up the bridge of his nose. The Predator knew some facts about the man holding the gun. Originally, he was sent back to take the man to the future for body parts, but for some reason, it all seemed to have gone wrong somewhere along the line. Now he sat in a chair in a dim, musty-smelling room, tied up with his own gun pointing at him.

A 27-year-old man called Barry was holding the gun, with an excuse for something called a moustache and a beard that looked like some kind of patchy fungus on his face. *Mmm, the slight distance of the gun from his face seems to be suggesting that things are getting slightly better*, The Predator thought.

"Well, you didn't want to talk earlier on when you were creeping around, did you? Yeh, why do you have a bloody gun on you? And why's it so light? I've used guns like these before, you know; I'm not a bloody idiot. Anyway, what's it made of? Tell me!" Barry articulated as he shuffled from foot to foot.

The Predator noticed, from his lower position in the chair that small droplets of saliva were flying out of Barry's mouth as he spoke... and they started landing on his face. A thought went through his head – *Oh god, I hope he doesn't have any funny diseases? He's probably got all sorts of ailments... I'll have to get a jab when I get back home?*

Then Barry shook the gun. *Oh, Shit!*

This is a much more scary situation now... I hope his finger is away from that trigger. I need to get out of this situation... His brain started to ramp up, as an exit strategy was in order. Glancing around the room, it was full of some storage racking, a cool room maybe. Then he noticed his backpack next to the exit.

"May I call you Barry?" The Predator asked in a calm voice.

"How the hell do you know my name?" he responded as a vacant look crossed Barry's face.

"A guess, maybe? You know what, Barry, this isn't the first time I've had a gun aimed at me today! To be honest, it's not been a good day at all. But you have a point and I will try to re-think my approach for next time!" The response came from The Predator, as he then spat something out that tasted downright nasty. Probably something that had been left in his mouth from the gun.

The Predator tried to remember if his gun had been anywhere dubious recently. *Mmmmm there was that time when I was in that pig farm... it did get dropped there... but it did get cleaned after. Oh shit... it's got brains on it, from when I shot someone point-blank from behind!* The Predator remembered as a queasy sensation went through his stomach. Then an amount of his concentration had to be used to stop him from throwing up.

"What the hell! You mucky sod... Stop bloody spitting, it's bad manners!" Barry responded.

Then, all of a sudden, the gun left Barry's hand as The Predator's foot kicked it. The gun twisted as it made its way up in the air with its previous holder watching in disbelief, mouth slightly open in awe at what had just happened. Then, realisation dawned that his advantage had now gone, along with the gun. It bounced off the grubby white ceiling to then be claimed by gravity as it started to make its way back to Mother Earth and, consequently, the floor. Both men watched this event unfold as they tried to predict the trajectory of the bounce and where it would end up.

Barry started to move over to where he thought it would land, but he was barged out of the way by The Predator who was now mobile but still partly attached to the dark old oak chair. As they both went to the floor at different places in the room, the chair smashed apart, and the captive man was now partially free. The Predator kicked the gun to give himself time. He started to free himself of the restraints as well as parts of the chair he was still attached to.

Both men scrambled to overpower each other as they individually grabbed for the gun lying on the floor. They pulled at each other's hands and arms, and – for whoever won – there would then be the issue of pointing it and pulling the trigger. They took different approaches as Barry swung his leg around and kicked the gun out of reach of both of them once again – it scuttled across the dirty grey tiled floor and out of sight.

Barry made a move and got free of the now unhindered Predator as he scrambled on all fours, then to his feet. The Predator did the same as he got to his feet, and then they both briefly stopped, staring at each other with their fists raised. It was as if they were in some badly made movie, each anticipating who was going to pounce first. There was fake ducking and diving, dodging and weaving, each trying to entice the other to make a move.

And then it happened. Barry lunged with a swift left to the face of The Predator. Then he stepped back to take a moment as a stinging shock went to his brain. He was not expecting that. Then The Predator launched a barrage of blows himself, as he lurched forwards, a left, right and left to Barry's face and one upper-body shot. Barry went down, winded and gasping for air after that last shot. Barry kicked the Predator's legs from under him, and both men fell back to the tiled floor. Scrambling on the ground, The Predator got on top of Barry; he now had the chance to get the upper hand by applying the pressure to win this fight. Barry lay on his back with his arms up, protecting himself so he didn't get knocked out. He then brought his leg up and around The Predator's torso to pull him off balance so he could get the upper hand on him. Barry then manipulated his body and started to apply a chokehold on The Predator's neck, squeezing as hard as he could to take the life from this man that had come to kill him. But Barry's arm was being slowly overpowered by the Predator as his grip was starting to give way from around The Predator's neck. And then he had no grip at all as The Predator was now free.

A punch to the face dazed Barry momentarily; he then saw the gun in his peripheral vision. The Predator started getting up and briefly stopped as he took in a deep breath to replace the lack of oxygen from the chokehold. Barry raced to get to the weapon, then picked it up as The Predator decided that it was time to exit this room and this situation. The Predator ran towards Barry and shunted him off balance to give himself a few more seconds and distance. He grabbed his backpack then the green wooden door frame exploded. The bullet, fired from his gun in anger, hit it.

This job is shit... I'm not getting paid enough, The Predator thought as he dodged around the corner, exiting the room and into a corridor. The white walls seemed to glow as they reflected the light to help The Predator on his way. The grey grimy tiles on the floor did not help him gain traction to get away, as his footwear slid on the tiles. He pushed on through as one stride after another gave slightly more traction and his speed increased, giving him the distance that he wanted from Barry.

Another shot whistled past him and hit the clear plastic doorway curtains which shimmered as the bullet pierced them, then went out the other side. The Predator pushed the curtains apart by using his backpack and they closed behind him. He slid one arm through the strap of his backpack, then the other, which would make it easier to run. Another shot, except this time the curtain deadened the impact of the bullet, taking the power out of it. Then gravity pulled it to the tiled floor and he heard the metallic sound of the bullet bouncing along in front of him. Another set of curtains approached, and The Predator negotiated them by parting them with his hands. His heart rate was heading to its maximum as adrenalin pumped around his body to help him get out of this situation and, with a bit of luck, keep him alive.

"I'll kill you; do you hear me, you cocksucker!" The voice came booming from Barry who was now running as fast as he could. The Predator could hear Barry going through the first set of curtains as he estimated how far behind him he would be.

The fear was now starting to lessen in The Predator's consciousness, as he knew he could get out of this situation.

Barry's only mission was to try to catch and kill this prick of a man that had come to mess with him. Yes, kill him! What had he ever done to deserve this? To be hunted down like an animal and put down! And why did he want to do that anyway? Barry's thoughts raced as anger and adrenalin pumped through his body.

The Predator now approached a set of red doors with a fire exit sign on them. He pushed the steel emergency bar on the right-hand door, using his weight and momentum to help him. With one movement the door swung open. It hit the outside wall then rebounded back with as much force as he had put into opening it. The Predator braced himself for impact as it hit his hands. The door briefly slowed him down but he pushed it out of the way again.

Exiting the building, the burning light of the sun hit his eyes and he briefly squinted until they adjusted to the new lighting conditions. The Predator then had his first bit of luck today, as he spied something that made his head turn slightly. He sprinted as hard as he could for his escape.

Making his way across the concrete car park which had clumps of grass and weeds growing out of the cracks. Then the sound of the emergency doors being flung open pierced his ears. The Predator was now waiting for a volley of shots from the gun that Barry had. He started praying that one of the bullets didn't hit him... which would be embarrassing. Being killed by his own gun that had been shot by a man that had outwitted him... called Barry!

As The Predator neared his destination, he stopped, took a deep breath in to calm himself down, then climbed on a dark blue and green Harley Davidson Street Bob. Inserting the key and praying that it was the right one, he turned it. The lights came on and joy filled his stomach and a brief smile crossed his face. Pulling the clutch, he then kicked the stand up and pressed the start button. The engine growled into life as fire spat out of the shortened exhaust. The noise and vibration shook the nearby windows like thunder on a stormy night.

Barry veered in a slightly different direction as he headed towards his Ford Focus ST. *No, I don't need to shoot this prick, I'll just run him over*, Barry thought then chuckled to himself. The thought of running him over repeatedly went through his mind. The key fob was pressed, and the doors unlocked as commanded. Pulling the colour-coded red handles to open the door, he jumped into the front seat, pressed the start button and the turbo-charged engine sprang into life. Then, waiting for the command from the driver's right foot, Barry thrust the red gear lever into first gear, lifted the clutch and pushed the accelerator down to its maximum. The persecuted tyres let out an ear-piercing noise as they span before finally warming up. The Focus lurched onto the road in pursuit of the bike.

The Street Bob was also being pushed to its limit as V twin began to produce all the power it could, out of necessity rather than desire. The rear suspension sat down with the power being passed through it, as it gripped the surface of the road. The Predator knew he had the acceleration with the bike, but not the cornering; as the car had that advantage, probably with top-end speed. He twisted the sponge-covered twist grip as he accelerated down the street. The wind and acceleration pushed him back, as he raced down the street. He glanced at derelict industrial buildings on both sides, with graffiti on some of them. The buildings had smashed windows, grit, and grime, and a general look of vacantness to them all.

Looking in the mirror, The Predator could see that his pursuer was on his ass – and to add to that, he had the gun!

A right corner approached, and he quickly applied the front and back brakes as he downshifted to use every type of braking that he could, but the weight of the bike doomed his stopping ability – it didn't slow down as he expected and he took the corner wide. That was not good, as the red car was slightly nearer to him now. It would probably take the corner easier than he could on the bike. Once again twisting the accelerator to pick the speed up, as the power went down to the road, the back end of the bike briefly twitched. The Predator could see a red dot of the Focus catching him in the mirror. The little sticker on it saying that *the object in the mirror may be closer than it appears*, did not help this situation; as he wanted distance from the Focus, not to be informed that it was closer than he wanted it.

A left turn now loomed and The Predator braked and shifted down slightly earlier to avoid overshooting the bend again. This time, he decided to trail-brake through this corner, and he kept the front brakes slightly on. This had the effect of shortening the bike's wheelbase, which promoted a tighter turning bike. *Much better*, The Predator thought as he passed the apex, then slowly opened the throttle to request the engine to pull him out of the corner. At the same time, the bike then wanted to sit up.

"Oh, bollocks!" The Predator exclaimed, as he noticed that the surface was going to change from tarmac to cobbled streets on the next bend; of all places, on a corner! Slightly easing off the gas and applying the brakes, he hit the smooth cobbles and, as expected, they jolted his bones to the core. *Bikes and cobbles don't mix*, he thought. He tried to decrease his speed but, as he had anticipated, the front tyre was not going to play ball. Down he went as the bike slid away from him, briefly trapping his leg, and then they separated company. He looked back, the best he could, to see where the red car was, whilst The Predator tried to slow himself down. At the same time as he uncontrollably rolled, the pain of the cobbled street started impacting on him. Finally, he came to a stop, glancing down at his battered, blood-covered body. He mustered his strength, then pushed himself to get to his feet as best he could.

The Predator then made his way to the left-hand side of the street. He glanced at the Harley Davidson that had spun on the cobbles, leaving a trail of oil and parts, which finally crashed into the kerb. An uneven throbbing came from the bike, then silence. Standing in the street, motionless, he was like a rabbit in the headlights of the Red Ford Focus as it ploughed toward him.

"I've got you now!" Barry muttered under his breath as he focused on the man – and only the man – that was in front of him. Barry wanted blood and he was going to get it.

"Twenty meters... fifteen... twelve... ten..." The Predator murmured, holding his nerve as long as he could. His fear was at a hundred and fifteen per cent, and then he quickly moved to his left; where now stood revealing the edge of a stone wall. The Focus hit it and curled around the wall almost in admiration of its strength. The crumple zones of the vehicle started to do their work. The crafted ridged shapes of the steel had to submit to the stone wall. The noise of all this energy being dissipated filled the air as the airbags fired, then the noise abated as hot liquids escaped to freedom.

No shooting, no movement, only gurgling noises from the car, which is what The Predator was hoping for. He sluggishly hobbled over to check on Barry, who was unconscious. He took his backpack off, placed it on the road, then opened it. Inside, there was a torch, some rounds for the Glock and the Transphone. He briefly looked at the piece of equipment in awe at how sturdily it was built. He hoped it still worked. He then took out a syringe gun. Then he fastened the backpack, picked it up and put it on.

He briefly looked around to see if anyone was watching. *Good, no busybodies taking photos.* He opened the battered passenger door, which creaked and groaned as a result of the impact. He slowly climbing into the car, then sat down next to Barry. Groans started to come from Barry, and The Predator injected him with a sedative from the syringe gun, to keep him under.

Light was streaming in through the car windows. The Predator glanced at his gun on the driver's side floor. He leaned down to pick it up and then quickly checked to see how many rounds were left; then he put it in a side pocket of his backpack. The Predator had all the time in the world now, and he was the current alpha male in this situation.

Setting the Transphone year to 2098, he took a slow, meticulous look around. One or two people were starting to appear on the streets now. Then, looking at Barry, he took a slow deep breath in and out. He grabbed Barry's arm and pressed the button on the Transphone. There was a humming noise started, then blackness enveloped them both as they were taken from August 2021 to the year 2098.

Twelve hours earlier.

Curly brown hair, 183cm tall, brown eyes with a brown mole above his right eye, slim but muscular. Mason Jones yawned and then smiled to himself as he felt the white silk sheets around his body. The regular sound of ticking from the clock to the left of him on the bedside table broke the silence. He tried to focus his tired eye on the light grey ceiling then took in a deep breath of the scrubbed air in the room. *Hmm, something smells different*, Mason thought, as he then looked to his left. The love of his life was lying there looking back at him – big brown sexy eyes and a wet nose... Barker, his golden retriever dog.

He smiled and then looked past Barker and noticed a female that he must have pulled last night, or did she pull him? All of a sudden, there was movement from her as she slowly sat up, stretched, and moved her head around as if to exercise it. She slowly climbed over Barker, then briefly stopped and smiled at Mason as her hair dropped onto his face. She then slowly put one foot and then the other on the floor.

"Touchdown!" she announced in a soft voice. She then turned, slowly made her way to the door and exited the room. Mason was wondering who she was as he watched a slight wiggle from her bare peach. Mason once again tried to make his eyes work properly, slightly squinting his eyes past Barker. In the space that the female had left... *Oh, a man!* Mason must have pulled him last night too – or maybe he came with the female? Or did the female come with him? It was all too confusing... *God, what a night that was...* He could not remember any of it at all. *It must have been a good one.*

He forced his sluggish brain to think. Yes, he did remember bits of the night. He had left his flat at around 10.00 PM, then went to the club. *Yes, that was it.* He then hit on some secretary with curly red hair, but the guy was not interested at all. *Oh well, his loss*, Mason thought to himself as he briefly touched his dick to assure it that everything was good.

Mason then vaguely remembered having a quick snog with a different secretary with blonde hair and a red leather skirt from some law firm. *Wow, what piercing eyes she had.* He remembered that one was brown and the other orange. Clearly contact lenses... or maybe tattooed. Mason was wishing she was in bed with him now rather than this random guy snoring at the far side of his king-size waterbed. *Had they had sex last night?* he pondered, once again briefly touching his dick, to again reassure it that it would get some attention at some point.

Mason lay there trying to think about what had happened. *God, my head is all blurry.* Had he been drugged or something? No, he had just drunk too much and partied too hard as he always did. He remembered being in the pink alligator club and getting a drink bought for him, but after that, he had no idea how he got home or what happened after that. *Maybe I was drugged after all and had to go through some debauched sex acts... with a bit of luck*, he thought as he smirked to himself.

Then a noise came through his bedroom doorway, presumably from the female that had got out of the bed earlier on. Who was that woman? Was she a legal secretary, CEO, or a hooker? Maybe the guy was the hooker and she had paid him. They must have been having some convention last night, as all he seemed to meet was lots of legal secretaries. He thought she had been there – maybe not? Anyway, her face did seem slightly familiar to him!

"Morning how's it going?" That was what he hoped the legal secretary would say as she walked in now covered by a light blue shirt with only three out of the five buttons fastened up. She promptly climbed onto the bed and over Mason and Barker, and then she took the position in between Barker and this random guy. Mason manoeuvred himself around so that he leant onto his right wrist to prop his head up.

"So, can you remember what happened last night?" Mason asked with a slight bit of anticipation in his voice – he had no idea what the answer was going to be.

"Can't you remember? Oh man, you must have been out of it!" the female responded as she looked at him, smiled, blinked and slightly tilted her head to one side. Why she did this Mason had no idea, but it looked so hot!

"Well, you and Claude got it on, and I watched... That's about what happened. Why?"

"Oh, no reason. I was just curious that's all. I can't remember... I was so wasted," Mason responded and looked away with a slight bit of shame at his response.

"So you just watched, as me and Claude got it on? Is this Claude by any chance? Did you join in at all?" Mason inquired as he tried to picture what may have happened last night.

"Well yes; when you and Claude had finished, me and Claude got it on. You watched us instead of joining in from the edge of the bed and then you were dancing on your own. Oh no, that was earlier, thinking about it. Errrr, I think you fell asleep," she responded, slightly sniggering at the thought and then smiled at Mason intensely.

"Okay, okay, do you want a cup of tea... coffee... juice?" he asked. He started getting out of bed, then put his feet on the cold white floor and briefly flinched at its temperature. *It should be warm... I bet the goddam heating is broke again.* Then while grabbing his dark royal blue dressing gown from behind the door, he stopped and briefly looked at the female lying on the bed looking at him, stroking Barker with Claude lying next to her.

"Ooh, yes please, coffee and toast," was the response that Mason got as this un-named female started snuggling into Barker and the bed again. *Why oh why didn't I nail her last night?* Mason pondered to himself. That was so unlike him; he was a man stud – or a man slag – whichever way you want to look at it. Men wanted to be him and females wanted him. He sniggered – *what a dickhead of a narcissist I am!*

"Okay," he acknowledged. As he made his way from the bedroom through a doorway to his left and into the open plan kitchen-come-living area. He

12

grabbed two mugs from the upper cupboards; one said Oliver on it, the other was just a blue-coloured one. He put the coffee in both cups, then milk and of course the sweeteners, and finally the water. The toast popped up out of the chrome toaster with the butter already on it. Mason put the four slices on a plate, then a whisper from behind.

"Me and you never got it on last night, I think Claude's still sleeping, you know!" came from his right side. Mason spun around ever so slowly and smiled. Who he thought was the legal secretary was now standing in front of him with only a shirt on. She slowly moved forward as she kissed him, then stopped. She pulled away slowly as she sucked on his bottom lip then let it go as it flopped back into position.

"Errrr, I think I need to go to the toilet... I have a small bladder, you know!" the legal secretary announced. She turned away as though nothing of any importance was happening.

"Okay sweetie, I'll be waiting for you," Mason said as he smiled at her. She made her way towards the bathroom and he gazed at her. *If she needs to go, then she needs to go,* Mason thought. After all, he didn't want any accidents... now that would be embarrassing for both of them. Although he had once had that happen, and it was not to be recommended...

The legal secretary slowly made her way to the bathroom, and Mason watched her go out of sight.

He quickly and silently moved to one of the upper kitchen units. He took his antique square red tin – the one with a picture of a London bus on it – off the top shelf of the unit. Twisting the catch, he opened it up to reveal a smaller round green tin inside. This was the place he kept his tablets for such an occasion like this – or just in case he got too drunk to get a hard-on like this! To be honest, it didn't happen that often, but he needed to be prepared as he had a reputation to uphold.

Panic started to enter the kitchen and then his head as he opened the green tin to reveal an empty box. Mason manipulated the tin in different directions hoping that a pill would manifest itself in front of his eyes... but nothing. He must have used them all last night, or the other guy must have used them. How did he know where they were? *Christ, is nothing secret anymore?* he thought as he started to scan around the floor for any pills that may have dropped. He did indeed see a silver foil packet and he knew that his luck was in (in more ways than one).

Mason smiled, and picked the treasured item up, carefully unpeeling the foil to reveal the prized possession. He then took out the blue tablet with a gold line through it and placed it under this tongue for a faster reaction. Mason knew that he had to stall for about five minutes for it to start working, and he bet the legal secretary knew this – that's if she had guessed that he would take something. Mason then quickly moved into the same position as before so she didn't notice that he'd moved.

Chapter 2

She made her way to the bathroom, the female also buttoned up her shirt, as it wasn't the warmest of places. As she entered the bathroom, a faint waft of lavender hit her sinuses. She smiled as it reminded her of the times she would go and see her grandma. Her grandma used to grow lavender and in the summer she would pick bits of the flower and have them hanging in her bathroom. Except the young woman knew that this was synthetic lavender – this guy wouldn't have anything like the real thing. No, he would go out and buy the smell, as nice as it is.

The bathroom was white with a blue line of tiles around the wall – nice and functional. She relived herself while having another glance around the bathroom. It had all the normal things – shower, dry and so on.

As she pampered herself, she glanced at the cabinet above the wash basin, and an urge took over her. She had to have a look in it, so she made her way to the cabinet, then open the mirrored door. Inside the cabinet were several brown medicine bottles, aftershave, skin creams, pain killers, and pain blockers, among other bottles and things that she couldn't identify. She could not believe how many various types of drugs he had. Then she noticed a silver wrapper lying on the middle shelf... Now, that one struck a chord with her and she smiled to herself. Picking it up and popping it into the top left pocket of her shirt, she then closed the door as softly as she could. She didn't want him to know that she had been snooping around.

Slowly making her way out of the bathroom, she glanced at the bedroom to her left. Claude was still fast asleep, which was good, as that meant that she would have this guy's full attention. She didn't want Claude in on the action with him for now... Let him sleep, bless him. After all, he had been a busy boy last night...

Mason was also having some thoughts and smiling to himself... *God, I hope this other guy doesn't wake up while she's screaming with joy.* Although for all Mason knew, he could be big downstairs! (But if he was, why didn't he remember him from last night?) Mason briefly remembered once that he'd had a threesome with him another guy and a female. Yes, that was not the best, as the other guy was big in every way, including personality. Mason was the second-best to them both. The woman hadn't been interested in him, it was all about the other guy pleasing her and her wanting him, Mason was basically a voyeur who wanted to be involved.

The legal secretary slowly made her way into the open area. Her hands were behind her back and she was visibly taking in a deep breath. Mason could see her chest rising and falling. She then made her way over to the window, stopped, then gazed out of it at the view. Snow... she hadn't seen that for some time. In fact, she couldn't remember the last time she had actually seen snow.

Mason made his way over to the window as he slowly and gently put his hands on the woman's waist, then slowly moved his hands around to her front. He slipped one of his fingers on his right hand in between the gap between the buttons on her shirt, then started to explore her belly button. *Mmmmm, an innie,* he thought, as his finger slowly made its way around the soft edge of it. He then felt the piercing in her belly button. He also felt the medication starting to kick in, and a slight amount of relief came over him. He now knew he was ready to perform the task at hand.

"Shall we get it on?" Mason said, as his hand started moving downstairs.

"Mmmmm, toast!" the legal secretary announced as she grabbed his hand and lifted it off her. She made her way over to the back of the counter in the kitchen so that she had a panoramic view of the area, then picked up a piece of toast and started eating it.

16

The legal secretary, sipping her coffee, then noticed that he was hard

"Do you want your drink?" she inquired as she took it over to Mason, who was now looking out of the window. She gave him the coffee. Mason drank it, smiled, and decided that nothing was going to happen. He moved around and sat on the green sofa, leant back and patiently waited. Legs crossed, he gazed at the legal secretary.

Standing to Mason's right with only the buttoned shirt on, she was eating the toast as if she hadn't eaten for years.

"So are we going to get it on or are we having breakfast?" Mason enquired, and then grimaced.

"I was going to," the legal secretary announced, "but you know what? Maybe another day. I want breakfast." She stood in front of Mason, legs slightly parted and most of her weight on the left leg.

"Oh, I see. So what's your name then?" Mason asked out of sheer politeness, hoping to defuse the situation and maybe claw back some of his dignity (as he sat there in his dressing gown that had now fallen open, revealing his chest down to his toes). *Maybe I'll put some clothes on, as the apartment isn't particularly warm,* he thought. Mason could tell that the legal secretary was also cold.

"Scarlett," she responded with a serious expression.

"Oh, that's a nice name," was Mason's response back, although he thought *isn't that a hooker's name? Oh god, if she's a hooker, she'll want cash next, God, I hope she's not charging by the hour… This is going to cost a fortune… and the other guy got all the action!*

"And what a nice sight that is!" a voice came from the other side of the room. Claude stood there fully clothed with a smile from ear to ear.

"Unfortunately, I have to go now, so I may see you two later," he announced. Then he shook his head slightly and laughed.

"Oh yep, okay, yeah… see you around," the response came back to Claude from both of them. Claude started to laugh again while making his way over to the only exit door in the apartment. He raised his left hand as a gesture of saying goodbye, and then let himself out of the door.

Mason started to notice a slight pain in his groin area as he moved around on the sofa to get comfortable.

"You look a bit uncomfortable there," said Scarlett. "It's a shame… If you hadn't been so eager, we could have got it on by now and you could have released that tension… But, hey, your fault." She then finished her coffee and started to màke her way to the bathroom.

"Um, is it okay if I have a quick shower? I don't want to smell of sweaty armpits when I go into work; I'm on duty at lunchtime." She then went out of sight into the bathroom.

"Sweaty armpits? On duty?" Mason shouted.

"Yeah, I'm a policewoman," Scarlett responded as she popped her head out of the bathroom and smiled.

"So you're not a legal secretary then?" Mason asked as he once again moved around uncomfortably on the couch.

"No that's my girlfriend, Annabella. She's the legal secretary." Then he heard the sound of the shower coming on. Mason just sat there thinking to himself: *Wow, who is this? She was someone else entirely different from the female I thought she was. What a ballsed-up night, last night was…* His headache had now gone, although he was in pain somewhere else.

"Music," Mason said to the AI sound system, and a song came on. *Mmmmm who was this?* he thought to himself, scratching his chin. A 1980s band called Squeeze from the UK he seemed to remember.

"No, classical," he then said. *That's better, some Mozart.*

"Coffee, Mason," he said to himself as he went over to the kitchen area that was placed in one of the corners of his open-plan flat. He often thought it was too small for him and Barker, but in reality it was probably the right size.

As you came in through the door entrance, the kitchen was on the right side and the dining table was in front of you. To the left was a small room that had a desk in it, and that was it. Further on down the room was the doorway to the bathroom and the only bedroom. Then, carrying on, there was a sofa and entertainment area, and at the end of the open-plan area was a glass door and balcony with a sea view. It was a nice privilege having a sea view and Mason spent many an hour entertaining on the balcony and just relaxing.

He loved the smell of the summer wafting in – it reminded him of his childhood. Mason had had a very nice childhood, living near the sea. His dad was a banker and his mother a homemaker. He had a brother that was eighteen months older than him – well, he would have been if he was still alive. He had

18

died of a heart issue as one could not be grown in time for a transplant. That was the reason that Mason had got into this line of work – to save people that needed parts. He knew that there was a slight moral issue with it and obviously it was a covert operation. Everyone pretended that it didn't happen – governments, the rich from the top down – but if they needed a body part to keep them or a loved one alive, oh yes, they would use the service. It was so hypercritical of them all. He made his way over to the bathroom and knocked on the door.

"Coffee is out, can I join you?" he shouted, then sniggered. A mumbled response came back, which prompted him to return to the drinks and take them out to the balcony. He turned the heaters on, as it would be cold out on the balcony due to the snow. Mason decided that when Scarlett had gone, he would have a quick shower, and go into work early.

Around five minutes later, Scarlett made her entry onto the balcony. She had on a short black skirt, fishnet stockings and a black body-hugging top. Mason looked at Scarlett and had no recollection of her at all. Wow, he must have been out of it last night, and he certainly needed to be careful with regards to his somewhat promiscuous sex exploits. Yes, he did go both ways, but in general it was one way or another for a night, not bringing a guy *and* a girl home. And look what happened.

"Do you have far to go then?" Mason asked as he sipped his coffee and sat down on the two-seater chair. Scarlet sat next to him then slightly cuddled in to get a bit of warmth.

"What's the tattoo?" Scarlet enquired, nodding toward it on his right arm.

"Oh, it's Geometric Symbolism," Mason replied as he held his arm up closer to Scarlet.

"I see!" Scarlett said with a slow, drawn-out response, as she looked at the tattoo. The tattoo was a big circle with what looked like an eight in the middle with a line running through it. To the side of the eight were two stars that were also in the larger circle.

"So why that tattoo?" she enquired.

"I like maths," was his blunt response back, as he covered his arm again. "So I'll ask again," he continued, "do you have far to go?"

"Oh sorry, no. Block G4 at Sharing estate," Scarlet responded as she then took a small sip from her drink.

19

"Cool," Mason replied, even though he had no idea where it was and, to be honest, didn't care to know as he didn't have plans to see her again anyway. Likewise, she probably had no plans to see him again.

"Well I'm off for a shower. Just let yourself out when you've finished your coffee, Scarlett," was his announcement to her. Mason finished his drink and promptly left the balcony. He made his way slowly to the bathroom with a slight stagger on the way.

Mason shut the door behind him and took a deep breath. *Geez, that was awkward*, he thought to himself as he entered the shower and commanded water at thirty-two degrees. He washed his hair, body, legs and feet. Classical music played in the background and the THC in the water also helped him chill. He took a quick check of his bits to make sure there was nothing there like a rash or something that shouldn't be there... The water started to wake him up, then Shaking his head he could not remember what had happened in the last twelve hours. *Oh at least I'm in one piece!* Out of the shower and into the dryer, a quick thirty seconds of drying; and all completed.

He gave his teeth a quick brush, applied some hair gel and took a deep breath, all the time praying that she had got the message and was gone. He made his way to the bedroom, to his wardrobe that was on the left. He took out some black combat trousers, a light blue t-shirt, a black Motorbike jacket and his Joker helmet. He put some socks on and a pair of black boots. A quick spray of deodorant and he was good to go.

He sheepishly made his way to the open area and looked around for Scarlett. *Yes, she's gone... good result,* he thought to himself. He had a quick look around as he grabbed his backpack. Then opened it up and checked the contents inside, then made his way out of the apartment, and walked past around ten doors to finally stand in front of the aluminium doors to the lift which opened automatically. Entering the lift, Mason turned and glanced at the wooden desk opposite with a single yellow flower in a glass vase. Above it was a random piece of crap that someone called art – some green and blue squiggly lines on a white background. He bet Barker could do better with her paw prints. A glance at his watch. *The dog sitter would be arriving soon.*

"Morning Mason, which floor?" the lift's friendly male voice asked.

"Basement, please!" was his response as he briefly looked in his backpack again to make sure he had everything. He remembered, to his embarrassment,

20

forgetting to take shells for his gun once, but, hey, he'd remembered the gun at least. Luckily for him, he didn't need the gun or he would have been dead. The lift quickly made its way to the appropriate floor, slowed down to a stop and the doors opened. Mason made his way out then crossed the floor with various cars parked in their appropriate spots.

Turning a corner, his prized possession was sat waiting for him. A smile crossed Mason's face.

Chapter 3

Before him stood the latest Ducati 8570k in classic red with black highlights and chrome mirrors. It was a thing of beauty. It didn't have the soundtrack of the older bikes, but it far outperformed the petrol engines of a bygone age. He missed petrol engines… the soundtrack of the exhaust… the smell… but this was the future. Yes, they were more demanding with the servicing, but they came alive when you started them, with the engine throbbing like a heartbeat. This one made a high-pitched whining sound at speed instead, but the performance was far superior.

Putting on his helmet, which had a bizarre retro-style design of the Joker's face on it, plus dirty teeth with one joker cards on the back. He made his way up to the Ducati and briefly stopped. Taking a deep breath, he straddled the red machine, gloves on and jacket zipped up. Then he snuggled his body into the seat as he laid forward, his feet rising on the electric pegs behind him. A humming started and slowly it rose off the ground.

"Morning Mason. Manual or auto? Also, destination please?" the female voice asked through the intercom system in his helmet.

"Errrr, auto and take me to command," he advised the machine. It started to move slowly forward as it hovered around ten centimetres from the ground.

Left, then right and up to the gates – the bike requested that the gates open and they complied. The Ducati then went out onto the street. Luckily, the snow had stopped and the road heaters had worked their magic as the snow had now turned to water on the roads. It didn't matter all the same, as he technically was not touching the road due to the mag plates to lift the bike, rather than having tyres.

He turned left and then the speed picked up. Mason grabbed onto the handlebar as the acceleration of the bike tried to force him off. One hundred kilometres came up in no time at all, as the bike made its way towards the slip road onto the skyway.

"Manual!" Mason commanded, at which the bike added a warning triangle on his heads-up display. Then he had control of this rocket ship of a machine. He moved his left foot slightly to firm it down as the bike accelerated. Mason leant with the bike as it took the curve of the entrance to the skyways, accelerating to 275 kilometres. The aerodynamics kicked in as the aerofoils started to play their part in stabilising the bike. The noise and feel of the rushing wind was thrilling as the speed started to climb to three hundred kilometres. The aerodynamics once again modified the bike's geometry to punch a hole in the air as best it could. Moving air at this speed was like moving through treacle as the friction tried to pull him off. He passed slower cars as they tootled along, their drivers sitting in them waiting to die of boredom or old age before they got to their destination. Yes, it was dangerous on a bike, although he had a safety bubble that would be deployed to protect him; if he had an accident. And he had every faith in the system working and keeping him alive. After what seemed like no time at all, the exit came quite rapidly. Mason applied the brakes and slowed down to leave the skyways.

"Auto," he announced, and the bike slowed down and exited the skyway. Moments later, he came to a set of lights and then onto the car park. The system made a flawless attempt at parking the bike up in the desired spot, then started to power down as the bike came to a rest on the floor. The fans kicked in to cool the lift mags and the on-board computer. Mason took a few breaths as he climbed off the bike and moved back to admire it as he removed his gloves and helmet. *This machine is the bee's knees*, he thought to himself and smiled. He turned then made his way to the lift, checking that no one was following him, then he pressed the button to request the elevator. The doors hissed open so that he could enter the lifts, and once inside they hissed shut. There was a slight sense in his legs that it was moving in a vertical direction, which subsided as the lift slowed as it reached his floor. The doors hissed open to reveal his boss standing in front of him, the Manager.

"Oh good, I wanted to see you as I have a job for you. Follow me to my office now," he barked at Mason, who stayed in the elevator. The Manager entered the lift as the doors hissed shut and the lift moved to a different floor. The doors opened again and both men exited the lift. They walked in silence down various bland white corridors, and they passed numerous people doing countless jobs for different amounts of pay. Then the Manager's office door opened automatically as they approached it and they entered a large, plush blue-themed office. Mason had never been in the office, but the stories of what it was like were always circulating round the building. To the left was a glass cabinet with trophies and ornaments in it, plus some photo frames. The main window could become a screen, but at present was a window that looked over the cityscape. A large hardwood and glass table stood in the centre of the room with glass screens with paperwork on it, which all appeared to be in order. The floor was covered in a dark blue plush carpet that you sank into when walking on it. It was the sort of feeling that you get when you walk on certain types of grass with your bare feet. The Manager sat down in an enveloping black leather chair, a statement of power, Mason guessed.

"Sit, Mason," was the request, so he took off his jacket and backpack and placed them on the carpet, along with his helmet and gloves. Finally he did as he was requested, and sat in the black leather chair opposite the desk of the Manager. The Manager pressed a button, then lead-cut glasses slowly rose from an opening that had appeared on the top of the desk.

"Drink?" he inquired as he started to pour the drinks even before Mason answered yes or no. The Manager then rose out of his chair and made his way around to the front of the desk. He grabbed his own glass, then handed Mason a glass full of what appeared to be scotch or whisky.

"Cheers," Mason said as he raised his glass towards the Manager, as if to subconsciously make an impression.

"Errrr, yeah, cheers. Okay, Mason, I have a special assignment for you. I don't know if you have heard, but Mandy War has been killed on a job. It is very sad. I hate losing an agent on an assignment, but this one is particularly

24

upsetting as it's been perpetrated by one of our own, Sage Boutella. Did you know Sage or Mandy?"

Then there was silence, apart from the low drones of the air-conditioning. The Manager took a large drink from his glass.

"Yes, I did know them, although not that well," Mason replied, knowing all too well that he was lying to this man in front of him. He knew that he had to keep his emotions in check as this was going to be a good tick on his career plan. He wanted to become the man sitting opposite him in the big plush leather chair.

"Good. Well it appears that Sage Boutella and one of Mandy's clients got together and killed her in 2019. Your job is to go back and eliminate them both. We cannot have people going around killing my agents and affecting the timelines. I mean, for god's sake, we do enough damage as it is, so we cannot have anarchists doing the killing. I have already started an investigation into why Sage has a Transphone. They are licenced, so how the hell does she have one? Jumping around time killing people with the other perpetrator, Jack Krupop. He was an assignment for Mandy, a Wayback that had been brought in for harvesting of his body parts. He escaped for some reason; somehow they got together and have done this assignation. We don't know how many timelines they have created or what they have done to get to the point of killing Mandy, but it's your job to take them out... is that okay?" The Manager announced all of this with his piercing eyes staring at Mason, waiting for the only answer that he expected.

"Yes, not a problem, sir. I'll read the report and get after them." This was the answer the Manager expected.

"Good... you have the full authorisation to go back with weapons to terminate them both. Also, when you are back in 2019, you have a parallel assignment to retrieve a Wayback. It's an urgent one as a VIP needs the part, which should be a simple job, then move onto Sage and the bloke who's with her. It really should be the other way round, but pressure from upstairs states it has to be this way. Are we clear?" This was snarled at Mason as the Manager sat back in his chair. For some reason, he spun once in the chair then sat looking at Mason.

"Yes, as I said, sir, all good," Mason responded. "I'll get the reports and set off back to get the first target, the Wayback, then go back and get the second

25

targets." Mason then finished his drink, got up out of the plush chair, picked his things up and started to make his way to the door, which slid open as he approached it.

"Good luck," the Manager said. Mason briefly stopped turned and smiled.

"Thanks. I won't let you down." Then Mason exited the office.

When he was out in the corridor, he took a few deep breaths to calm himself down at the news that had just become knowledge to him – of Mandy's death. He had known Mandy quite well as they had gone through training together and he was surprised that the Manager had not checked up. They also had had a few meals together when they'd undergone training, but they'd kept their relationship purely professional all along. Mason had wanted to take it further, but she always made it clear that nothing was going to happen. Now and then, Mandy would invite him over to her place for drinks and she would tell him all her woes and how things just didn't work out how they should. Mason would drink, listen, and then go home. Heaviness had fallen on his heart now, and the only way to lift that was revenge. But revenge on someone who he also had feelings for, this was not a good day at all! Mason made his way down the corridors to his red mean machine. As he got to the lift, he stood next to a tall female with bright red hair in a ponytail.

Chapter 4

A glance to her left, "Hi, Mason, I hear you have the job?"
"Yeah, hi Sadie. Yeah, I've got it," he responded to Sadie without looking at her.

"Well it was inevitable that someone was going to get killed sooner or later. We've had such a good safety record. I bet the Manager was in a mood when he saw you?"

"No, he was pretty calm, actually." Then there was silence as the elevator doors opened. Mason, like a true gentleman, let Sadie enter first. The descent of the lift was also in silence, then the doors hissed open and they both exited.

"Good luck, Mason, you'll need it, bud." These were the last words Sadie said as she headed off in a different direction to him. Mason headed over to his Ducati, making sure that he wasn't going to be jumped or something stupid like that. He then briefly stopped to admire the piece of red machinery in front of him. *What a work of art*, he thought to himself as he stroked his chin pondering on the recent events and news. Yes, he was sad about Mandy – he had known her for some time. She was a friend and very good at her job. He would never admit it but she was probably better at the job than him.

Then his thoughts turned to Sage and the guy with her. He knew her all too well – they had flat-shared when training, so he knew her very intimately indeed – all her quirky things – and even her uncle Callum whom he hadn't seen for years. *How old would Callum be now? Was he still alive? Should I go and see him before I go back after Sage? Probably not... it may alert her somehow. Yes, Sage and I had had some fun when we were training,* Mason smirked to himself as he put his helmet and jacket on then climbed on the red machine and started it. There was a brief delay and then a few clicks from the Ducati as it started to hum, lifted off the ground and hovered – as if pacified for a moment – before it leashed its power to accomplish speed.

"Morning, Mason. Manual or auto? Destination please?" the female voice once again asked. There was silence as Mason thought for a moment or two.

"Auto and home," were his instructions to his Ducati. The bike started to negotiate its way out of the car park to its destination. Left, right and to the security gates at the exit, then it turned as it headed to the Spiralling slip road and up onto the skyway. Mason noticed that it was starting to rain, so he pressed a button on the dashboard that made the screen lift. It covered him now rather than just keeping the wind out of his face. He was still not fully protected, but as long as he was moving, the aerodynamics would manipulate the raindrops past his body (although when he didn't move, his legs did get wet).

As he passed the cityscape, sadness filled his heart again concerning what had happened and what he had to do. He had taken people out before, but not when he knew them. It was all unsanctioned and the documentation, in reality, was a joke. If he got caught in 2098, he would be toast. No one would help him out, even though they always said they would if he was arrested. He'd be charged and sentenced without anyone helping him.

What he was doing in his day-to-day job was technically illegal, but there was a line and he was crossing it. Mason often wondered how they got funds to run an illegal organisation like the one he worked for. It was probably like all the other organisations that the governments ran. No one talks about it and everyone denies that it exists, but all governments want to have the upper edge and the United Kingdom's government was just the same. Then to add to that what would happen if he got caught in another timeline, he dare not even think about that; and what would happen to him.

The bike started to slow down as his journey was coming to an end. It negotiated his exit and spiralled down the ramp and onto the main streets again. The bike navigated left, right, through the crossroads, and then to its final destination about one hundred kilometres from Leeds. When you are travelling at around 250 kph, it's not that long a commute.

The red machine glided up to his apartment block, 1K8. It was a nice area but the building was a little old. It didn't have one of those fancy parking things that store your vehicle on the roof. It was old school with a security door that he approached. The Ducati slowed down to let the doors complete their job of getting out of his way and letting him in. The bike made its way round to its designated parking spot and glided to a stop. It slowly lowered itself then powered itself down. Fans came on and strange noises appeared as it did some self-care to prolong its life expectancy. He noticed that the bottoms of his trousers were damp and he let out a slight sigh as he alighted from the bike. Briefly stretched his arms and back as he reached for the sky and then relaxed. He felt a presence behind him and then heard a voice in his left ear.

"That's a nice bike. I'll take the backpack and your wallet, okay?" Clearly, this person did not know who they were dealing with, which was unfortunate. They were going to pay for this, as Mason was not in the best of moods. He turned his head and glanced at the perpetrator. 167 centimetres, about sixty-five kg, female, shoulder-length brown hair, around thirty-two years old.

"Do you really want to do this? I'll let you walk away now... Please walk away, okay...?" Mason said in a calm and controlled voice.

"Fuck you... I have a gun, just give me the bag and the wallet," she responded as she pushed the barrel of the gun harder into his back as if to enforce that she was not going to walk away without what she wanted. And what she wanted were the items that she had requested... without any argument.

"Okay, I give in." Then he slowly moved into the gun barrel, slowly lifted his hands as if to surrender... then he explosively turned, putting one arm over the top of the assailant's arm then wrapping it around so that the arm with the gun in it was locked and couldn't shoot at him. Then with his right hand, he grabbed her neck and forced her off balance and down to the ground. A swift punch to the face dazed the attacker and he then removed the gun from her and took a few steps backwards. Now the weapon was pointing at her as she lay on the ground dazed.

"I warned you… now get up and piss off. I'm keeping the gun," he shouted at her as he stood a meter or so shaking. Adrenaline was flowing through his veins and the gun was pointed and primed to fire.

"I think you've broken my nose, you bastard," she screamed at him as she sat up and started to check to see if it was indeed broken. Blood was starting to run out of the left nostril by this time, although initially she didn't notice. Consequently, she was smearing blood over her face unaware of this act. She looked at this man that had hit her in the face, completely disregarding the fact that only moments earlier she was quite happy pointing a gun in his back and threatening him.

"You should be bloody ashamed of yourself for hitting a female in the face. What sort of man are you?" She started to get up onto her feet unceremoniously; Mason could tell that she had a bit of concussion as her eyes were slightly glazed – also, her balance was not the best as she swayed in front of him.

"I'll tell you what, you won't do anything stupid. If you want, we can go up to my place and you can clean yourself up. I do feel bad but that's what happens when you point a gun at someone," he announced as he lowered the gun and then checked the slide to see if it was loaded. No, there weren't any bullets in it so he then removed the magazine and put the gun down the back of his trousers and the magazine in his pocket. But all the same, he didn't know her, and if you play with fire you may get burnt, which is what had happened to this female. In one respect, she was lucky that he only disarmed her instead of beating her up or killing her.

"So do you want to go up to my place or not?" he asked once again as the assailant stood in front of him slightly rocking.

"Okay, I suppose so," she announced as she unceremoniously moved towards him.

"Are you okay to walk?"

"Yes, why wouldn't I be? Maybe because I am a female that's been beaten?" she rebuffed back at him.

"This way," Mason announced as he rolled his eyes at the females comment, then slowly made his way to the elevator. He kept his distance from her to be on the safe side. Deep down, he knew this was not a safe or good idea, but he felt bad about what he had done to her, which marginally shocked him. As they got to the lift, the doors opened. Mason signalled to the female to enter the lift first which put him in a position where he didn't have his back to her at any time. The lift jolted slightly and moved up to the appropriate floor – level five, room five. As they left the lift (to some strange soundtrack of birds singing), they made their way down the corridor to his room door. It had the word five on it, in black letters. The door clicked open as it recognised him, then he entered his flat. He knew that he had his back to the assailant but she was walking slowly behind him – a few meters away, so not close enough for her to attack him. As she entered the flat, she stopped.

"The bathroom's through there and to the left, okay?" he gestured to her. "I'll make a cup of tea for you!" he hollered and pointed again in the general direction of the doorway. She responded with a low-volume groan, making her way slowly past him to clean herself up.

After about five minutes, Mason went over to the bathroom and knocked on the door.

"Are you okay?"

"Yeah, I am, thanks," she responded, sounding a bit more upbeat. After another minute or so she appeared to look much fresher.

"Your tea's over here," he gestured to the cup on the kitchen benchtop that had a picture of Micky Mouse on it.

"Thanks," she said in a sheepish tone, not giving him eye contact at all.

"I'm Mason," he announced, to try and break the ice. Mason hated silence – it always came before something bad.

"Karen… or you can call me Kaz."

"Okay. Nice to meet you, Kaz. How's the nose?"

"It's okay, I suppose! I'm sorry that I tried to rob you, but that's what I have to do," Kaz said as she started to drink her tea.

"I get it, but you're lucky that I didn't break your nose or even kill you. You know you can't go around shoving a gun in a person's back and expect to get away with it."

"Well, I normally do," she announced, glancing at him with sad eyes.

"I'm not arguing – I'm just saying it's your call," Mason rebuffed. He drank his tea out of a cup with a picture of Superman on it.

"Okay, when you've finished, I'll escort you out the front and you can be on your way."

"Can I have my gun back, please?" Kaz asked as she finished off her tea and put the mug down. Mason thought for a moment about his answer and what he should do now. On the one hand, the gun was hers – if she lived on the streets, she may use it for protection. But on the other hand, she would no doubt try this again and maybe get hurt or killed. It was a real moral dilemma and he wasn't her keeper.

"So where do you live then?" He asked his quick question to help him decide.

"Oh, I live on the streets. Why?" Kaz responded with a slight bitterness in her voice.

"Oh, no reason. Just asking!" He smiled at her and handed the unloaded gun to her, then the magazine separately. Kaz took the gun and put the empty magazine in her back pocket. Then she stepped back and pulled out what looked like the same magazine. She slid in the magazine and pulled back the slider on the gun. It was now loaded with a bullet in the holder.

"Get the fuck down on the floor and put your hands behind you!" Kaz screamed at him.

"For god's sake!" Mason mumbled to himself as he calmly did exactly what he was told. Inside, he was so annoyed at himself for falling for this trick. He was embarrassed with the situation, especially as he had tried to be a good guy. Yes, he had hit her in the face, but she had pointed a gun at him and he didn't know it was empty at the time. She moved closer to him, still pointing the gun at him. She took out some zip ties and promptly tied him up as he lay face down on the floor.

"I want a bag," she shouted at him.

"In that cupboard over there at the end of the units," he responded, nodding his head in the general direction. She went over, putting the gun down the back of her jeans. Opened the door and took the bag out. Over the next twenty minutes, she ravaged his apartment, taking what she thought would be worth something, to the point where her bag was bulging with items.

"Are you happy now?" Mason enquired with a sarcastic tone to his voice.

32

"Yes, thanks, sorry, but you're too nice. Too trusting," she responded. Kaz then came closer to him. "Can I get out okay or do I need you?" she asked him in a polite voice.

"No, you're good. You can get out. You only need one code to get in," Mason responded, still lying on the ground.

"How am I going to get out of this?" Mason asked as she made her way over to the door and pushed the handle down.

"Not my problem, babes," was the response he received as she opened the door.

"Hey, Kaz how many kids do you have?" Mason asked as he lay on the floor tied up.

"Two. Why?" was the response, as she stopped and glanced back at him.

"Oh, I thought it was three due to the size of your ass, that's all." He smiled in her general direction. Kaz immediately turned, marched over to Mason and then gave him two swift kicks in the ribs as he lay there on the floor.

"One for each kid, you dickhead. Oh, and one for good luck." She screamed at him as she kicked him again. Then turned and stormed out of the room with his bag full of his stuff.

Mason lay there for a few minutes letting the pain subside from the three kicks Kaz had given to him as a present. He was thinking about how the day was going so far; to be honest, it was not going that well. After a few more moments, he started to manoeuvre himself to his knees, then to his feet. He made his way to the drawer that contained the knives. He picked a small one then made his way into the bathroom and spun around so he could see what he was doing with the knife. Mason then started cutting the zip tie that was holding his hands secure. Slowly but steadily, he cut through the item… then freedom.

He made the call to the building security to check his apartment room camera, the exit and garage camera, then gave them a description of Kaz (if, of course, that was her real name). Mason was not a big fan of cameras in his flat, but it was part of his agreement with his tenant and his contents insurance was free if he had them. But the downside was obviously that the feed could be tapped into and he could be watched without his consent. But this was one of those instances where it was good that he had them. After the job he would contact the insurance company, and of course; add a few things on. After all, he had to get his insurance credits back.

Kaz had taken some valuables, but most of his real ones were in the safe. Luckily, she wasn't smart enough to pressure him for the location of it. After all this excitement, it was time to prepare for the jump back in time and start his assignments. He made his way to the shower and stripped off. "Water, cold," he demanded as the shower came on and, oh, it *was* cold! He washed his hair, face, body, legs and feet, all in a total of seven minutes. Dried himself, then made his way to the bedroom, then the wardrobe to get his clothes and gear for the jump. Combat trousers, t-shirt, toiletries, Transphone (all charged up) and charger, warm jumper coat.

He went over to his safe; put his thumb on it to get his weapon of choice, the Browning M99pc, a Polly carbonate and Kevlar state-of-the-art piece of equipment. Invisible through detectors in the past and it was hard for the current security system to also spot. Even the bullets were undetectable, that was of course if you got the top-of-the-line ones that didn't leave a trace – even on impact they shattered, not leaving a slug or any other trace to identify the gun. Then he had the Glock17 Gen 7, his second weapon, but sometimes it was his first choice, nice and reliable. Putting all the items in his trusty backpack, he was ready to go and make some credits.

Mason pondered the two missions that he was embarking on. The first job was a straightforward one of capture and deliver to 2098. The second would not be straightforward and he would need to be on his A-game for Sage. Mason also didn't know what the second target was like. For all he knew, Sage had either trained the target into a killing weapon or he may be a waste of space. Mason would need to keep an eye out for him. He moved over to the window – the rain was coming down. He decided to get a Goober to make the jump back to 2025 to do the first part of the job. Mason called it in; picked his backpack up and headed to the foyer of the apartment to wait for it to arrive. On arrival, the car pulled up at the front but didn't pull under the overhang of the building, which meant he had to walk out into the rain to get in. This always happened when he ordered one of these – *why didn't it pull in under the overhang so that people didn't get wet? So frustrating,* he thought as he made his way to the Goober, starting to get wet.

The journey to Command was not eventful at all; Mason looked through the reports on his first target, which came across as being a standard job, apart from just one red flag – that he served in the British army and was called Barry, twenty-seven years old and 175cm tall, give or take. It may be an issue, as he would have skills that an ordinary Joe public wouldn't have, but Mason had tackled worse before.

The rain was steady, as it always was this time of the year. Mason requested some music, and birds tweeting came over the speakers of the car. It was better than nothing, but not what he wanted.

Pulling up outside Command, he alighted out of the Goober and made his way to security. The system sensed one gun – the Glock17 Gen 7 – but didn't detect his browning, although he did declare it to them. After a short walk, he made his way to the transit room and lodged the appropriate paperwork for the jump. Then he entered the dark brown walled room with a white ceiling that always gave him goose pimples for some reason – he didn't know why. Also, not understand why the walls were such an awful colour, but never mind, he would only be in there for a few minutes. The date, time and year for his first jump was set. Then he took his backpack off, got his Glock out, put the backpack back on, took a deep breath and pressed the red button on his Transphone. A humming started, and then it went dark.

The darkness started to clear as Mason tried to grasp where he was in his new surroundings. Mason immediately moved to a hiding position, as he needed a few moments to understand what had happened. Moving to a different location, he then passed a desk on top of which were a Glock handgun and a set of Harley Davidson keys. He checked the firearm to see if the Glock was loaded or not. He emptied the magazine and put the gun back and put the keys in his pocket, then slowly moved forward.

"Hey!" came a voice from behind him. He spun around and his target was there. Mason briefly noticed a fist flying towards him and then the impact of it… and the shock and trauma… and then darkness started to envelop him as unconsciousness came…

Chapter 5

A beeping sound came from the Transphone and nothing happened.
"Mmm that's interesting," Sage said.

"What is, whys it not working?" Callum asked as he stood there looking at them both.

"Signal it says, very unusual. Okay Jack a change of plans, it looks like we are going back to get your things except a longer way!" Sage stated, slightly smiling at him, hoping that he had made the right decision.

"I'll order a Goober for us," Sage announced.

Jack had a confused look on his face but said nothing. Then he started laughing at the whole weird situation he was in. Sage glanced back and thought it was nice to see him happy for at least one moment.

"Why can't we just go from here?" Jack asked inquisitively.

"It uses a lot of power, and it's easier to track and we have a week signal for some reason. Best go to the normal place."

The Goober arrived and Sage said her goodbyes to Callum. There was a slight tear in Sage's eye as they walked down to the waiting vehicle, then climbed in.

"D 127 block nine," Sage said, as the Goober's doors closed. It completed all its safety checks then slowly exited the street on yet another journey. Then the vehicle spiralled up to the skyways. This was not a high-priority job and it chose the slow lane of 150kph to get the customer to their destination as safely as possible.

"Do you want some music, Jack?" Sage enquired, as Jack was just sitting in silence looking out of the window.

"Errr, yes, anything please," he responded as they went down the skyway at a steady speed. "Can we have some Portishead on, please?" Sage asked the vehicle. Eerily, almost immediately, the sound of Dummy by Portishead filled the cabin.

"How are you feeling, Jack?"

"I feel sick inside, but I'm not going to throw up," he responded without breaking his glance at the view outside the car. The slow sultry tones filled the air as they made their trip. They slightly slowed down to exit, then spiralled down to the regular streets below. Taking a left, right and some more turns until they slid to a smooth halt at the destination, and then the door hissed open. Sage had a bad feeling about this jump. She paused briefly, but put it down to paranoia. Sage got out first, grabbed her backpack and put it on. They made their way down an alleyway to the end, then moved across some redundant land towards a disused building. *This must have been an old factory at some point time in time,* Jack thought.

"I feel as though I've been here before," Jack said as he briefly paused and looked around.

"We play with time, Jack! Changing timelines. For all we know, we may have done this before. Come on, we're in the open!" Sage stated as she glanced around uneasy at the journey they were on.

"God what a stench of crap," Jack shouted out as it hit his nostrils. Sage ignored his comment as she went through a door, turned into a room then into another empty room that had a few chairs in it, with two next to each other. Sage took a brief look at the chairs and their positioning, took her backpack off, then sat down. She pulled the Transphone out of her backpack then checked her weapon was loaded and put it back in the backpack.

Jack sauntered into the room then looked on as she manipulated the gun, sliding the various parts. He tried to remember if he had ever shot a gun, but he came up blank.

"Okay, Jack, date, time and destination please," Sage requested so she could put it all in the Transphone. She started putting her backpack on, waiting for the response.

"Make it the Friday, that's when I met Mandy in the pub at around five."

"The address?" Jack relayed the address and Sage put it in the Transphone.

"Okay, all in," Sage responded after a few seconds. She got up and moved over to the white spot that was on the floor and then looked at Jack.

"Come on Jack, I don't hurt. Just hold my hand and don't let go, okay!"

There was a slight pause from Jack then he slowly moved to stand next to Sage. He took her hand and they could both feel that their hands were clammy. Probably anxiety or was it a connection?

She briefly explained what was going to happen again and Jack said he understood. Sage then pressed the 'go' button on the Transphone. A humming sound started, and it started to get darker and darker until darkness completely enveloped them both as they transported through time, and then they appeared outside Jack's apartment.

"I feel sick!" were Jack's first words in 2019 – and he then promptly threw up on the floor. Sage dropped his hand and moved away from him, as she didn't want puke on her shoes.

"Are you okay?" she asked a few moments later.

"Could they be waiting for us in there?" he asked as he wiped his mouth on the front of his t-shirt. They both stood looking at the building opposite them, with thoughts of what may or may not be waiting for them inside.

"I'm not sure about this. Can I think about it?" was Jack's response as he rubbed his chin. Panic was starting to flow through his brain to the point of overload. He was beginning to feel anxious about all this, and a churning feeling started to develop in his stomach.

"But on the good side, it's not raining." He looked at Sage, then smiled.

"I know it's all a shock, Jack. Come on, let's grab a drink at that café down the road. It's only about a five-minute walk, I would say. I'll get them," Sage acknowledged as she returned the smile back at Jack.

She thought about the situation and tried to put herself in his shoes. *It must have been so hard for him? Told that you have to leave your life behind, everything you have ever seen or known all has to be left behind. On top of all that, a psycho bitch is out to kill him if she doesn't then death in car crash is waiting for him. Well that was one time line, but this is a different time line now.* A smile crossed her face.

"Errr, yes, okay, let's do that," Jack agreed. Sage nodded then started walking, as she took the lead of Jack at a slow, steady pace so that he could keep up. Jack made a conscious decision that he didn't want to catch up with this female, as she would want to talk to him, and he wasn't sure that he wanted to talk to her now. A sad cloud swept over Jack as he watched the cars, trucks and buses go by. *No skyways, strange buildings or anything like that – just smelly, noisy vehicles. This is as good as it gets – cutting-edge technology, but he had seen the future and it was so, so different. Yes, it was like what was portrayed in the movies – alas, that was the problem. It was nothing like this, his life, memories and friends would go on forever.* He felt nauseous again – with the residual taste of puke in his mouth, his stomach was in knots, *probably the anxiety* he thought.

Jack kept hanging back, and Sage kept looking back at him, indicating that he should hurry up. They both made their way down the road to the café. They arrived at an old-fashioned cake shop– it had some tables inside so that it could also be used as a café. On display were buns, cakes and all sorts of other delightful things in the window, plus various sandwiches to also be taken away or eaten inside. Sage briefly stopped to admire the delights in the green wooden-framed, glass-fronted shop. She glanced at Jack as she smiled softly at him to try and put him at ease. He responded with a grimace back at Sage.

"My shout, what do you want?" she asked as she entered the café, a doorbell sounding to alert the staff that they had a customer. Sage went up to the counter and was greeted by a slightly overweight older woman with a lovely smile.

"Yes, what can I get you, dear?" She smiled then waited for the response.

"Errr, I'll have two ham and cheese sandwich please and two coffee's. Latte's, if you don't mind," was Sage's response as she glanced out of the window at Jack who was gazing at the world.

Jack watched an Austin Martin Vantage pass by until it turned the corner and was gone. He was not feeling himself, his head was spinning, and he felt sick to the core. All the same, he had to go through this, as he knew his life possibly, probably, maybe depended on it. Jack then finally followed Sage into the café and he noticed she was ordering. Sage went over to a table and sat down waiting for Jack to follow her – except he was mulling around the shop in a strange dazed way, looking at pictures of flowers – anything that he could do to delay the conversation that he was going to have to have with Sage. Jack was not ready for the decision he had to make shortly. Yes, he had made it in the future, but now he was back in his time it was all different. He felt sad but he was also hungry, so he had to eat something. He slowly made his way to the table, and finally sat down opposite Sage at a slight angle, but didn't give eye contact. Then… silence!

When the coffees were ready, the old lady behind the counter shouted Sage's name out. Sage and Jack got up and they moved to the counter where they picked up their coffees and sandwiches. Then made their way to their table and sat down. Jack then shifted his chair to sit opposite Sage in silence, with no eye contact once again. They both started to consume their drinks and food with not a murmur from each of them, and the silence became unbearable. Who was going to crack first?

"You know, Jack, a decision has to be made regardless of what you want to do. You know the consequences if you do nothing. And you know what will happen if you do something. I know I keep going on about it, but you have to realise why," Sage explained again as he sat opposite her still in silence, eating his ham and cheese sandwich and drinking his latte in peace.

"Look, Sage, I was in a prison cell and I woke up with a gun pointing at me, but I think I've been patient with you and all this. How the hell do I not know that you've not drugged me or hypnotised me? Or I'm still asleep in my cell? Or you're a con artist? Answer me that, Sage… if that is your name? Female from the future! Ha!" he barked at Sage then continued eating.

"Look, Jack, I get what you're saying. I can appreciate that it's hard for you. I'm not trying to rip you off, drug you or anything; I think you know this deep down. I'm trying to help you, Jack," Sage responded and looked intensely at him, trying to come up with a more convincing story or a different approach to this situation. She came up with nothing. Jack picked his coffee up and took another drink out of the disposable container. The doorbell rang to alert the staff of a new customer. Sage looked over Jack's shoulder, as most of his torso was obscuring her view of who was entering. Then she was able to see a young mother with a baby strapped to her front in one of those hippy carrying pouches. Behind her was a man, 183cm tall, curly brown hair, slim but muscular.

"Jack, I beg you, please don't move, don't look round... Just sit there and drink your coffee," Sage said politely in a quiet voice.

"What?" was the response from Jack, even though he did actually hear the request. He complied with the instructions with regards to moving but he was not quiet.

"I will explain if we make it out of here. Please... I'm begging you to be quiet and still. Just drink your coffee."

Jack had a feeling that this was not good, although why did he believe her all of a sudden was unclear to him, but he complied anyway. The male and female's reflection could be seen in the window. Jack wondered which one Sage was hiding from. The female with the baby? Or the guy who looks like he means business? Yep, it was the guy that looked like a hitman, Jack presumed. The guy made his order to the nice old lady, then stood waiting around the counter talking to the female with the baby as a distraction, probably a time-waster until his coffee was made.

"I'm not being funny, Sage, but I think I look peculiar just sat at the table, don't you?" Jack asked as he dared not move as instructed.

"OK, just try and look normal... Let's move seats?" Sage suggested.

"Really? If we both get up, he will look over as it's so obvious."

"Shit!" Sage blurted out as she raised her hand to slightly cover her face, just in case the man looked in their direction.

The man was joking with the female, then started making baby noises at the baby to amuse himself or the baby. He then glanced over at them both.

"Quick, kiss me, Jack," Sage said abruptly. Jack complied, knowing exactly why she had asked. The man's coffee was completed, then he took his glance off of them as his concentration was shifted to a new job at hand, putting sugar into the takeaway cup with a lid on it. Task completed, he turned, left the shop, and went out of sight.

"Who the bloody hell was that? What's it all about?" Jack barked at Sage.

"This is bullshit, you know. You need to be upfront with me for god's sake, Sage."

41

"Jack, I have been trying to get it into your head about how serious this all is, but you have been putting it off," she announced to him as she finished her coffee.

The old lady started to clean tables, and when she got to their table she briefly stopped.

"Sorry to interrupt, sweethearts, but are you Sage? Well, that nice young man who just left told me to say hi to you, Sage."

Sage's face went white as she realised that she had been recognised.

"Come on, we have to get out of here!" Sage ordered Jack.

"Is there a back way out of here, please?" Sage asked the women abruptly.

"Yes, the toilets are through there, darling, and there's a back door... Why?" she responded, as Sage rose from her seat, quickly making her way to the back door. Jack made no move and just looked at Sage. Sage looked back and stopped.

"Jack, come on! Look, this guy is after you – and probably me! This is not good, trust me. We need to get out," Sage shouted. She started to make her way by following the sign on the wall.

"Okay, I'm coming," was Jack's half-hearted response.

Chapter 6

As she got to the door, she stopped, and Jack nearly ran into the back of her. She slowly popped her head out of the doorway, to see if she could see anything. This also gave her a chance to have a look at the lay of the land, and which way they would be running. There was a brick wall that was about two metres high, and luckily there was part of it that was knocked down (possibly by a car or a delivery van).

"Jack, we'll make a run for it over to that bit of the wall that's knocked down, then take it from there. Just keep close and follow me, okay? We need to move… Do you understand?"

Before getting a response from Jack, Sage was gone. She sprinted out of the back of the establishment, across a small car park to the escape route through the wall. Jack followed, looking left and right, then nearly falling as he tripped over his own feet – his toe-capped work boots were not the best of running gear. Sage jumped through the broken wall and Jack followed, except he caught his right foot on a brick, then face-planted on the pavement the other side of the wall. Sage briefly stopped to help him up.

"No, go on, I'm right behind you," he shouted, getting himself up as he chased after her. They ran for some time, although it was hard work as Jack had

43

his steel-cap boots weighing his legs down. Sage was expecting to hear a gunshot at any time before they got to safety. Sanctuary came in the form of a shopping centre. They both ran through its car park, trying to not get run over by the customers' cars. There was much tooting and beeping as the general public lost their cool at the two idiots running in front of them. The drivers were on a mission to get parked up, get in a shop, buy things and get out as fast as possible... or waste their lives away looking at useless crap.

Finally, they both made it in through the front doors and then into the main area with lots of people - which meant security cameras!

"This way!" Jack shouted to Sage, as the tables had turned – he was the one with the knowledge. Sage followed Jack for once; they made their way through the shopping centre, trying to be as inconspicuous as they could without running. Kids were screaming and some people did glance at the two of them moving down the mall, passing sports shops, banks, hairdressers, and so on. They stood out in the crowd, all sweaty with a sense of urgency... but they weren't just trying to get the latest consumer item at a discount, they were trying to be safe.

"Through this door," Jack shouted. Then down a corridor, left, then into another room, which at first glance looked like a changing room.

"I did some work here a few years ago, so I know the layout of this place," Jack explained, as he sat down on a fixed wooden bench. Sage sat next to him and they both hyperventilated in unison for a short time.

"So Sage, I think I have been pretty damn patient with all this... Who is he, then? You were shitting yourself in that café. To be honest, I have played this game long enough, I think it's time for a few more answers," Jack told Sage.

"Who is he? Oh god, he's a fucking killer, end of! I trained with him. Errr, we had a thing together... that's the only reason he's given us the heads-up. He's called Mason! What can I say... Honestly, he's better than Mandy and me. Although his Achilles' heel is that he loses concentration on the job. He's focused, then he'll decide that he's going to try and chat up a female that he has just bumped into on a job. I don't know if Mason does it to put himself under pressure, but he always comes up with the goods." Sage explained all this as she was controlling her breathing. Her head lowered slightly at the situation. She knew they were in trouble, but Jack had not grasped the seriousness of it all.

44

"So what are we going to do then?" Jack asked as his body language portrayed the same feeling of helplessness as he was confused, with the story of this person from the future who's going to kill him.

"Look, we don't know if he's after you, me or both of us, but for god's sake, the likelihood of him walking into that café in this time... I mean, the odds are so out of this world. We'll presume that he's after us until we find out different. So, Jack, it's the same question. What the Hell are you going to do? Because as far as I'm concerned, I'm now being chased and I need to look after myself." This was the blunt response to Jack's question, although this time she didn't look at him – her thoughts were on how to stay alive with no weapons and with a killer after them.

Jack's frustration with the situation then boiled over with a barrage of direct questions to Sage about the whole situation.

"Let's put this on the table, Sage. What evidence do you have that I'm going to be killed? Show me. Yes, you have taken me to the future, and according to you, we are being chased by a killing machine. Where's the evidence? You want me to play along with all this? Enlighten me, please. For all I know, that guy is a random guy. All I have is this story you've told me. You may have taken me to the future, or maybe you drugged me, and I dreamt it all. Can you show me something – anything – now?"

"Honestly Jack, I could show you photos, newspaper stories... but you would say I had forged them, so I'm not going to bother going down that road. You have to use your gut-feeling on this one, maybe go out on a limb, I was in your dreams when we went to the future, which must mean something, for god's sake," Sage responded as she got up. She glanced away from him then started to pace around the room, thinking of what else she could say to persuade this person that it was all true.

"Jack, in your dreams, did you go to a gig with a female called Mandy? Did you errr... did you meet a man in the future who gave you a mug of tea and on the mug it had a Star Wars picture of a Tie fighter? When you first met the man in the future, did he hold a gun at you? Did you go for a ride in a Goober? How do I know all these facts if it was a dream, Jack?" she asked. She then stopped, stood in front of Jack and glared at him, hoping that he would remember some of the things. She then witnessed the proverbial penny drop. *Bingo!* Sage thought to herself, *he's in!*

Chapter 7

This coffee's good! Mason thought to himself as he sat on a park bench opposite the café, observing it and the patrons inside intensely. It was apparent that Sage was starting to panic – he could see that her body language had changed from before. Maybe she had just realised that there were going to be consequences resulting from Mandy's death. Did she think that she could steal a Transphone, go jumping around in time executing people and get away with it? *Interfering with the running of the agency? The job the organisation have an obligation to their customers, legal or illegal to provide parts that were required to keep the wealthy and powerful alive....* Mason thought as he took another sip of his coffee.

Taking out the Transphone from his backpack, he then went into the program to find the search mode and turned it on. This would help him locate Sage's Transphone. That's how he was going to track them, just in case they decided to do a jump or two, to try and shake him off of their tail. Unfortunately, it did take time depending on their location. If both units were in the same year it would find hers faster than if she had jumped period and destination. But the more times it had to find them, the inbuilt artificial intelligence would locate them quickly. But he had the waiting game on his side as he was in no rush to make the kill. He liked Sage and it would be more fun in the long run, as he would get paid more for the job. The thought made him smile at the credits he would earn and the fun to be had.

He took another drink and observed Sage and the guy – *James? Jo? No, Jack* – move to the back of the shop and then out of the rear as they fled for their lives. Maybe they thought they were so smart to come up with this clichéd plan. If he was going to kill them, they would be dead already. No, he wanted to let Sage have a chance, which would make it more interesting for him. Mason didn't give a toss about the guy, but he did have a soft spot for Sage.

Mason remembered a party that they both went to many years ago when they were training. It was at one of his friend's houses, Jonathan, although they all called him Johnno. Johnno was tall and skinny, just an average guy. Although he did like his weed if the truth is known, probably a bit too much! Johnno was studying engineering, and Heather was studying clothes design at the same university. Heather was so hot it was unreal – small in stature, funny, intelligent, chatty, curvy, beautiful eyes and cute with long black wavy hair with an infectious smile. A smirk once again crossed Mason's face as he thought about her. But the thing that made her different to nearly any female he had ever met was the conversation! She was obsessed with talking about female matters in a random chat; she would announce in general conversation some amazingly tantalizing hot one-liners.

Her conversation was so crude, yet so different and funny that it would stop a discussion at a hundred meters! She would glance at her stunned audience, smile at everyone, get up and leave the room, only to return about ten minutes later as though nothing had happened.

Heather was always bringing up, tantalising discussions, comments that would send any hot blooded male into a daydream about her. Her looks, intelligence and her gutter mouth were not what you would expect in one person. She had a presence that no one he had ever met in his life had. To top that, she had always stuck in his memories. Mason shook his head at the thought then sniggered to himself.

Anyway, he was digressing in his daydreams. He remembered that he and Sage went to a party once at Johnno and Heather's house; he couldn't remember if Mandy was there or not, but it didn't matter. So they arrived at the front door and straight away Sage pointed out that she could see smoke coming out from the cracks around the door. It appeared that the house was on fire, although music was still pumping from inside.

Mason opened the door and smoke enveloped them both like a winter's fog as they entered the house. It seemed that Johnno the host had acquired – okay, probably stolen – a smoke machine. It was smoggy, with the smell of cannabis in the air as they entered through the doorway. They immediately passed some people snogging each other's faces off. They negotiated their way around them through the mist, making their way through the house. They jolted into other obstacles on their way as they both carried down the yellow-painted walls of the hallway. They bumped into strangers, or maybe even friends, although due to the murkiness they had no idea at all who these people were. For all they knew, these were aliens invading Earth or maybe they were just here for the party.

They carried on with their journey to the back room. The party had a theme of the 1990s indie scene – there were the clothes and there was obviously the music and the drugs to accompany it. Music was blasting out, songs from The Happy Mondays, The Smiths, The Stone Roses, New Order and so on. The music playing was mostly the Manchester sound.

Mason remembered bumping into two wheelie bins full of cold water and bottles of beer. He and Sage got a bottle each then started to wander around this big Victorian house enveloped in smoke. They slowly moved around the house checking it out, venturing into different rooms. They had the feeling that this was a student's residence or something similar as no normal person wouldn't allow their house to be used like this.

They finally came back to where they had started as they passed the wheelie bins again and headed into the back room at the back of the house. Mason then remembered the joint that Johnno had tried to make, with about three roll-up papers all stuck together to make one long joint that was about twenty centimetres long. The issue was that there was so much marijuana and tobacco in it, they couldn't draw on it. So in reality, you couldn't keep it going or even get high from it. It was such a big joint that it couldn't be smoked. Johnno had attempted to roll this massive joint for some reason, and God only knew why! But it was an engineering failure, so Johnno as an engineer got a D off his mates for Didn't Work.

He then remembered other bands being played like The Fall and Inspiral Carpets. The party guests had all put on period baggy trousers, jumpers, T-shirts with a retro smiley face and of course the hats. God, that party was so, so good; then he remembered the funniest part of it all was that one of the neighbours or someone had called the police to shut it down. Ironically, Johnno knew the police officers that arrived. They joined in with a few puffs of a joint, thanked Johnno, then left. How bizarre was that? Not your ordinary fun police, the type that wants to stop people having fun as they are working, so why should you be having fun if they're not! *They're all evenly balanced with a chip on both shoulders* – that's what Johnno used to say. God, he was so funny.

The party went on for several hours; fun was had by all with the consumption of beer, vodka and THC. At the end of the night, they both went back to his place. As they went through the front door, Sage stopped and he bumped into her. She turned, slightly moved her lips closer to his, millimetres away from Mason's. Then there was a moment when they both knew that they were too wasted to do anything about it. Sage took a step back and went to the spare room for the night. *Mmm, what could have been*, Mason thought to himself. He'd always thought that maybe they would hook up one day, but alas they never did and he always regretted it.

Mason observed them both running away like frightened mice. He sniggered to himself as he watched the guy fall over and faceplant the floor. *Ooooh, that must have hurt; this is going to be a fun job, as the guy is clearly an idiot.* Mason finished his coffee and looked at his Transphone. It was still searching, but that was not a problem. He got up and started walking in the direction that they went in.

After a short brisk walk, he noticed a shopping centre sign and then decided that (A) that was where they would have gone and (B) he could look at some shops on the way. *A win win situation...* Making his way across the car park, he stopped in a safe place and took the Transphone out and checked it – bingo, it had found them. He slowly walked forward, briefly stopping to have a good look at the Transphone again and immediately got beeped by someone in a car. Mason glared at the female sitting behind the wheel, but then realised that the car didn't fly so it couldn't go over him. He was slightly appreciative that she just didn't knock him down.

They were both hiding in a storeroom (or some room like that) inside the shopping centre. As he made his way to their hiding place, Mason stopped to glance at some brown leather shoes in the window – *mmmm, they seem very nice* – then he looked at what he was wearing, and decided against getting them for now. Maybe some other time.

Checking the Transphone yet again, he noticed that they were on the move now. He decided to turn off the central mall walk way and intercept them. He took the backpack off, then got down on one knee as he looked in a pocket of it. *Yes!* Mason smiled to himself as he pulled out a watch that was linked to the Transphone so he didn't need to keep getting the big bulky thing out. It would show him all he needed to know on the timepiece instead.

Mason made a snap decision; it was best practice to sort the shopping centres surveillance cameras out before he engaged his targets. He decided to load a small one-hour virus onto the camera system. Mason went into a folder on his Transphone and found the camera system relatively easily – then hacking it was also easy. He went into another folder and several options came up. Picking the virus which he was going to use on the system. It would shut the system down as though it had decided on its own that it had to do an update now. The beauty was that it could not be stopped. This would keep happening for an hour or so, then if anything happened – such as death carnage or mayhem – the cameras would not capture it, as it would be doing an update. He also included the mobile phone camera tag of 800 metres. So if some nosey parker decided to take pictures or videos of anything that may be happening, their phone cameras would not work for an hour or so. He launched the virus. Then put the watch on.

Glancing up, he noticed the targets coming out of a doorway. Sage headed his way, then all of a sudden stopped and turned. Mmm she must have realised that she was going the wrong way. Protecting himself from being seen, Mason pulled out his gun from the backpack and checked the chamber to make sure it was ready to be used. He then pushed the gun down the back of his trousers, to keep it there until he needed it – which may be soon... He put the backpack on and checked his watch to see the location of the targets. One red dot flashed on the small screen as it was tracking their Transphone and not the person. Mason went into the camera system to make sure that they were all down. No busy-bodies' phones will be videoing him making a hit in broad daylight, good all cameras were down also. He got to his feet, then started moving in the direction the watch was giving him. As he made his way out to the car park, he briefly stopped. Spotting them just passing a McDonald's outlet, Mason jumped into action as he went a different way to get a better view and position. He bounded into a slight jog to get slightly closer, and for a cleaner shot. His priority was Sage – the guy would be an easy target to finish off – he couldn't even climb over a wall without falling. Mason stopped by a wall – yes, there they were. Much closer, walking across the car park thinking they were safe. He chuckled to himself. Bracing himself up against the wall, Mason thought, *shall I just wound Sage to make this go on a bit longer? Or go straight for the headshot?*

He squeezed the trigger and the safety released itself, allowing the gun to be fired. The shot began its journey at high speed as it forced its way through the air, splitting it metre by metre to its final destination. The side screen of a red van that was moving in front of them exploded and covered them both with glass. They stopped, looking at it in disbelief.

Sage grabbed Jack by the hand and pulled him down to hide behind the car they were next to. By this time, the van had stopped, and the driver was walking around the front of it, unaware that he had just been shot at. He stood there aimlessly looking around, hoping that someone would give him a clue as to what had happened. Other nosy bystanders and onlookers stopped to have a look. The driver turned and then started making his way toward some teenagers, presuming that they had broken his window, by throwing something at it.

"In the van!" Sage ordered Jack as she ran around the back of the van and jumped in. When Sage was inside, Jack opened the door and climbed in the other side; Sage rammed it in first gear and hit the still-running engine's gas pedal. The van lurched forward, leaving the driver standing in the car park stunned, stranded and wondering what had just happened.

"Noooo!" Mason said under his breath as he launched another round out of the handgun to try and intercept one of his targets. This slug's journey was more successful as it went through the back window, carried on down inside the van, through a particle-board wall in the van, then got the taste of flesh. It continued its journey out of the front windscreen, leaving a painful cry from the victim of the bullet. The slug had now lost its power and momentum; its journey of only a few seconds came to an end. The deformed bullet was now a waste of material in this throwaway society.

The red van clipped a trolley being pushed by a man, and its contents went scattering everywhere – bread, eggs, bacon, lettuce, cauliflowers and the most precious of goods, a pack of six beer bottles smashing on the ground as the golden juice spread all over the impact site. With a sharp tug on the steering wheel, the van veered to the left as it curb-hopped out of the car park with screeching tyres, the impact of the suspension bottoming out on the bodywork. Dirt and rust lay where the van had landed after its short but sweet flight through the air. An oncoming car screeched to one side as the driver turned the wheel to avoid this out-of-control red van hurtling towards him. Veering in another direction, he almost hit a pedestrian on the pavement and then nearly smashed straight into a signpost.

"Sorry," Sage shouted out of the side window as the van sped by, then made its way onto the right side of the road and out of sight of Mason.

"Time to get out of here!" Mason muttered to himself as the general public started screaming and running in various directions. Panic, terror and fear played its part in the event that was unfolding. Mason joined in with the chaos to look less conspicuous. He alighted from the location into a jog. Looking for a pursuit vehicle, it then came into view and a smile once again crossed his face.

"It's okay, it's okay, slow down, Sage, the shooter is far behind us now. We don't want to get pulled over by the cops, do we?" Jack said as he put his hand on top of Sage's white clenched hands on the steering wheel. She started to ease off the gas and the van slowed down to a more legal speed.

"Keep going along this road. How much fuel do we have in it?" he asked with a grim tone.

"About half a tank. Why?" she responded as she briefly glanced at him, then back at the road.

"I have somewhere that we can go, so you keep driving, and I'll tell you where to go, okay?" Jack moved uncomfortably in his seat and he then moved his right hand towards his left side.

"I need to get rid of this backpack. It's so bloody uncomfortable trying to drive with it on," Sage announced as she started to struggle to remove it while driving. With all the excitement that had just happened, she forgot to remove the backpack before she began to drive. It just wasn't one of the essential things that she had thought about.

"I'll hold the steering wheel, and you take the backpack off, okay?" Jack said in a calm firm tone, as he took control of the direction of the van. Sage wriggled out of the backpack, then threw it on the floor of the van. She took control back then glanced at Jack and smiled – she was now comfortable and not being shot at. She turned the radio on and the pleasing sounds of music filled the van.

"Who's this?" Sage enquired, to take the tension out of the air. Knowing that Jack was quite clued up on music.

"It's La Freak by Chic..." Jack responded, with a slight undertone to his voice. "I think we need to stop."

"Why?" the response came back at him with a glance.

"Errrr, because I think I've been hit, and I need a piss!"

"Hit! Where have you been hit?" Sage asked. The van veered on the road and Sage corrected it as they nearly hit a wall.

"In my left arm... please pull over into this garage car park," Jack pleaded. Sage did what she was asked to do. The red van locked its wheels on the chalky-gravel surface and came to a stop, with a cloud of dust surrounding them. Sage applied the handbrake, then killed the engine.

"Where are you hit?" She turned her body to face Jack to assess the situation.

"My left arm at the top!" She moved closer to have a good look at the damage.

"I'll get out to have a better look." She jumped out of the van and ran around the front to the passenger side door, then opened it and leaned into the van.

"This might hurt!" Sage started to inspect the wound. She grabbed her backpack from the footwell, and opened it up. She started to hunt around in it for something. Then pulled out a small pouch and promptly unzipped it, taking out a pair of scissors. She then cut Jack's clothing to get a better view of the wound. After a few seconds of peering, tutting and prodding, the diagnosis came.

"Look, Jack, it's not life-threatening, although it does need some stitches. I'll do it later on when we're in a safer place," she explained to Jack as she started to get the appropriate equipment out to do a temporary job.

"What are you doing?" Jack enquired as she placed a small patch over the wound.

Sage then started to put the equipment back together in her trusty backpack, threw it back in the footwell, went around the van, climbed in, then started the engine, and they were off on their journey again.

"We need to get a move-on – where's this place you were on about?" Sage asked as she changed gears with a crunch.

"Oh, carry on down here for about another ten Ks; you'll see a church – take a left there. About a hundred metres up that lane on the right is a road with a big tree. On the opposite side of the road, go down that, follow it round to the left of the fork and there's a barn. We can stop in there for a bit." He explained this while looking out of the window of the van and holding his arm. He then turned the heating up.

"I'm cold," Jack said out loud.

"Hi, I'm Sage, nice to meet you, 'Cold'!" She glanced at him, then turned away to look at the road.

"Yep, probably shock, Jack," Sage explained to him, as she followed the instructions impeccably. The road was a bumpy dirt road. Sage took her time but they were soon at the designated point. She pulled up in front of the doors; Jack got out, unlocked the doors and opened them. Sage drove the van in and out of sight of the world. When inside, Sage killed the engine, then let out a sigh. She lowered her head for a few moments to compose herself, then looked at Jack who had sat down on a straw bale to the side of the van. His demeanour was not good, with his head down on his right hand.

"Well then, Jack, do you have enough evidence now to believe me?" Sage asked as she climbed out of the van. She wanted an answer to the question she had been asking for several hours now.

"Yes," was all Sage got from Jack in a soft and defenceless voice.

"Good, you believe me – so what's your answer then?" she immediately barked back at him. She got the backpack, placed it down on the floor in front of him and started to open it.

"I don't know… I suppose I don't have much choice, do I? If I stop here then this man will get me, so I have to go with you, don't I?" he declared as he looked at Sage with his brown eyes that looked slightly watery.

"Come on, let's look at that arm. Sit up!" Sage waited for him to shuffle into a better position. Then started to clean him up with some alcohol swabs from her first aid kit.

"Errrr, no... no, Arrrr, that hurts," Jack screamed out.

"Oh shut up! I've seen bigger cuts on my toe," her response came back as she was now concentrating on threading the bent needle to stitch his arm.

"This may hurt a bit. Bite onto this bit of plastic." She shoved the plastic – which she'd found in the backpack – into Jack's mouth, then promptly dug the needle into his arm and started to stitch it up.

This brought back a upsetting memory of getting stitched without any painkillers. Jack remembered a time when a big piece of wood had hit him on the head and split it open. He recalled just standing there – he had been confused but not knocked out – blood oozing from the wound on his head. His workmates had all shown concern for his well-being by taking him to the hospital. When they had dropped him off, they made sure that he would be seen. They left him and went to the pub. Jack had promptly fallen asleep in the hospital waiting room with his head injury.

He remembered getting up and going to the triage nurse to explain what had happened. All of a sudden, he was taken into a room and then the nurse started to stitch his head up without an anaesthetic. Jack got about ten stitches on the left side of his head and was kept in the hospital for observation for the night. When he was on the ward, this lovely young trainee nurse was looking after him. Jack did think about getting her number but didn't bother. Smiling to himself as he daydreamed, he bet the nurse was good in the sack, as nurses seem to have a bit of a reputation for being very experimental.

"Aww, that hurts. Why are you being so rough with me?" Jack complained as he snapped out of his daydream. Sage held his arm still and finished off what she was doing.

"There all done, now take this tablet that she produced from her bag," Sage announced as she straightened up in front of him, smiling with satisfaction at the work she had just done.

"What is it?" Jack asked as he glared at it.

"Pain killers... All good now, Jack. We need to keep moving. Honestly, he will find us soon. The thing is, I need to have a weapon; you know, something to shoot back at him. So the only plan I have at the moment is to get one as soon as possible. The only thing I can think of is to go to the future, get my weapon and try to take him out. What's your thought on that?" Sage asked as she stood in front of him, legs apart by about 300 centimetres, with her hands on her hips, intending to present as a person that means action.

"Yeah, whatever," the deflated response came back.

"Hey, why don't you go and look in the back of the van, you never know what might be in there!" Sage suggested, for one of two reasons: one to take Jack's mind off the situation and, two, she was hoping that there was something of use there. Jack got up and went round to the back doors and Sage accompanied him on the small journey. He lifted the handle to open the red van's door; *wow, nothing at all here apart from space and air.*

"No wonder it was so fast," Sage said out loud. She started to laugh, and Jack slowly joined in.

"How do you feel now?" Sage enquired as they stood looking in the back of the empty van.

"I was convinced there was going to be something in the back, as the owner had built a wall to stop you looking in."

"Yeah, me too. Oh man, look, you can see the bullet hole in the wood," Jack responded slightly more enthusiastically than he had been moments earlier.

"Come on then, let's go!" she said in a firm tone.

"Go where?" Jack responded with a look of fear on his face.

"The future. We need to get out of here, and I need to get weapons," she announced whilst making her way to the passenger's side of the van, then got her backpack. She then put it down on the floor to get the Transphone out. Jack stood there watching as she started typing something into the unit.

"Okay Jack, remember this will seem funny. I have to be holding or connected to this, and you have to be connected to me. So you'll hold my hand, remember? I'll press the button; there will be a humming sound like last time. It will start to go dark, then, after a short time, it will start to get lighter, and we will be in 2029. OK. Any questions?"

"What about my mum and dad's things?" Jack asked as he stood there with big sad eyes, like a naughty boy that was being scolded by the teacher.

"We'll come back for your things when I get something to protect us with. I'll also show you how to use a gun. Oh, the tip of the day, when we get there, please stay still —it's for your safety. Just let me take care of things, okay?"

"Why, what will happen if I move?" Jack asked as he started shifting from one foot to the other.

"Because if you move, you may get shot!" came the blunt response.

"Oh! Mmmm, okay, although I'm still not sure about all this. Are you sure that we'll come back? Remember, I'll have nothing... that's if I'm alive!" Jack said as he slowly moved closer to Sage.

"Promise!"

"Okay, let's do it!" He grabbed Sage's hand and then squeezed it tightly out of fear. Nearly instantly, Sage could tell that his hand was clammy.

"Okay, one, two, and three!" Sage announced, then pressed the button, and as she said it, it started to go dark.

Chapter 8

Mason stood in the shopping centre car park; he needed a vehicle of some kind. He looked around the car park frantically for one, but it was hard due to the commotion he had created. He was not sure if Sage would do a jump straight away or not, but he needed to chase after them just in case. If they jumped, he would follow them through the jump, although it would slow things down in his pursuit of them. If not, he would follow them in a car or whatever he managed to lay his hands on.

Then he heard something that caught his attention. A liquid-cooled v-twin – initially, he thought it was a Harley Davidson with a badass exhaust system on it. Glancing at the machine, no, it was an Indian Chef Bob, black with 1133 cc of American muscle. Mason ran over to the rider, a well-built man around a hundred kilos with a grey beard, a black helmet and wraparound sunglasses on.

The bike stopped behind some cars as chaos was still everywhere. With screaming people, and cars trying to get away from the danger zone. The rider was trying to manoeuvre the bulky bike into a position where he could get past the cars in front of him.

"Hey bud, I'm borrowing your bike. I'll try and not scratch it, although I can't make any promises," Mason announced to the rider who stopped what he was doing, then looked Mason up and down.

"Piss off! I'll fucking knock your teeth down your throat!" the response came back to Mason as the man stopped what he was doing and climbed off the bike, breathing in to make himself more intimidating. Reality had settled in as the man realised that this guy who wanted to take his bike had pulled out his gun and stood there with it in plain sight pointing it at him.

"I'll need the helmet also," Mason insisted. The man took it off and handed it to Mason, with anger bubbling up inside.

"Go on, you can go now," Mason instructed and slightly gestured with the gun, as he didn't want the man jumping him when he was putting the helmet on. As instructed, the man glanced at the bike then left the incident behind as he ran into the distance.

Mason put the helmet on and started the Chef Bob, the exhaust roared with anger and venom – it wanted to be let loose. He pulled the front brake as he spun the bike around on the spot in the direction where the van had gone; then he slowly let off the front brake and the bike started moving forward as instructed. The pursuit was now on; he started dodging people kids, and cars that were randomly going in all directions. Due to the low ground clearance of the bike, Mason made his way out through the proper exit of the car park. He turned a tight corner in pursuit, and he could feel the left peg lift due to him scraping it on the road. *Jeez, I need to watch out for that, I don't want to lose a foot or something,* he thought to himself as he went up the gears, blipping the throttle to help shift gears without using the clutch. He knew that they had a good start on him, but he didn't know where they had gone anyway. He spent about twenty minutes riding down a dual carriageway. He laughed to himself as he passed through a speed camera, riding past cars, trucks and vans – but not the van he wanted.

Mason pulled over at a siding, got off the bike, then took off his helmet and the backpack. He placed it on the seat of the bike and removed the Transphone to check if he was catching up with them. The Chief Bob sat waiting for some more action as the lumpy engine ticked over. In the process of Mason looking at the Transphone, his bag fell to the ground.

"Good they haven't jumped yet, they're about fifteen Ks or so in front of me!" Mason mumbled to himself as he made a mental note of the directions, then bent down and put the Transphone back in the bag that was now on the floor thanks to the Chief Bob V twin engine.

He put the backpack on his back, and climbed on the bike. He kicked the stand out of the way and slammed the bike into first gear, then opened the throttle. The back end sat down on the suspension and lurched the bike forward in pursuit of the prey.

"Okay, there's a church. It's left there, then about a hundred meters up that lane on the right is a road, there should be a turning. Mason turned as he noticed a big tree on the opposite side of the road. He went down slowly, following it around to the left of the fork. A barn came into view.

"That must be it," he said out loud to himself, although he knew that they both probably had an idea that he was around due to the noise from the bike. Maybe not the best form of transport to pursue someone in the end, but it was fun all the same. Stopping the bike and putting the side stand down, Mason shut the engine and dismounted it. He briefly paused as he squatted down behind a drystone wall. Removing his backpack, he rummaged in it for some binoculars. He looked through them as they focused themselves on the target – he could see no sign that they were in the barn. No movement, nothing… the doors were shut. It looked like a deserted barn.

Mason was in two minds whether to leave it until the sun went down or go straight away in the daylight. He had no idea if Sage had a gun or not. Glancing around he noticed that it was quite an open approach to the barn. Taking a second look, he spotted that the wall went all the way to the back of the barn, so he could have cover from them until he was almost there. Mason had another advantage – his gun – although he may have lost the element of surprise thanks to the bike. A glance at it to check it out. *What a fun piece of kit.* He though, but he needed to focus on the job at hand.

He put the binoculars away and took out the Transphone once again to check to see if they were in the barn or not. Yes, they were still in the barn so that made his mind up – he would go now. He put the Transphone away and took out the Glock, checking it was loaded, then he put the backpack on. Mason crouched down behind the wall and slowly made his way round to the barn. The wall was not the highest, but it was doing its job of hiding him. After a few

60

minutes of this, he was next to the barn, and he slowly and quietly made his way round to the wooden doors at the front.

Mason noticed a crack in the doors and he carefully spied through the slit to see where they were. No targets in sight, just the van. Mason took a few deep breaths to control the adrenaline as he carefully started to open the door with the gun at the ready. He creeped through the gap he had created in between the door. The van was in view with its rear doors open. *Interesting*, Mason thought to himself as he made his way slowly towards the vehicle, trying to keep out of the sight of the rear-view mirror in case they were sitting in it. He didn't want them noticing movement behind them. Mason got closer and his pace picked up as he moved towards the van's front door. Then pointed the gun at the side window – nothing! Quickly turning with his gun raised, his knees bent so that he could move faster, and scanned the perimeter in case this was a trap.

"Where the hell are they?" he said out loud to himself. Quickly moving to cover and squatting down, he took a deep breath to control his emotions. Mason slowly panned the area again just to make sure, then decided that the place was safe. He lowered the gun and decided that he could relax slightly. Taking a few more deep breaths, and his body slowed the process of producing adrenaline.

"They must have jumped!" he said once again to himself. Then walked over to a hay-stack, took off his backpack then sat down. He removed the Transphone to check out their position, but nothing! They'd gone but as yet he didn't know where or when, as the Transphone was still trying to calibrate itself to their new time and position. But every time they did a jump it would be able to find them faster.

Mason knew he had time to kill – maybe about twenty-four hours or so – but first he would have a look around the van to see if there were any clues in it. He checked the driver's side and noticed a bullet hole in the windscreen… then the blood. Yes, he must have hit one of them in the shoulder or somewhere around that area. He seemed to remember that Sage was driving, so it must have been the male with her. Wishing it had been Sage, although he would be slowing them down, and if he got in a fight with him he know where to concentrate the attack – not that the male would be much of a match for Mason. Deciding that he would go and get the bike, find a hotel and take it easy for the night. Maybe a few beers.

The plan was made, the backpack was put on, and he left the barn and made his way to the bike. Putting the helmet on, fastened it tight (but not too tight), turned the key and Chief Bob roared into life. Remembering that he had passed a hotel during his chase, Mason made his way back the same way that he had come. Except this time, it was a leisurely ride with the cool wind hitting his face to keep him awake. His fingers were also starting to get uncomfortable with the cold as the sun was beginning to set and the atmospheric temperature was beginning to drop. Cold but very awake, Mason pulled into the car park, found a spot, killed the engine, and silence then surrounded him. Making his way over to the entrance, he passed several flash cars – a Porsche, Jaguar, and Bentley, to name a few – and he wondered how much this place cost! Not that cash was an issue to him, he could make or take as much as he wanted, just by accessing poorly protected bank computer system; compared to what was being used in the future. Move some money from an unsuspecting company or whoever he decided to take it from. Darkness had fallen as Mason pushed one of the double glass doors open, and then he was greeted by warmth. It was nice on his cold face as he took the helmet off and made his way over to the counter and placed it down. A portly man with rosy red cheeks and slicked-back hair in a black suit was standing on the other side of the counter.

"Yes sir, can I help you?" he inquired with a French (or maybe Belgian) accent as he glared at the helmet on the counter as if to say "remove that!"

"A room for the night, please," Mason responded, ignoring the man's fixation with the helmet's position. He glanced around the foyer, which was a very spacious area with lots of seating for people to discuss first or third-world problems and solutions that they may or may not decide to act on.

"Yes, we have a room for you, sir." He placed the bill in front of Mason as if to say "can you afford this place?", then glared at the helmet once more. Mason pulled his card out and paid for the room.

"Room twenty-two, sir," the desk clerk announced as he handed the key card over. Mason decided to play a trick on him as he walked away, leaving the helmet on the counter.

"Sir, sir, your helmet!" the clerk shouted out.

"Oh, thanks! Send it to my room please." He smiled at the man, turned, then made his way to the lift. All the time, he took notice of the different people and the layout of the building. *Hmmm, that's interesting... the bar is through there,*

I'll pay that a visit later on. He pressed the lift button but still observed the area as he waited for the lift doors to open. The doors opened, and an empty lift greeted him. It's amazing who you can meet in a lift and the conversations that go on, with everyone listening as they all stand there pretending not to.

He was once in an elevator in New York, and by the time that it had reached his floor he had met a female, wowed her, and invited her to his room. They then went on to spend the night together, that was such an easy pull. He'd thought it was Christmas, although he did end up with STI; which probably explained why she was so fast to jump into bed with him. Probably punishment from her or some divine power to tell him to keep his pants on.

Mason shook his head and smirked to himself as the lift doors opened. Then he made his way to his room, passing chrome picture frames with paintings of dogs and horses. Then on down the cream-coloured walls and carpets of the hallway to a white door with a gold door handle, with the gold digits twenty-two. Touching the key card to the pickup on the door and there was a click. He pushed down on the handle as the door opened, and then the lights came on.

The room was nice but nothing special. His backpack came off first, then he took the gun out and placed it under the pillow, just in case. Then removed his Transphone and adapter, and plugged it in to charge it up. Going over to the minibar, Mason took out the vodka, poured it into a glass and downed it in one. Chuckling to himself, he wondered why he had bothered with the glass, but he had! A deep breath in, then out! The decision was made as he turned to leave the room to go down to the main bar in the hotel.

In the bar, patrons were all stuck-up toffee-nosed pricks, all with marbles in their mouths. Mason hated the rich in any time zone, but they did pay his wages. Most of them had had it all handed to them on a plate, with no clue about life or the price of it. Mason slowly made his way to the bar, passing white leather seats with the gentry looking him up and down, as he did not fit in so well. Chrome and glass were all around the saloon area with dark bits of wood here and there. An open fire was at the far end of the area with an old lady who sat there, probably drinking port.

He noticed an Asian female, on her iPad, sitting on her own at the corner of the bar. Mason moved over to sit at a right angle to her – then he just stared at her. After about twenty seconds, she glanced up at him and then back at her iPad.

"Didn't your mum tell you it's rude to stare?" the female acknowledged Mason's stare.

"I never had a mother. She died giving birth to me," Mason replied to the female.

"Oh, I am sorry, I didn't mean to be nasty," she responded to him, then looked up as she beamed an adorable smile.

"It's okay, I'll let you off this time if I can buy you a drink?" Mason said as he rose from the chair and stretched out a hand.

"Hmmm, is this a ploy to get me drunk? I will have a gin and tonic please," the female answered as she put her iPad down then slightly repositioned herself on the barstool. Mason ordered the drinks from a bartender who was in a white tuxedo with slicked-back black hair.

The drinks arrived and he put them down on mats in front of them. Mason gestured to move closer to the female and she responded warmly to the idea.

"Okay, I'll let you off with the mother thing, just this once." Mason picked up his drink, took a small taste of it, then smiled in the direction of the female. Some light piano music played in the background to help with the ambience of the room.

The conversations went to and fro all night, and the drinks went down quite smoothly; finally, it was last orders. Mason smiled internally as he knew he was going to have this nice warm female snuggle up to him tonight – all he needed to do was seal the deal. He knew that she was on business, on her own, engaged, but not happy in the relationship.

"So do you want to fool around tonight?" Mason asked directly, which he always thought was the best policy. He wanted to know where he stood, and if he should continue pursuing the female or not bother wasting his time.

"Gosh... oh, golly you are direct. Are you as direct in the sack?" she bluntly asked as she finished her drink and placed the glass on the beer mat.

"Well, I can be if you want," my response was rebuffed back at her.

"You know, there is an old Asian proverb. It goes like this: just because I'm drunk, it doesn't mean I'm going to sleep with you!" the female said as she stood up (slightly wobbly). "Goodnight Mason, I hope you complete your task." She smiled at him, picked up her iPad, then slowly and confidently walked away. Mason was transfixed on the hypnotic sway of her walk.

"Well, bedtime for me!" he said to himself, as he made his way in the same direction to the elevator. The female was still waiting for the lift. The doors opened and they both got in the lift. As it rose to their appropriate levels, the silence was very awkward. The music in the background didn't help the situation as they both had their eyes transfixed on the doors.

"Well, this is my floor," Mason announced, half-heartedly hoping that it was the woman's floor too. Exiting the lift, the female wished Mason a good night and the doors closed. He was on his own.

"Well, to bed and sleep for me," he announced to the world.

Chapter 9

I t started to get bright… then there was a big blue sky… then the heat. Quite a change from the UK in any year.

"Where are we?" Jack asked, then bent over to throw up.

"Jack, remember to keep still," Sage shouted as she started to type a code into her Transphone.

"All good now… you can throw up!" she announced, then moved away from him as the stench was quite pungent.

"No, I'm good," Jack said as he slowly rose from his bent position, then wiped his face with a tissue that Sage handed him.

"Oh my god, you have a swimming pool! Can we go in it later?" Jack shouted out as he span around in the garden like a child, forgetting that seconds earlier he was throwing up.

"Well, I wouldn't as it'll be cold, and god knows what bugs are in it. Come on up the stairs."

"What's that? It's… it's a dead body… what the… he's… oh, god it stinks!" Jack announced then started making a gagging sound as he slowly backed off from a decaying adult body that lay outside the back of the house under the shade of the veranda. The dry pool of blood surrounded it with parts of his intestines and limbs being eaten by maggots. Jack could see them moving with the excitement of the feast they were gorging on. Body parts were missing, probably eaten by anything else that was hungry.

"What's happened to him?" Jack started to dry-retch again, with the stench that filled the air. Sage moved closer to the body as she put her hand over her mouth to combat the disgusting odour that was making its way up her nostrils.

"He's a burglar. Or was. The guns took him out."

"What do you mean, guns took him out? You said we are off to 2029?" Jack said as he was still trying to throw up at the same time as he slowly moved away, metre by metre from the body.

"Welcome to Johannesburg," Sage announced. She moved away from the body with no emotion, as though it was a branch that had fallen from a tree rather than a dead man lying on the concrete. She unlocked the door to the house, then entered.

"What do you mean, Johannesburg? Do you mean South Africa?" Jack wanted to make sure that he was on the right track.

"Yep, Johannesburg, South Africa." She disappeared out of sight into the house and Jack followed. When inside, he looked around the kitchen... Worktops, walls, ceilings and tiles, all in white, made the place look stunning against the dark grey doors of the units.

"Is this your place?" Jack asked as Sage took off her backpack, then grabbed the Transphone and plugged it in to charge. She then vanished out of sight through a doorway without saying a word. Jack followed her curiously as usual down a white plain hallway. Numerous spotlights shone down on him. She went out of sight once again through a doorway off the hall. Jack followed and they were in a bedroom. Sage opened the wardrobe door and inside was a black steel gun safe. Sage entered the combination and the door clunked. Moving the handle and opened it and an array of firearms presented themselves to them both. Sage grabbed at one of the guns then took a magazine off a shelf in the cabinet, put it in, pulled the slide to load the chamber and put the safety on. She then held it out to Jack.

"Oh, no, no, no, I don't know how to use a gun, I'm not interested," he protested to her as he put both hands in his pockets.

"Well, after what's happened today, don't you think you should be?" Sage snapped back at Jack, who stood in front of her with a stony face, just glaring at Sage in defiance at what she wanted him to do. Sage could see the cogs ticking over in his mind as he weighed up the pros and cons. Slowly taking his right hand out of his pocket, he then held it out, as he knew that she was right this time.

"Okay, this is a Remington 1911 R1. This has a safety grip that you manually operate with your thumb. Look: safety lock on, off, on, off. Okay? It has seven plus bullets and one in the chamber." She then handed him the gun. Jack took it gingerly from her hand. He looked at it as if it was a baby's soiled nappy.

"It's a Remington? Is that the make? Do they make shavers as well? Why 1911? Was that when it was made? What's that all about?" The questions started to come from Jack.

"Er, I don't know if they make shavers, but this company make guns, and the '1911' is when it was patented, I think." Sage replied to Jack's questions, a slight smile crossing her face.

"This is my favourite – a Glock G17 Gen five pistol; I like my Glocks, they're nice and reliable. So I have seventeen shots. This one was made in 2098… even though they use plastics in the 2019 version, this one is completely made from carbon fibre rather than with some metal parts. Even the ammunition is completely carbon fibre. I don't know how they do it! Before you ask another question, Jack, all I do is shoot them. This all helps with the weight; it also gets through customs a lot easier – that's if I ever had to." Sage took a magazine out of the gun cabinet and put it in the Glock. "It doesn't have a safety as such, it's this little trigger attached to the main trigger, you see." She then showed Jack the gun's safety and smiled.

"Come on, let's have a play?" They moved out of the bedroom, down the hall, through the kitchen, and onto the patio where the dead body was.

"Right, as I said, there is no safety on this like yours or other guns. I'll show you later, got it?" Jack's response was zero as he stood looking at her with his arms down and his gun pointing at the floor.

"So you point and pull the trigger." The weapon fired in the direction that Sage was pointing it, and a ricochet bounced off the wall.

"Your go. Remember to take the safety off," she said as she watched him. He slowly turned to face the wall that Sage had just shot at, lifted the Remington and stood there motionless.

"Jack, take a few deep breaths and slowly pull the trigger," Sage urged him.

"I can't do this... No, I just can't," Jack announced as he slowly lowered the gun.

Sage moved behind him and nudged his elbow as if to tell him to have another go.

"You can do this, Jack. Take a deep breath and pull the trigger," Sage said in a soft but forceful voice.

Once again, Jack gradually raised the gun, as he took a deep breath and pulled the trigger. He took one shot, then two more and he started to smile at the experience of what he was doing.

"Good, Jack, well done. Okay, shoot the body," the instruction came.

"What? No! No, no," Jack responded as Sage pointed her gun at the body and shot at it without looking.

"Well, he's dead anyway, so if you can't shoot a dead body, how are you going to shoot someone in front of you who wants to kill you?"

"Hmm, you're right, I suppose." Jack pointed the gun at the dead body lying on the ground, except now blood was trickling out of the corpse. He stood there, his gun pointing at the body, but he could not shoot it, even though he wanted to.

"It's okay Jack... Take your time... deep breaths and slowly squeeze that trigger... okay?"

The gun went off and the bullet entered the body, which moved slightly from the impact of the bullet. Jack then fired a second and a third at the body.

"You see, you lose your humanness. It's just a lump, not a person, and that's what you have to think. You're not shooting at a person, but a thing, or you'll be dead," Sage stated as she popped another shot into the body, then casually moved into the house with Jack following.

"Safety on, okay!" she shouted. Jack pointed the gun inadvertently at Sage as he looked at it to check if the safety was in fact on.

"Wow, what the hell are you doing, Jack?" Sage used her hand to redirect the weapon away from her face.

"Man, you have to be careful where you point that thing. It could go off. It's not a toy, you know."

"Sorry Sage... I'm so sorry I'll be more aware of what I'm doing with it," Jack responded as his face went a bright red after the smiting he had just received.

"Okay, put your safety on, weapon down. Also how many shots have you fired?"

"Err I don't know!" He responded, then looked at the gun as though it was going to tell him.

"Seven Jack, you shot seven. You must count them, so you know when you're going to run out, Okay!"

"Yes, yes I will." A soft tone came back with puppy dog eyes to match.

"Okay take your clothes off, I'll wash and dry them and then you can have a shower Oh, I think there's a dressing gown behind the door. While you're doing that, I'll also cook some food. I'll shower later on and then we can relax and hopefully have a good sleep, how's that sound?"

"Err. What about the guy chasing us?" Jack questioned as he put the gun down.

"He's called Mason, and he's good at his job. He's a slightly better shot than me and thinks outside the box. He looks after himself, you know, trains at the gym a bit. I qualified with him initially; he can be a machine but loses interest easily. He's diagnosis with ADHD. He does take medication for it but forgets now and then to take it. Let's hope he's forgotten his meds or he will be a pain in our ass. It'll take about twenty-four hours or so for him to find us this time, although the time will shorten the more jumps he does chasing us. Hence why we have to use this time wisely. So go and have a shower. Leave your clothes out in the hallway, okay?"

Jack did as he was told; Sage took both guns to the gun cabinet, ejected the magazines from both weapons and cleared the chambers. She reloaded them to the maximum then inserted the magazine again and pulled the slides to bring both guns online as weapons of death. Then she took out the holster and slid the guns into their appropriate ones. When that task was completed, it was time to start washing the clothes. Then she made her way to the kitchen, putting the weapons down on the counter. The next job was to see what food she had in the house for them to eat for dinner. Jack emerged in his dressing gown and sat next to Sage. He pushed the guns to one side and looked at his plate. A smile appeared on his face as he started to devour the beans on toast. They ate the meal in silence.

"That was nice!" Jack stated before shoving the last piece of toast (with a hint of three baked beans on it) into his mouth. Then he got up, grabbed Sage's empty plate and placed it in the dishwasher.

"You'll make someone a good husband if you keep that up," Sage said and started to laugh.

Chapter 10

Movement, "What time is it?" Jack asked curiously.

"Oh about eight-thirty... why? You know, Jack; you haven't given me your decision yet," Sage said, looking at him as he washed his hands and looked out of the window at the night.

"About what? Should I stay in 2019 to be hunted down or move to 2098 and... oh, what will happen? Oh yes to be hunted down? Which one, Sage?" Jack turned and glared at her.

"That's not fair, Jack. I didn't start this; I'm here to help you out... to try and stop you from being killed." Sage diverted her eyes from connecting with Jack's.

"Oh yes, you and your friends out to get poor Jack, to stop him being cut up for parts for the rich and famous. Thanks," Jack aggressively voiced back as he stood in front of her with anger in his eyes.

"So when does it stop, Sage? When I'm dead or when we are both dead? What will happen if we get lucky and kill this guy? Will they send a terminating robot after us both? When... when will it stop?"

"I don't know, Jack. Yes, they will probably send someone else, although I don't think it will be a terminating robot," Sage said, smirking at Jack to try to calm the situation down.

"Well, to me it looks as though I have made my decision. I'm with you, so I suppose I'm off to the future, but I still want my two things when it's all over. That's all I have left of my family... no brothers, sisters, mum, or dad... just me – good old Jack Krupop. I'm off to watch TV in the front room if that's okay?" With dejected body language, Jack made his way into the front room in silence, turned the TV on and started to channel surf.

Sage sat briefly in silence looking out of the window. She could see the street lights flickering like stars in the sky, and she took a moment to reflect on how bad it must be for Jack. She too had realistically no family. She noticed that it was starting to rain.

Everywhere they went it bloody rained. Sage remembered a time her and Mason got caught in the rain. They were on a job in around the year 2035 and the car that they were using had broken down. Mason was useless at anything mechanical. They were driving along a country road to pick some farmer up and the car just cut out. Everything, engine, lights, radio, windscreen wipers, the lot. Mason had pulled the car to the side of the road and sat in silence for a moment or so. She remembered looking at him and thinking how attractive he was with his five o'clock shadow and moisturised face. He then popped the bonnet, got out and started doing something in the engine bay. Sage got out and moved around to the front of the car. Mason was doing nothing apart from tapping the engine with his gun.

"What are you doing?" she asked.

"Well, Sage I have no idea what's wrong with it! So I thought I would tap it a bit. Then I'll get in the car and tell you I tried to fix it. Then when it won't start, I'll say it's knackered, as though I know what I'm doing."

Sage remembered having a look at the car herself, although she could not find anything wrong with it either. Their destination was about a Kilometre or so down the road, so they started walking down the pictures country lane and got soaked. Mason had put his arm around Sage to keep her warm, as it was November in Scotland and the weather was not the warmest at that time of the year. Sage remembered that she always wanted things to slowly go further but it never did. She felt a fuzzy feeling in her stomach as she remembered that day. That was always the feeling she got when she saw him. She knew that she had always had a crush on him. Sage had felt it earlier today in the café when she first spotted him. She knew that he did not feel the same about her, and killing them both would be easy for him.

She got up and took two beers out of the fridge, then made her way to the front room with them as a peace offering to Jack. Entering the room, briefly stopped, then moved over to where he was sitting. He glanced up at her with red eyes and it was obvious he had been crying.

"Sorry Sage," was all Jack said.

"It's okay Jack, I get it! A beer as a peace offering!" He smiled as he took the beer then moved over to one side of the sofa. Sage sat down and put both feet onto the couch to be comfier.

"I know you are Jack! What are you watching?"

"Crap." He changed the channel

"Oh yes, Fawlty Towers… this is so funny. It's the rat one. You know the episode with Basil, the rat," Jack announced, quite excited as he shuffled in his seat.

"My favourite one is the German episode," Sage responded. They both watched TV together as they spontaneously laughed at the jokes.

"So what are the sleeping arrangements then, Sage?"

"Well, we can have separate bedrooms or sleep in the same bedroom for protection, but no hanky-panky. It's not like that, it's well… you know what it's like," Sage said as she got up and took the empty beer can off of Jack.

"A roadie?" she asked.

"Why not?" Then she made her way into the kitchen, to grab another two beers.

Sage checked the Transphone too. "Good, nearly 100 per cent," she mumbled to herself. Glanced out of the window, picked up both guns, then made her way into the front room. Jack was asleep on the couch. *Hmm, do I wake him or not?* she thought to herself.

Sage left him and went to bed.

Chapter 11

Mason woke up alone, which is not how he wanted to wake up. But it helped him out, as he didn't have to make up some lie – to whoever was in bed with him – about what was going to happen next. No awkward explanation about what had happened in the night either, so he counted his blessings all at once. Glancing at his Transphone, seventy-six per cent located, maybe a few hours more to get their location and year! Thinking definitely time for him to order breakfast, shower, shave then maybe clean his gun as he had a feeling that he was going to be using it today. He didn't want it jamming on him when he wanted it to work, which could get him killed. Mason phoned for room service and ordered a full English breakfast and a pot of coffee. After about ten minutes, the doorbell rang. He got up and quickly decided that he'd best not answer the door stark naked, so he put the dark blue hotel dressing gown on (with a random emblem on the left sleeve), then opened the door.

A wide-smiling female was standing in front of him with a trolley. Hopefully, his breakfast was on it, under a shiny steel dome.

"Morning sir, did you have a good sleep?" the female announced in a bubbly manner. She pushed the trolley in, then stood waiting for her tip. Mason gave her five pounds and smiled politely but he was pissed off. *Yes*, he thought, *they get paid crap wages, but then they want a tip for doing a job they are already getting paid to do. A bus driver doesn't ask for a tip, or a policeman. Oh, I caught a hardened criminal speeding in a car today, do I get a tip?* Granted, the female was polite during their brief encounter, and she smiled once again and left.

Mason stretched and then moved everything onto the small table and started to consume his breakfast. He switched the TV on and unfortunately there was only boring breakfast TV showing. Three idiots who have no idea about life, sitting talking about crap and getting paid to do it. He switched channels several times until he finally got to a music channel. A 1980s channel popped up with Culture Club singing *The War Song*. Not his favourite song by them and not their most popular, but it brought back memories about being in a nightclub on New Year's Eve. It was such an outlandish night as he was out with his mate Max, a nice guy with dodgy teeth. Ironically, Max had found a diamond ring on the pub floor; he did think about handing it in but then thought against it. In the end, he gave it to a female he was seeing as a present. Max was like that, a genuinely good-hearted guy.

The two of them went to various pubs and ended up in a seedy nightclub. The DJ started playing *The War Song* as the first song of the New Year, then a scuffle started next to them. They both got covered in beer as the fight started to spread, just like it does in one of those old cowboy movies. Within seconds, about thirty people, male and female, were fighting on the dancefloor. Beer glasses smashed as this tornado of anger and rage spiralled out of control. The lights came on as the five or so bouncers started to try and stop the fighting, but got caught up in the fiasco. People were running and screaming in all directions, through the fire escapes, main door, and even hiding in the toilets. It's amazing what can happen in such a short time.

Mason briefly stopped eating, smiled to himself, then continued with his burnt toast, egg and not-so-burnt tomatoes. After finishing, he cleared the table, picked up his backpack to remove the gun he had used earlier on, along with the cleaning equipment, and then he sat down at the table. He put the towel down on the highly varnished surface (to protect the parts rather than the table). A waft of burnt gunpowder drifted up to his nose, which reminded him of weapons training. Once, when he was doing guns training with Sage, she didn't check the breach and the gun went off. Luckily, it shot into the floor, and everyone in the class covered up for her, as she would probably have been suspended on the spot – if not worse.

Mason stripped the gun down until it was just parts on the towel. He gave them a quick clean and inspected the parts. Then started to reassemble the weapon in reverse order. Mason tried to fire the gun without touching the safety tab. *Seems good.* Three or four times he pulled the trigger and reset it, and a sweet clicking sound came from the weapon as he pulled the trigger. He reloaded it, slipped the magazine in and pulled the slide back. *Good to rock and roll, ready to take them both out*, he thought. Mason made his way over to his Transphone that was charging; yep, he had a destination and a time to go to now. Playing in the background now was Wham and Wake Me Up Before You Go-Go. He picked the gun up, glanced at the TV, smiled and put the firearm back in the backpack and placed it in the wardrobe for safekeeping.

He then made his way into the bathroom and took a long hard look in the mirror. *Hmm, the laughter lines seem to be getting a bit too big and too many.* He decided that when he was back in his own time he would get them taken out. The operation would not take long and would be relatively cheap. He jumped in the shower and started to wash. He smiled as he knew he was quite buff with the amount of time he spent working out, but not to the point that he looked deformed.

When drying and dressed, he retrieved his backpack and put all his belongings in it. Briefly glanced around the room to make sure he had not left anything, then headed to the door and exited the room.

Making his way to the lift, he passed the female again delivering someone their breakfast. The lift doors opened with a high-pitched squeal. A man in a black jacket and white shirt with a black bow tie exited the lift, nodded in Mason's direction and then was gone. Entering the lift, he then pressed the ground button and a squeal came from the doors again as they closed. Mason did not remember the noise last night when he used it, but things do break – that's nature. A Musty smell in the lift as it plummeted down, then jerked to a halt. The doors opened, except this time in silence.

"How strange," Mason mumbled to himself as he exited the lift then noticed another man in a black jacket and white shirt with a black bow tie. *Must be a party or something on,* he thought as he made the short walk through the foyer to the checkout desk. A slight aroma of that morning's breakfast wafted up his nostrils. A mature female with short black hair was behind the counter. *Hmmm, no ring,* Mason thought to himself as he hit her with the smile, charm and the low husky voice.

"Was your room to your liking, sir?" she enquired with the generic question, as she made uneasy eye contact with Mason.

"Well yes, although a bit lonely in bed!" the response came back as the female averted her eyes and a slightly red tinge started to show on her face.

"Oh, what a shame, sir, I'll pass that on to management. Maybe maintenance can have a look at that?" the response came back, slightly flirtatiously, Mason thought.

"Yes, it's a shame I'm not stopping another night," Mason responded and threw a glitzy smile.

"Yes, it is, sir, although you may be lonely again," the female responded as she appeared to become uneasy with the conversation. Mason stared at her intensely, just for a bit of fun. He wanted to put pressure on her for some reason, but he didn't know why. He had to get onto the job at hand of terminating Sage and the guy with her.

The female tapped some keys on her computer, then glanced at Mason. She smiled and slid the bill onto the counter towards him. After paying, Mason smiled, then turned to make his way to the bathroom.

"Thank you, sir, I hope you have a nice day," she said in a slightly raised voice.

Mason didn't respond to the female as he made his way to the public toilets, with the backpack now in hand. Once inside the toilet (it had mirrors and four sinks to his left, urinals to his right and stalls in front of him), Mason had a quick look around to make sure that no one else was in.

"Good, good…" he mumbled to himself. He entered the stall, locked the door and put the toilet seat down with his foot – after all, he didn't want to touch it! Removed his Transphone, put his backpack on. Then entered the relevant coordinates, date and finally the destination of Johannesburg. Before moving to the future, he decided to email his Manager in 2098 with regards to how his mission was going and what he planned to do! Briefly pausing, a strategy popped into his head. Yes, he could go after Sage, but when all was said and done, he had all the time in the world. What he could do is pop to 2019 and hit a club. He had had a good sleep and could go for a few hours and party, not drink too much, maybe do a line or two, possibly pull someone... Then he'd jump to 2029, it was as simple as that. The Manager wouldn't know as Mason knew how to wipe the memory of jumps. The Transphone was fully charged and he knew where they were. He deserved some fun... he had been working hard chasing these two and not had any kind of break at all.

The toing and froing of right and wrong were playing out in his mind. Mason looked at the time and destination on his Transphone screen and made the call. He went into his favourites list and clicked on the destination. The year and coordinates changed – destination: Party Time! He pressed the button on his Transphone and it started to go black.

Chapter 12

Then, seconds later, the light started to arrive as his destination became clearer. He quickly glanced around to check he was where he wanted to be – he was in a storeroom, Bingo. As always, the light was on, and the smell of disinfectant wafted up his nostrils, with the familiar chemical smell. Numerous cleaning products such as mops, buckets, spray cans and cloths all standing on the floor in no particular order.

Mason opened the door to the small cupboard (it was locked but you could exit it from inside). A blurry wall came into view that stretched to his left and right with a door at both ends. Various coloured graffiti covered every flat surface, dim blue-tinged lights adding to the effect. The strong smell of dope entered his nostrils and a smile crossed Mason's face. He knew that he would be having a good relaxing time for the next few hours and then go back to work. The door to his left opened and a tall man walked in then glanced at Mason as he passed by and carried on down the hallway.

Mason had to dump his backpack as he wanted to party. He knew that he was in the right place, Amsterdam 2019, before Covid had hit the world. He had had his jabs so it would not bother him. Covid was a pussycat compared to what came in 2037. That was called Cast! Ironically this came from a small meteor that had crashed into the Earth earlier that year. The scientists took it and did experiments on the rock and woke up an organism which killed you in days if you breathed it in. It entered your system through your lungs and killed your white blood cells. Millions had died; the world shut their doors to each other. Even wars had to stop as it was killing so many soldiers. The scientists made a drug to combat this issue and the planet sighed with relief.

There was a yanking feeling from his shoulder as his beloved backpack left it, then it was in the hands of someone else. Mason turned as he witnessed a person running away with it. Five metres, seven metres, nine metres. Mason started the chase after the backpack, Transphone, gun – the lot – his life was in that tartan backpack.

"Hey, you fucker, I'll kill you!" Mason shouted in the hope that the robber would just drop it with fear, but he didn't. The thief went through a doorway into a sea of people, smoke and music. A Panic at the Disco song was playing, but he was focused on the backpack. The heavy smell of pot hit him and he wanted to stop to breathe in the atmosphere, to join in, but Mason knew that this was not the time. He was focused on his bag that was now starting to get closer as the crook was pushing people aside, which meant less obstacles for Mason, as the gaps were already there. Just like when cars on the motorway jump behind an ambulance.

They moved through two open doors and into another room (now playing in the background was Jimmy Hendrix's Voodoo Child), Mason was angry now and he was missing out on all of this because of this dickhead. *When I get hold of him, I'm going to make this arsehole pay for all this,* Mason thought to himself. He went past more people as they all watched in awe at what was happening. In reality, they had no idea that a time machine was in the backpack of this thief.

The thief hit some stairs and started to ascend them two at a time. Mason then hit them, as metre by metre he was catching this crook. At the top of the stairs, the man turned right then barged by some females, knocking them to the ground. Mason arrived at the top of the stairs with the debris of female bodies, legs and handbags everywhere. To accompany that there was screaming and shouting. Jumping over these hurdles, Mason then exited the building. Around four metres behind him now, and Mason would catch the robber. The thief

81

glanced back and Mason noticed that the man tried to increase his speed to get away. Mason knew it was a waste of time as he was focused on this person and the prize. They ran down the street, passing and dodging people, to his left, right, then in front of him. Then, out of nowhere, the thief threw the backpack to his left. The tartan backpack went through the air, spinning, and landed in the centre of a canal. Mason bounded over some railings, leaping through the air after the bag. The bag and Mason hit the water nearly simultaneously. After a short swim, Mason captured the prize, and the thief got away. Mason held the bag aloft to try and keep the contents dry and useable. He knew he had fastened it properly for such an incident, but wanted to make sure. Mason swam to some steps nearby then slowly climbed out breathing heavily; he thanked the gods that he had the bag and its contents in his hands once again.

When out of the water, crowds of people stood watching the spectacle that was unfolding in front of them. A dripping Mason, now on terra firma with his backpack in his hand, slowly walked away from the gawping bustle of people. Thirty seconds or so later, he was far enough away from prying eyes and phones, Mason put the bag down on a bench under a street light, he held his breath as he opened the bag. It did exactly what it should do and that was to keep everything in it dry. Letting out a long breath of relief, he took out the Transphone and put his destination back in for Johannesburg. He put the wet backpack back on, prepared himself mentally and, as normal, he took a few deep breaths to calm himself down. He could feel his heart racing as it always did before a jump. The apprehension of whether the jump would go well. Would he jump into something that would kill him? All these factors had to be taken into account. He took a quick glance around – there was no one to be seen! He pressed the button on the Transphone – the humming started, and darkness engulfed him.

Chapter 13

The darkness cleared, except it was night-time. Mason did not move, apart from instinctively crouching down onto one knee as he took a few moments to reconnect with himself and his surroundings. It was warm in the night air as he listened to the outside world of nature at work – crickets, the wind in the trees, the human world of cars travelling. In the distance, a burglar alarm was keeping everyone awake.

Mason moved slowly to the bottom of a set of stairs then eyeballed the surrounding area, his eyes still getting used to the lack of light. He removed his backpack, took the gun out and checked that the chamber was loaded. Deciding that he needed to stash it, he then pushed the backpack into some bushes that were situated to his left. Moving slowly up the stairs he counted them – one, two, three, four, five and six, then the top. *You never know when that bit of information may come in handy,* he thought.

At the top, he once again glanced around at the house that stood in front of him. It looked empty as the lights were out, although it was not guaranteed that no-one was inside. Approaching the door, he moved to the side of it, then slowly glanced in through the window. All he could see was a kitchen, although there were signs of some life – he could see two cups and some dirty plates left out on the worktop. How long had they been sitting there? They could be hours old – or years? Hopefully, this is them! Mason was not a hundred per cent sure; the tracking told him where they had jumped to. To get to their current location would require more tracking, which would mean more waiting.

Mason's self-drying clothes were near enough dry by now. He did not completely understand the technology – just that when they got wet or damp, they shorted out to create heat that consequently dried the items. It was all a bit too high-tech for him, although the main thing was that his underwear was now nice and warm. Mason's heart rate was now quite high, as the adrenaline had once again started working on his body. He could sense his breathing was also elevated as he slowly picked the lock. Once that task was complete, he slowly slid the door open to keep the act of surprise on his side.

"Oh shit!" he said out loud to himself as a squealing alarm went off. Quickly, he made his way into the kitchen. He also didn't know the layout of the house. Mason deliberately went slowly through the kitchen to a door on the other side. The squealer was doing its job as the piercing noise intruded his ears, trying to make him leave the building. But it was also forcing him to lose focus on what he was doing. Looking around in the darkness, he could see that there was only one white door. Making his way quickly, he stopped and slowly opened it. It was dark and he looked down the hallway. His breathing was starting to slow down now as Mason was in the zone mentally and professionally and had near enough blocked out the squealer. The light automatically turned on, which made him wince as it hurt his eyes. He moved his head quickly out of the light and blinked to readjust his eyes in the now changing conditions.

Sage heard the alarm going off and grabbed her backpack and guns. Luckily, she had made a point of sleeping with her clothes on. She had also decided to pack Jack's clothes in the backpack. He should have had the clothes on but fell asleep in the dressing gown before he could put them on. She moved to the bedroom door, stood to one side and took a deep breath, then opened it. She took a quick peep out but saw nothing. Then made her way down the corridor, through the door on the left and over to Jack, who was unbelievably sleeping through all the noise.

"Jack, Jack, wake up!" she screamed at him, shaking him simultaneously.

"What, what?" the response came back.

"Oh god!" His brain started to get into gear.

"I have your clothes in my backpack, get them out, get dressed, here's your gun. We will exit out of the front door, okay?" Sage ordered. Then she span around and pointed her gun at the door, just in case anyone came through it shooting. Jack complied by getting dressed in around twenty seconds or so, and then he was good to go.

"Okay, pull the slide on your gun and let the safety off. Get behind me and please don't shoot me!" Sage requested. Jack did as he was told. He could feel his heart pumping with excitement, anticipation and fear. His palms started to sweat with all the adrenaline going around his body, and he had a sick sensation in his stomach. *What am I doing in this situation? This should not be happening, is it a nightmare? Oh yes, it's my new life?* Jack thought then nodded to confirm the plan.

Sage led them both as they made their way towards the door. She then turned right, down the corridor and slowly opened the front door. A swift glance, good, no potshot, so hopefully the intruder was not waiting for them outside. Jack made his way out first; Sage looked back and could see a shadowy figure down the hallway in the light. Anger started to creep in as she felt violated that some piece of shit had decided to come into her house. Was it a stranger? Was it a burglar? Was it Mason? She didn't know! All she knew was that this person should not be in her house. She must have forgotten to put the external guns on last night or the sensors had missed them. Either way, she would be looking at the system tomorrow.

She could see that the person was going into the area where most of the bedrooms were, including her extra guns and ammo. Sage could not remember if she had locked the safe or not, but regardless it was too late to worry about that now. The figure stopped as it moved back, then turned and looked at Sage. She could not see any facial definitions of who it was, but she was convinced that it was Mason. She could feel it in her stomach. A twisting gut wrenching sensation came across her, like a wave of emotion.

The backlighting and the light from the moon trickled down the hallway probably meant that she could see him better than he could see her. The movement from the person in her sights telegraphed that only one thing was going to happen. Sage was doing the same as him, they stood still with their guns pointing at each other. Who was going to fire the first shot? Sage knew he had a weapon but Mason didn't necessarily know she had one. The time seemed forever, as the hallway light went out on the timer – as did the squealer. Silence now. This triggered Sage to take the initiative of letting the first round off. She knew that it was a hit, but she also knew that Mason did use a vest when he thought that he was up against it. She moved to the right side for cover as a volley of three rounds came at Sage, hitting the wall to the right then left but not hitting her. Several rounds then came from her left, to her surprise Jack was joining in. Sage pushed him behind the wall and out of the way as he stood in an open space waiting to be hit.

"Jack, focus. I'm going to get you some rounds off. You run to the top of the road, turn right follow the path that's parallel to this road. At the bottom, there are some bushes – hide in them, okay?"

"Yeah, okay," was Jack's response to the instructions. Sage did what she said she was going to do.

"Go!" Sage screamed out, and Jack did as he was told.

Sage released one shot, then a second. The person shooting back hid in the doorway out of sight in the hall. Sage instinctively waited until they showed their head again, then released rounds four and five. She turned and started to sprint into the night to the designated place she had told Jack to go to.

Making her way up the street and into a poorly lit park with trees and bushes, then down the path to meet up with Jack. Sage was buzzing now with all this excitement. A brief memory popped into her head about what it was like training. The job that they did, you would think would be relatively easy. Go and pick a random up! But so many times it was not that straightforward – the person would attack them, run, or even have guns. Spotting Jack exactly where she had told him to meet her, a smile came across her face. Probably more with relief that he was safe rather than anything else. She stopped and took two very deep breaths as she tried to control herself. Jack appeared to be breathing quite normally, which she was happy about. He was not freaking out like she had expected, that was also good. Although she did notice that his hands were shaking. Ironically, she had thought about not even filling his gun up with bullets, but clearly that would have been a bad call as he seemed quite happy to shoot at people when he had to. Although clearly, shock from this had not set in yet.

"Okay, Jack, we will have to go into the shanty town on the other side of the major road. Do you understand?"

"What? Shanty town?" Jack blurted back.

"Look, Jack, the Transphone and my backpack are back at the house. So we have to lose him, kill him, whatever. Then go back and get it, then do a jump, OK?"

"Where is it?"

"The Transphone's on charge in the house. I'm sorry, I didn't expect him so fast. It will get faster with him finding us the more jumps we do." Sage then released the magazine, and started to fill it up with bullets that she pulled out from her pocket. She put the magazine back in and pulled the slide back to make sure it was good to go. Then slotted it in the back of her jeans.

"Give me yours?"

Jack complied. Sage took the gun, loaded it and handed it back to him.

"Don't point it at me, please!" she requested from Jack once again.

"Sorry, although the safety is on," he countered.

"Not bothered, we need to work on your safety in a gunfight, and your shooting, but that's for another time. Thanks for joining in, though – you made a difference in that shoot-out. How are you feeling?

"Oh, like I'm on edge. I'm shaking a bit also!"

"That's the shock, hopefully you'll last the night before it all kicks in. Come on follow me." Sage briefly stretched, then rushed out from the bushes, looked around just in case he had stumbled onto them hiding. Making her way into the darkness.

Jack rushed after her and noticed a sign, Luping Avenue, and made a note of it. Then they went down a ginnel and took a slight right as they ran at a reasonable pace through some sort of truck or car park, and out onto the other side. They then stopped as Sage momentarily looked for traffic, then bolted across the road.

"Where are we?" Jack shouted out to her.

"Pretorian Street," was the response as Jack followed her like a leach this time – he didn't want to get lost. He made mental notes of landmarks such as buildings, houses – really anything he could see, that may help him in the future, just in case he got lost.

Mason looked round the corner once again to expect a volley of rounds, but there was silence. *She's gone!* he thought. Then he did a controlled rush to the door and out into the front garden. He knew exactly what she would be doing; *she'll be going to the shantytown to do the jump.* Mason made his way down the road – he turned left, then passed some bushes. He made his way to a major road, and in the distance he could see two figures running towards Pretorian Street. He would not put any credits on it, but he knew that that was them as he picked his pace up to try and catch them.

Sage made her way down a dark opening. Apprehension was starting to play its part with what may be waiting for them inside this place. Jack had no clue where they were going – he could feel butterflies starting to flutter in his stomach at the unknown. His internal monologue once again told him to make notes of where he was going. Jack needed to remember in case they got separated at some stage, so he could at least find his way back to the house if he needed to.

A burnt-out car and truck stood at the side of the road, *a good reference point,* he thought. Following Sage in the dark was not that easy as there were dark bits then light bits. Sage then ran under some trees and turned right onto another dirt road. Jack followed, and the stench of sewage, rotting food – maybe even death – engulfed his nostrils to the point of nearly making him throw up. A thought popped into his head. There was no time to relieve himself of the last food he had eaten, knowing that the guy after them would just shoot at him on the spot as he emptied his stomach. God, how embarrassing that would be – being shot dead while throwing up. A memory, one time when he was younger: he had been out on a big night out with his mate. Jack came home, went to bed and woke up the next morning with a slight hangover. He made a rash decision to have cornflakes for breakfast, with milk. Within five minutes the milk had curdled in his stomach and he was upstairs with his head down the toilet, throwing up. That lasted most of the day – he felt ill for about twenty-four hours. As of that day, he never drank and then had cereal the next morning, especially with milk.

But that was a few years ago, and he was now in South Africa being chased by a guy who he didn't know, who was trying to kill him. He could see Sage under the glow of the moon as the alleyways between the shacks closed in with a claustrophobic feeling. He took a variety of turns – left, right, right, and left – he had no notion where they were going or where he was. All that Jack could do was just keep following Sage. The next thing he knew, he was face down on the floor.

Chapter 14

Jack pushed himself up, then pressure from behind him pushed him down again.

"What's bloody happening?" Jack blurted out, as he was so confused.

"Watcha doing in my place, white man?" The deep-toned voice came from behind Jack's head. Then he felt his gun been removed, as he tried to struggle his way free. Now the pressure of what seemed to be his gun was on the back of his head. This person came closer and whispered in Jack's ear.

"I'm gonna kill you, fucker." Jack heard the click of the safety go off.

"No, no, no, no! Please, no I have cash!" Jack screamed out.

"Do you?" the pressure immediately released itself as the person got off him.

"Staan op. Empty yorr pockets, then I'll kill yoo," the man stated in broken English that was just about good enough for Jack to understand. The moonlight cast a shadow from the building that covered the man with the gun. All Jack could see was the hand and the gun pointing at him. He slowly got up. Jack knew he had no change, no cash – nothing, just his wallet and a set of house keys. This was a fucked-up situation. He could feel himself shaking with fear – or was it adrenaline again?

He fumbled around in his pockets then threw the items on the floor in front of the man holding the gun. The assailant stared at the items and immediately went over to them, bending down to pick them up. Jack made his move, kicking the mugger in the head, just timing it at the point where he bent down to pick the items up. The power of Jack's kick impacted on the assailant's head, reeling it to one side. Dazed, the gun went off randomly, the man grasping to consciousness. Jack then ran over immediately and unleashed a second kick to the head, and silence came from the mugger now.

Jack bent down, retrieved his gun, then quickly looked around for his wallet and keys which were still in the same place that he had thrown them. There was a voice, then a shot from god knows where hit the steel sheeted building beside him. Jack was once again in fight or flight mode, except this time it was flight. He scurried through an opening – hopefully out of sight of the person shooting at him – to potential safety. Another shot ricocheted off the wall to his left as Jack knew that someone was once again after him. Was it the man from the future trying to kill him? Was it a random person who lived around here? Who the hell was it?

"Jack… Jack are you still there?" Sage softly shouted out, stopping then turning to check if he was still there – no he wasn't. She waited for Jack to join her but he didn't. Slowly, Sage started to make her way back the way that she had come, but there was nothing. The light wasn't good, noises could be heard, then there were some shots, but Sage couldn't make out where they were coming from.

What should she do? She could wander around this place looking for Jack and maybe get into trouble herself? Or she could just hope he can find his way out – he was quite resourceful. Although the lack of response from Sage shouting was a bit disturbing.

"Where oh where is he?" she mumbled under her breath. She glanced at her watch – eleven twenty – she turned and jogged back past a small phone tower (a tin shack), turned the corner and ran straight into two men. One of them immediately grabbed her right arm, then her left. Sage started to struggle and her right arm became free. A quick hook to the jaw of the guy jolted him enough to release her left arm. She went to grab her gun but her jaw was thumped. A floating and spinning sensation started to come over her, and unfortunately, Sage knew what this meant… Then there was darkness.

90

Jack moved left and then right, jumping over rubbish, running through small puddles and streams of liquids (he didn't dare think what was in them). He had no idea where he was, or the destination, but he believed he had lost the assailant after him as the shots and voices had stopped. He stepped to one side of the path, then moved into the darkness to rest, holding the gun ready. He prepared himself mentally for an encounter that he hoped would not happen in the next thirty seconds. After about what seemed like hours (but was probably around a minute), he let out a sigh. Starting to relax as the shaking slowed down, he took several deep breaths to calm himself, then put the safety back on.

OK, what the hell am I going to do now? Sage is missing, I have no idea where the hell I am... What am I going to do? Jack thought to himself, as he also tried to control his breathing again.

OK, Jack, you have been in this position before (allegedly)! Except this situation is only ten years in your future and you have a gun that you know how to work! Except you're not a hard-ass gun-toting motherfucker, are you Jack? He thought again. He then started to snigger, probably out of fear rather than anything else. He got up and peered around the corner of the building he was hiding behind. The moonlight lit certain areas up in front of him and covered other parts with darkness.

Bingo! A Ute... maybe there's keys in it? Or it's already been hotwired, then I can get out of this place... Jack thought as he quickly scurried over to it and tried the door.

My god! It opened – what a stroke of luck! Jack smiled. *This is not going to happen,* he thought as he lowered the sun visor down. The keys fell on the driver's seat. He held them up in the moonlight to see if he could find the right one. After a few attempts with different keys, he turned it in the ignition and the dash lights came on.

"Please start, please start!" Jack mumbled as he turned the key. The engine started to crank over slowly at first, then faster. He pressed the gas pedal to help it start, and after a bit of coaxing the Ute came to life, rattily, but it was a runner. Jack noticed the engine oil light was still on with the engine running, but he was not concerned as it wasn't his Ute. He needed lights to see where he was going.

Then lights came from the building next to the truck. He pushed the clutch down and rammed it into first gear then let the clutch up. It veered foreword, lurching back, then forewords then back, as if it was the first time he had ever driven a vehicle with a manual gearbox. Whilst he was moving forward, he fumbled with the storks and buttons, then finally, he got headlights. He followed the wheel tracks of the dust road as they went left and right. Grabbing for the seatbelt, it eluded his hand at first, then he grasped it and clicked it in. Jack felt much safer for some reason with it on. He took a sharp left then went straight as the shanty started to become less dense.

"Noooooo!" Jack screamed out as lights appeared in the Ute mirror, realising that he was now been followed. Every gear change was not the best and it was clear that this Ute had seen better days, many years ago. The synchromesh in the gearbox had gone in second as the gears ground every time he tried to engage the gear from third. Finally, he came to the main road and turned left, regardless of any traffic that might be coming down. Jack needed to boot this piece of shit and lose the following vehicle. He had no idea what it was that was following him but he hoped that it was a bigger piece of shit than the Ute he was in, not a new jazzed-up Ute with a top speed of a zillion miles an hour.

His foot was pressed as hard as it would go to the floor, and the engine pushed out as much power as the tired components would do under the circumstances. Something was rattling quite fiercely from the engine area – either the camshaft or the rockers. All Jack did was hope that they wouldn't let go as the engine screamed its ass off.

Approaching a set of lights, he prayed they'd change to green and they did! Keeping his foot to the floor, he sped through them. Glancing in his mirror to see where his pursuers were. Not good – they went through the lights; they also appeared closer... Looking to his right, he noticed a long brick wall whizzing past, and darkness to his left. Jack glanced at the radio and smiled. He pressed the power button on it, hoping it would work. A slight glow came up and the sound of god knows what, some people talking in a foreign language. He pressed the eject button on the unit and a cassette popped out, bouncing around the cab and onto the floor. The radio then kicked in. The sweet sound of the song *Down Under* by the Australian pop band Men at Work filled the cab. This took the edge off the chase as he could at least sing along to try to calm himself down.

The adrenaline was pumping through his veins, putting him on edge as he fidgeted in his seat. Jack covered more distance, then another nightmare approached in the form of a set of red traffic lights. He indicated right and his right foot hovered over the brake pedal. Then the decision was made – he planted the accelerator pedal instead and ran the lights. Jack took a deep breath, as the glass shattered and the vehicle started to spin, then rolled onto its side. Jack looked down at the road as it skidded under his left shoulder. The Ute came to a stop. Dazed and shaking, he released the seatbelt and fell slightly. Quickly he used his legs to push the windscreen out of the way. Jack climbed out of the Ute as he tried to comprehend what had just happened. He could see his pursuers just arriving at the intersection. There was a man driving – a female was stood on the tray behind the cab, with a rifle or something in her hand. Sat in the middle of the road with steam billowing from under the smashed bodywork was a Toyota Camry. Jack thought it must have hit him as he had run the red! His pursuers' Ute stopped and both parties left the vehicle. Jack froze to the spot, not knowing what to do. Chance once again presented itself as a do-gooder or Samaritan, whichever line you want to go down, had stopped to see if Jack was okay. This was quite clearly his day to be a motherfucker badass as he promptly jumped in the person's car, engaged drive, then floored it. The wheels briefly span until they acquired a grip and he exited the scene. Glancing in the mirror to see what the pursuers were doing. They were running back to their Ute.

A snigger at what he had just done, then Jack tried to make sense of where he was going. He noticed a white fence to his left but had no idea what was behind it or where he was. The kind owner of the vehicle had left the radio on. It was playing Billy Idol and *Rebel Yell*! The pumping beat inspired Jack to drive as though he had stolen it, which he had! If ZZ Top came on, he knew he could lose them, he thought, as he was starting to enjoy this.

There was a slight kink in the road, then another set of red lights presented themselves to him. He glanced in the mirror and saw that his pursuers were still in the background, but Jack made the call to slow down for the lights. Bingo, the lights turned green and his foot floored the accelerator once again. Trees on both sides hurtled by as he picked speed up then braked as he came to a T-junction. Left or right? He didn't want to end up in a dead end; this was not the time to start procrastinating, as he needed to get moving.

The lights once again in the mirror were getting closer. Either way didn't look particularly good, but the choice was made. He looked in the mirror again – yes, there they were, bearing down on him as the car veered right for about fifty meters then he took another right turn. Once again, there was a straight road and he picked the speed up.

A shot hit the back of the car but seemed to not do any damage. The car was performing well as the engine screamed and the auto box went up and down the gears perfectly. He braked again heavily, racing around a right bend into another T junction. He recognised it as he turned left and went down the road he had just come up, except the white fence was on his right side. He held his breath as he approached another set of lights at speed, and he ran the red that had just shown itself.

After more driving at speed, Jack then arrived at the accident that he had just created. Once again he started to indicate left at the set of lights. Why did he do that? To give his pursuers an idea of where he was going? Or just out of good driving habit? Except this time he slowed down, but not too much as the lights were green. He didn't want to have another accident at the same place. Glancing to his left, people were standing around looking at the accident. A man stood under a streetlamp pointing at Jack as he entered the junction and left in one move. *Probably the owner of my getaway car,* he thought.

He accelerated out of the corner and down what he suspected was the main road that he had previously come down. He then noticed a sign to confirm this. Jack was driving like a demon, the Corolla which he had stolen was running well. He chuckled to himself – what a badass he thought he was. Taking a few corners, passing a few cars that were driving at the speed limit. He glanced in the rear-view mirror to see where his pursuers were. Yes, the headlights were getting smaller and smaller and a large smirk crossed his face.

"Shit, shit!" screamed Jack as he approached a set of red lights and cars! Taking to the grass to his left, he slowed down to avoid a person on the pavement, then glanced left and right to see if anything was coming. The car selected first gear, the engine screamed, and the car bounced when he came off the curb and onto the road and started to pick up speed. He checked the mirror again and the lights were there pursuing him with no remorse. On the radio, *Whip It* by Devo was playing, then Joy Division, ironically with a track called *Radio*. It wasn't his favourite song, nor was it the liveliest tack for a high-speed drive, but it slightly settled him to the task at hand of getting away from his pursuers. He passed cars, vans and trucks at speed, and the headlights of the Ute were once again getting smaller.

Gunning the car through a corner, the suspension bounced and the tyres screeched whilst seemingly just about keeping him on the road. Then he got onto a straight bit of road, picking the speed up again. He took a glance yet again in his mirror and could see the hunters, although they were further back as he was outperforming them now. Catching more cars again, choosing his moment to pass one, two – then he hit the brakes as all the wheels locked up in a squealing noise. Bearing in front of him was a truck on the other side of the road, blocking him from passing the third car. Jack hit the fast peddle again and the Toyota's gearbox kicked down, then lurched forward, screaming from the engine as it started going up gears – second then third. The back window shattered as they were now on his ass shooting at him. *How did they catch me so fast?* he thought. Jack didn't want to waste his bullets randomly shooting back at them; to be honest, he had no idea how many shots he had left anyway. *What am I going to do?* he thought. *Drive until I run out of petrol, and hope they ran out first? Oh, and hope they don't hit me as they kept shooting.* Another shot went through the headrest of the passenger seat.

"Fuck!" Jack screamed out. An explosion of dust and fluff came out of the headrest, causing him to wheeze and sneeze as it filled the cab. He grabbed for the window winder but there was nothing – it was missing. The dust was starting to annoy him now, and his coughing was getting worse. He glanced down at the centre console, *oh yes, that's the key*, he thought as a smile crossed his face. He turned the fan switch to full, and air started to blast into the car. Particles of dust and fluff headed out of the back window that was conveniently partly smashed, which helped with the task. Glimpsing at a burnt-out car and truck, Jack knew exactly where he was and a decision was made. I'll pull over, run, hide in the bushes and hopefully not have to shoot anyone. He hit the brakes and the pursuers ran into the back of the car. The car started to go into a spin from the impact of the pursuers' vehicle, and its screeching filled the air. The Ute's driver was struggling to keep it on all four wheels as it snaked past Jack. Physics took over and the Ute spun onto its side – then, after a brief slide on its side, it stopped. *Hmm, the second vehicle I've smashed tonight... I hope they're both insured,* a slight bit of thoughtful humour from Jack. The car had come to a stop, facing in the direction of the pursuing Ute that was now on its side. Steam started coming out of the front, then there were tell-tail signs of flames as black smoke joined in. More smoke started to billow from the front of the vehicle with wisps of flames. Jack's heart was pounding, although his head was light – maybe from the shock or head trauma, possibly adrenaline, or maybe lack of water. He had no idea; all he knew was that he had to get away from them, but he couldn't move as shock and fear played a part.

"Get out, get out get out! Let's go, Jack," he mumbled to himself. Opening the door and another shot whizzed by him. His legs felt weak as he staggered, slowly picked the speed up, then ran towards the burnt-out car and truck. A volley of shots went over his head. Jack started to trace his way back and passed various houses and buildings that looked slightly familiar to him. He did not look back, he just kept running until he got to some bushes. He quickly moved into them and waited silently.

Trying to calm his breathing down once again so that he made no noise. The Remington 1911 R1 was pointing in the direction where his pursuers may appear. *Hope I've lost them,* he thought. His mind was racing with all sorts of possible outcomes. Was he going to die? Be wounded and torched? Or had he lost them? He mentally made a note that if they fired at him, he would fire back to kill, but if they didn't he would let them go.

They appeared, running towards him, then slowed down, chatting to each other and pointing in various directions. Changing direction, they made their way towards the bushes then went by. Seconds later, they come back and stopped in front of the bush with their backs to Jack. The pursuers had a brief conversation that Jack could not make out. Then it happened, exactly what he didn't want to happen. It was something that Jack had no control over. He sneezed. The dust from the car had finally played its part. Both the assailants spun round and lifted their guns. Jack let two rounds off, one hitting each of them. The left person went down straight away, dead by the look of it, as a haze of blood filled the air from his head. The right person lurched to one side, returning fire with a volley of shots randomly into the bushes, not at any particular target. Jack squeezed the trigger as he let two shots off and then there was a slight noise as the second person collapsed to the ground, presumably dead.

Jack stood in the bushes silently with the gun held up, waiting for one of them to move, but nothing. He felt cold and sick inside knowing what he had just done. Then he threw up retching what was in his stomach. Finally, crawling out of his haven of the bushes, Jack made sure that they were both dead, by kicking them both a few times. He slowly moved closer to the dead bodies, gun raised and shaking. He checked their pulses. He had seen it in so many films where they came back to life, then shot the good guy. Jack could smell blood and death, which made him gag, then he threw up again onto the road. After some time of being bent over and gagging, coldness crept once again through his soul, then the shaking continued. Seconds, minutes passed. He mentally told himself that it was him or them. He then slowly headed up the road to the house that Sage would hopefully be waiting in. Jack decided that if no lights were on, he would wait outside.

Chapter 15

S age could feel a rocking motion, like being in a small boat, swaying gently in the lake. She remembered the long summer days when she would go on the lake, fishing with her uncle. She felt a slight sense of tightness on her wrists, but Sage did not comprehend what it was, as she started to struggle to breathe. There was a coldness on her back for some reason – what was happening? Her ankles felt strange, then the pain from them started to become intense. A hot sensation came over her. Voices, yes, voices started to enter her consciousness. This tranquil state that Sage was in was weird. The chatting was unclear but excited, then there was laughing – yes, she could hear laughing. The voices started to become clearer as they got louder and louder. She slowly opened her eyes and all the pieces came into place.

Sage's vision was blurred, but after a few blinks, her eyes started to focus. She looked around the room, which was dark apart from the moonlight that was streaming in through the windows.

Groggy, she looked down and noticed her hands were tied by some rope to a chair. Someone was tying her feet also. Realisation kicked in! Slowly she started struggling, thrashing her legs as she tried to twist out of this nightmare. Then she started screaming to try and get someone's attention. A hand quickly came over her mouth to shut her screams up. Tears started to well up in her eyes. It started to sink in, what they might have in store for her. Sage stopped and the hand removed itself.

The other man came over and grabbed her jaw, then moved her face left and right. He then tilted her head so that she was facing him. He stared at her. His eyes filled with darkness from his soul, then a large smile crept across his face, as he looked down at Sage.

He said something to her that she didn't understand. He then smiled again at her as his hand clasped around her neck; the hand squeezed slowly tighter as all hope of breathing was now cut off. He moved his face closer to hers. There was a smell of stale breath as he spoke.

"Fok jou (*fuck you*)."

Sage understood that, then he let go of her neck and stood up. Instantly, she gasped for air, as she needed to conserve her energy and choose her moment. The man then took his shirt off and threw it to one side. Sage's eyes followed it as she noticed her gun lying there. He turned his back on her as he moved away. Then the rest of his clothes came off, and he started to prepare himself.

Sage, anticipating what was going to happen, tried again to twist, screaming, trying to kick herself out of this situation; hoping that Jack would turn up and kill them both.

"Stil teef of ek sal jou nou doodmaak (quiet bitch or I'll kill you now!)," the now naked man shouted.

Panic was at an overload in Sage's brain. The other man standing to the side of Sage started laughing. He then slowly started to undo his belt. The naked man stood in front of Sage, and she could tell he was ready. She could see him picturing in his mind what was going to happen. The briefest of smiles crossed his face in anticipation.

Sage struggled again, twisting, trying to escape from the binds. She also knew what was going to happen. At this point, she started mentally preparing herself for it. A final struggle, twist of her arms and legs as Sage put every ounce of energy into it. A creak, crack and a groan.

The struggling paid off, as the wooden chair started to fall apart. Sage ended up on the floor with various parts still attached to her limbs. Grabbing the chair arms, she now had weapons, although other parts of the chair were constricting her movements.

"Teef (bitch)," the naked man shouted as he quickly moved towards Sage. She swung the chair arm, which connected with his face. His eyes glazed over and down he went with a thud on the floor.

"Fokken teef (fucking bitch)," screamed the other man as he started to move forward, then stopped and glanced at his unconscious friend on the floor face down.

"Yes, you are thinking now, aren't you?" Sage mumbled as she slowly climbed out of the parts of the chair that were still around her legs, whilst keeping her eyes fixed on the man. She was now free. Glancing at her beloved gun lying to her right on the floor.

The man looked at it and started to move towards it then stopped. Sage got to the gun first and quickly grabbed it. The second man realised that he had lost his power over this helpless female. Now he was looking into the barrel of the Glock.

"Oh yes, it's a different story now, isn't it?" Sage screamed aggressively at him. She took in a few deep breaths. She was still gasping for air. The pain from her ordeal was starting to pass, although her legs were shaking with fear, anger and rage.

"You see, this bitch has a gun," Sage shrieked at the man as she slowly moved around to get a better position as the other man was starting to come round. She was mentally telling herself that she needed to keep calm or she would make a mistake; then they may get the upper hand again. A glance at the gun and she could see the barrel shaking at the end. *Focus on them, not the gun.* She mentally told herself.

The man on the floor looked up, resentment and rage in his eyes. He then started to slowly get up but stopped, as he realised what the situation was. Sage gestured for him with the gun to get up. He did as he was commanded and stood in front of her, naked. Sage could see hatred in both of the men's eyes as they stared at her like wolves waiting to pounce.

"Ons gaan jou doodmaak (we're going to kill you)," the naked man said in a sadistic tone as he slowly moved his index finger across his throat to gesture it getting slit. Then he moved forward. Sage pulled the trigger and shot him in the scrotum. He went down, screaming as he grabbed his balls as if to try and stop the pain. The second man stood still with his jaw slightly open in disbelief at what he had just seen.

"You see, if you had just let me go, this wouldn't be happening, would it?" Sage calmly announced to him.

Silence came from the man still standing. The other man was in between whimpering and screaming as blood oozed out of him. Sage looked at the man standing and pointed the gun at him.

"Nee, nee, nee, nee, nee, nee, asseblief nie jammer nie, jammer (no, no, no, no, no, noooo, please no, sorry, sorry)," he pleaded to Sage, then collapsed to his knees looking for mercy. Sage held the gun, waiting to make a decision. Put this monster out of his misery, or let him go? If she let him go, Sage knew that other females would be treated the same. They would be put through more than what she had been put through. Her training and luck had got her to this point, but this small pack of men would no doubt prey on any female they wanted without mercy.

The decision was made; the trigger was pulled and the bullet went into his forehead, execution-style. The man's body slumped to the ground, as did Sage who collapsed as the feelings, emotions, hurt, and revenge flowed through her all at the same time. Sage had no idea how long this torture had been going on for. She gagged, then retched as her body tried to purge out the adrenaline, suffering from what she had just been through. Then she looked at the naked man who was now quiet, but still alive. He was staring at her. Sage pointed the gun and put him out of his misery too.

After a short prayer to mentally help herself out, Sage rested for some time to allow her strength to come back. She then slowly got to her feet and momentarily paused as her eyes welled up with tears, with the relief that it was over.

She glanced at the two perpetrators in the light with no remorse for what she had done. They will hopefully be in a place where they deserve to be. She took a breath and composed herself, then moved to the door and the exit.

Outside, Sage was on full alert. She glanced at a car sitting on bricks and went past it towards the main road. Jumping at every noise she heard – fear was still playing its part with her emotions and head.

Sage then remembered that she was been chased by a killer. *Can this night get any worse?* she thought. Sluggishly and methodically, Sage made her way past the bushes that she and Jack had hidden in earlier. She briefly stopped in the shadow of a tree, then noticed two bodies on the ground. She looked at them and wondered who had killed them. Jack, Mason or a random person? Then started to move again towards the house – she did not want a shootout knowing that she was not mentally or physically up for the fight. Not to mention the lack of ammo, although if it happens then so be it.

"Psst, Psst." A noise came from the bushes outside the house. Sage gradually lifted her gun. Then there was movement from the direction of the noise and slowly Jack emerged from the bushes.

"God, I'm glad to see you!" Jack announced as he slowly made his way over to Sage then wrapped his arms around her in a cuddle.

"Oh my god, you will not believe what I have had to go through tonight to get back here. Do you think it will be okay to go inside? Mmm, you smell funny..." Jack announced as he backed off and then tears welled up in his eyes. He then gestured towards the house with his gun as if to change the subject.

Sage mentally told her self this was not the right time to let go. She had to stay strong and focused even though she felt nauseous. They had both been through a lot recently and needed to get through this night together.

"Errr, well the door's still open. I'll go in first, and you follow me, okay? But I'm running low on ammo," Sage said as she took a deep breath in and tried to be the calm one. Moving to the door she pushed it slowly open. All that greeted her was silence. Sage slowly made her way down the hallway noticing impact marks on the wall from the earlier shoot-out. Systematically, she went through the house as it became more apparent, there was someone inside; Sage was not going to bet any credits, she knew who it was.

Chapter 16

Mason waited, preparing himself for what may happen. He knew that a white male going into such an area would be a dangerous act. Mason could not understand why Sage went, into such a place at this time; you wouldn't even go during the day. Maybe she was desperate.

Arriving at the main road he looked left and right, not wishing to get knocked down by a passing car or truck. He picked his speed up to a jog with his gun ready – he knew that his magazine was half empty. Now each shot would have to count. Quickly, but in a controlled manner, he made his way under a tree then into the shantytown. The moon was quite bright as he glanced up at it. No clouds in the sky. He stopped at a corner, then with a hurried glance he moved forward. He performed the same task at every exit, corner or what he perceived as a danger point. He systematically made his way forward, although realistically he had no idea where he was going or where they had gone. After a few moments, he concluded that it was a waste of time. They could be anywhere! For all he knew they had jumped. He couldn't check on the Transphone if they had, although it probably would not have registered yet anyway.

"What do I do now?" he mumbled out loudly as he moved into the shadows of a building. The stench was unbearable. He was now at a lower perception of alertness. Mason decided that he was looking for a needle in a haystack. How was he going to find them – there must be hundreds – if not thousands – of places they could be hiding? Fear was also teasing him. Mason's stomach was knotted up with panic inside. He turned and started to move back the way he had come. There was a brief noise from the main road – a truck – then he heard some screaming to his right, which soon stopped. *Not my problem,* he thought. He had enough on his plate trying to find the duo.

After a few minutes, he was back at the main road. Then he moved to stand under a tree as a Ute went speeding past him. About twenty seconds later, another Ute passed. He watched both of their tail lights go into the distance and realised that he was hungry. That made the final decision for him – he would go back to the house, wait for them and maybe make some food for himself.

Making his way back, Mason sauntered along to the edge of the main road, checking that he was not going to get hit by something. He passed some bushes on the right-hand side then went up the road to the house. It was as he left it – with the door ajar. The smell of gunpowder greeted his nostrils. He entered through the doorway and closed it behind him. Mason had a feeling that no one was home, but all the same he raised his weapon and did a quick sweep of the house. Food was all that was going through his mind at this point, then the notion of a shower.

He started to scan around the kitchen – he looked in the fridge-freezer, then finally onto the cupboards. A smile came across his face. He pulled out a tin of baked beans and frozen bread. He microwaved the beans and toasted the bread, and ten minutes later he was sitting eating his meal of choice, beans on toast. He had always decided that if he was given the last meal, it would be beans on toast. A smile crossed his face and then he devoured the food. After finishing, he put the plate in the dishwasher, then it was shower time. He entered the bedroom's en-suite bathroom, he turned the shower on, then set the temperature and stripped. The shower was a bit cold so he turned the heat up to adjust the temperature. As Mason always did, he started from the top and worked down – from his hair to his face, arms, and then down. He remembered the female in the hotel room that morning and he started to get turned on.

104

"What the fuck?" he shouted as the shower door opened, just at the wrong point!

"Hands up!" he was ordered. He did as he was instructed, which left Mason in a slightly compromising position...

"Hmm, a bit busy eh, Mason? Did I catch you at a bad time?" the voice said as a female stood in front of him with a grimace on her face. She could not help but look at his manhood standing to attention.

"Hey, Sage, nice to see you."

"Really!" Sage said in a sarcastic voice.

"What's happening? Oh, I see!" Jack blurted out. He then realised what Sage was looking at, got embarrassed and moved away.

"I'm not going to ask if I can finish what I've started," Mason voiced as he climbed out of the shower. He stood in front of Sage on display. As a result, his manhood slowly shrivelled up.

"Okay, where to now? The bedroom?" he said in a dry tone, smiling.

"Grab that towel, then walk in front of me and don't try anything, Mason. The night I've had, I will just pop one in the back of your head without a second thought, okay?" Sage announced in an aggressive voice. He did as he was told, although she kept her distance from her prisoner just in case he tried something. Jack was watching in silence.

"Okay Jack, tie him to that chair, there's some cord in the second drawer over there – she gestured towards a drawer in the kitchen. Jack followed her instructions as he tied Mason the best he could.

"Is he secure?" she asked as she slowly lowered the gun that was pointing at Mason.

"Yep, all good, although I'm no knot expert, you know!" the response came back from Jack. Finally, Sage was happy that Mason was restrained and not waiting to ambush them. Making her way over to the fully charged Transphone, she turned on the security system to maximum alert, just in case someone had seen them going in and out of the house. Maybe they thought that there were some easy targets inside.

"I'm off for a shower!" she stated, then slowly made her way out of the kitchen.

"What happened to you? You don't seem yourself!" said Jack.

He then rushed after Sage. Finally blocking her way into the bedroom, he was not letting her go anywhere until he had an answer. Sage looked at him as tears started to well up in her eyes.

"Jack it's been a very traumatic night for both of us, I'm off for a shower... please, please let me go!"

"No, no, there's something wrong isn't there?" Jack insisted, he persisted in blocking her way.

"I was attacked by two men tonight and nearly raped. In the end, they suffered and they're dead. Happy now?" With that bombshell of news, Sage barged her way past Jack and into the bathroom. She closed the door and checked her gun – it was empty! A good job she didn't need it. Then she took a breath as the tears finally streamed down her face. She stripped and entered the shower. Frantically she tried to wash off the smell of the attackers, any guilt and the rest of the night.

Jack stood in the bedroom in silence, not knowing how he felt about what Sage had said. Anger started to well in his stomach. He knew he had to release it in the near future. The bed.... He started punching the mattress as hard as he could, until he became physically exhausted, he then slowed down. He turned and sat on the bed head between his hands.... After some time and lots of tears, he decided that he needed to do something to take his mid-off of what had happened. As he calmed down he noticed that his arm hurt from the gunshot wound earlier on. *Mental note get pain killers off Sage when you have the chance...*

Having seen how Sage had reloaded his gun earlier on, he decided to reload it just in case something happened while Sage was in the shower. He had a heavy heart and wanted to rest, but decided to check on Mason first. Jack did not say a word to him even though he wanted to ask him questions. Like, why are you doing this? Who are you doing it for and how can you live with yourself? Mason just smiled at Jack as he sat there with a towel covering his modesty.

Jack rolled his eyes then made his way to what he would call the armoury room. Placing the gun on the desk, he sat down and started to pull the Remington magazine out, then loaded some more bullets into it. He heard what sounded like gunfire – *it can't be,* he thought to himself as he carried on with his task at hand. After what seemed like five minutes (but was probably only seconds), then pulled the slide and loaded the gun. Jack started to slowly make his way out, gun raised towards the kitchen.

"Oh shit, he's gone!" was the solitary announcement that Jack made as he entered the kitchen. Slightly lowering the gun out of shock at the missing prisoner. Realization kicked in and he raised his gun, then slowly started moving backwards out of the room. Turning, Jack quickly rushed to the bathroom, then burst in. Sage stood in front of him completely naked. Jack could not help but to give her a once-over glance. Then shame tapped him on the shoulder as he remembered what she had been through only a short time ago.

"What the hell are you doing? Can I not have bloody five minutes of peace?" Sage screamed at him.

"I'm sorry, but he's escaped," was the response back from Jack as he covered his eyes after seeing everything. He turned to look away out of embarrassment.

"What do you mean he's escaped? You said he was tied up? For god's sake, are you trying to kill us both?" Sage yelled once again at him. She finished climbing out of the shower. The only time she could get away from the turmoil of the night had been destroyed.

"Well, knots are not my strong point... I did say," he announced back.

"Oh, thanks for telling me that now, I should have done it myself. You're as useless as a one-credit watch, really you are!" she shouted at him whilst pulling a towel off the rail and wrapping it around her. Her guard, Jack, watched out for an attack from Mason.

"Give me the gun!" She held out her hand, then promptly took the Remington off Jack. Sage knew her gun was out of bullets.

"Stay behind me, Jack," Sage slowly and systematically made her way through the house. When she was happy that Mason had left, she made her way over to the chair then picked the cord up and looked at it.

"I should bloody strangle you with this for doing such a crap job. I asked if it was good and you said yes!"

"Sorry, Sage." That was all she got back as she made her way to the sink to get a drink of water. Then placing the cup down and she made her way to the Transphone. Sage looked at the screen on it, then did something with the device. The next job was to hitch up her towel again.

"Did you open that?"

"Open, what?"

"The patio door," Sage clarified.

107

"No!" Jack responded as he looked at it with a vacant look.

Turning off the security system and raising her gun, then slowly went through the doorway; out onto the patio. Jack had no idea what she was doing but followed her as it started to become apparent. Now there were two bodies on the patio. The man from earlier on and now another man, which was Mason.

"Oh, well he got what he deserved," Jack blurted out as Sage slowly made her way to the body then bent down to check if Mason was dead or alive.

Mason had a vague, dreamy smile; he looked at Sage. She noticed his eyes light up.

"What's the dickhead saying?" Jack blurted out.

"Nothing. Mason, ignore him," Sage softy said back to this dying man.

Mason was mentally asking himself questions. Why had he taken this mission? He never wanted to kill Sage, which is the reason she was still alive. He lay on the patio completely naked, yet there was a warm euphoria engulfing him. He knew that this was the end – he was starting to feel sleepy. The initial pain from the three shots he had taken had subdued. When he saw Sage's face, all the pain went away. Only love was in his heart for this female in front of him.

Sage put her hand under his head to comfort him.

"I'm sorry, Mason."

"It's okay, Sage, it's all in a good day's work, you know," he said as he raised his right hand. Sage grasped it. A tear slipped out of his left eye. All sorts of feelings were enveloping him. He realised his life was ending – the confusion and fear, but at least he was not alone. Sage was with him.

"It's a shame we never got it on, Sage, I could have made you happy."

There was pain and then a smile crossed Mason's face. Then he was gone. Mason let out a sigh then… nothing. His hand went limp.

"Mason, Mason." Sage knew it was over. She never knew how he felt about her, but she also felt the same way. Tears ran down her face as she once again realised why she had got out of this business.

Sage sat next to her fallen friend and enemy, then said goodbye to Mason. Getting up with her head down and a solemn posture, she passed Jack and made her way into the house. Jack followed then realised that she wanted to be alone when she moved through the kitchen to the bedroom then closed the door behind her. Jack was going to ask if she wanted anything but all he could hear was Sage sobbing.

Chapter 17

Once in the bedroom with the company of silence, Sage started to reflect on her position in life. Was it all worth it? She was not employed – she just did the odd job here and there, bar work mainly, some shop work, any odd jobs for a few credits. She had no lover, man, or husband on the scene. This was a chink in her armour; she did like that, but maybe it was time to change.

Sage had no children, none on the way, not even a twinkle in her eye. And the good points in her life? She was jumping around in time, having a blast getting shot at, and attacked – although this was not her current life, this was a past life she was reliving again. To top it off, for some weird reason she was helping a stranger, who could not tie bloody knots. Could her life get any worse? Yes, she had just lost a friend that was trying to kill her, but in reality, Sage knew that he would have probably killed Jack and left her. Well, she would have hoped that that was his plan anyway.

What was she going to do now? It was like her life was one big event of banging her head against a wall. No matter how hard she tried, she got nowhere, but everyone else seemed to be moving forward – apart from Mandy. She was the cause of this all.

Sage looked at the gun sitting on her lap. It did look tempting! All she needed to do was point and pull the trigger, then it would all be over. The running, the fear, the anxiety of trying to think about what to do next. But what about Callum? Would he be okay without her? He would be devastated, if she was killed while working, but he would understand. All she would be doing is putting her trauma, agony onto him. Sage knew that she needed to put it all mentally in a box, to deal with later. Yes, currently it would relive her, but what about him, and even Jack? Jack would be a sitting target.

The noise of a cup smashing on the floor in the kitchen reminded her that she had Jack. She had taken this task on and would finish it or it would finish her. Anyway, it would not be fair on him, so she made a pact to revisit this mental place at a different time when she was alone to think her life over. After taking a few deep breaths in and out, she glanced at her shaking hands then looked in the mirror. She saw a very bedraggled Sage. Smiling at herself out of irony, then winked just out of amusement.

Standing up, she then put the gun down on the bedside table. She locked the bedroom door, then went over to her backpack and took some items out of it. She took a glimpse at the mirror again, then made her way into the bathroom, dropped the towel on the floor and turned the shower back on. Climbed into the shower and started to vigorously wash herself to try and get the smell, dirt, blood and thoughts of the night off her. Glancing down at the floor where a combination of colours washed away, intertwined with her tears, as the water swirled around then went down the drain and was gone.

Sage was washing and washing to try and disinfect herself from the night, the death and the attack that had happened. This process went on until the hot water started to run cold. Climbing out, she dried herself, cleaned the mirror with her right hand then once again stared at herself. This went on for several moments. She moved closer as if to enlarge her view as she looked into the backs of her eyes, trying to see what was going on in her head.

All sorts of thoughts spun around about the night and what had recently happened. This would stay with her to her grave unless she did something about it. She realised that she was so, so close to being raped tonight. And why? Because two men could not control their urges? No, they were animals and finally got put down like the animals they were.

Moving to the bed she lay there, trying to block the night out. She then started thinking of all her past lovers. To be honest, there were a few, but they all treated her with respect and never forced her to have sex with them. Although some of them only had sex with her rather than making love to her. She pursued this to try and take her mind off what had happened, with nice thoughts and deep breathing, and by remembering the first time she had sex. A slight smile crossed her face as she remembered that she hadn't known if he was in or not – never mind whether he had finished or not! But it did get better from there on.

Number four was not the biggest but, god, did he know how to turn her on! Then the next one was a big guy, but only thought about himself and when he had finished, then that was it. His interest in her – with making her happy – was over. She had about thirty seconds of frantic action to make sure she was satisfied, and that was it, game over. The next one was obsessed with weird stuff, something she was never that big into, but she did it just to please him. Sage could never grasp that at all, why did guys like strange stuff? But luckily, that lover didn't last long at all due to his bizarre behaviour and lack of loyalty to her. Bumping into him in a restaurant with another female was not a good advertisement for him as boyfriend material.

Then her thoughts shifted again. What was she going to do next? Yes, Mason was out of the way, but someone else would come after him. What were they going to do? The options that she could see were to go to her Uncle Callum's house and ask him. Or try to negotiate with the Manager or kill him off. He was a person that Sage never really got on with. Try and blow up the jump system or delete herself from it somehow. Jump and ditch the Transphone then hope that they don't find either of them. Keep running and killing their assassins, whilst hoping that the Manager got bored or they ran out of players or maybe they would be killed, to end it once and for all. It was a mess, one that she should sleep on. Hopefully tomorrow she would feel better and more like herself. She glanced at the dark maroon curtains, got up and tweaked them; as there was a gap in the middle. The defence system was on, and they were as safe as they could be.

No, why should she have tonight's thoughts for the rest of her life? She did have the power to sort this out and forget it. Sage reloaded her gun with ammo, put clothes on, got the Transphone, set the place, time and date, then pressed the button and everything went dark.

In what seemed like no time at all, the darkness cleared, although only moonlight was creating any light. Sage glanced at the time. She needed to move, as she knew that the other her would be running down the alley soon. She quickly made her way down past the corrugated sheeting. Then raised her gun and moved into the shadows. Voices could be heard and a shiver went down her back. Moving slowly out of the shadows.

"Hey!" She spoke softly and with a wavering voice. Sage could feel her hands shaking as she pointed the gun at the two men. The two men had not heard her at all as they were engaged in conversation.

"Hey, you fuckers!" she shouted louder. This time they both stopped talking and looked at her, then turned to face her as they realised that she had a gun.

Sage moved slowly closer to them, gun raised. She gestured that they go in the shack that they'd previously had her tied up in. They both stood in silence in front of Sage.

"Forgive me, God, but I must do this," she mumbled, then pulled the trigger and the man on the left went down, then there was a second bullet for the man on the right.

Glancing out of the window, she watched herself run by, unaffected by these two dead animals. The memories would now start to fade away on what these two men had done.

Sage took out the Transphone that was stuck down the front of her jeans. Clicked on its last time, pressed the button, and it went dark.

Arriving back in the bedroom, she once again looked at the dark maroon curtains. Then, after putting the Transphone on charge, stripped and climbed into bed and pulled the covers over herself. She looked at the lamp that sat next to her, touched it and it turned the light out. Then she brought her legs up so she was in the fetal position and pushed her hands between her legs as if to comfort herself with what had happened to her. Closing her eyes, Sage thought that this was possibly the worst day of her life. But she knew that some of it would disappear.

Jack stood looking at the door that Sage had shut for a moment, then decided that he should go and check the external doors for safety. As he did this, he went over to get some water and put the kettle on. Glancing at the two bodies outside under the night light, a tear rolled down his face. What a waste of life – gone forever. All their thoughts and emotions, and experiences gone for good. These sorts of things upset Jack as it brought the reality of all this into perspective – how frail humans and humanity are. That one piece of lead in the right place can end it all forever.

A click broke his concentration as the kettle boiled. He poured the water into a blue cup, then started to remember his parents and how they were not around anymore. It troubled him like a cloud of sadness covered him. Both were dead. He had no brothers or sisters – he only had himself in the world. Jack was so grateful for Sage going out on a limb for him. She must have such a wonderful heart. She could have stayed in 2098 and just thought, *sod him! I don't know him, so why bother!* But she hadn't, she had honour; she was a wonderful human. To come through time to put her life on the line for someone who she didn't know, it humbled Jack. Slowly making his way to the bedroom that he should have been in, when the shootout started earlier on, rather than sleeping on the couch. He headed down a corridor and passed the armoury, to the end room.

On entering, the walls were dark blue and had a light grey ceiling rather than white. There were light blue curtains and a single bed, draped in a cream cover, to the right of the room. A lonely TV on the wall was all the room had for furnishings. Sparse was what came to Jack's mind. He placed his gun down beside the bed, then made his way over to the window. Glancing out, he could see street lights twinkling as time was passing on. The moon was very bright tonight – he had found that out earlier on when he was running from the guy – Mason – who was after them both. Yes, the dead guy outside his room, who Jack could see in the moonlight lying there with what looked like a cat sniffing him – possibly thinking he was supper or maybe dinner. Who knows? He pondered for a few more moments about what was going to happen. What was he going to do? What did Sage have as a plan for him, her and them? Shutting the curtains, Jack smiled to himself at the fact that he had survived another one of these days. His thoughts then went to Conner. He could not remember the last time he'd had a chat with Conner.

Sage had said that it all started when someone called Mandy had taken him to the future for body parts, or something like that. Then with the events that occurred, he got accused of murder and then it all started to spiral out of control. Jack stripped and then climbed into bed, and he looked up at the ceiling for a few minutes before turning the light off. He closed his eyes and plummeted away into a disturbed tormented nightmare of a sleep.

A beeping sound went off. It was Sage's alarm on the Transphone. Someone was on their way. It didn't always pick the signal up, but this time it had. Sage jumped out of bed then quickly put her clothes on and grabbed her backpack and Transphone. She rushed out of her room and down the corridor to Jack's room. Bursting in with urgency, Sage turned the light on and viewed Jack face down with the covers on the floor. His bare ass showing, he was twitching and his mouth was open, there were slight signs that he had been dribbling on the pillow.

"Jack, we have about five minutes and counting. Someone will show up wanting to kill us, so get up or you're on your own."

Jack jumped like he had been electrocuted. Sweating with the night parcels he was having.

"Errr, bloody hell, I'm naked, Sage. I haven't slept well at all!" Jack blurted out as he covered his bits with both hands.

"Really you're going to be self-conscious now? You'll be dead if you don't get up this second. Just grab your clothes and get dressed in the car."

"You have a car?" was the response that came back to Sage.

"Of course I do! Do you think I'm stupid?" Sage picked his gun up, put it in her backpack and left the room. Jack grabbed his clothes and trainers; he exited the room also, following her naked but covering his modesty with the clothes. He systematically dropped socks and trainers, then picked them back up so he could follow Sage.

"Come on and turn the light out when you leave," Sage shouted. Jack did as he was told, and followed Sage who was waiting for him. They made their way out of the front door, closed it behind them. Sage pressed the remote on the key fob and the garage door opened up. A Subaru Outlander stood there with the bonnet open and some wires leading from it. Sage disconnected the wires that were obviously from a battery charger.

"No good having a getaway vehicle with a flat battery, is it?" Sage stated as she climbed into the car. Jack threw his things in the footwell of the passenger side then got in.

"Ooh, that's cold!" he complained as the cold leather touched his bum. Sage started the car, then engaged Drive and floored the accelerator. She came out of the garage at speed, then pressed the fob again, the door started to close behind them. They were on the run again…

Chapter 18

The Chief was sitting, looking out of the window and pondering whether he was going to have a BBQ later that night or not. Yes, these were issues forced upon him by society. It would be unhealthy, with the large amounts of alcohol which him and his friends would consume; not to mention the burnt red meat (although it would be tasty!). But it was better than the alternative of the cardboard food his wife Pia tried to feed him – that stuff was put together in a factory and then she dared to tell him it was healthy. At least his meat roamed freely in a field eating grass and mooing!

But the sky was blue (although getting a bit cloudy). The decision was made, it was BBQ night! The Chief made his way over to his desk then clicked on various names on the address book that came upon on the clear glass screen.

"Dictate," he said out loud, to prompt the computer to start working.

"Barbeque, my place tonight, 1900 hours. I'll provide the food and the fun; you bring yourself, alcohol and the drugs!" The words appeared as the computer typed them up onto the screen. He glanced at the text to make sure that it all made sense.

"Send!" was his next command, and the computer did as it was instructed. Then the message went into the digital world. The Chief started to check through his emails to see how Mason was doing but there was nothing. He sat staring at the screen, then started thinking about this issue. Mason was usually very prompt with his reporting. The Chief had not received anything from him recently, which was not a good sign at all. He thought this was all starting to become too hard. He just wanted Sage out of the picture, then his life could go back to how it was: steady. He needed to cover his bases. He decided to send someone, just to check and see how Mason was going – but who? Mandy was out of the picture, it was a shame Sage was also out of the picture as she was good. Now possibly Mason was also out of the picture. He could send Jodie – she was a bit unorthodox, but she did get the jobs finished. Although the slight issue with her was that she did end up killing some of her clients accidentally (so she always said). No it had to be someone else.

"Abbie Praxia's number?" he asked the system, and instantly got a tone. It dialled the number and the line rang. After around five rings it went to the answering machine.

"Hi, I'm probably doing something, but if you leave a message, I may get back to you… if you are worthy of it!"

"Hi, errr, this is the Chief. Can you call me back as soon as possible? Thanks." He took a brief pause as he thought about adding more to the message.

"End." The phone hung up. Well, it was time to go, as he had a BBQ to start up before his seven or eight friends came round to take the piss out of each other, drink and maybe do drugs until the morning. He smiled to himself – he loved his three-day weekend. He promptly got up, turned his computer off and left for home.

****

There was a vibration from Abbie's phone – she ignored it, as there was an interesting conversation coming from the table next to her that she was listening in to.

"I bumped into your girlfriend at the doctor's yesterday," a short, balding old man said.

"Which girlfriend's that?" responded a tall grey-haired man.

"Tracy, you know?" the short man said as he took a drink.

"Tracy?" the confused tall man said as he sat thinking who this man was referring to.

"Yes, the one on reception that you always go on about when you've been to the doctor's."

"Oh yes, Tracy. What I would like to do to her... if I could get a hard-on, anyway! I bet she's been around, you know?" the tall man responded.

"You're a mucky old man; I hope you choke on your drink." Then the short man glanced at the bald man.

"Yes, well, you can only dream of your youth, many, many years ago." Both men, most likely in their nineties, started to laugh out loud, as they sat in a café front discussing their youth, and their past adventures, from lovers to wives and fighting.

Abbie loved listening to them both chatting away – they did this in the same coffee shop at the same time every day. It was the same routine for her nearly every day. Whoever was there first would take up the entire table with their belongings. Then the second man would arrive and start moving them about, putting the items on the floor or just being annoying. After that, there would be a joking argument or maybe one would hit the other on the back of the head in fun. This would instigate the man who arrived first to stand up and ask the second man if he wanted to take it outside or did he want his false teeth knocked down his throat? The response would be some sort of abuse, like that he couldn't win a fight with a paper envelope. Then hilarity would ensue from them both, as they shook hands and laughed about what fun they had just had.

Abbie enjoyed her coffee before she went home to her apartment in one of the high rises in the city. About five minutes after the two men's conversation had finished, she decided to look at her watch. How strange that the Chief was calling her so late in the day, he must be desperate! Why was he phoning her? Surely he would phone his blue-eyed boy Mason or one of the other purple circle people? Abbie decided that she would ignore the call and go home. Then maybe she'd call him later on, or even wait until tomorrow to do the task that he wanted her for.

After a brief moment of clarity, she finished off her coffee then redialled the number to have a conversation with him. The phone rang and all she got was his boring answerphone. It was the standard message: "I'm sorry, I'm out and I will get back to you." What it probably should have said was: "Sorry I'm pissed at the moment, I'm probably having a gang bang with my mates. I'll call you back when I get my dick out of this person (whoever it is)."

The Chief had a reputation around the place. Was it true? No one knew, but the fact was that it kept going around the building, and you never know when there may be something in it. "No smoke without fire," was what her grandma used to say. Abbie was not of the same slick bread as Mason. She was younger, at only twenty-eight, with striking blue eyes, shoulder-length blonde hair with a green rinse through it. Her look was slightly wilder-looking than Mason's chiselled buff model look. Abbie had a slightly strange build; she looked overweight except for her muscular thighs, arms, and shoulders with a flat stomach to finish off. The body shape was due to her hobby of gymnastics. She wore glasses but changed to contact lenses when she needed to. She liked her look, with the glasses, most of the time.

To top it all off, she had a bubbly personality. She had tattoos on her arm of vines and leaves going up to her shoulder. Her nose, tongue and ear were pierced; yes, she stood out in the crowd, which is exactly what she wanted. Abbie did not want to be one of those sheep that conform to everything and follow rules. When she had joined up to the company, she looked so different, but there was a plan. Abbie went through the tests, and the training of the company, and got the top scores. After the scores, she got friends, then the contracts came. After that came all the commendations of best this and top of that. Abbie knew that it was time for her to come out of her shell. The metamorphosis happened like a butterfly or a moth. A beautiful creature that stood out in the crowd, in any timeline, in any place.

She looked up at the sky as the rain started to fall ever so lightly. People started to run as though it was plasma acid falling from the sky, but it was just rain! She smiled to herself, then finished her cup of coffee, and ordered a Goober to take her home. Glancing at the two old men chatting away about what they had done with their lives and how long they had left. Four minutes twenty-three seconds later, the Goober stopped in front of Abbie. She stared at it, the rain bouncing off the bodywork to create a slight halo effect. Abbie got up from her chair, glanced at the two old men, then rushed to the vehicle to climb in. There were the usual pleasantries from the on-board computer, including the question of destination.

"Block four, Aiden zone, please. There's no rush in getting me home. A standard ride please, not a high-speed one," Abbie requested as that was slightly cheaper than the high speed rides that broke the speed limits. You paid for it in the credits you were charged, which was fair enough. The Goober then powered up and moved off into the lane. It made its way down the road, then turned left and onto a winding part of the section.

"Oh, put some easy music on please," Abbie requested as she made herself comfy.

The Goober headed up the curved ramp and onto the skyway. Some background music came on that Abbie didn't know, but it was better than nothing. The seats were covered with what looked like sheepskin wool but they were obviously fake. Looking out of the window as the rain was now lightly coming down.

Tall and slender, squat and long, the cityscape was coming to life as the darkness started to creep in and the lights of the buildings started coming on. The other cars were of various colours and shapes, although generally they were the generic teardrop shape. Other vehicles on the skyway, trucks and motorbikes among others, were all powering on to their destinations.

Abbie had a bike licence but didn't own a bike at the moment, it was impractical for her to have one, and Phil would no doubt object. But she always thought that it was cool riding a bike in the rain, with the aerodynamics keeping you dry as though it was magic. Abbie was always awed at the future she lived in when going back to do a job and watching programmes on the TV like Star Trek; it was amazing that she was living in the future that the programmes were trying to predict.

Keeping to the centre lane, the Goober moved along at a steady speed. She lived on the fifty-first-floor apartment with a west-facing view, which gave her amazing views of the sunsets in summer and winter. Abbie loved sitting on the balcony with Phil, who also loved to sit staring out at the sun setting. They would be snuggling into each other under a warm blanket and a glass of mulled wine. On the odd occasion, they would do some meditating together, but that was not that often as Phil was not that big on all that crap. Finally, the Goober pulled to a stop at the destination under the large overhang that led to the

119

entrance of the building. Just as it stopped, the electronic female voice came over the speakers once again.

"Thank you for your company today, it was enjoyable. The fare will be taken from your account. Have a nice day." The door hissed open and Abbie climbed out. Glancing at the wet road, she could see that the rain was now falling slightly heavier than before. On approaching the building, she placed her right hand on a glass screen about head height. Once again, a generic female voice thanked Abbie and hoped that she'd had a nice day. *Hmm, everyone hopes I have a nice day?* she thought sarcastically.

The green-tinted glass doors silently slid open and Abbie made her way into the large hotel-like foyer. Looking at the people that were milling around, Abbie smiled internally – she was happy that she lived in such a nice place. Noticing the hard black marble floor, she made her way over to the lift. With a stroke of luck, she arrived at the lift door and it simultaneously opened. A well-dressed man and woman, both in suits, stood in front of her. Abbie walked into the lift and noticed that the man was slightly red in the face as though he was embarrassed. The lift immediately recognised her from the chip in her wrist. She had only lived in this apartment for about ten months, so she did not have full access to its facilities yet. Abbie looked at both of their reflections from the mirrored doors. She thought that they were probably going to a function or maybe the restaurant on the top level. The only access Abbie had at the moment was to the building and her apartment. After a year or so, Abbie hoped that she would be accepted by the building committee, to be given full privileges of the building. This would include the gym, library, bar, free Goobers and restaurant. She smiled at the thought of her and Phil going to the restaurant for the first time.

She then felt the lift speed up as the G forces compressed her body into her legs. Then as it slowed down, she became lighter and the lift dramatically braked to the point that it stopped. A thought crossed her mind, that the journey in the lift would be hard on someone heavy; Abbie was at her normal weight of sixty-eight kilos. An advertisement for wedding rings that was being screened at her from the back of the lift doors cleared as they slid open. A large mural of a tree greeted her eyes as she moved out of the lift.

She turned right, then glanced back at the couple in the lift who were now gently kissing. A smile crossed her face as she started walking slowly down the plush corridor to her apartment; number 5116. The soft dark green lush carpet could now be felt under her feet; it was like walking on spring grass. Various random pieces of artwork were placed on the cream-coloured wall. At the end of the corridor was a full-height window with a view of the city. She finally arrived at the door, the chrome numbers on the light ash wood sparkled in the light. She put her hand on the chrome handle and, without any effort, the door opened, so she entered.

"Hi, I'm home!" Abbie shouted out as she took her shoes off at the door, then placed them on the rack. The small hallway led straight into the living room then onto the dining room. Basically, it was one big space with different names for different areas. Abbie could hear music playing in the background. Frank Sinatra was singing *Fly Me To the Moon* – not Abbie's cup of tea, but Phil liked him so that's what they would listen to.

"On the balcony, babes, watching the rain coming down and snuggled up!" A voice came from the direction of the kitchen. Abbie made her way over, walking on more plush carpet, except this time it was blue. Passing the white coffee table and black leather sofa to arrive at the kitchen doorway. Phil was sitting on the outdoor sofa, under a woollen blanket – she was wearing a back-to-front baseball cap. *How are the 2060s?* Abbie thought as she made her way through the stainless steel kitchen and picked up the pre-made coffee that Phil had placed on the counter worktop as a welcoming gift.

"Is it cold outside, love?" Abbie asked as she made her way onto the balcony. She was greeted by Phil's smile – it was the smile that had first hooked Abbie's heart. That fateful rendezvous in the city seemed so long ago. A nightclub called The Garage, a disused car garage that used to fix petrol, diesel and the odd early electric cars. It went out of business for some reason. This was surprising because the hydrogen fuel cell had been introduced in the mid-2030s. Then the next breed of transport came to fruition as more exotic propulsion systems appeared, like the mag plates. The car lifts, jacks and tools were still in the building, although barriers were around them to stop the drunk or drugged idiots from climbing on them. The music was of all sorts, as there were different rooms –electronic, classical, the seventies, eighties, nineties, two-thousands, mid-century and now. Abbie was moving into the 70s room and had got her drink knocked out of her hand by Phil, who had clumsily bumped into her. They had glared at each other, but something clicked; then that smile.

Her heart was pierced with an arrow from Cupid. A tingling sensation came over her. Abbie smiled to herself as she remembered that time. The song that was now playing was Elton John – *Bennie and the Jets*, which reminded Abbie of the night, every time she heard it. She remembered that they chatted for a bit, then moved into different rooms and danced until a song by a band called Cigarettes After Sex came over the speakers. It was so in the moment, the song was called, *You're the Only Good Thing in My Life*.

They had danced slowly and close, and that's when the first kiss happened, on the dance floor in a crowd of strangers. Yet they felt all alone in each other's arms. At that moment, it felt as though no one else was in the room, just the two of them. Then, to spoil the moment, a guy had bumped into them both and started mouthing at them as though it was their fault. Abbie remembered looking at Phil's smile, then she had swung a right hook that connected on the drunk's jaw and he was sent spinning backwards into a group of guys. They grabbed him and shoved him in the direction of the bouncers and he was gone out of sight. By the time that it was all over, *Parklife* was on by Blur! A great song – not the most romantic song by any stretch of the imagination. The Knowledge did a live version of *Parklife* on one of their retro live albums, which she owned. They had both danced all night, with intervals of passionate kissing until the club closed. When they finally exited, the lights in the club were up, which hurt their eyes. Both were shattered and they agreed to go back to their own pads to sleep and to meet up the next day.

Phil hadn't moved in with Abbie yet, but it was only a matter of time before that happened. It had been talked about, but nothing was set in stone and there was no time scale. Abbie put her drink down on the outside table. She moved around, sat down and snuggled next to Phil. It didn't take long until Phil's hand started to wander. Abbie was also in the mood; she placed her right hand on Phil's head as she briefly played with her hair, then down to the cheekbones, then moved to the neck, kissing Phil softly. She slowly undid the top button, then the second and down to the third. Abbie continued down south until every button was undone. With both fingers, Abbie slowly parted the white garment to reveal Phil's chest. Abbie had noticed the moment they met that Phil had a lovely smile, piercing eyes and curvy body. Even in the darkness, the light seemed to illuminate her for some reason.

"You smell of flowers, Phil. Have you been using my shower gel again?" Abbie asked inquisitively, yet jokingly.

"I may have!" She planted a kiss on Abbie's lips that seemed to last for a long time. Abbie knew that this was a distraction from the question. Pulling away, Abbie gazed at Phil.

"Oh bless you, Phil... I love you."

"Philippa!" was the correction Abbie received.

"Oh babes, whatever." Then their lips touched again, except this time their tongues were involved, as Philippa's hand slowly made its way into Abbie's top. Then she touched her skin, slowly moving around her back to pull her in closer. The rain was starting to come down harder now and the wind was also starting to pick up. They briefly stopped as they snuggled under the blanket for shelter. Their blanket had inevitably outlasted its usefulness as it was getting wet. The water started to penetrate its way in, interrupting the two lovers under it.

"Come on, let's go inside," Abbie suggested as she placed a small kiss on Philippa's forehead. They both got up and headed inside, into the warmth and security of the apartment. Locking the elements outside – the rain and wind could not get to them now. Inside, the passion continued as they made their way over to the couch, briefly both standing and admiring each other in the light.

"Lights down, fifty per cent," Philippa requested. She moved closer to Abbie then with both hands grabbed her.

"That's mine!" she announced as she squeezed with passion. Abbie smiled.

"Let's go to bed." She grabbed Philippa's hand, leading her to the bedroom.

The next morning, Philippa heard the shower going, as she lay on the bed naked, thinking about what had happened that night. She Loved Abbie so much and the way they played together, but she did want to try a man again. Now and then it popped into her head, the difference in the body's structure and smell. She started to remember her first boyfriend, Jo Eggbut. What a name, it was as though someone had thought of it as a joke! They were eighteen and made out in his car (not the most romantic place to lose your virginity). He was self-indulgent, as he wanted to be pleasured first. The whole experience (which didn't last long for her). This was the only time she'd had sex with a man. As for her, the experience was not good. Philippa remembered the comment that he said after he had tried to rock her world – "Come on, I'm meeting my mates in ten minutes." This was the line he gave Philippa after he had finished. They had both promptly put their clothes on, then met up with his friends.

Philippa then heard the rumours that she was a shit lay, although it didn't stop one of his mates, Greg Goodwin, coming up to her and saying, "Do you want me to show you how to do it?" Philippa believed that he was under the impression that he was doing her a favour. She declined the free lesson that had been generously offered to her and decided to try females, which she enjoyed so, so much. The tenderness, warmth, softness, and kindness... the list goes on. No farting, face rash from the stubble, grubby fingernails, over-sweating body (although a bit of body odour could be a turn-on).

Philippa grinned to herself thinking of Abbie, then the devil herself appeared with a towel around her. The water glistened in the light on her skin.

"My turn," Philippa said as she got up then made her way to the doorway that Abbie had just come through.

"Are you watching my tush?"

"You bet I am, and if you don't hurry I'll smack it."

"It won't be the first time," Philippa responded as she went out of sight.

Abbie took out her knickers, bra, jeans and a yellow t-shirt with a tree on the front, then systematically slipped into them all. She glanced in the mirror and checked herself out as she combed her hair.

"There, you're beautiful," Abbie announced to herself, then burst out laughing at the vainness of the comment. Abbie was not vain at all; she could wear work clothes and work on an old car engine, getting dirt under her nails if she wanted to. She used to do that with her older brother who restored old cars with petrol engines in them. Not desirable by some parts of the population, who keep on about how the Earth's going to die! Well, they have been on about it for about a hundred years now and guess what, it's still going strong. There are colonies on the moon and Mars, and humans are exploring other parts to colonise.

She picked up her Transphone and checked the message from the Chief. It was a brief email explaining that Mason had not contacted him and could she go to the quadrants he was last at to find out what the hell he was up to?

She made her way over to the wardrobe and pulled out her trusty backpack. She as always checked that everything was inside. Clothes, credit cards, carbon fibre Colt Defender 1911 with her initials, AP, etched into the handle, spare rounds and so on, with other items of various descriptions. The one thing that was missing was lip balm – she headed over to her bedside cabinet to grab one, and she added it to the backpack. A girl must have her lip balm, you never know when you might need soft lips. Just as Abbie was set to go, a vision appeared in front of her: Philippa was wearing a towel on her head and nothing else.

"Are you after it again?" Abbie, stopped in her tracks.

"Have you got the time?" the response came back at her.

"Unfortunately, hot thing, I'm going to have to go. I don't know how long I'll be, okay?" Abbie announced as she picked up her backpack.

"All good, babes, stay safe! Because who's going to do the washing if you don't?" the response came back. Abbie went over and softly kissed Philippa on the lips, then made her way out of the apartment and took a short walk to the lift. In the lift, she ordered a Goober to the office where she would do her first jump from. As the lift descended, she noticed that the advertisement on the lift door was now for trips to the moon. Abbe had thought about a holiday, but wanted warmth rather than no gravity. She made her way through the foyer and waited outside for the Goober to arrive. It glided in front of her and the door slid open. She jumped in and noticed that the rain had now stopped. The vehicle set off, then stopped all of a sudden, as a man walked in front of it, unaware of what he had done; he had been concentrating on his conversation with someone.

"Give him a toot, car, to wake him up." Abbie shouted out.

"Sorry policies will not allow us to be aggressive. Please keep seated, we are setting off," the computer explained to Abbie.

"I'll be as downright aggressive as I want," Abbie mumbled under her breath.

"Pardon, did you say something? The voice enquired.

"No, just drive please," was the response back. The Goober made its way to command – it wasn't a long journey, although the spray was still hanging around, now and then the wipers would come on.

"Do you want any music on?" the voice enquired.

"No, it's all cool, thanks," Abbie responded as she thought about Philippa. Abbie loved Philippa with all her heart, but deep down Abbie knew that Philippa was not a hundred per cent into their relationship. Abbie could not put her finger on it, but they needed to talk about their future. She looked out through the spray on the windows as the Goober passed other cars. Abbie looked at the passengers who all looked happy in their little bubbles of metal, carbon and glass. Completely ignorant of anyone else and the issues they may be having. But how many of them were happy? Or maybe playing along as that was the easier way to go about it. Who was cheating, and who was being cheated on?

Abbie thought of Phil – she was happy and she loved her. The Goober glided on through the rain, which was now coming down quite heavy up to the point that the traffic slowed down. The Goober finally arrived at the destination, gliding to a halt in front of the main door of a building. The car's doors slid open and Abbie climbed out of the vehicle, almost forgetting her backpack. She was still thinking about Philippa and the issues that were bubbling underneath their relationship. She had a heavy heart; she took a deep breath and gazed around at the bustle of people. Then she looked at the Goober she had just exited. The next passengers were climbing in. A man and a woman – do they look happy? Are they together? Are they work colleagues? Either way, they slid off into their lives as the vehicle went out of sight.

Entering the front door through security, she declared her weapon, even though the security system didn't detect it. After she used the lift, she took a small walk down a clinical white corridor, as she headed to the transit room. Pushing open the hardwood door, she entered an office and filled out the appropriate paperwork for the jump. Then there was around ten minutes of waiting for everything to clear with no conversation with anyone. These people did not talk to anyone as low as her. The all-clear came and she entered a dark brown walled room with a white ceiling that just didn't look right. She never knew why it unsettled her, but it did! A low humming was always audible, regardless of whether the room was being used or not. Abbie set the date, time and year for her first jump. She calmed her slight nervousness by taking deep breaths, then looked at her Transphone, pressed the red button on it, and then a humming sound increased as it started to go dark.

The darkness cleared and it was night-time. Abbie moved behind the wall at the foot of the stairs, then instinctively crouched down onto one knee as she let her eyes adjust to the light for a few moments. It was silent, apart from the wildlife, and that made it a bit disturbing that nothing could be heard. Then

126

there was the sound of a car – *oh well, at least someone else is alive in this time,* she thought to herself in her position of safety.

Abbie made a move slowly to the bottom of a set of stairs, then stopped. She heard something at the top of the stairs. Hiding behind the brick pillar, she slowly took off her backpack and got out her night vision goggles. Putting them on, then gradually moved her head. Yes, just as she thought, it was loaded with weaponry as part of the alarm system. Slowly, she moved behind the pillar again. Then took off her backpack, and removed her Colt Defender 1911and checked the chamber – it was loaded.

She put the backpack back on, then deliberately moved from behind the pillar and took a shot at the first sensor, then the second. Bits of the sensors rattled to the floor. Then, she waved her left hand as a target – *good, nothing,* she thought and cautiously stood up, hoping the defence system was now down for the count. *Good nothing,* she though and breathed a sigh of relief...

Then moving up the stairs cautiously, just in case there was a third sensor. Systematically counting the steps – one, two, three, four, five and six then at the top. Abbie glanced at two bodies, one black and one naked white male. The house looked empty – the lights were out. Abbie made her way to the door, then snuck a look in through the glass; all she could see was a kitchen. Although there were signs of a shoot-out and a chair stood in the middle of the floor. *Interesting,* she thought to herself as she tried the door. It slid open.

Making her way methodically through the dark kitchen. She didn't know the layout of the house at all, but her night vision goggles were a godsend as she tried not to bump into anything. There was a white door in front of her, she slowly opened it – there was more debris on the floor. More evidence of a gunfight. She looked around, then the hallway light automatically turned on. *What the!* The light startled her initially, although luckily the night vision goggles protected her eyes. Her eyes started adjusting immediately to the brightness, she looked at the rest of the house like a cat looking for its prey, Abbie soon concluded that no one was home.

Slowly letting down her guard, she made sure that the front door was secured, then made her way to the kitchen. A brief search for a rear light switch. It was tucked away on one of the walls. Once located, with a quick flick of the wrist the area outside was illuminated. Eyeballing the two bodies outside, Abbie knew that the naked body was Mason, but she had no idea who the other one was. She made her way out to confirm that it was Mason. Then bent down to look at his face and check for a pulse. Due to the blood loss, he was dead. The rumours were true – he presented well, having a physique like an Adonis. Abbie glanced down and another myth was confirmed, about his endowment. There had been rumours that he used to be a porn star on the side, which always made Abbie snigger.

Quickly looking around, there was a grey sheet or something in the corner of the garden. Picking it up, Abbie shook it to make sure there was nothing untoward in it – she didn't want to get bit by a puff adder or something like that! Then placing the sheet over him as a slight mark of respect, especially after the lack of disrespect she had shown only a few seconds earlier. Then there was the task of finding his equipment – they didn't want that falling into the wrong hands. She took off her backpack then got out her Transphone, typing some keys on it. Then a noise came from the bush, which showed her where Mason's Transphone and backpack were hidden. Picking it up, she placed it on top of Mason's body. Abbie set the Transphone to home and pressed the red button, then stepped back. There was a twenty-second countdown, Abbie stood looking at the body. Mason disappeared from the place where he was lying on his final journey to the year 2098. He would hopefully be picked up and dealt with. Abbie now knew that this was now her job, like it or not!

Taking stock of the situation, Abbie sent an email explaining everything to the Chief, and her plan of waiting at the location until her Transphone connected with Sage's. This would give Abbie a location and time to pursue them both. Moving inside, she was getting bit by the local insects that were after her blood. She made a cup of tea, picked her backpack up, then moved the chair into an obscure part of the kitchen, just in case Sage walked in, and set down the trusty backpack next to the chair. Abbie plugged in her Transphone to charge, then pulled the slide once again and checked that it was ready to go, should she need it. She didn't want to be in the position where she was pulling the trigger and nothing happened – that would be hilarious! Or maybe not? She sat down and made herself comfy, then started to go through Mason and Mandy's reports. It was starting to become clear to Abbie that the two people that she was tracing were quite good at killing off their pursuers. Abbie didn't know Mandy or Mason personally, but she did know that they were proficient at their jobs. She knew that they were both well known in the ranks. She was going to have to be careful or she would be the next name on their list of dead and dusted!

Going into Sage's file, the penny dropped. She was previously employed by the company? This was not good – not good at all – she would have had the same training in capturing, evasion and killing, just like Abbie. But the guy she was with was a mystery. Why was Sage helping him? Why was she doing this? What part was he playing in all this? Checking out his file, Jack seemed a normal guy. Had he had some special top-secret training or something? He was the one that had killed Mandy, so he must have some skill set, but what was it? Sitting in the dark with a cup of tea, waiting for these two killers to come back, deep down, Abbie hoped that they didn't return. She knew that she would be outgunned and maybe end up like Mandy and Mason.

Chapter 19

The unmistakable drone of the boxer engine was all Jack and Sage could hear as they sat in silence. Jack clumsily finished getting dressed; Sage was driving now to the speed limit (although five minutes earlier, she was driving like a lunatic, screeching tyres, revving the engine into the red).

Jack looked at the radio as he thought, *shall I put it on or not? Will it work?* The car looked okay, so he had a bet with himself that it would work. He reached over and turned the system on – white noise came over the speakers. He pressed the pre-set buttons on the system to see if anything came on and then realised that it was on AM, not FM. Jack briefly stopped to check out what buttons did what, then proceeded to press the band button, as some African music came on. More buttons were pressed and some sweet, sweet music came across the airwaves – *I Don't Care* by Ed Sheeran and Justin Bieber. It wasn't his type of music but it was better than nothing. The next song was *Jump* by Van Halen – *wow, that's a song.* He remembered his dad playing it when he was younger. He would dance around the room like Dave Lee Roth, trying to do the jump that the singer did on the video, but failing miserably at it. Jack internally smiled to himself; he missed his dad, although he never really showed it. Jack then remembered the video to the Bieber track, *I Don't Care.*

He seemed to remember that they were both sitting next to a swimming pool, posing. Well, Bieber was with his top off, wooing the females with his hunky, tattooed body. This brought out a snigger from Jack.

"What you laughing at?" Sage asked as she glanced at him and then put her eyes back on the road.

"Oh, nothing. I was just thinking about this video, that's all!"

"Is this the one with Bieber posing by the pool?" Sage asked, as she then braked heavily at the traffic lights that had just changed to red.

"Don't want to run them, do we!" she said. She glanced left and right to see who was around.

"Yes, that's the video – why?" The response came back at Sage as she lifted the clutch and they set off again.

"Oh, he was quite cute; I met him on a job once. Bieber was okay, although he had a lot of "yes" people around him. You could tell he was a nice person at heart, but maybe the press presented him like they do to sell papers, make news, whatever... I don't know... I liked him," Sage explained and then yawned.

"Yeah, I get what you're saying; I think he gets a bad deal off the press," Jack, then turned to look out of the window.

"I'm knackered; I could just do with a good sleep, except someone else is now after us. The alarm went off on the Transphone. The only way we'll get a bit of peace and quiet is with another jump, which will give us about twenty-four hours respite at best. But where to?" Sage said as she looked at the road ahead intently.

"Well, let's look at this logically. Could we go somewhere, then get on a train or something? We could sleep on the train and still be on the move. I would imagine that that would throw them off for a bit longer. I've never been to Paris, you know!" Jack hinted to Sage, then glanced at her. He noticed that the moonlight etched out the features from the side. Starting to notice her face, her jawline and her nose. It was strange, but all the time that they had been together, this was the first time that he had actually looked at her. Was she married? Did they marry in the year two-thousand-and-whenever-she-was-from?

"I'll think about the train, Jack."

"Can you explain it to me again, Sage?"

"Explain what?" was the response as she shuffled uncomfortably in her seat, unsure of what Jack was going to ask her.

"Well, why you are helping me?" Jack noticed Sage appearing uneasy with the ambiguous question.

"Do you want me to drive?" Jack asked as he thought he should take a turn. Maybe this was not the time to start questioning Sage.

"No, it's all good, we don't have far to go now," Sage responded as she turned up the heating slightly.

"So why are you helping me?" Jack asked again. After a slight pause, he could see the thought process going on in Sage's head.

"Well, it's like this. It'll be sketchy, okay, so bear with me. A female called Mandy came back from the future to take you to 2098, where you would have been chopped up for parts in the future and sold to the rich, as the rich only want real parts from a real person. I presume you escaped and we bumped into each other at some point. To be honest, I don't know or remember what happened after that. Probably the reason for that is that some event happened – possibly the point that you killed Mandy. That has changed the timeline, so in reality what did happen then was wiped clean as a new timeline stated instead."

"But I've never been to 2098," Jack insisted.

"No, that was a different timeline, so you won't remember it. Originally, me and you went back to kill Mandy before she took you, I would say; and we succeeded. As soon as Mandy was dead, she couldn't take you to the future. So you never went to the future and that timeline ended – and then a new one started. The police had your fingerprints and CCTV footage so as far as they're concerned, they have all the evidence that they need to put you away. So you got arrested for murdering Mandy, even though you; the Jack sat next to me didn't technically do it. But another you in a different time line did. Do you understand? As they say, the rest is history. It's slightly more complicated than that, but I think that sort of explains what happened, okay?" Sage glimpsed at Jack, then smiled to try and reassure him.

"Okaaaaay, I... sort of get it, but how did you find out? Jack asked.

"An email I sent myself," Sage responded while pulling the wash/wipe to wash the windscreen...

"What would happen if I bumped into myself then?"

"I don't know. Probably nothing... Ask a scientist, I'm just a user of the technology," Sage said. She looked at Jack again. Then an uncomfortable silence fell in the vehicle for about ten minutes. Only the radio played music to break it. Songs such as Kate Bush's *Babushka*, The Beatles with their hit *She Loves You*, and Pink with *Walk Me Home*. All random tracks from random years.

"Where are we going?" Jack asked as they kept driving.

"I don't know... I'm running out of plans. I'm just not in the mood for all this shit, Jack." Randomly, Sage put the car indicators on to pull over, as the vehicle slowed to a halt.

"So what do you want to do then?" was the question directed at Jack, as she slightly turned her body to face him. Sage turned the radio off, then only the engine could be heard ticking over under the drone of silence.

"We have someone else after us already; we could end up dead. But as a short term plan, I do like the train to Paris idea. It will give us time to sleep, then we might be in the frame of mind to come up with some sort of plan on how to stop this, apart from us both being killed. Which I don't want to happen, okay?"

"Whatever you think, Sage. You're the boss – I'm just tagging along. Are you okay? You don't look it. Have you been shot or something?" Jack noticed pain on Sage's face as the moon shone through the windscreen.

"It's been a hard night for us both and things have happened that I want to forget... I will forget them soon." A slight smile crossed her face as she tried to reassure Jack that everything was okay, then she turned off the engine. All that could be heard now were crickets and the breeze as they made their way around the outside of the car.

"Well Sage, when we got split up, I had to shoot someone. Then I got in a car chase all over the place. Then I had a car accident and stole another car, and to top it all off, I shot two more people. So I can shoot live people as well as dead ones now," Jack said as he referred back to the earlier incident in the back garden with the corpse. Jack was just trying to break the silence.

"But it seems it wasn't as distressing as your night, Sage." Jack opened the car door and climbed out. He made his way around the front of the car then opened the driver's side door. He held out his hand to Sage. She took it and climbed out of the car. Then Jack clasped Sage's face with both hands, smiled at her and embraced her body with both of his arms.

"It's going to be okay in the end, you know. It's an adventure we are on and we will come up with a plan to stop this. We just need a break, that's all, Sage," Jack said softly in Sage's left ear.

"You know, Jack, you're doing really well. You are coping with what you have gone through tonight, you should be proud of yourself that you are still alive. Trust me you're not just tagging on. You are a killing machine!" Sage announced as she pulled away from Jack, smiled at him, then kissed him on the forehead.

"Okay, let's go from here to London, King's Cross, then we'll jump on a train to give us some breathing space. It's a good plan and it's yours, Jack," Sage said, then they parted from their embrace. She walked to the back of the Subaru Outback, opened the boot and grabbed her backpack. Then made her way to the front to use the car headlights as they were still on.

"Well, are you ready then, Jack?" Sage enquired as she put the backpack down on the ground.

"So we're going to use my plane, then?"

"Yep, we are, but remember this is not a sightseeing tour. It's a means for us to get a bit of rest, okay? We'll take it as it comes," Sage explained as she got down on one knee, rooted around in the backpack, then pulled out the Transphone.

"Gun, please," Sage demanded as she held out her hand waiting for the item.

"You have it, remember? I feel safer with it, can I have it back?" Jack asked.

"Oh, yes, I do! We are off to London. You shouldn't need it there and the backpack will shield it from the metal detectors when we get on the train. But if they want to look inside we are knacked." She stood up, fastened the backpack and put it on.

"All good then, Jack?" she inquired again and smirked at him.

"Errr, yes, I'm as good as I'll ever be, I suppose."

"Okay, you know the drill, don't let go. So what year are we going to?" Sage inquired.

"Maybe a few months after I got arrested? I don't know? You make the call."

"Okay, it sounds like a plan, my man!" Sage said back at him as she set the time, date and location. Come on then, hold my hand and let's do this."

"What about the car? Aren't we going to burn it or something?" Jack asked.

"Oh Jack, you watch too many movies. Someone will see it and it will start getting stripped down for parts. Hand please." Jack complied.

Sage pressed the button and, as normal, there was a humming, then darkness enveloped them both.

Chapter 20

The boredom, darkness, and tiredness were starting to take their toll on Abbie. It had been a long day for her. She repeatedly checked her Transphone to see if it had connected with the two people that she was chasing. No, nothing, just the calibrating sign that always comes up when you don't want it to. Deep down, she knew that they would not be back, but had to wait, just in case.

As time passed, it became more evident that Abbie's hunch was right. They were not coming back, although she could not sleep, just in case they did. They would no doubt make sure she slept for a long time, just like they had done to the other two, dead. Several coffees later, Abbie was awake and buzzing with anxiety, feeling twitchy. Her back was aching as she sat silent with one earplug in, listening to some music from Chapter 245, her favourite band. As the sun started to emerge, Abbie made the final decision that they were not going to show. She slowly got up (her legs and back protested) and put her backpack on, then moved outside. Opening the Transphone, she put in the coordinates and time and pressed the button. Darkness enveloped her and she was gone.

"Touchdown!" she mumbled to herself as she appeared again. She looked at the dark brown walls and the white ceiling – yep it didn't look right, but she wasn't an interior designer, but she was back in 2098. She made her way out of the room and down the hallway. No one said anything to her as she passed security then went out of the building.

Abbie was going to get a Goober, and then noticed a Microtaxi. A smile crossed her face… now and then she did like to drive; it gave her a sense of freedom. Quickly making her way over to the white vehicle, she pressed the amber-coloured button on the side just behind the door. An electric whine accompanied the door's opening. Climbing in, she pressed the green-lit start button. The screen in front of her came to life, as she clicked various buttons, then engaged manual drive. A squeaky female voice came over the system with some disclaimers; *if this or that and the other happen, you're on your own and you owe us credits.*

"Where to, please?" the annoying voice requested.

"Block four, Aiden zone," Abbie replied. Then the price came up on the screen to let her know what this privilege would cost.

"Yes, I confirm manual drive," Abbie, said out loud, and the car started to move.

It headed down the road, then sparingly up onto the skyway. She picked up speed as she went through the gears. As each gear was engaged, she was pushed back into her seat. She felt the excitement and exhilaration of being in complete control of her destiny and life. A wrong move at these speeds and it would be too late before the electronics could take over to try and stop someone from killing themselves. It wasn't long before she arrived at Block four of Aiden zone. After manually parking the car up, the vehicle went into cooldown mode. The door opened with a whine, then Abbie climbed out with a grin on her face and her heart pumping with excitement. *That was one kick she got out of her job, going back in time and feeling free and alive rather than constricted by laws on everything that you do.* She thought as the smile stayed on her face.

"Thank you for using Microtaxi, your account will be deducted the appropriate credits," the voice stated, then started to diminish in volume as Abbie walked away from the vehicle. She glanced back; it had already headed off to do its next job. Abbie approached the building where she took the standard procedure of placing her right hand on a glass screen. The female voice thanked Abbie and hoped that she would have a nice day. The green-tinted glass doors slid open and Abbie made her way into the building. She made her way over to the lift, then pressed the elevator button. There was a slight wait for the lift, then the doors opened. Abbie walked into the lift and it immediately recognised her, as always.

"Good morning, Abbie, how are you today?" the voice announced to her as she felt the lift speed up to her floor. The advert on the doors today was about moving to the moon! The lift doors slid open and a big mural of a tree greeted her eyes as always. She turned right then walked down the corridor to her apartment. As she put her hand on the chrome handle, the door clicked open and she entered. Walking through the living room, she noticed everything was still off. It was morning, and Phil was probably still in bed; so that was her destination. Abbie headed towards the bedroom and took off her backpack as quietly as she could, so as not to wake Phil. She stopped outside the door and started to remove her shoes, jeans, and top, but left her bra and pants on (those were Phil's job to remove). They didn't have sides – the first one in bed slept the furthest away from the bedroom door. She didn't know why that was the rule but it seemed to work. Opening the door and slowly making her way to the bed, Abbie pulled the cover back.

"Err Hi?" a male voice came from the bed.

"Lights," Abbie shouted, and they came on.

"What the fuck are you doing here? Who the fuck are you?" Abbie screamed at the person that was in bed with Phil.

"Oh my god, babes, I'm so sorry... you shouldn't be here... Oh crap," Phil responded.

"It's pretty bloody obvious you weren't expecting me. Get the hell out," Abbie screamed again at this person.

"Who are you? the male asked as he lay there with everything on display.

"I'm her partner; get the fuck out of here!" Abbie's response came back at him as she looked around for something that she could use as a weapon. She quickly moved over to the dressing table and picked up a steel comb with a sharp end to the handle. He slowly got up from the slumber of the bed. It then became apparent that he was starting to get aroused with one naked and one semi naked females in the room, regardless of the situation.

"Get the fuck out before I cut your dick off and feed it to you," the response came back from Abbie.

"Okay, sister, I'm on my way… Stay cool about it all," the he said as he started to get dressed. After a few minutes of this, he then casually made his way to the front door with Abbie following. He opened the door and smiled as he left the apartment. Abbie slammed the door behind him. The next thing to sort out was Phil. Abbie stormed through the apartment into the bedroom. Phil sat in bed with her head in her hands.

"What the hell are you playing at? You slag! Get the fuck out of this bed! You're out of here. You can collect your things another day."

"Oh please, please, babes, I'm sorry, I didn't mean to do it. It just happened," came the excuse back from Phil.

"Oh, he accidentally fell into bed, I presume, oh, let's have a guess, did he accidentally shag you? Get out, before I kick you out!" Abbie screamed at Phil as tears rolled down her cheeks. Phil got out of bed and slowly moved to pass Abbie and start putting her clothes on.

"I'm sorry." Phil stared at Abbie but got no response. Then she moved out of the bedroom and to the front door.

"I'm so, so sorry, Abbie. I didn't mean to do it. It was an accident, and I won't do it again, honest. Let's make up, please."

"Leave," was the only response. Abbie moved to the front door and opened it. Phil went through the opening and was going to say something but knew it was a waste of time. Abbie slammed the door behind her. She turned and made her way to the bedroom, to sit on the bed. She took in a few deep breaths, and the tears came streaming down her face.

Chapter 21

The darkness started to clear, then it took a few seconds to get their bearings. A slight amount of light entered through a small window towards the top of the wall. Jack and Sage found themselves in what they thought must be a storeroom.

"Oh, this is great, well done!" said Jack sarcastically as he started looking around the small room. Tins of this and that stood on some shelving that had seen better days. In one of the corners stood a mop and bucket and next to it was a mousetrap, with a dead mouse in it.

"Hmmm," was the response as Sage tried the door handle to see if the door would open.

"No, that's locked! We can't get out through the window! Soooo... I will pick the lock," Sage announced with a slightly happy tone in her voice. She took off her backpack, put it down then put the Transphone back in it. Then started rummaging around for a few seconds, then took out Jack's gun and handed it to him. She removed something and lifted it in triumph in front of Jack's face, as though she had won a prize. It was a small tool of some kind. Jack just gazed at it.

140

"What's that?" he asked inquisitively, as he tried to focus on it in the dim light.

"Oh, it's a tool to help me pick locks, it's good for so many things. She started to change the small bit at the end of this futuristic implement. Jack thought to himself, *I wonder if it's like a sonic screwdriver out of Dr Who.*

Sage put the tool's point into the lock, although it didn't appear to fit. She tried to manipulate it to go in, and Jack could tell that she wasn't having any luck. Sage was starting to huff and puff with frustration at the situation she was in. She knew Jack was watching and wanted to prove to him that she could get them out of this predicament.

"Do you want me to have a go? Jack asked casually.

"Well, if you want!" the response came back as she moved out of the way and handed it to Jack to let him try.

Jack pulled out his gun from the back of his jeans, which only moments earlier he had put there. Pointing the gun at the lock and let off a shot. The noise in the closed cupboard was deafening to them both. Bits of wood and dust started to fly around in the closed environment like confetti.

"Wow, that was loud, has it worked?" he asked as the door lock was now in bits, just as it would have been if it was a movie.

Wow, one thing in the movies that seems to work, his inner monologue said as he then sniggered to himself, *how cool was that?*

"For God's sake, Jack, everyone's going to know we're here. Then it's question, question, questions, and guess what – we don't have any bloody answers to give them, do we... Oh god, you're a fool... a bloody idiot... but it worked. OK rant over," Sage smirked at Jack and turned what was left of the door handle and slowly opened it. Jack exited the room first. A voice came from his left.

"Hey, what are you up to?" a man in dark blue trousers and a similar coloured top inquired.

"Oh, there's two of you, is there?" the second question came to them both.

"Err, mate, a moment," Jack shouted as he moved over to the guy. Jack then indicated that they should both move away from Sage, who just stood there not having a clue what was happening.

"Look mate, it's like this," Jack announced in a soft voice as he turned his back on Sage. The man was now looking at Sage slightly strangely.

141

"You see that chick? Well, she's a bit of a nympho! She likes sex in strange places. So we've just done it in that storeroom. I'm sorry but, you know, man to man, I can't say no to a shag, can I?" Jack whispered to the guy who just stood there speechless. He then looked at Sage again and smiled at her.

"Well you shouldn't be down here, but if you've done it already then errr... Where else have you done it?" he asked, as a smile crossed his face and he once again glanced at Sage.

"Well, you know the mile high club? We're gold class members in that club, oh which way to the train station?" Jack told the guy, then asked the question; as he nudged him and smiled.

"Yeah, yeah, okay mate, just go that way to the station. Go on." He then pointed down the corridor past Sage.

"Cheers, bud." Then he winked, turned and walked up to Sage.

"Smile at him and say bye," Jack told Sage when he has got within hearing distance of her.

"Oh, yes, and thanks."

Sage did as she was told, then smiled. The man winked back at Sage. They made their way down the cream-painted corridor and a concrete floor which led them to some wooden doors.

"What did you say to him?" Sage enquired.

"Nothing much. I told him you were a nymphomaniac!" He glanced at Sage as he pushed the door open and went through the doorway. Sage followed in silence and they emerged at Kings Cross train station. Sage stopped in her tracks as realisation hit her.

"What's wrong?" Jack enquired as he stopped and turned towards her.

"We're in King's Cross! Oh my god, we are in King's Cross station," Sage stated with an extremely excited voice.

"And the issue with that is...?"

"Harry Potter. I've seen all the remakes and the original ones." Sage had a glow on her face and a smile from ear to ear. The only word that Jack could think of to describe Sage was awe.

"Yes, Harry Potter, platform 9¾ is over there," Jack pointed, then started moving in the direction of it, as he just knew that they would be going that way. He passed various people to his left and right, dodging all sorts of individuals who appeared to be deliberately getting in their way, as people seem to do when you are in a rush.

"Oh yes, no sightseeing – I seem to remember! We only have an assassin on our tails, don't we? So let's look at some movie prop," Jack sarcastically stated to Sage as he walked slightly in front of her.

"Okay, okay, I'm coming I'll look another day," replied Sage as she followed begrudgingly.

"You do know we are in the wrong station, don't you?" Jack said out loud.

"Yep, we need to be in Saint Pancras, but the Harry Potter thing isn't there," Sage said back at him.

"So you deliberately put us in the wrong station to see the Potter thing?" Jack enquired, then glanced at Sage and rolled his eyes.

"I may have!" she responded, looked at him and smiling.

They moved out Of King's Cross to King's Cross Square and over to a big sign that pointed to various places to go. Then made their way across the square, past numerous people – all the normal Londoners and presumably a few tourists for good measure. Jack could see people taking selfies of themselves next to this and that, but probably very boring pictures, he thought. *Oh, this is me next to a lamppost, a wall, a poster, and so on.* They passed a café with some chairs and tables to their right with no one sitting on them. To the left, some London cabs were waiting for a customer. The smell of smog and excitement filled the air. They both kept moving forward. By this time, Sage was walking at Jack's side with her trusty backpack and a grin still on her face.

They stopped briefly, looking left then right for traffic as they crossed the road. They realised it was the modern part of the station that they needed to go to. There were bold letters above the entrance of the station saying the words St Pancras. Going through the glass doors, they made their way to the Eurostar platform. And finally ended up at the ticket office. Sage got the ticket's and put the numbers into the Transphone to adjust something with the tickets.

"What about the guns?" Jack announced with panic in his voice as he stopped in his tracks. Sage came up to him closely so that she could talk to him softly.

"Well, the metal detectors won't detect them as they're not metal. We'll put both clips in a bag then put them in the backpack in bits.

The bag is a stealth bag, which means that it will show them normal things that are just pictures such as toothpaste and toothbrushes. It's something that's stitched into the lining of the bag. Pretty cool, eh." Then with a smile on her face, Sage slowly moved over to a quiet area, took the backpack off and opened it up.

"Just a minute Jack, don't do anything. I'm jamming the CCTV for about an hour." She tapped away on her Transphone.

"Okay, all good it's down."

"What do you mean? It's down?" Jack asked curiously.

"Well, when a camera looks at us, the program will block it from seeing us." She smiled at Jack once again and gave him a cheeky wink.

Jack passed her his gun, then Sage took the clip out of the gun and put it in the backpack out of sight of human eyes. Sage did the same with her gun and then tied the backpack up again and put it on.

"Obviously, if they want to physically check the bag, we're knackered, but that's a bit of a chance we have to take. I normally don't go through border controls to avoid that sort of shit. Errr, I need to get two tickets." Sage started tapping on her Transphone.

"Okay, we have a train in about forty-five minutes. I'll get that one." Sage tapped out some more then looked at Jack.

"All good, come on," she advised Jack as she started to walk up to the entrance. Jack took a deep breath in and out a few times then trailed behind. They both followed the route that they had to take, as shown by the signs.

"What about passports?" Jack blurted Panicking behind Sage.

"We have tickets, I have attached our passports to the tickets. They will compare the pictures on the tickets and let us through." Then walked on.

Sage put the bag through the metal detector. As this happened, she looked at Jack and winked at him again. No sirens went off! Sage picked the backpack up from the other side and put it on. Jack had to take his belt off because that set off the alarm. Then he was through and a smile crossed his face as he glanced at Sage.

"Wow, that was easy," Jack had a bounce in his step.

"Hmm, don't count your chickens, we have to get off at the other end, you know." The response dulled his enthusiasm for the trip.

"Oh yeah, do you think they'll check it?"

"I don't know, Jack, I can travel to the future but I can't look into it," she responded then sniggered at her witty joke. They got onto the train and took their seat, then waited to start moving. Then there was a banging noise as the couplings of carriages started to take the strain and the train slowly started to move out of the station. The carriage was clean, although the air was stale with a smell of something that Sage could not put her finger on.

"Hey Sage, do you think this will work?" he said, slightly leaning forward.

"Oh, it's a good plan. They might be waiting for us at the other end, and then again they might not. It depends how on the dice rolls… if we're located or not. And if they do find us, they then need to get to the station in time. I would be waiting, but to be honest, the chance of them seeing us in a crowd is slim. We'll take some precautions when we arrive in Paris, just in case," Sage stated as she started to make herself comfortable in her seat (to hint to Jack to shut up and sleep, while they had the chance to do so).

Jack made himself comfortable and looking out of the window at the trees, houses, and various buildings all passing by, with the sun rising from behind them. The noise from the rails on the steel wheels was hypnotic – it permutated through the suspension and into the carriage. Jack did the same as Sage and started to snuggle down into his seat and close his eyes.

He opened one eye and took a quick glance at her – he could tell that she was already asleep. He opened his other eye and started looking at the other commuters on the train. He did not feel safe, because he didn't have his gun! How strange, only hours, days ago he had never shot anyone, now he craved his gun for protection. How quickly human nature can change when it needs to.

A screaming child as always could be heard in the background of the train noise. To his left was a businessman with a dark brown suit and brown shoes with a moustache. It gave the man the distinct look of a 1970s porn star, at which Jack sniggered. Oh, what was the name of the star in the movie Boogie nights? It wasn't important, but this guy could have a lead role in it without any problem. Opposite him was a semi-attractive female maybe in her mid-forties or early forties, with dark brown hair that was pulled back as far as it could be and tied with some elastic band or something. She was wearing a white blouse buttoned to the top. This accompanied her tight business trousers and black high heel boots. She took a glance, smiled at Jack, and then she got up and slowly walked down the centre aisle, probably heading to the toilet, he

145

presumed. Jack couldn't help himself but he had to have a look at her, just to make sure he was right in his assumptions. Yes, she stopped outside the toilet. He was only guessing her age – for all he knew, she was in her twenty's and had a hard life.

Jack glanced out of the window then back at the table opposite him, and he noticed something that the porn star was holding. Bloody hell, there's a gun on the table! His heart started pounding; the adrenaline once again flowing through his body. He kicked Sage to wake her, but nothing; she was out. The guns were in the backpack and he couldn't get them. He kicked her again but she just would not wake up. Jack decided to get up and go for a walk. Hopefully the man with the gun would follow Jack, thinking Sage was not with him – especially if he made it obvious that he had seen the gun. Jack glared at the man as he passed him as if to invite him. He made his way down the carriage in the same direction that the female went earlier on. Jack couldn't help but notice that everyone seemed asleep. He looked back – yes, he saw the reflection of the man get up in the window. Then he lifted his right arm, pointed the gun in Sage's direction and pulled the trigger. The sound was deafening, and Jack froze at what he had just witnessed. *Run!* was his reaction as he went down the corridor to the end and opened the door to get into the next carriage. His heart was pounding as the adrenaline once again pumped around his body. The corridor formation had changed. The seats had all gone and had been replaced by walls. *This must be a sleeper car*, he thought as he quickly made his way down the corridor, checking behind, making sure that he was not being followed.

"Spcccccc, in hear!" he heard from behind him as he noticed one of the doors open slightly. He stopped, then quickly made his way back about maybe a metre or two and the door opened wider.

"I'm here," the voice commanded him. He checked to see if the porn star assassin was following him. No, he didn't see him, so chances are he wouldn't know where he was hiding. Jack entered, shut the door behind him then locked it. Turning around, the female from earlier on was standing in front of him. Jack then noticed that she had a gun pointing at him.

"Errr, what are you doing?" he enquired as he stood still. This was not happening, for fuck's sake, he had a porn-star assassin after him outside, and a bitch pointing a gun at him now.

"Strip!" she said to Jack, as he stood there in awe at the situation he was in. "Why?"

"I don't know, just strip!" the female screamed as she raised her right eyebrow, then smiled to embellish the situation. Jack knew he was in a sticky situation, although what the hell he was going to do he didn't know. He started to slowly undo his belt, then pull it out of the loops of his trousers, throwing the buckle end around the female's wrist. He yanked on it, then pulled her hand and body towards him.

Jack moved to one side, then grabbed the gun and pointed it towards the roof and it went off; light debris from the roof came showering down on them both. Then a struggle started as they both had their hands on the gun, except the female had her finger on the trigger, which seemed to be getting pulled randomly. The gun went off again as they moved around the small room, banging into the wall, window, and the door. Jack got the door handle violently pushed into his back, with the pain to match. Boom – another shot went off. They both went to the floor to gain supremacy over the other. Jack was on top, except the gun was pointing towards his shoulder. He slowly overcame this with his strength advantage, but it was not as easy as he would have imagined. This female was strong, she must work out! The gun went off again and the window in the carriage shattered. Glass showered over them both. The wind now was part of this as it whisked around, throwing what it could. Then all of a sudden she was on top and using her strength and body weight to slowly move the gun in Jack's direction.

"Who's going to win?" she asked Jack, and then she leered at him. The gun was slowly moving towards his face. Jack started to try to move his head out of the way of the barrel that was heading towards him. There was another shot, except this one missed his left shoulder and shattered the carriage floor.

He lifted his knees and started to slide down between her legs as the gun slowly made its way towards his head. His feet were pressed against the wall – he gave a swift knee to the small of her back, then she lost balance and went toppling over him. The gun was dropped and it skidded across the floor. This was his opportunity to try and get on top of this situation. He grabbed the gun. Now he was the one randomly shooting off rounds at the floor hoping one would hit the female. The grappling continued. Slowly they both got to their feet and once again like some sort of ritual mating dance moved from various parts of the small room wrestling with each other. They both moved towards the smashed window. There was a falling sensation, and screams as they fell through the shattered opening in the carriage.

"What, what, what," Jack shouted out as he came out of his torrid dream. Startled, he looked around with embarrassment, then he realised what had happened. Sage sat opposite him smirking, the porn star moustache man glanced up from his laptop along with the semi-hot female who also glanced up from the book she was reading, and frowned at him. She must have realised that he was dreaming, probably by the confused look on Jack's face.

"Do you feel better?" Sage enquired, then glanced out of the window.

"Oh I feel knackered, but I suppose I'm okay for now," was the response as Jack then threw in a yawn for good measure to emphasise that he needed more sleep.

Jack noticed some music in the background, but could not decipher where it was coming from. It must be the porn star who had earphones in? Although he couldn't tell what was being played. Forgetting the music, he then realised that he'd slept through the journey that had taken them through the tunnel. They were now on French soil. The train made its way past buildings, fields of various colours with trees scattered along. Roads with cars, trucks, and at times farm vehicles. Then the train went under bridges, whilst more train tracks started to merge into each other. More and more lines ran parallel to them, with trains going at different speeds and directions. Jack jumped, as a train passed his window the opposite way, then was gone.

They entered the Gare du Nord, which looked a very similar age to King's Cross station in London, if maybe a tad older. The train slowly went over the various points; all sorts of clicking could be heard from the wheels under the carriage. They slowly pulled up at the platform. Probably ninety-nine per cent of the passengers stood up to grab their cases in anticipation of getting off. Jack and Sage just sat waiting for the train to clear.

"Look, someone could be waiting for us. We just have to get off and out of this place as fast as possible, okay? We'll try and mingle with the other passengers. Try to stay close to me or someone in front of you. Especially if you can walk behind someone taller than you. If we get separated, we'll meet at, say, the Eifel Tower tomorrow at twelve. No, one pm! Okay, Jack?" She leaned back, hoping that she had covered all the bases at once. Then smiled at Jack to try and comfort him.

"It will be fine, trust me. I feel it in my waters," Jack added.

"Oh, I feel so much safer now your waters are all good," Sage responded. The train had ground to a halt and passengers started to slowly move, then disembarked the train. They both stood up as the carriage was starting to clear now, and they made their way to the door. Sage briefly stopped and put her backpack on, making sure it was secure on her back.

They disembarked from the carriage and started to mingle with the crowd. Both of them moved closely behind two tall people. Jack noticed that they were chatting away to each other in what appeared to be American accents, maybe Canadian. The conversation appeared to be about baseball, although he didn't care. All he wanted was to get out of this situation alive, without a shootout or being killed.

A sickening sensation was coming over him, with all this running, jumping and shooting he just wanted to go back to his life of being an electrician. He pondered on the good old days when he got up, went to work, came home, got drunk with Conner and went to gigs. Oh, but not randomly chatting to a female in the pub that wanted to take him, to the future, and chop him up for body parts. No, no, that had got him into the situation he's in now. No, he wanted to chat to females that wanted to kiss him, maybe marry him and have kids with him. He could live to a happy old age in a boring suburban life if that's what he wanted. A tug on his right arm snapped him out of his daydream; he glanced and followed Sage's lead as they moved behind a wall.

"What's wrong?"

"Just mixing it up. We'll do the same behind these two coming, okay?" She indicated towards two tall women walking towards them.

"Okay," Jack responded as he looked at both of them.

They slipped their way out and started walking behind the two females. One of them glanced at Jack as if to say what are you doing? Jack's response was to smile back, which seemed to appease the woman's curiosity about the situation. The two women walked slowly along the platform, with their conversation appearing to be taking most of their concentration. Jack had no idea what they were talking about, as they appeared to be speaking in German. They both got further along the platform then into more open space, but at the same time mingling in with more people. Sage grabbed Jack's hand again; once again she started to manipulate the direction that they were going in. They started to move towards a side entrance rather than the main one. Sage had decided that the main entrance would be where she would wait for them, hence the reason to avoid it.

"What are we doing?" Jack asked as he followed, stooping to try and not stand out in the crowd so much.

"Just shut up and follow me," was the barked order towards him, and he did exactly as Sage commanded. They made their way through a door, down a corridor then to some fire doors at the end. Sage briefly stopped, took her backpack off, took a tool out of it then promptly did something to the magnetic switch. She pushed the escape handle and the fire doors opened. Jack expected an alarm, but nothing. Sage placed the tool in the backpack, then put it back on. They casually made their way through the now open doors – out into the sunny city of Paris.

Jack followed as he always did, then smiled as the warmth of the sun hit his face. It reminded Jack of holidays in Spain with his mum and dad when he was a teenager. Then his thoughts ran into another holiday memory, of when he was in a hotel also with his mum and dad. Maybe the same year maybe another, he couldn't remember. He had been bumming around the swimming pool, the table tennis table and the snooker tables of the hotel. Every time he was there, he noticed that this female was there, not looking at him but just hanging around. After a few days of this, Jack decided that he would go up to her and ask for her name. Surprisingly enough, she didn't burst out laughing but told him, "Jane!" They chatted for most of the day; then they arranged to meet in the hotel disco the following night. The disco was held in the lounge at night for all the residents of the hotel. It was a children's disco that played the normal radio music of the time and older stuff. Culture Club, Funboy Three, Bananarama, to name just a few of the older bands' songs. As the night went on, Jack and Jane moved away from their appropriate parent's view to a more secluded area, outside in a dark alley. That's when Jack got his first kiss, which moved on to snogging. He also managed to grab hold of the girl's right boob through her bra, for the briefest of seconds. Jack smirked to himself thinking at the time *what an accomplishment for a young boy!* The downside to the story was that Jack never saw her again. Over the years, he had wondered what had happened to Jane. Maybe she had been grounded or maybe her family had left the hotel the following day? It was a chance encounter between two young teenagers who would never bump into each other again.

Reality once again kicked in, as he tripped over a curb on the road and nearly fell flat on his face. He picked his speed up, as Sage was leaving him, due to his daydreaming. Finally catching Sage, they both dodged left, right, and right-left past Parisians who probably didn't think anything of two people running through the streets as though someone was trying to kill them. He followed Sage quite closely now and she turned left. Jack had to do an emergency stop, as he had shot by the alleyway. Inside, it was dark with high walls on both sides. The sun could not get in, and the cold and dampness could be felt in the air, which hit them both. Sage stopped and Jack stood opposite her. She was breathing quite heavily. She leant forward and rested her hands on her knees. The light was poor, although Jack could see her chest heaved in and out to get oxygen in her lungs. Feeling embarrassed, he diverted his eyes before Sage noticed.

"I think we're okay, Jack. If they were out there, we would have been shot at a few times by now. We'll wait here for a few minutes, then go to this place I know; maybe get some food after, okay?" she announced with a pant of breath in between the words.

After a few minutes, Sage stood up then led the way to this mysterious place she was talking about. Jack was pondering what it might look like. Old, probably, and knackered! Or maybe it was a friend she had or another ex-boyfriend's place? Maybe he was away being a spy or in the SAS. They passed shops and cafés with stylish Parisian females and males sitting drinking coffee. Elegant, stylish, sophisticated – the look said it all, that they were not on vacation, they lived in Paris. Next to them, the tourists looked like tourists, scruffy and out of place. Dogs were everywhere – big, small and all crapping and pissing to their heart's content over the Parisian pavements.

They walked for about fifteen minutes before stopping outside a doorway, then they climbed two marble steps. Sage grabbed hold of the brass handle doorknob, turned it and the door opened. Jack half expected it to creak as it opened, but no, it travelled like it was on silk hinges. Sage entered the building, then moved down a long and dim corridor with marble tiles on the floor and walls, and at the end was a lift. Sage pressed the lift button, and after a few seconds the doors opened. It was quite small inside, with enough room for about six people. Pressing the floor button, she was the only person that knew where the hell they were going. They started to go up to the second floor. After a jerky stop, the doors opened and they both walked out. Jack let Sage lead the way down another dim corridor then through the door at the end, then to the right. A counter with a very attractive man stood behind it. He had every hair in place, a five o'clock shadow, and pearly white teeth.

"Excusez-moi, parlez-vous anglaise," Sage asked.

"Of course, Madam," the husky response came from the man, although Jack at that point turned off and looked out of the window that was opposite the desk. Looking down onto the street below, he could see people milling around. Sage started moving again as she followed the man.

"Jack!" Sage called out, as she made her way to their room with the man from behind the counter.

He appeared to have an air of composure as he paraded in front of Jack and talked to Sage. Jack didn't like this guy, a smiley smooth-talking French bloke; he straggled behind them both down a corridor. Eventually they reached a white door that had a number nine on it. The man opened the door for Sage, then said something smooth and suave to her in French. They both laughed, as he gestured for them both to enter the room. Sage did, and then he looked Jack up and down as if to pass judgment on Jack being with Sage. As Jack passed the French man, he smiled at Jack. Jack grimaced back to show his disapproval of the want to be model and his swagger, then shut the door on him.

The room was small, with a funny shape to it and a window that looked out to the road. Jack looked around the place; the bathroom was nice and clean. Then he made his way to the bedroom and stood motionless, just looking.

"It's nice, isn't it, Jack? What's wrong?"

"Errr, well, there's only one bed and one chocolate on the pillow?" was his response as he picked a chocolate up and ate it without saying anything.

"Yes, I know, we'll have to share. Didn't you hear us talking about it? You don't mind, do you? There's no bathtub, so you can sleep on the floor if you want?" Sage proposed as she took the faithful backpack off.

"No, no, no, it's okay, errr, it's nice. Hey, look an empty chocolate wrapper under the pillow. I bet it's the cleaner, they always do things like that." He smiled out of discomfort from his comment as he pretended to have found the wrapper he had just consumed the chocolate from.

"Okay, I'm off for a shower, then I'll clean the guns. After that, we'll get some food, okay?"

"Yep, errr, can you show me how to use the time travel thing?"

"Errr, maybe I'll show you later on!" Sage responded in an evasive way. Then she made her way into the bathroom and closed the door. After a few minutes or so, Jack could hear Sage singing, but he could not figure out what it was she was singing. Maybe it was some song from the future? He wasn't bothered; it was just nice that she was singing. Then she started on another song – *Wonderwall* by Oasis, was the ditty she was killing. The door opened and Sage appeared with a towel partly wrapped around her.

"Your turn!" she directed Jack. He sat gawping at a semi-nude female in front of him.

"Errr, yeah okay." He got up then entered the bathroom, closed the door, locked it, undressed, showered, dried, and put the same clothes back on. Exiting the bathroom, Sage stood in front of the mirror in a pair of white pants and a bra. Jack once again averted his eyes then moved over to the window, he looked out of it while Sage dressed.

"Okay, let's go, then," Sage shouted at Jack as she stood at the door with her backpack in her hand. Jack moved from the window and looked Sage up and down. He smiled.

"What about cleaning the guns?

"I did it when you were in the shower. Do you want one or not?"

"Errr, no it's okay, I'll leave mine here."

"No, it's not okay, we'll take them both. Put this in the backpack and I'll keep one down the back of my jeans. She lifted her t-shirt to slide the gun down the back of the jeans. Jack did as he was told and then they made his way to the door, exited the room and shut the door behind them.

153

Chapter 22

The water cascaded down on Abbie's face and mixed with her tears. The concoction of emotion flowed down over her body. The water was warm, and Abbie was trying to use it to clear her head, soul and mind of Phil – and what she had done to her.

What a bitch – what an absolute bitch! Abbie thought as she slowly washed and massaged her body from head to toe, making sure that every part was given some tender loving care. Finally, she was complete in her task of self-care. The torment of what had happened was mostly washed away. But Abbie knew that the mixed torture of her broken heart would stay longer and come back again in waves of emotion and anger. It would all no doubt be triggered by something or someone in the future. She climbed out of the shower then looked at herself in the mirror. The face staring back at her. Abbie looked into her own reflection. Seeing that she was troubled deep inside.

"Sod her, sod them all! Look what she's lost." Abbie adjusted her posture to promote her image in the mirror. She then promptly but slowly spun around, with her arms up above her head to accentuate her legs, hips and torso. No, she was not the tallest, sassiest, or even best-looking female on the planet... but she did have a heart of gold, she was a hard worker, and she differently didn't need

154

this type of shit in her life. The decision was made; she would be taking a sabbatical from females and love for the near future. Celibacy may be the wrong word, but she definitely needed a break. Drying herself the old-fashioned way, with a nice soft white fluffy towel. More self-indulgence and pampering once again to help her get over this drama. Abbie knew that work was calling – work which would mean possibly killing or being killed.

Note to self; take Phil off the will when I get back from this job. Abbie didn't want that cheating cow getting anything if the worst happened to her. She exited the bathroom with the towel wrapped around her. Then she stopped and promptly untucked the towel, which dropped to the floor. She stood near the window, a completely naked female. No one could see in, so why did she need to cover herself up? To be honest, if someone was looking through her window and was shocked and wanted to report her, then sod them – they shouldn't be looking.

Abbie smirked to herself. She made her way into the bedroom and took a deep breath, briefly pondering on what she was going to do.

"Music random, female power," Abbie shouted out. A second or so later, there was a piano intro, then a female voice with touching lines came on over the system. It was a female anthem that had been copied many times through the years. The one that came over the system was Gloria Gaynor and *I Will Survive.*

Abbie smiled at the song as it started to penetrate her soul, her femininity. She stood in front of her full wardrobe trying to decide what to wear. Then the decision was made quite quickly. She knew that she would wear the same as she always wore for work. Jeans – black or maybe blue – a black T-shirt and a pair of trainers, probably dark blue or maybe black, or possibly her Doctor Martins boots, black.

She moved over to the wardrobe and took out the appropriate items. Knickers, bra, black jeans, black T-shirts, socks and then she pondered: *trainers or Doctor Martins?* This time it was going to be Doctor Martins, just in case she had some ass-kicking to do and, boy, did she want to kick someone's ass.

"I'd better clean the gun!" Abbie mumbled. She used her finger to unlock the gun's safety, she took her choice of gun out, a Browning Hi-Power Classic 9mm. Nice and reliable, with a punch to it. Fully polymer carbon, not detectable at all with a jamming chip in the handle. No hiding behind things with this baby on hand. It was not the newest model around, but she liked it, and it liked her. The marriage was complete, as weapons go. She went and got her backpack, then made her way over to the desk in the bedroom, sat on the chair, took the gun out, made it safe then quickly cleaned it. She briefly checked again what was in her standard backpack. She placed the gun in with extra shells, clothing, first aid, and her Transphone, among other knick-knacks.

A plan was forming in Abbie's head, as to how she was going to capture these two. She had completed some research regarding her targets and one thing stood out. They did have a weakness. It was pretty good, and a bit adventurous, to say the least. She would have to get out of her comfort zone on this one though. Probably not the most kosher of plans, but if the job gets completed then she gets her pay and maybe a bonus too. This may even get her in the purple circle and everyone will be happy, apart from the two dead people. But Abbie can live with that part! Anyway, she's already probably going to hell due to the things she's done in the past – these two are just to add to the list of bad things.

Then moving to the kitchen. Now playing was Pavilion with their recent rendition of some old song from the late 2000s. She quickly made a cheese sandwich.

Yes, the plan could work. All she needed was the proper leverage to get it to work, and she knew what it would be. Now excitement started to come to Abbie's job, as she briefly forgot about the torment that her heart had recently endured. Yes, this would make her feel better. With a bit of luck, she may even be able to imagine that the two people with bullets through their heads are Phil and that bloke, whatever he was called.

She poured a glass of milk and finished off her sandwich, then she glanced out of the window at a clear blue sky. Putting her plate into the dishwasher. Then grabbed her backpack and a short dark blue denim jacket, she glanced around the apartment briefly, checking it out, then exited.

Abbie ordered a Goober on her way down in the lift. The advertisement in the lift this time was about guitars. The Goober was waiting for her outside. She climbed in and tried to relax but inside a rage was brewing. The journey was a standard one that took her back to Control. Excited the Goober and passed security without a word or glance. There were a few documents and permits to complete and she moved to the centre of the room. Abbie felt a sinking sensation in the pit of her stomach as the humming started. As always the anxiety of not knowing if it would work sprang in her mind. *Would she be pulverised in to a millions atoms and spread through time, or end up where she should be? Statistically it should be ok, but you just never know*, she thought. Darkness started to enveloper her and she then jumped back in time.

She immediately huddled up as the cold hit her – she was not prepared for this. Why the hell didn't she check the weather forecast? That's a rookie mistake, but she knew that she had been distracted. A few cars were still on the roads as the light was fading. Abbie turned left and made her way down a slight incline past various shops. A bus passed her, and the turbulence from it made Abbie lose her footing on the curb. She fell down and hit the floor, frustrated and angry bubbled her inside. Feeling unladylike, she got to her feet. Then there was a gritter, which came right up to her, peppering her legs with stone and salt. It was a good job she went for the Doctor Martins and not trainers, or else her feet would be freezing.

After a bit of a walk, which helped her mentally, Abbie reached her destination. The Jolly Rodger pub, she entered through the door, then shook herself off. She smiled at the punters who were all looked at her standing in the doorway. In the background, a Katy Perry song was playing. She made her way over to the bar, looking around again as she waited. A nonchalant female came over to her and gave a slight nod of the head, which Abbie took as *what do you want?*

"A pint of lager, please."

"What type?" the barmaid enquired.

"Any," the request came back towards the barmaid, a slim female with shoulder-length bright red hair and brown eyes, with far too much lipstick on (and maybe too much Botox). She moved away, picked up a glass and started pouring the lager. She came back and clumsily placed it in front of Abbie as it had overflowed and then pooled on the bar. Abbie paid for her drink and moved the glass onto a beer mat. Abbie gave her a wink – *you never know,* she thought. Then Abbie remembered that she was on a sabbatical from females, and love in general. The barmaid glared at Abbie then went away.

Now playing was some song she knew but didn't know who sang it. Making her way over to the colourful and chrome, nice-looking jukebox, just like the ones in the classic films of this era. She checked out who was playing. *Smack*

My Bitch Up by The Prodigy. Then moved over to a seat, taking off her backpack and placing it on the floor. She was sitting in a position where she could see everything that was happening.

Abbie started to think about how she was going to do this and how it was all going to play out. In general, these plans worked, but there are so many factors that can throw them off into a spiral which can be hard to get out of. The best thing was to just play along and see how it went. Then the target walked into the Jolly Rodger. Abbie couldn't hear what the target said, but he must have ordered a pint of something, as it was placed in front of him. The seconds and minutes slowly passed by, and Abbie sat waiting for her chance to pounce on the target. This was taking forever... maybe a new approach would work? She got up, put her backpack on and made her way to the jukebox, drink in hand. Abbie looked at who was now playing, The Stone Roses with a track called *I Want To Be Adored*. Abbie spun around quickly – bingo, beer all over her!

"What the hell are you doing?" Abbie shouted as she jumped into action.

"Oh hen, I'm sorry... I'm sorry. I'll get ye another one, Okay?" the target responded.

"Okay, I'll have any lager. I'm off to the toilet to dry myself off."

"Which one do ye want?" the response came back as Abbie moved off to the toilet.

"I'm okay with any," Abbie responded as she walked away. When she was inside the toilet, Abbie glanced in the mirror at herself. *Stage one has been completed,* she thought with a smirk on her face. She started to dry herself off with the hand dryer. A touch of nervousness was starting to creep in. *Why is this happening now?* She controlled her breathing for a minute or so, which seemed to work. She emerged from the Ladies with the target stood at the bar, watching the TV. He glanced at Abbie making her way towards him, instinctively straightening himself up to give a good impression.

"Hi, I hope you're dry now? I'm Conner." Then he glanced at the TV without asking for her name. He promptly pulled a face as something happened on the TV he didn't like.

"Do you like football?" Conner asked as he stood facing her, but his head was twisted to look at the TV.

"A bit. Who's playing?" Abbie asked out of manners rather than interest.

158

"Oh, it's a big one. Rangers and Aberdeen at Aberdeen, you know?" his response came back as the halftime whistle went and his focus changed from the TV to Abbie.

"I'm Abbie. Nice to meet you, Conner."

"Aye, nice to meet you too Abbie. To the Rangers!" Conner announced as he raised his pint and drank fifty per cent of it in one go. Abbie also responded, "To the Rangers," and promptly drank her pint in one.

"Eh, you're a canny lass, Abbie. Do you want another?" Conner asked with awe in his eyes at the drinking action he had just seen.

"Yes why not, why not indeed..." she responded back at him. Conner promptly finished his pint off and ordered another two. He burped while waiting for the beers to arrive. He presented one to Abbie, then Conner clinked the glasses together and drank a slow but good measure out of his pint.

"So what are you doing after this then?" Conner asked as he noticed that the second half of the match was starting.

"Nothing much. We could go somewhere a bit quieter and maybe a bit warmer," Abbie suggested as she could feel a breeze flood through the pub as a couple walked in.

"Er, yes, that would be a good idea. There's a kebab shop just down the road – we could go in there, and then there's a pub a short walk past that," was his response as he systematically tried to head the football in the net; similar to what the player was doing on the TV.

"Yeah, that sounds okay, Conner." Abbie then drank half of her pint and smiled at him. She could tell that Conner wanted to watch the match, but was trying his best to be polite towards her.

"If you want, we could go after the match. That's if you want to watch it anyway?" Abbie let Conner know, which did seem to cheer him up as his head turned in the direction of the TV, back to Abbie, then to the TV again. Thirty minutes later with lots of Ooohs and Ahhhs, the match ended. One-one, a fair result with no red card to the Rangers, which did go down well with Conner.

His attention then turned to Abbie and also to his stomach. He drank his pint then suggested the kebab shop again. *Wow, what a gentleman this guy is,* Abbie thought to herself as she promptly smiled at him and nodded in agreement. Conner led the way out of the pub. Outside they tried to keep warm with a brisk walking pace. The kebab shop was not too far, just as Conner had suggested.

Being honest, it was just as she had anticipated it would be. The kebab shop was not the cleanest, Abbie told herself that street traders in Asia cook the best food on the streets and this was about as clean as theirs.

Mild meat, onions, peppers, and tomatoes, the food of kings. Conner put everything on his gherkins, chilli, peppers, and the lot. As he consumed it, Abbie could see sauce dribbling out of his mouth and slowly running down his face. Slight beads of sweat were starting to form due to the hot spices. When both of them had finished their kababs and warmed up a bit.

They slowly made their way to the next pub and Abbie was starting to get slightly worried again with the situation. The plan was going well; he was slowly lowering his defences regarding her. But she knew that there was a job to do, and she had to just roll with it. They finally reached the second pub, The White Lion, which had a picture of a White Mountain lion on the board flapping around in the wind above the entrance. They went through a small tunnel then continued through two wooden doors that shut behind them. The heat of the pub hit them and they started to sweat! Was it the change of temperature, or the chilli in the kebabs? *Probably the kebabs,* Abbie thought. The bar was on the left-hand side with a step halfway along the floor of the long pub. In reality, it looked very similar to the Jolly Roger but more modern. In the background was Justin Bieber singing some love song. Abbie knew this because of the massive video screen playing the song.

"What do you want, doll?" Conner inquired as he leant casually against the bar. Abbie wanted to tell him to shove his doll up his ass but she bit her tongue.

"A pint please. Um, I'm just off to the toilet, okay? Where are they?" He pointed at the toilets to show her the way. Abbie walked over and glanced at a red and blue sign, 'his' and 'hers', on the wall. Inside the toilet, she stopped at the washbasin, washed her face, placed both hands on the counter, and slowly looked up at herself in the mirror. She took some deep breaths to calm herself down again.

"It's going to be okay, Abbie, just play along. You're holding the cards, not him." She smiled at herself for reassurance and then moved to dry her face – there was only a hand blower on the wall that would only let you dry your hands, not your face. This always annoyed Abbie, that the idiots that came up with such a stupid invention. She remembered the dryers where you could spin the nozzle and point it where you wanted. The only thing she could use was toilet paper. Afterwards, she checked in the mirror to make sure that there were no bits of toilet paper stuck to her face. Abbie emerged from the powder room and made her way to the bar where Conner was waiting.

"You found it okay?" Conner asked with his distinctive Glaswegian accent. He smiled at her in a sweet way and his eyes said it all.

"Yes, thanks," was her response. Then the conversation started over several slow drinks, and their chit-chat went on for some time. Now and then they would have a drink, they even threw in a shot and a glass of water to help them on their way. Abbie thought this guy was a very complicated, intelligent, and curious person indeed. Honestly, she was starting to like him. He didn't seem like his profile at all. He told her about his childhood and his upbringing in Glasgow, about his sisters and brothers and the full story of how hard it was at school. Also, he chatted about the pubs he used to frequent in his youth, his friends, nightclubs, the lot. Conner opened his heart with stories as though they had known each other for years.

The bell went – it was last orders. Abbie looked around. They were the only people left, along with the staff, who wanted to go home as soon as possible. Making their way to the door, the barwoman stood waiting to let them out into the wild cold night. They both stood looking through the glass windows of the door, knowing how cold it would be outside.

"How far away do you live, Conner?" Abbie asked as she put her backpack on and zipped up her jacket (which was not suited for this type of weather, even though it was from the future, and made of superior materials to the jacket that Conner had on). It was still only barely up to the job.

"About fifteen minutes' walk. What about you? How far do you have to go?" he responded back to Abbie, then he smiled at her again. For some reason, she felt a small tingle in her stomach. What the hell was happening to her? *You're on a job, not a date,* she internally told herself.

Then shockingly, Abbie found herself responding with a smile. "Oh, I'm a good 45 minutes away," she said with a white lie. She hoped he didn't ask where she was going, because she had no idea.

The door was opened by the barmaid and the cold air hit them as they ventured outside to the street.

"Which way you going? I'm going this way," Conner asked.

"Me too!" Was Abbie's response. It was head down and hands in pockets time as they walked as quickly as they could. The wind was starting to pick up even more now – it penetrated through their clothes and down to their skin. As predicted, about fifteen minutes later they arrived at Conner's place.

"This is me, do you want to come in to worm up?"

"Errr yes please," Abbie responded. Conner took his time opening the front door, which was at the side of a shop front, as he was shivering quite a bit. He just could not get the key into the cylinder to open the door. Finally, he managed to unlock it and he nearly fell in through the door. Abbie followed near enough straight away to get out of this harsh weather.

"Are you okay? You can have a nightcap? You can also try and order a taxi from here and wait if you want."

"Thanks, I'll see how I go."

Conner started to climb the dark stairs, with Abbie following.

"Isn't there a light?" Abbie asked before she tripped over something.

"Errr no, lassie, it needs a bulb," he replied. When they reached the landing, Conner opened another door then turned the light on. He entered his flat, still closely followed by Abbie, who was on the hunt for warmth.

"Errr, it's a bit of a mess, lassie. Tomorrow is my tidying day!" Conner stated, then he fluffed some cushions up to take away the fact that it was not the best-kept place. *He's a guy living on his own,* she thought. *What else should I expect? Who does he need to impress to keep a place tidy? Although it would be an idea if he maybe had two days a week to tidy things up.* She chuckled to herself at the joke she had just made up. Abbie slowly moved around the room looking at the things and nick-knacks. She was shaking in her cold clothes, although this place did seem slightly warmer.

"I presume you want a cuppa to warm you up?" Conner asked. Without waiting for an answer, he put some water in the kettle, then put it on to boil, then scratched his nose.

"Sit down, love; do you want a blanket or something? I bet you're freezing? I know I am." The kettle started boiling. I'm just going to put something a bit warmer on. Conner said, as he made his way into another room.

"I, um, you can borrow a jumper if you want?" What do you say? Conner shouted from the other room, as she could hear him scuffling, presumably changing his clothes. Abbie was lost for words, this guy was so nice, and it was

162

going to be hard to follow through with the plan. Reappearing he moved over to the boiled kettle, stopping mid-move, and looked at Abbie.

"Well, what are you going to do then? Do you want a jumper or maybe a blanket?" Conner said, looking directly at Abbie as he made the tea.

"Sugar?"

"Sorry?"

"Do you want sugar in your tea?" Conner asked as he stood waiting for a response, spoon in hand.

"Yes, I'll have a jumper or blanket, please."

"It's on the bed."

Abbie got up and went to the bedroom. For some reason, the bed was made and the room was very tidy, not like the rest of the flat, which was a bit of a surprise to her. Sat on the blue quilt cover was a crocheted blanket that was all sorts of different colours. It looked like someone had made it out of all the leftovers of wool that they'd had.

She made a mental note that she had to keep close to her backpack as her gun and worldly possessions were in it, like her Transphone. She exited the room with the blanket wrapped around her as tight as she could have it. Straight away Abbie started to feel warmer.

"Sit... please sit, your tea is there. I presumed you didn't want sugar – and to be honest, I don't have any anyway," he announced, gesturing to the cup of tea, then he started to chuckle to himself. Abbie sat down and then glanced at her backpack sitting on the floor. It looked as though it was close enough to get to if she needed anything out of it. She knew that she had spare clothes inside it, but decided against using them and letting Connor start thinking about why she had spare clothes in her bag. Abbie glanced at the cup of tea, which was in a blue and white striped mug. Conner had a Brown mug with a flower on it.

Abbie could not get over this guy, with his quaint Scottish accent, and thinning brown spikey hair. Okay, he had a bit of a beer gut, but lots of guys in this period do, due to all the hidden sugar, carbs and so on. Some music arrived in Abbie's ears, it was apparent that the stereo had been put on.

"Who's this?" Abbie inquired. No response came from Conner he came and sat next to her.

"Hey, I'm telling you now, there's not going to be any hanky panky," Abbie bluntly announced. Connor got the message as he looked at Abbie. Abbie's

163

heart slightly cracked as she could feel the intensity of his gaze started to penetrate her sole. All of a sudden she felt quite hot, and flapped the blanket like wings to cool herself down. She was falling for this guy, but why? She was into females, not guys. It was all confusing for her. Conner slowly moved closer to Abbie. There was a long stare into each other's eyes, silence.

"How's your tea?" Conner asked with his voice an octave or so lower than normal. This was all too much for her. All these questions were starting to come into her head. *Am I not into guys? Have I been fooling myself all along, am I actually into men or both? Has he drugged my tea?* Conner pulled away from her – had she missed her chance? A chance for what? She was not interested in men. Although this guy was different... he didn't seem like a dickhead.

"If you want to stop that's cool you know Abbie. It's not the best night to be going out again, especially now you've just got warm. I'll sleep on the couch tonight if you want, or we can sleep in the same bed, that will keep us both a bit warmer," Conner suggested. He then finished off his tea.

"As I said, I trust you; we'll sleep together. That's it, to be honest... body heat allegedly is the best way to warm up when you're cold," Abbie stated, she could feel that she was getting cooler again. After the intense stare from Conner that had that brought her emotions racing. Another slow sloppy song was now playing, mentally she rolled her eyes.

"Who's this then?"

"George Michael. You're still cold aren't you, petal?" Fancy a dance to warm you up?" Conner got up and held out his hand to Abbie.

Silence was all that Abbie could muster; this was not going well at all. He was such a smoothie, but she could not resist the offer. The next thing she knew, they were dancing ever so slowly. Abbie's head automatically rested on his shoulder. His hands were clasping her around her back, and she felt Conner softly pull her body towards him.

What was going on in her head? Had the cold got something to do with all this? Maybe she had hypothermia and was not herself at all?

"Come on, let's go to bed, lassie, it's warmer there." Conner smiled then he gently clasped both hands around Abbie's face. He gently pulled her closer and softly kissed her on the forehead.

He moved towards the bedroom door, stopped and glanced at Abbie. She followed.

Chapter 23

They made their way out onto the Parisian streets. Sage briefly stopped, looking left then right. She glanced at a church clock – 2.14, it said.

"This way!" Sage commanded. Jack had no idea where they were going but he was undeterred.

Jack viewed the Parisians moving around the city, the buildings and the smell of Paris, and he smiled. This was a slight distraction from what appeared to be the norm for them – running and been shot at. When would it end? He didn't know, but it was time to enjoy himself in Paris. As he had know idea how many hours, days there would be before he was killed!

"Do you know where we're going, Sage?" he asked as he walked a touch faster to catch up with her.

"Sort of, but maybe not! We will see! It should be just around this corner." Sage stopped and glanced at Jack, then beamed.

"This is it." She made her way to a midsized café with a black wrought iron ornamental table and chairs outside. Around the outside area were some low walls and large plant pots with shaped bushes in them to add some greenery to the establishment. There were full-length glass windows which probably opened up when it was summer, to give an alfresco feel about the place. That would mean the Parisians could be seen even more when socialising. The café was not full, but a selection of patrons had already picked their spot; to admire and be admired by the passers-by.

"Such an idyllic place, don't you think?" Sage said, as she gracefully negotiated her way across the street and to the table that she desired, towards the rear of the open area; but not inside the café. In the background some music played, although Sage did not recognize it.

"Hey Jack what's playing? Sage enquired as she sat down.

"Errr, I don't know, sorry," came the response as Jack stood looking around at the various people and buildings to take in the atmosphere. He then slightly moved the chair to get a better view of the café and sat down.

"Do you want to play a game of people-watching?" Sage asked. Jack was sitting at a forty-five degree angle to her.

"People-watching?" His response was not enthusiastic.

"What about the people trying to kill us? Or have you forgotten about them? We need to come up with a plan to end all this, Sage."

"Don't worry about that at the moment – enjoy Paris! I have a plan anyway. Just chill, they won't try anything here – there are too many people around.

"Hey, look at that man, Jack, over there in a black and white striped t-shirt, with the crew-cut hair. He's in his early thirties, holding a baby. Do you see him? Look at the female sitting with him. Would you say she's a similar age – hmmmm, maybe his wife or girlfriend? Can you see her next to him? She has long black curly hair and she's smiling ever so intensely at the man and baby. Presumably he's the father of the baby. Well, Jack, what sort of life do they have? I wonder if they're married? Not married? Or friends? You know, questions like these are always popping up in my head. Do you see how much fun it could be, just sitting and watching people?" Sage then shuffled to make herself more comfortable in the chair.

Sage knew that she was trying to escape the reality of the situation that they are in for a few moments. It had been a bit of a roller-coaster over the past few days for them both except she needed a break from Life, reality, an escape if only for a few moments.

"Yes I see them, leaving! I know what people-watching is you know! And yes, I get it, but what about our small dilemma of people trying to kill us?"

"Jack, please chill for five minutes, okay; I beg you?" The response was tainted with a drone in her voice, and directed at him with a look to match.

"Okay, if you say so." He moved his chair again to get a different view of the area. Then he started the task of people-watching.

"What about that man crossing the road, mid-fifties, carrying some paperwork in his right hand, thinning hair, white shirt, beige trousers, and I believe his fly is undone. What about him then, Sage?"

"Well, Jack, maybe he has just forgotten to pull the zip up after going to the toilet."

"Or, has he just had sex with his secretary?" Jack jumped in. Sage looked at him and rolled her eyes at the comment.

"Really, Jack?"

Sage noticed a few tables away a man in his mid-fifties. Then she moved closer to Jack, so he'd be able to hear her better and she didn't need to talk so loud.

"What about him then? With a light blue and white shirt, a pair of trousers and trainers? Sat on his own. What's he doing with his left hand in his pocket?" Sage enquired. Then the man brought out some change and put it on the table. He sat there a few moments longer, drinking his cappuccino.

"Errr, it looks like he's getting change out of his pocket, and now who's lowering the conversation, Sage?"

Sage then noticed at the far end of the café a man in a wheelchair with blue-rimmed wheels. He was wearing black trousers and shoes, and a white shirt with lines printed on it that looked like a grid. He had dark-framed sunglasses and dark hair that was shaved at the sides. He had a fashionable five o'clock shadow, which was sculpted into a beard. On his knee was an item that looked like a guitar box or something similar. A man pushing him was wearing dark green combat shorts, a black t-shirt with the random number 629 on it, and some sort of random symbol. He also had black trainers; a black baseball cap turned the wrong way around, dark sunglasses, and a backpack that appeared to be full because it was low on his back. Following a few paces behind them both was a Scandinavian-looking female, slightly shorter than the man in front. Around her thirties, pretty blonde curly hair, that was tied back. She was dressed in a white t-shirt and cut denim shorts with trainers on. Strangely she was also carrying guitar boxes similar to the man in the wheelchair. They all sat down at a table and looked around, then held each other's hand as if they appeared to start praying. They did this for about twenty seconds, then smiled at each other. Sage thought that it was good that people could do that in the open without feeling intimidated.

"What about that group with the man in the wheelchair then, what's their story?"

"Oh, it's obvious, Sage, They must be musicians, maybe buskers? You don't need to be a detective to figure that one out. Look two guitar boxes and maybe the other guys the drummer?"

A slightly frumpy waitress approached the three of them. She was dressed in the standard white blouse and black skirt, and tied-back blonde hair. The waitress had beautiful olive skin which made her look a lot younger than Sage imagined she was. Sage believed she was about in her forties but looked thirtyish. The waitress took their orders, smiled, then moved away as did Sage's observation.

"What about her, Sage, on that table over there? Late forty's female with browny red hair that's a bit scruffy. Wearing a white short-sleeved cotton blouse, that had delicate flowers stitched on it. Look, her top buttons open.

"Oh yes, with a light blue long pencil skirt. It sort of matched the top. Although her shoes did not go with the outfit at all – red trainers! That is not the future – I should know." Sage announced, then laughed out loud. She covered her mouth to stop the laughter; as people from other tables glanced at them both.

"I'm sure people do the same to us, Jack. Oh, look at him and her? I wonder what they are up to? If they only knew we are time travellers being chased by an assassin!" Jack then joined in with the chuckling that was going on between them.

He then noticed the fashion statement of the day.

"Sage, on the other side of the road! The tall guy with the sides of his head shaven and with a Mohawk, red-rimmed sunglasses,

"Yeh, he has a posture of *get out of my way, I'm important, I'm the alpha male in this city and I'm the man,*" Sage added, with her pretend male voice to emphasize the vision they had just seen.

"What do you think he does, looking like that?"

168

"He's probably a multi-millionaire businessman, student, or unemployed," Sage replied with a touch of humour to her voice.

"Okay, what about the two young females sitting opposite each other, like they're in a meeting. One has light brown hair tied at the back with an elastic band or something like that. She's in a white summer dress that's just above her knees. A pair of white stilettoes and a white handbag. Do you think there Prada or Channel, Sage?"

What's she drinking? Sparkling wine or champagne? She looks high maintenance, or maybe she has a good job… say, a lawyer? There is no ring on her finger, maybe she has a lover or maybe she is the mistress. But the question is. Do you see her friend Jack, light brown hair! Unfortunately, she has on one badly cut leopard skin print dress that goes just above the knees! To be honest, Jack, the dress is probably a size two too small for her."

"Meow, Sage, that's a bit catty!"

"Well, what do you expect, dressed like that? Also, why is she drinking a pint of lager? Very unladylike."

Sage grabbed her chin to give the impression that she was thinking about the dilemma she had just described.

Jack sniggered and let out a slight noise that alerted Sage to the fact that he was having some fun. She glanced at him and through him with a broad smile.

Sirens started to fill the air from one end of the road, as a police car made its way down. The echoes of the noise hit the buildings and bounced around; it was slightly painful. Cars and trucks tried to move out of the way as the police car passed them. People stopped to stare at the vehicle as it passed. Then the excitement was over and they disappeared into the distance. Everyone started to get on with their lives once again as if nothing had happened.

Sage then glanced at a two females sitting down, mid to late-twenties. One had brown hair. She wore a khaki green denim dress, and had no bra on. Sage could tell that gravity was starting to take its toll over the short years of her life. Maybe her mother should have introduced her to bras. It was not flattering at all. *What a bitch I am!* Sage thought to herself. Then she reflected about the fact that most females are bitches to others.

The other female had a white top, denim shorts, blonde hair tied up at the back with a clip, and tortoise shell sunglasses. They both were systematically on their phones.

"Look, Jack, the musicians are going." Sage pointed out as they got up to leave the café, slowly mingled in with the crowd and went out of sight. The game carried on.

"Oh, they didn't play a song! Oh well!"

"Well, I suppose we can see if anyone is coming for us?" Jack announced as he glanced at a waiter that was heading in their direction. Not tall, about 165cm, slim with greased black hair that looked like a Lego head haircut and a small slim moustache.

"Bonjour, que puis-je vous obtenir, madame, monsieur? Je m'appelle Claude et je suis à votre service."

"Excusez-moi, parlez-vous anglais?" Sage enquired with a very good French accent, which Jack thought was quite sexy.

"Oui madame."

"Hello, what can I get you, madam, sir? My name is Claude and I am at your service," he said with a French sensual accent, then smiled at Sage showing his perfect white teeth (with a gold filling in his right canine).

"Errr, a skinny latte for me. And you, Jack?"

"Errr, the same, please," was Jack's unsure response. He was not expecting to drink yet as they hadn't looked through the menu.

"We'll look at the menu to see if we want any food in a minute or so, okay?" Sage then responded as the waiter winked at her, smiled, and made his way to another table.

"Did you see that?? He winked at you. The bloody waiter winked at you. How up his own ass he is."

"Calm down, Jack, he's a Parisian, maybe? That's what they do, I think?" Then grinned.

A group of boys around fifteen years old, all moved slowly by the cafe. Sage noticed one of them slightly nudge his mate. The gang of boys all looked intensely at the female in the leopard skin dress. When they had passed by they glanced back, and a hive of conversation was had between them all – probably about what they had seen, and no doubt their imaginations were running wild.

Sage then noticed a single white male was performing pilates for some reason on the opposite side of the road, which was strange, to say the least.

Random cars passed by – Renaults, Mercedes, Fiats, a few scooters, and Lamberts.

170

"Oh look, Claude's coming back with our drinks," Sage announced and a massive smile appeared on her face. He put the drinks down, said nothing, then made long eye contact with Sage and smiled at her. Sage's heart fluttered at the thoughts that started going through her head. She watched him slowly walk away and his hips swayed side to side like a male model.

"So many people coming and going in this cafe, I bet they make a fortune every day," Sage stated, then took a drink out of her cup.

"Mmm, that was smarmy of him, wasn't it? Looking at you like that, all sloppy?" Jack stated. He then took a drink out of his cup. "Mmm, that's nice." Then he grinned.

An African female and attractive looking male walked in and stood looking for a place to sit.

Claude the waiter entered the scene, as a smirk crossed Sage's face of *what if*. Sage couldn't remember what the percentage of Parisians that were unfaithful to their husbands or wives was, but she knew it was quite high. Once again she ever so briefly imagined herself being seduced by him, or maybe by a similar type of Parisian with his sexy language and tone of voice.

A car backfired to their left and Sage glanced in the direction of the noise. Then a red mist filled the Paris air which had exploded from Claude. Then a second as he was forced back onto the table, as though some invisible elastic band had snapped tight. Cutlery fell to the floor smashing, as did Claude. The backfiring sound kept randomly going and screams started to take over as humans started falling to the ground. Sage realised what the noise was, gunshots... The impact from the bullet hitting Claude twice and killing him as he collapsed to the ground in a heap. His body was motionless with blood slowly oozing out onto the floor. Sage could see the African female that had just arrived get up and start to run, and then she fell to the ground. The handsome male at the same table got up, briefly stood motionless then ran into the café and out of sight. She noticed people running around, and realised what was happening; and what they needed to do.

Chapter 24

Sage screamed "Down! Down… get the hell down, Jack." As she hit the ground instinctively and pulled out her gun from the back of her jeans. She loaded the chamber and threw her backpack to Jack who had heeded Sage's instruction to react. She glanced at him; he was now rummaging around in the backpack to find the one thing that he needed, his weapon. Random shots rang out in the air. Bullets could be heard flying over their heads with a whoosh and impacting the wall behind them. Debris splintered over the floor, with dust in the air.

The hairs on the back of Sage's neck stood to attention and the adrenalin once again kicked in. Sage started to take deep breaths to control her emotions, as she always did in these situations. She needed to be calm and as cool as she could be in this situation. She had to look after herself and hopefully Jack too, then maybe try and stop innocent people from being murdered.

She was hiding behind a plant pot at this point and Jack appeared to be in a relatively safe place. The windows in the cafe started to shatter as a volley of bullets went through them. Then Sage noticed the frumpy waitress inside the café. She had been hit, although she was slowly dragging herself to the back and out of sight.

"Throw me the backpack," she screamed at Jack who was making sure that his gun was loaded. He did as he was told and Sage put the backpack on. It had everything they needed to get out of this situation – ammo and the Transphone.

Sage glanced over the road, she could see the palates man was running away. Then he suddenly slowed up and arched his back, stopped, then fell to his hands and knees. He finally hit the ground, lying on the floor face down, presumably dead. Sage was hoping he was just wounded, although no movement came from him.

"What's happening?" Jack shouted at Sage, as a car ran into the lamppost just outside the cafe. Steam billowed from the front of it, although no one got out of the vehicle.

"I think it's a terrorist attack," was the response he received back from her.

"What do you mean a terrorist attack? We need to get the hell out of here!"

"Or take them out?" Sage finished his sentence off and threw Jack a hard look. Once again, bullets hit the wall behind them and covered them in small bits of brick.

"Er, take them out? Won't that mess everything up or something?" Jack responded. He winced every time a shot went off.

"Yeah, you're right, even though we are changing the future massively anyway. Come on, follow me." She crouched down, then moved behind some furniture that was on its side.

"Look there's one over there!" Sage announced. She pointed at the female with brownie red hair and a light blue long pencil skirt that was now hitched up. She was sprinting down the street and then a car smashed into her – the car kept going down the street. She was thrown into the air, her body twisting, her arms flailing around. She landed and there was no movement – her body was contorted and her head was facing the wrong way.

"Jack, are you listening to me?"

"Yes."

"OK, at the moment they think no one has any guns. As soon as we engage, they will all start firing at us. Do you understand?"

"Yes."

"So on the good side, that allows people to get away. On the bad side, we are their number one targets. But hopefully, we can take them out, OK?"

"Are we good Jack?"

"Yeah, let's get them." He then winked at Sage.

She braced her gun, ready to get a cleaner steady shot. Sage then lined up one of the gunmen – he was just about in range, shooting at anyone or anything that moved. Sage took in a deep breath, then slowly squeezed the trigger. The gunman pivoted as the slug hit him in the shoulder. Grasping what had happened, he turned his weapon in the general direction of Sage and Jack. Sage let another round off and this time it was good, as he stopped shooting then fell back to the ground, presumably dead. The shooting briefly stopped as the others realised that one of their comrades had fallen. A brief silence, then they started shouting again. A volley of bullets peppered their position then stopped. Gunfire was now coming from further up the street. Sage looked over from her cover to see what was happening.

"It looks like there's another two, and they have headed up the road. Come on their getting away." Sage got up and climbed over two bodies. The female with light brown hair tied at the back, in a white summer dress that was now covered in blood, and the light brown haired female, with the leopard skin print dress. Sage knew that they were dead due to their wounds.

"Don't look at them, Jack!" she shouted. Then she ran towards the man who was doing pilates. She grabbed his arm and pulled him behind a car that had crashed into another car. She took cover and bent down on one knee. Sage knew before she checked for a pulse that he was dead, but she checked anyway.

Jack followed her and he also jumped over the two bodies. He couldn't believe what he was witnessing. Only minutes earlier, they were having a drink and a chat, now they were all dead. As he made his way over to Sage, he noticed the two females running down the road to safety. One in a khaki green denim dress and the other in denim shorts, with blonde hair.

"Is he dead?" Jack asked as he knelt beside her.

"Yes." That was all she said. She glanced around to check that she would still be covered by the cars, as she got up and went over to the terrorist to see if he was still alive.

"He's dead," Sage announced. She got up, then looked at Jack who was puking in the street behind the cars.

"Come on, Jack, stop that bullshit!" she shouted at him, then started to move after them in a crouching manner with her gun at the ready. Sage moved forward a little, then took cover after the shoot. She used the vehicle that helped to keep her covered. It was a systematic approach that she had used several times to hunt someone down.

"Oh my god, it's the guy in the wheelchair! The sneaky bastard," Jack mumbled. He looked at the dead terrorist, then wiped his mouth with his arm, trying to get rid of the taste of vomit. He grasped that he was standing with his back to a set of terrorists, in a shootout, in the middle of a street. He turned then crouched and looked for Sage; she was making her way after the terrorists. Jack ran after her, keeping under cover, he didn't want to lose her again. He was quickly catching Sage. Jack noticed two of the boys with their skateboards lying in the street, dead. Their baseball caps were lying next to them, covered in blood. More blood was on their skateboards and the road. He finally caught up with Sage. He crouched down beside her.

"Are you ready for this, Jack? Because once we start this, they will either run or shoot back. That could mean we end up dead, okay? Get some ammo out of the backpack." Jack complied in silence and handed the bullets to Sage. They both loaded their weapons and pulled the slides back.

"I'm crapping myself, Sage, but let's get them." Jack noticed the fashion statement of the day. The tall guy with the sides of his head shaven with the Mohawk. He was running and then his right knee gave way as blood sprayed out of it. He fell to the ground. The female terrorists slowly walked over to him. They stood over him for a few seconds with the power of his life in her hands. Then they pulled the trigger, executing him.

Jack stood up in silence, appalled at what he had just witnessed. For some reason, maybe anger or fear, he let off two rounds in her direction but one missed as it hit the building behind them. The second shot hit the road in front of her. The terrorist spun around and let a volley of shots off in their general direction. Sage and Jack hid behind the wall that they were using and waited for them to stop.

"What the hell are you doing, Jack? We need to be a bit closer than that. By the way Jack, I'm shitting myself as well, but we will have to try and forget about that for now."

"Sage, I think that's the blonde with the man in the wheelchair."

"Agreed."

175

They both slowly and simultaneously looked over the wall; they could see her running up the street to catch the other terrorist. She kept glancing back to check if they were being followed. Then she stopped and shot the man with thinning hair, a white shirt, and beige trousers carrying paperwork. Sage knew that he had already been shot as he was on the ground, but that was the point that she finished him off. The paperwork started to blow around as his grip on life and his paperwork let go.

"Come on," Sage said as she got up in pursuit of them, with a quick sprint to get within about fifty meters. She stopped behind a van, then got down to one knee, steadied herself, and let off another two rounds but missed. The murdering was starting to stop as the Parisians had mostly hidden by now, fled, or were dead. The terrorists were starting to pick their pace up. They had realised that it was time to get out of there or be shot by the police. Sirens were now starting to come from every direction. Jack caught Sage up, just as Sage got up and made her pursuit after them again. Then it happened! The terrorists split, the male went right and the female went left.

"What do we do, Sage, split or not?"

"No, keep together," she replied and turned down a narrow cobbled street.

"Come on," Sage shouted at Jack as she moved out past the apex of the corner and out of sight. Jack followed ever so slowly, then hurried up as Sage started to run again then stopped at the end of the street. Jack caught her up, they both stood in silence. All they saw were cars everywhere crashed.

"There!" Sage shouted as she noticed that the female had just gone around a corner.

"Come on!" Sage started to run in the same direction, with her gun in her hand ready to shoot – and at the same time this female she was chasing was also running around the streets of Paris brandishing a gun. Sage and Jack came to the corner with the weapons held up in anticipation of what might be around the corner. Sage took a good long breath and held it, as she slowly ventured her head around the corner. *Good, no one there, waiting to blow my head off,* she thought. The female was running down the street, but they were closing in on her. She glanced back, briefly stopped, then went into a building.

Sage ran after her, slightly blinded by anger and revenge for the innocent people that had been killed. She was closely followed by Jack, who was also looking out for police – as well as anyone that may be trying to kill them both.

176

They got to the building entrance; Sage slowed down once again and raised her weapon just in case. She realised that the terrorist had gone inside the building and the pursuit was now on. *Where did she go? What room was she in? Was she hiding in a room to hijack us both and end this?* Thoughts flew through her head. A bead of sweat started to manifest itself on her forehead. She thought about how they had both been through a lot together in this lifetime and the previous one she had had with Jack – even if she could not remember any of the prior events, as it was in a different lifetime, different Jack and a different Sage.

She slowly moved in through the oversized doorway, then entered a hall. The hallway was cold with a tiled floor, white doors on both sides, and at the end of the corridor there was a door. *Probably the staircase,* Sage thought. A strange smell of oldness mixed with cleaning products filled the air.

The adrenaline from the run was well and truly working throughout her body now, Sage was pumped for action. She could feel it in her veins as the heightened senses started to kick in. A shot rang out. It echoed in the building as the bullet penetrated the cream-coloured plaster. The wall next to her exploded then coved Sage in powder.

Chapter 25

Sage took a quick retreat to safety. A moment to gather her thoughts, then another glance around the corner to see where she was! No shots, nothing, she was not there, slight relief; then a shot. Sage could feel the energy of the bullet as it flew by her. It displaced the air around her face then impacted the wall behind her. *It must have missed me by centimetre's,* Sage thought as she bobbed her head back to safety. Then another deep breath as Sage briefly pondered on how close that was. Jack stood next to her, ready to do what he needed to do. She looked at him, and in return he glanced back – no words were exchanged but she knew he had her back. Sage briefly waited then took some deep breaths in out once again. Then glanced at her hand, it was shaking slightly. *Good, I'm wired*, she thought. She slowly moved her head around the corner. The terrorist was nowhere to be seen. Sage let out her breath slowly in hope that she would not get shot at. She moved forward into an open and vulnerable position. But the echoing in the building gave away the terrorist's position, as footsteps could be heard. She was running up the stairs to the next level.

"Are you okay?" Jack inquired. He waited for Sage to make her move.

"Yes, we'll take our time with this one; I think she's not the best shot." Sage gradually made her way down the corridor, then slowly through the doorway at the end. She glanced at a staircase in front of her that was not that well-lit. Caution was on the top of the list. She climbed the steps to the landing. At the top, there was a round window to her right, then there was a second flight of stairs. Sage had a gut feeling that the female had gone through the door rather than going up more stairs. Sage had been counting the number of stairs the female had run up, then she had heard the door close behind her. Sage stood to the side of the door then opened it, and another gunshot filled the building with an echo. The bullet entered the wall on the opposite side of the landing. Then the sound of a door closing. Sage went around the corner in pursuit down the hallway to the door at the end then stopped. Sage heard quick footsteps and put two and two together.

"She's going downstairs," Sage shouted out in hope that Jack would do something. Sage went through the door after the female, she glanced her turning the corner on the landing. Sage thought of taking a shot but she knew that she was running low on bullets, and to be honest the terrorist couldn't have too many left either. Another shot went off and Sage tried to take cover. Sage got to the bottom of the stairs, made a quick dash then entered the hallway that she had originally been in, but there was nothing. No bullets, just police sirens and then Jack's voice.

"It's okay, Sage, I've got her." She looked to the side where the terrorist was on the floor bleeding with her gun near to her hand. Sage picked the gun up. She bent down to see if she could stop the bleeding or at least get some information off of her. Sage was aware that maybe someone had heard the shooting and if so, had probably called the police. So, time was ticking as it didn't look too good for the terrorist, who was on the floor bleeding out, with no future, and the two innocent parties were standing over her with guns.

"Well done, Jack, that was a good move and a good shot." She then threw him a glance to hopefully underline what he had done.

"Thanks." That was all she got back, as he started retching and then spewed up once again.

"So what's your name?" Sage asked the terrorist.

"Go to hell," was the reply she got. Sage glanced at the blood-stained wound at her abdomen, and manoeuvred her knee to apply pressure to it – not to stop the bleeding but to apply pressure to inflict pain to persuade this person to talk. A scream came from the female – the desired effect was reached quite easily.

"Okay, again, what is your name?" Sage asked again as their eyes were locked.

"Jaqueline."

"Okay then, Jaqueline, where are your friends hiding and where are they going to meet? Oh, and names?" Sage asked and slightly applied pressure again to coax Jackeline to talk. Jaqueline begrudgingly told Sage the name of the hotel and then the street.

"Room number, please." Sage put slightly more pressure on the wound to encourage her once again to reveal what she wanted.

"Arrrrgh, stop, stop, okay, thirty-eight... room thirty-eight. Stop... oh, please stop," she pleaded.

"Names of your associates?" Sage asked, then applied pressure to the wound.

"Basher and Roman," was the reply.

Sage looked at Jack. "We have to finish her off – you know that don't you, Jack?"

"Yes, I know, she'll grass us up." A shot rang out in the building. Jack lowered his gun as the wisp of smoke from it briefly lingered where the barrel had been. It was pointing at Jacqueline's head.

"Let's get out of here, Sage." Jack started to move towards the door then stopped.

"Police outside... there must be a back way out?" Jack yelled. Sage had already started to go up the corridor in the general direction of the back of the building. Voices could now be heard from behind them, as they tried to quickly make their way to the back without making a sound. Door after door was locked and it was starting to come to the point that they may have to use their weapon to open one of the doors.

"They'd have found the body by now," Sage said. Voices and whistles could now be heard in the background. Sage stopped at a door and tried the handle.

"It's locked." Then she used the butt of the grip on her gun to smash the glass. The sound resonated through the building, and as predicted the police caught wind of what was happening. Sage used the gun to push some glass out of the way then pushed her hand through and grabbed the handle to open the door from the outside.

"How did you know it would unlock?" Jack asked as Sage pushed the door open, then took back her arm through the window. Except her hand was bleeding, not much, but enough to make a mess on the door.

"I didn't, it was a guess. Come on, let's get out of here," Sage announced as she moved forward, through the door opening. Jack followed – he glanced and saw men appearing at the end of the corridor.

"Go, go!" he shouted as they both burst into a run. Whistles could be heard from behind them. They sprinted down a street into an alleyway.

"I think we lost them," Sage said as she realised that she had a gun out in broad daylight, with no way of realistically explaining the reason why they were in Paris with guns.

"Come on back up here." She moved back down the way they had just come and slotted the gun down the back of her jeans. Then went around the corner and stopped as a police car approached them. She instinctively grabbed Jack and pushed him against the wall. Sage kissed him ever so gently, and he responded by kissing her back. The kissing became stronger, then his tongue started to explore her mouth. It was then forced out as she started to explore his mouth. Jack's hand slowly clasped her waist. He then squeezed and pulled her closer as they started to touch each other. Sage could feel Jack getting hard, as her hands grabbed his hair and moved his head with passion. The breathing was starting to become heavier, faster as both of them started to get excited with the situation they were in. The excessive amounts of adrenaline that was in their bodies, flowing through their veins, needed to be used up. The police car drove by them. Sage was enjoying it all a bit too much, but she pulled back and stopped the kissing. She glanced at the car heading down the street and out of sight.

"What the hell was that all about?" Jack asked, slightly out of breath.

"Look, Jack, they are probably looking for a male and female in the street. We fit into that and guess what? We have guns on us. So, we could well be the terrorists. Affection in public places does not go down well, hence the snogging. I bet the cops in the car had a treat watching us though." Sage said as her cheeks went slightly red out of embarrassment.

"Oh yeah, I've heard that before!" Jack said then coughed to try and deflate his embarrassment.

"Anyway, what are you on about? Do you think I have the hots for you or something?" Sage asked as she looked up and down the street to try and decide which way to go.

"Haha, noooo why would I think that? It was for the cop car that's all! Haha" Jack's eyes were transfixed on Sage for a moment, and then snapped out of it before she noticed his gaze.

"Come on, lets get back to our room, and we can debrief there," Sage said as she started walking off in what Jack thought was a random direction.

"Debrief? We're not in the army, you know. Anyway, why wouldn't you have the hots for me? I've seen the way you sometimes look at me," Jack rebuffed sarcastically as he followed Sage.

"In your dreams, Jack… in your dreams." Minutes later, they stood outside the doorway of their hotel and they climbed the two marble steps once again. Sage opened the door and, as before, there was silence. Drearily, they made their way down the long and dim corridor that had an odour similar to the other building they had killed the terrorist in. This building appeared to have more lights, although they didn't make much difference. Jack noticed the marble tiles had grains of what looked like gold or something – *maybe it's painted on*, he thought.

Sage pressed the lift button, a number of clunking sound's, then once again the lift doors opened. The hairs on the back of Sages neck stood on end as the sounds of sirens could be heard. *Probably the police, ambulances and God know what else*, she thought. Played in the background the city noise could also be overheard. They entered the lift in silence. The sounds of the mechanics nearly took over the noises of the city, as they slowly moved to a higher floor. The doors opened with a rattle and they both wearily walked out, Jack let Sage lead the way once again to the door at the end. They passed the counter and this time there was a female there. Jack glanced at the olive-skinned brunette and smiled, although he carried on walking behind Sage down the corridor, took some turns and got to their door. Sage opened it and made her way in.

"Are you okay, Jack?" Sage stopped, turned to him, and then looked him in the eyes.

"I'm knackered, Sage. I feel like I want to sleep for weeks." Then he lifted his right hand to show Sage how it was shaking.

"That's the adrenaline, excitement, fear trust me. You will sleep, then there'll be the nightmares and the trauma of what has just happened. I do have some tablets to help you out with all that if you want them, okay Jack." A smile and a glance into his eyes followed.

"Oh how's your near death gunshot wound?" Sage inquired, whilst trying not to laugh...

"It's not funny you know!" then smirked back it her.

"Ok, ok I'll take them after I have been to the toilet," was the response as he made his way to the toilet to relieve himself, and then he threw up again. Sage made her way to the bedroom and shut the curtains. She then took her backpack off, placed her gun down and started to take off her sweat-sodden t-shirt. She peeled off her damp jeans and then Jack entered the room.

"You look like a ghost, Jack," she smirked at him.

"I feel like I'm dead," he responded. Then put his gun down and started to take off his clothes in the same don't-give-a-damn manner.

"Hear take this tablet for, well everything... It will help you with the pain, trauma and sleep. Not that you will need anything to help with the sleep." A smile towards Jack, as he took the tablet. Next, Sage took off her bra and knickers, and the climbed into bed. She looked at Jack who was standing in front of her completely naked. He then climbed into bed and pulled the sheets up to cover them both.

"Cuddle me," was all that Sage said. Jack obliged by sliding an arm under Sage's head, then she placed her head on his chest. Her right leg slowly made its way over his left leg and she snuggled into a comfy position. A tear rolled down Jack's cheekbone as the shock and realisation started to hit home.

Yes, he had been in a shootout in Johannesburg and shot people, but this seemed real, whereas that didn't. Maybe it was because he had seen dead bodies lying in the street, executed by the terrorist parasites. Innocent men, women, and children, all unarmed and couldn't have hurt the terrorists. Shutting his eyes, Jack could sense that Sage was already asleep, and he was quickly engulfed by darkness.

Chapter 26

This was different from what Abbie remembered and definitely different from Phil. The kissing, the touching over her body, the tenderness... Abbie could not remember guys being as tender. He pleasured her as though he was not expecting anything in return! She experienced several orgasms from his silver tongue, squirming with delight and embarrassment at what was happening to her body. The shivering came over her in waves of joy, then it was the moment of truth as he slowly moved and positioned himself. Abbie thought about her vibrators and sex toys; although very good in 2098 they were no replacement for the real thing... He started to slowly move in and out of her. But nothing was vibrating – this was real, from a flesh and blood male. It wasn't some plastic item that would need charging (although it would go on for longer than he probably would). Still, you never know! Which Abbie did think was a slight advantage over the real thing. But this was special... The speed slowly picked up and he kissed her on the cheek, forehead, and lips. More orgasms started to unfold and she was just enjoying the journey. This was so, so good and different from what she was used to. *You could never beat the touch of a woman,* Abbie thought, *but mmmmm this is nice,* as she came again. Abbie was in a glow of happiness – she could never remember being treated so well by a man. They both climaxed, and the moment was full of joy, pleasure and happiness.

Then there came a grunt, and like a bad movie it started to go slightly pear-shaped as Connor lay on top of her like a dead piece of meat squashing her into the bed. Reality kicked in as he started to go limp inside her. He tried to get a bit more mileage out of it, but it was no good. He rolled off her and lay motionless in silence. Abbie could now breathe, she contemplated what had happened.

Conner looked at the time on the clock next to the bed. He made a slight noise and rolled onto his side with his back to her. Abbie took this as *it's all over and I have to get to sleep*. This did not sit well with her. He had got what he wanted but what about what she wanted? Yes, she'd had many orgasms, yes she'd enjoyed them, but she wanted cuddling, caressing... Yes, they had met tonight and had sex, but it was a moment that no one else shared. This was only between both of them; it was a twinkling in time that could not be taken away.

There was a noise – Conner had started to snore. This is not how it happens in the movies at any time. A feeling started to brew from inside her. Rage. This underlines why she preferred females over males – men are self-indulgent dick heads. Abbie could not believe how taken she was with this man. That she had put doubts into her head, that she was doing the wrong thing.

Oh, bless, he's so sweet! No, he's a self-centred pig. The feeling of anger bubbled inside her, trying to escape. This was helping her, and it allowed her to go to step two of her plan. Now the likely outcome would be to get to the end of the mission, this was quite clear. She had had doubts that she could complete what she had to do, although now that was different. Surprisingly, all it took was a grunt from a man to do this. To push her over the edge, something so small in his eyes, but in her eyes massive. Abbie lay in a damp patch which reminded her of the pleasure she had had and how it had gone stale from her host. She slowly moved and climbed out of the bed as the cold caressed her body. Yes, she could have cuddled up to Conner's back, but no! It was a sign of weakness in her, and she was not weak. No, she had briefly wavered, but he was going to find out what she was made of.

Abbie made her way to the bathroom to freshen up. She turned the tap on to hopefully warm the water up, and she then put both hands on the sink and rested on it. She lifted her head slowly and looked at herself in the mirror. She had a quick wash with lukewarm water as quite clearly the hot water system was turned down. She thought about the years that had passed her, and the time she had had that would never happen again.

Then Abbie made her way out to her backpack. She opened it up, and its interior light came on. Then pulled out some clean underwear whilst trying not to be too noisy, and moved around the flat to collect her jeans and other various pieces of clothing, and dressed.

Snoring was coming from the bed area as Conner was fast asleep. She removed her gun, then loaded the chamber. Briefly Abbie stood in the night light that was being provided by the moon, thinking about what she was doing and why. She pondered once again about the past – Phil and her deceit. Then thought about Conner and how he had shown her what she was missing, then shown a different part of what she was missing. She was glad of what he had shown her. She moved to the window and looked at the moon. It looked the same in any timeline, just like people. Self-centred, devious, and self-indulgent – sod them!

Then a decision was made. It was time! She made her way over to the light switch and turned it on. Groans came from Conner, but nothing to be too worried about. Oh no, the poor, poor man was probably exhausted from servicing the little lady. She glanced at the kettle that was stood waiting to be used, picked it up and made her way over to Conner.

"Rise and shine, your worst nightmare is here," Abbie announced as she slowly poured the cold water over him.

"Err, what the fuck... what the..." was the response as Conner came out of his comatose sleep. His eyes opened wide as he stared at the sight of a gun barrel being pointed at his face.

"What the...! Why... why are you pointing a gun at me? Where did you get it from? I don't get it!"

"It's simple. I'm using you as bait," was the response. Abbie smiled at him – the revelation that she was having was quite uplifting.

"Bait? Bait for what? Fishing?"

"Bate to capture your friend Jack. Now get up and sit over there," was her instruction. Conner pulled back the sheets – he was completely naked under them. Abbie could not help but look at Conner's manhood. A smirk crossed her face again as she briefly remembered how close he was to changing her to the other side. But it was not to be – females were not just different, they were better, end of! Abbie knew that there were good men out there, it was just a matter of finding them – but they were so rare.

"I'm bloody cold."

"Get some clothes on then," she ordered him. It was a slow process as he started to saunter around looking for various parts of clothing to complete the set. As he was putting his socks on, he stood up and then fell over onto the bed.

"For god's sake, it's not hard to put your socks on, is it?" Abbie announced as she bent down to pick up his t-shirt to help him out. At that point, she felt an impact on her left side and then one to the back of the head. She dropped the gun, knowing what was going on. Conner was attacking her. She brought her forearms up to protect herself until she came up with a plan of response. The gun was on the floor but it seemed that Conner had not seen where it had gone. Abbie took the beating initially, but then she started her response, running headfirst into her assailant. He was forced backwards and into the wall – the desired impact. A groan came from Conner. Then there was an influx of punches from Abbie – left, right, left, left. One to the stomach again and some headshots. Conner had lifted his arms to protect himself but she could tell if he was hurt. His guard started to go down. Abbie could see a vacant look come over him as he started to go light-headed. At the same time, his legs became like jelly as the trauma caused by the ongoing punches. It was overwhelming his neurotransmitters, which were all firing simultaneously. Conner had vacated his head and slid down the wall. He ended up unconscious on the floor. Abbie stood there watching him, fists ready to dish out more pain; whilst he lay on the floor.

Abbie briefly stood over this man that she had just knocked out, in some primal show of strength and victory. Then humanity kicked in and she checked that he was still alive.

Abbie quickly went over to get her gun. Next she needed the backpack, and some cable ties to make sure that this didn't happen again. How embarrassing to be caught out like that, with him pretending to be struggling to get dressed. Abbie shook her head – *What a fool, falling for that old trick. Did I just fall out of the idiot tree? Oh well, at least I came out on top. Those boxing lessons were worth the credits indeed,* she thought to herself. The win also pleased her competitive streak. She had a quick look around for a chair to sit him on so that he couldn't get away. Moving him to the chair was a task in itself, as Conner was deadweight, but Abbie was able to secure him to it.

Next she had to let the prey know what was waiting for them, then to set the trap to catch them both. Abbie had the bait that was now tied up on the chair unconscious. She glanced at him once more, motionless and secure.

Hi Sage,

Just to let you know that I have Jack's friend Conner tied up with a gun to his head. I suggest you come and visit me, obviously unarmed. Then we can settle this slight issue we have. You know where I am as you have the info at the top of the screen.

Remember, this is my job.

Kindest Regards,

Abbie. xxx

Abbie looked at the message on the screen, then chuckled at the *kindest regards* comment as she hit the send button. All she was doing was inviting them to join her, just so she could execute them both, even though the email did seem to suggest differently. She would complete her task, go back to 2096, get paid the bonus, and have a few weeks off maybe a holiday or hit some clubs. Was she ready for that sort of life with all the work of trying to get a partner? She looked at Conner and a brief feeling inside suggested that maybe she would possibly look for a partner of either gender as you only live once.

Making her way to the kettle, she decided that it was coffee time! She had no idea when they would arrive, or even if they would show up at all. For all she knew, Conner was nothing to Jack, and if that was the case she would need to come up with something else.

After making the coffee, Abbie covered Conner with a blanket. She didn't want him to be cold. Then she moved the chair to a position in the room that gave her the best view. She put the TV on, covered herself with a blanket, and reloaded her gun. She prepped the Transphone as a hasty exit would be required. Then she put the backpack on, made herself comfortable. Then the waiting game started…

Chapter 27

Jack and Sage woke up nearly at the same time, entwined in each other. Jack had his left arm under Sage's head in the same position that they went to sleep in; Sage had her right leg over his left leg. The warmth from their bodies was nearly unbearable, due to thick covers hemming them in like prisoners.

Looking at each other, they lay motionless. Both were thinking the same thing, but neither one had the guts to do anything about it. What do they do? Do they kiss? Do they look at each other longer? Maybe just have a conversation? All these questions and more were simultaneously going through both their minds...

"This is awkward, isn't it?" Jack finally said. He knew that he couldn't hold the silence any longer. To add to this dilemma, Jack was starting to get hard but knew that it was not the right time to even think of anything like that. Jack started thinking about electrical drawings and other tedious things. He had seen this trick in a movie or some TV show. Their lips were centimetres away from each other. *Is something going to happen?* Jack briefly thought, then he went back to thinking about electrical drawings. His urge was returning.

"I'm off to the toilet," Sage announced then untangled herself from Jack, and promptly got up and made her way to the bathroom. Jack watched her walk to the door. Light was coming through the split in the curtains but not enough to fully drench Sage. She closed the door, and moments later Jack heard the shower come on. He lay in the bed thinking about what had just happened, the closeness, the smell of her.

He got out of bed and made his way to the bathroom. He noticed that the door was slightly open. Should he enter or not? This was a dilemma indeed. He stood at the door for a few moments. It opened and Sage stood there with a towel around her.

"Oh Jesus, you scared me, Jack," Sage said in a frightened voice.

"Oh er, sorry, I was just waiting to go to the toilet."

"Oh, you should have just come in, it's okay," Sage replied, moving past Jack to the bedroom.

Jack entered the bathroom to relieve himself. As he was doing this, he chuckled to himself, even to the point of shaking his head at the embarrassment of the whole situation.

"She must think I'm either stupid or a snooper," Jack mumbled and continued to chuckle.

He then had a quick shower, dried himself then wrapped the towel around himself and made his way to the bedroom.

Sage was standing naked with her back to the doorway in the bedroom. She started to put her bra on. Deep down, Jack was sad but relieved. He didn't want to complicate this situation any more than it was already.

"So what's the plan, Jack?" Sage asked as she turned her head and smiled.

"Regarding what?" he responded whilst he was putting his trousers on.

"The terrorists, of course!" Sage answered as she pushed her head through her t-shirt. Sage started to put her socks on, then the rest of her underwear and finally her jeans.

Jack stood looking at Sage getting dressed. He could smell the freshness of her shower gel or whatever she used. It was so potent.

"What's your shower gel?" Jack blurted out before he had time to engage his filter.

"Oh, it's from the future, with fewer chemicals in it!" Sage specified as she looked at herself in the mirror.

Then a ping came from her backpack. She moved over to pick it up. Searching for the source, she quickly found her Transphone. She opened the screen and noticed a message.

Hi Sage,
Just to let you know that I have Jack's friend Conner tied up with a gun to his head. I suggest you come and visit me, obviously unarmed. Then we can settle this slight issue we have. You know where I am as you have the info at the top of the screen.
Remember, this is my job.
Kindest Regards,
  Abbie. xxx

"What's that, a message?" Jack inquired as he stretched his neck to try and see what it said.

"Er, no, no, nothing, I don't know… what can we do about them?" she replied as she returned the Transphone to her backpack.

"About what?"

"The terrorists, Jack!"

"Well, what about using the Transphone? Let's say, take the terrorists out before they do any mindless killing?" Jack announced and sat on the edge of the bed. Looking down at the floor, he thought for a moment.

"Er, well, yes. I suppose we could go back, take them out, and save a load of lives at the same time. That's a good idea Jack. That's the reason why the Transphone was developed, to do such a job," Sage responded as she tied her laces up.

"Well, let's do it now then? Make sure you're fully loaded, with spare ammo. We'll go back and kick some terrorist ass," was her comeback, then picked up her gun.

Jack put his trainers on and then made his way over to where his gun was laying. They both filled up their magazines and pulled the slide back to load the chamber.

"I'm all good to go," Jack stated, as he shoved the gun down the back of his trousers and covered it with his T-shirt. Sage picked the Transphone up and started to put the day, and time location in it and then stopped and looked at Jack.

"So when do we go back to?"

"Er, maybe an hour?" He shrugged his shoulders and pulled a face to emphasize that he was uncertain.

"Hmm, we got to the room at around twelve forty-five, okay? We originally left the hotel to go to the cafe at around two-fifteen after freshening up."

"Okay, we'll say an hour and a half then?" Sage said and then waited for the confirmation response from Jack, who as always shrugged his shoulders and said nothing. Sometimes he added a grunt that indicated that he was happy with the decision that had been made for him. Sage completed the task of inputting the information and glanced at Jack.

"Well?" was the response she gave him as he stood in front of her. They got into position, and Sage grabbed Jacks hand so that they were connected to each other, glanced at him and pressed the button on the Transphone. A humming started. Then, as before, everything started to go black. Moments later, the light started to come back and to Jack's surprise, he was standing in the same place as before the jump. It was as though he had briefly closed his eyes rather than travelling back in time.

"Hey look, two chocolates," was all that Jack said. He picked one of them up, promptly opened it, and stuffed it into his mouth without a thought for Sage. Then he glanced around the room, then put the empty wrapper under the pillow.

"Was that nice?" Sage asked as she watched him devour the chocolate.

"Er yes, oh sorry, did you want one? There is one left!" Jack glanced at it as if he was going to eat that one also.

"Don't even think about it," Sage glared at him. He started to reach out for it but pulled his arm back before grabbing it.

"Come on, let's go, before you get the other one. We need to be out of here." Sage spoke with a slight tone of urgency as she put the Transphone in the backpack, then made her way to the door. Jack glanced at the chocolate lying there but thought better of it. Following Sage, for some reason, he had a swagger to his walk.

They both made their way to the lift and out of the building before they bumped into themselves arriving for the first time at the hotel. Making their way down the Parisian streets, they took in the smells of coffee, and croissants.

"Look, we know where they are hanging out, why don't we just go to the hotel?" Jack announced. They both stood looking at the cafe that they had been sitting in when the shootout started.

"Yes, I think we have time." Sage looked at the church clock in the distance.

"I think it's this way." Then she moved off in the direction at a quick pace and the walk started to develop into a jog. Jack scanned around and then followed. Making their way to the hotel, Jack was once again looking at the Parisian people. They all looked so fashion-conscious in their suits and dresses. The warmth of the sun was a slight change from the norm, which made Jack happy. Outside, the hotel looked magnificent in the daylight of Paris.

"We'll just catch our breath, for a second or so, I want to get some composure before we go in," Sage stated as she took a few deep breaths.

"So what's the plan?" Jack enquired, as his eyes were transfixed on a leggy blond in a hugging blue dress with a very open cleavage area.

"Put your tongue away Jack, it's embarrassing." Sage took off her backpack and rummaged around in it for a few seconds.

"I have this! She passed a small black wallet to him. Jack opened it up and burst out laughing.

"Oh my god, what a picture, were you on drugs when you took it? Why are your eyes so red? FBI? The Federal Bureau of Investigation? Who do you think you are, Dana Scully? For god's sake, we are scraping the barrel now. Do you have one for me? I could be James Bond?" Jack stated then passed it back to Sage as he was still sniggering out loud.

"Really, Jack! I get that it's not my best picture, but it's all we have, okay?"

"So then, what's the plan?" Sage glared at him, waiting for an answer.

"Well, er, I think we should go in then show them your FBI credentials, and see what happens," was his response, then he started sniggering again. He started to make his way up the stone steps of the hotel. Then he went out of sight, through the doors of the hotel.

Standing in the foyer, briefly taking in the layout of the area. Then Sage arrived seconds later and stood by Jack.

"Over there, Sage," Jack gestured with a nod of his head towards the counter and the concierge who was standing behind it. There stood a large male with bushy thick black hair. He was wearing the hotel's uniform which was snug fitting.

"Okay, stand back and leave all the talking to me," Sage stated as she made her way over to the counter.

"Excusez-moi, parlez-vous anglais?"

"Yes, madam I do. Welcome," the concierge replied in a husky French accent, then smiled.

"Welcome, what can I do for you?"

"Well, I have a slight situation. It's like this, I am with the FBI and I'm looking for a female and two males that are in this hotel. Intel has said that they are possibly in room thirty-eight. Can you please confirm that?" Sage held her breath as she showed the man the FBI ID, then smiled back at him. The concierge held his hand out and took the ID off Sage to have a closer look at it. Once it was in his hand, he intensely glared at it, then at Sage.

"I have never seen one before, Madam." He commented, as he once again glanced at the photo, then at Sage, then back at the photo.

"Can you tell me if they are in, please?" Sage asked as firmly as she dared and held out her hand to regain the ID – as if to say there would be no issue at all with the ID.

"Well, I shouldn't, I suppose, but as you are with the FBI..." he stammered then scratched the temple on his face. The man looked left and right as if he was looking for his boss or someone higher than him to give the okay.

"Please, time is of the essence," Sage commanded. She could feel the anxiety starting to build up inside her. But she knew that she had to keep the part going and stay cool, to pull this off.

"Well, okay," the concierge replied, then punched a few keys on the computer in front of him, and smiled.

"Yes, they're in, although I'm led to believe that there may only be two people in the room Madam. Shall I phone up and let them know you're here?" he enquired as he automatically picked the phone up.

"No, no it's okay; we will visit them in person. Thank you. You have been ever so helpful." She smiled at him.

"I think I should let my manager know you are on-site, Madam. Do you want security to help? Shall I call the police?"

"No, no, it's all good, we are just going to ask them some questions, that's all," Sage replied, then she started to move away.

"Okay, Madam, thank you," he shouted back. Then his attention was taken up by another customer.

They made their way over to the lift through the foyer. There were plants to the left and right, and various black leather seats scattered around. The white ceilings and walls brightened the area up, and a large mirror on the main wall looked back at the counter that the concierge was behind. Sage glanced to check that he was busy with another customer. Some relief came over her that he was not phoning someone straight away. Jack pressed the button and they waited for the lift.

"God, that was close. I thought he wasn't going to buy it," Sage announced as she looked around the area to familiarise herself.

The doors opened and two females holding hands walked out, one with pink hair, the other with blue. Both wore orange t-shirts and jeans and they started laughing loudly as if to say *hey look at us, we're having a really good time!* Sage and Jack glanced at each other, then moved into the lift as a slim bald male started to follow them in.

Sage lifted the ID, nearly shoving it in the man's face. He stopped, said something in French (Sage and Jack had no idea what it was), rolled his eyes and turned to leave the lift. The doors shut, and both of them started to laugh.

"I cannot believe that people fall for it, I really can't. I need to get one of my own." Jack said as he shook his head with disbelief.

"Well, it works, 99 per cent of the time on people. They just fall for it! I've used it loads of times to get into places. I once used it at a ski resort. That was so much fun, I'll tell you about that later on." The lift stopped at their floor. There was a chime and then the door opened. They both looked at each other and moved out into the corridor. Then looked at the signs on the beige wall, the arrows showing them which direction the various rooms were in.

"This way," Jack stated as he moved in the direction of the room, then stopped about three rooms down from the desired door.

"Okay Jack, I'll knock on the door and tell them it's room service. The door hopefully will open, and we go in guns blazing. With a bit of luck, it will be three clean shots, then three dead terrorists. Are we good with the plan?"

"Errr, don't you think we should make sure it's them first? And don't you think we will be making a lot of noise, Sage? And also the man at the desk said that there were only two people in the room!"

"Oh, mmm, yes sorry, I'm getting ahead of myself. OK, maybe one of them is out! So we go in guns raised, if we get a target that has a gun, we shoot to kill, okay?" Sage said as she looked up and down the corridor and then pulled out her gun.

Jack said nothing – he just nodded; they made their way to the door with the number thirty-eight on it and stopped. Both stood to one side of the door. Looking at each other's fear, which was evident. Sage mouthed *OK?* Jack nodded once again. Sage knocked on the door and tried to put on a French accent to add to the originality

"Service de chamber," she shouted, then pulled a face as if to say *I'm not sure that that was right?* Nothing happened, so Sage knocked again. Around ten seconds or so later a fumbling could be heard coming from the door, and then it started to open. Sage shoved the door open with her shoulder and raised her gun. Jack was behind her, gun raised, looking for his first target.

"No, Jack, no, no it's not them," Sage screamed out as she lowered her weapon that had been trained on an Asian man who had run to the back of the room and was now shaking with fear.

"It's okay... okay, we're sorry," Sage said to him, then slowly backed away, slightly bowing at the same time to try and show some respect. Sage then showed the man the FBI ID card. This appeared to calm the situation down slightly. Jack had also realised that maybe this was not the right person they wanted, as a large female was lying on the bed in red leather pants, boots and a bra. She tried to scream then put her hand over her mouth, that stopped most of the sound from exiting. The female also appeared to be have a whip in her hand; Jack raised an eyebrow slightly at the strange sight in front of him.

"So sorry, love, so sorry... wrong room, wrong room... FBI, FBI..." he said. He could see fear on the female's face. Jack glanced at Sage, trying not to smile, although it was hard not to. This was not what they had expected at all. They both slowly made their way to the door as they repeated the word "Sorry."

Once outside, they looked at each other and started laughing at what had just happened.

They moved down the corridor towards the lift. They stood in silence, pondering over the situation that had happened.

"What now, then? The bitch must have given us the wrong information," Jack blurted out.

"I have no idea at all. Maybe try and take them out at the café." Was Sage's response as her shoulders dropped with deflation.

The bell chimed and the lift doors opened. Out walked Jaqueline holding one coffee. She had a carrier bag hanging from her left arm and she was wearing a white blouse and a dark blue pencil skirt.

Looking at each other without saying a word, they watched her go around the corner and briefly out of sight.

"Is that who I think it is?" Jack broke the silence.

"Yes, I think it is," was the response as they rushed to the corner and Jack peered around to see which room she went to. Out of sight again, she turned another corner onto an additional corridor. He hurried once again and poked his head around to see which room she went to. She was knocking on a door about halfway down the corridor. After around twenty seconds the door opened – she went into the room and then the door shut.

"Come on, let's see what room number it is?" Jack said as he moved off in the direction of the door.

"No, no, wait, Jack," Sage shouted as softly as she could. But it was too late as Jack stood outside the door. He then turned and made his way back to where Sage was standing.

"What are you trying to do?" Sage said in an aggressive tone.

"What's wrong? Take a chill pill, Sage!" was the response she got back.

"What if someone had opened the door and you were stood there looking stupid?"

"Oh, I look stupid, do I?" he responded.

"No, no, no, you know what I mean. Someone could have heard you outside, and opened the door with a gun in their hand then just shot you – that's what," Sage said with a tone of apology in her voice for calling him stupid.

"Okay, it's room forty-two."

"So, what's the plan then?" Sage inquired, as they both just stood looking down the corridor in the general direction of the room.

"We need to know if the three of them are in the room still or just the two, don't we?" Sage said, then scratched her head.

"I'll stand outside and listen if you want?" Jack volunteered to do the task at hand.

"No, no, we will have to use hope again, and hope they are all in. Although she only had one coffee in her hand!"

"Or maybe two of them didn't want a coffee. Stop over-analysing everything. Come on, let's do this," Jack blurted out.

"Okay, okay, I get that you're becoming bored, anxious or whatever, but we could both end up dead. So what's the plan? "Sage asked again.

"Why is it my plan?" Jack questioned Sage.

"Well, you came up with this idea and to be honest you're on fire at the moment with ideas, so I'm running with it."

"Okay, Sage. Well for me, it's the same plan as before. We go, knock, you say room service in that French accent. When it opens, we overpower the door, go in guns raised and shoot anything with a gun, and take them out. What do you say?"

"Wait here," Sage said as she started to walk down the corridor to a trolley. She looked around very suspiciously then picked something up. She quickly turned and started to make her way toward Jack with a smile on her face.

"What are you doing?" The simple question came from Jake in a whisper.

"I've seen it before; the maid leaves the master card on the trolley so that she doesn't lose it. Sometimes they have it on a string or a lanyard, but I had a hunch that hers would be on the trolley. Sage lifted her arm and the card dropped out of her hand like a magic trick. So we will go to the door, using the card to open it, then we can take them by surprise. Does that sound like a plan or what?" Sage smugly announced as she stood in front of Jack with a grin of contentment. She knew that the plan she had come up with was a good one.

"Er yep, that sounds like a plan indeed. Come on let's get this over with." Jack started to move in the direction of the room and Sage followed him. As before, they stopped and stood on each side of the door. They pulled out their guns and checked the slides, just to make sure that they were loaded and ready to be used.

"On three... One, two, three..." Sage swiped the card, the door clicked open, she pushed the handle down and burst into the room. Quickly making her way in, then down the dimly lit corridor with her gun raised. Jack followed, gun raised.

The sight was not what she was expecting; Jaqueline was sat on the bed reading a magazine! A partly naked man was standing next to her.

"What the--" Jaqueline and the man said simultaneously. Then Jaqueline started to make a move for her gun on the bedside table. Sage squeezed the trigger and let off a round that hit her in the back of the head. The slug continued its journey out of the front of her skull, pulling blood and brain matter out with it and ending its journey in the wall. The wall was now covered in the remains of Jaqueline brains, blood and skull. The body immediately slumped on the bed as a motionless piece of meat. By the time that this had all happened, the man was standing in front of Sage, hands raised.

Fear had started to take over. The man started to talk in a language that Sage did not understand.

"Speak English," she said with her gun pointing at him.

"I'm sorry, sorry, I have done nothing wrong, I don't know who she was, she said she would give me a good time. I don't know about the gun, I'm a poor man. Please!" the random man blurted out as he stood in front of Sage, pleading.

"The other one's not here," Jack announced. He came out of the bathroom and checked the wardrobes just in case. After that, he went and shut the door to try and control the sound; then he moved back towards Sage and the man.

"What's your name?" Sage asked.

"Basher, why?" he responded, then smiled.

"Where's your mate?" Jack directly asked then lifted his gun and pointed it at the man.

"I don't know what you are on about... Who? What other man?" was the reply he got.

"I will ask this one more time: where is the other one?" Jack moved closer and pointed the gun directly at the man's face.

"Go on, shoot me, you piece of shit, I'm not going to tell you or the whore anything! Go on, shoot me!" Basher furiously started.

Sage let off a round into his kneecap which exploded, a haze of blood spraying everywhere. The man collapsed onto the floor, screaming with pain as he rolled around grasping his exploded knee.

"Fuck, fuck, fuck!"

"So where's your mate? Shall I do the other one or do you want it in the balls?" Sage asked him in a calm voice, then moved closer.

"Fuck off, bitch." Was his reply as he spat in Sage's direction, except nothing came out of his mouth. Sage could see on his face that he was in vast amounts of pain, although his screaming was starting to quieten down. She thought he was going to pass out.

"Hey, hey, for the last time, where is your mate? I'll do the other knee!"

"Arrgh, I don't know, he's gone for a coffee." The reply came back as he rolled around on the floor which was covered in blood.

"He's not going to tell us anything, you know," Jack said to Sage as they both stood there watching this poor would-be terrorist squirming around in pain in a sea of blood.

"Yeah, I know. I would put him out of his misery, but I think of all the innocent people that he was going to kill, and you know he deserves it, piece of shit."

"Yep, I know what you mean," Jack responded.

A click came from behind them both. They both lost interest in the man on the floor as they slowly turned to view a figure. A man was standing in the doorway holding one coffee.

Sage raised her gun to shoot.

Chapter 28

The Manager sat in his office looking out of the window as he drank a cup of tea from a green fine bone china mug. The waft of the fragrance drifted up his nose and made him content. He was thinking about the day, which had been a slow one. Not the best of days; he had had better ones.

The morning had started with a meeting of command team leaders and their bosses, which implied that he was under the microscope and probably some shit was going to fall in his lap. The meeting was held in a large office on the next floor up from his. In it, there was a dark, highly polished oak table with twelve white leather chairs. On the table were two large jugs of water in the centre on white coasters. The walls were white and clinical, and the ceiling was a light grey. Place – cards marked the spot and location you had to sit, so he could not move to where he wanted to be. The Manager sat facing the window, which was not the best seat! The high-rise view distracted him or anyone else that was in that position, all sorts of movements could be seen happening outside.

To add to that, in the morning the sun would be glaring in through the full-height windows, making whoever sat at that side of the table hot and uncomfortable. This was torture to the person's eyes. He had sat there many times in the past. Even if you asked for the blinds to be turned down, the request would be denied, because it would make the room dark for everyone else. The Manager had once pointed out that the lights could be turned on or up. This was shut down as wasting power and costing the company credits, and was he going to pay the extra cost? He had thought of replying to that with a yes, although bit his tongue on that occasion. It was all designed to unsettle the person under the microscope. He had seen it work many times before when he sat on the other side of the table.

Straight away, they started to turn the screw on him. All the shit that had happened recently – with one of his agents, Mandy, her death and the consequences of that. Then The Manager defended himself by updating them on his pro-activeness of sending in Mason, to try to get the focus off himself, but he knew that he was flogging a dead horse with that idea.

The two leaders of the assault on him were bitch Winchester and bastard Salford. *Okay, so you're shagging each other, but don't pick on me for that*, he thought as he tried to not wish both of them dead with a hard, stare as he sat opposite. *What the hell did she see in him?* he thought as he sat gazing at Winchester. She was in her mid-thirties, slim(ish), always well-presented, shoulder-length auburn hair that was clipped up. She always put on too much makeup, although the reason for that was that she had bad skin. Underneath all that make-up, he imagined she was quite pretty.

Salford on the other hand was in his early fifties, ninety-five kilos, give or take ten, with thinning to bald hair, a grey beard that was sculptured, sweating armpits, and a gut to match, oh and married with three kids. Their relationship was a joke! Did Salford think she was with him for any reason other than promotion, credits and status? The rumour flying around was that she didn't love him, and was also dating a lawyer on the side. This was all he could think of, as he got his arse chewed by both of them in turn!

Yes, Mandy had messed up. Yes, he was in charge, blah, blah, blah, he thought and then let loose.

"But let's look at it this way. I wasn't there and neither were either of you! So we don't know exactly what happened. We can only assume that certain things happened. Mandy should have known that it was a dead end. Yes, the target, errr, Jack was lucky, but that's how it goes when you work in the field, as you would know." He aggressively defended his position, also knowing that neither of them had served in the field. Because they were in the position of

202

pushing pieces of paper. They loved to talk the talk but in reality, knew nothing of life and how the job went.

After an hour or so of the same questions asked in different ways, The Manager glanced at the other two monkeys at the table who were keeping quiet. He knew they were glad that he was getting his ass chewed up, which meant that they weren't. The Manager got his orders and he agreed, even though he knew that he wasn't going to do what they asked. He knew they would forget, as they always did. They just had to prove their power to themselves.

In the next meeting, whenever that would be. The two of them would have forgotten what they had said and agreed on. Their focus would probably be on one of the other two baboons, Davis or Morris.

Winchester and Salford said their last bit of bullshit, then looked at each other and smiled.

Oh, how sweet! The Manager thought to himself, they all got up and exited the room. Salford even opened the door for Winchester, bless. They both exited. The Manager gave out a sigh of relief, as he stayed seated in his chair for a few moments to let the room clear, this also gave him time to calm down.

"Well, I think we got off quite well, what do you think?" Davis stated as he got up from his chair.

"Oh yes, if your department runs well, it's all good, Davis!" Morris responded as he glanced at The Manager and smugly smiled.

"Sod off, the both of you. Just piss off," was the response he gave them. Then he got up abruptly and his chair fell over.

"Ooooo," was the response from both of them! He took a deep breath in and picked the chair up. Then he grabbed his info pad and left the room in silence. He didn't give the two of them eye contact, because he was not in the mood for a bitch conversation. The time would come and revenge is sweet.

He made his way to his office and glanced out of the window at the blue sky. Not a cloud in sight. About time, it seemed like it had been raining for weeks.

He finally arrived at his office and briefly stopped to check his mood; after all, he didn't want to take it out on his secretary. He took a few deep breaths again, in and out, in and out. He was now composed enough to face her. He opened the door and quickly passed by her, heading into his domain. Shutting the door firmly behind him. He made his way to the desk, grabbed a glass, and poured himself a drink to chill himself out.

He decided that he'd best check up on Abbie, to see how she was getting on. It had been some time since he had had anything from her or Mason. He also prayed that nothing had happened to her. God, he hoped she wasn't dead. That would probably mean a written warning, if not his job. He glanced at the clock, what was he going to do today? And whose ass was he going to chew, as shit only goes downhill?

There was a knock on the door and Kimberly entered.

"Sir, you have a call from your wife, shall I put it through?"

The Manager pushed his chair back into the recline position and put his feet on the desk.

"Err, yes please, Kimberly, put it on the screen."

"Hi Pia, how's it going?" The Manager enquired as he took another drink.

"Oh, I'm shattered. Just got in from a twelve-hour shift, so I'm off to bed. Oh, and remember, I'm in again tonight so I won't see you until tomorrow. I may stop at my mum's, she's closer to the hospital, okay? Oh, I see you're drinking? Is there one for me, Pav?"

"Yes, there's one waiting for you, darling. Oh no! Someone seems to have drunk it. It's all cool; I'll get something to eat on the way home. I'll see you tomorrow night or whenever. Have a good one."

"Thanks, Pav, love you." Pia blew Pav a kiss then the screen went blank. She was a good, hard-working wife. Good to look at, and a lovely person with certain enhanced parts, which he loved. The issue was that she loved her work more than him, and her shifts were wrecking their marriage. They had spoken about her changing shifts, but she loved being on Accident and Emergency at the hospital. She was in charge, she loved the power, and Pav got it because he loved the power also in his job.

Time was ticking away today, but the reports he had to do just sucked the time out of the day. *Gosh, how time flies when you're not having fun*, he thought to himself, then took another drink. Well, it would be some takeaway tonight! Maybe he would watch a movie or the news? Mmm, see what's happening on Mars or even how the crisis on Pluto is going? No party tonight for him; it was at home on his own time. Sod the reports! Pav thought to himself, as he started to turn his equipment off. *Mmm I was going to phone*

Abbie, oh, she'll be ok I'll do it tomorrow. He thought. Then picked up his jacket and once again gazed out of the window. He could see the sun setting. *Another day of my life gone, how many more do I have?* he contemplated as he stared out of the window.

There was a knock on the door and then the voice of Kimberly, his short-term temp secretary, entered the office. She was always well-presented in a pencil skirt, short brunette hair, early forties, pretty, and voluptuous, with mysterious green eyes. It was strange how she had got the job. One day his other temp just didn't arrive and thirty minutes later Kimberly rocked up.

"I'm off now, if that's okay?" she requested in her soft well-spoken voice. She stood at the door waiting for the answer, which seemed to take longer than normal.

"Sorry, yeah, yeah thanks for today," Pav responded. She exited the office, then the door clicked shut. About twenty seconds or so later there was a light knock, then the door opened again.

Pav looked in the direction of the door to see who it was.

"Yes Kimberly, what is it?"

"This is so not me! But, well, a new bar has just opened down the road. I know you have not had the best of days, and I was wondering if you wanted a drink, just to unwind? If you don't, then that's all cool."

"Er, well, it has been a crap day, Pia's working late again."

"Yes, you said the other day that you thought she was. Well, it's your call. I was just asking." Kimberly turned and started to leave the office.

"Kimberly, just a minute... Okay, just one, but that's all."

"Whatever, I'm not forcing you, it's your call," Kimberly stated, then stopped, and looked around at The Manager. Then she started walking slowly out of the office as if she was waiting for him. He made sure everything was turned off and he exited the room.

"Lights off!" he announced, which was his last job for the day. Then he left the office and the electronics did as they were told.

They walked down the white-walled corridors of the building, passing various people that appeared to still be working. Unfortunately, this included Davis whom they bumped into.

"Night. Have fun, kids!" Davis said then smiled at Kimberly and winked in the direction of Pav who was trying to make some distance behind Kimberly.

To not get the tongues talking in the office, Pav silently mouthed the words *piss off* to Davis, who smirked at him as he passed. They both made their way out of the main entrance into the fresh air and the warmth of the sun.

"It's this way," Kimberly said as she headed in the direction that they should go. After a short walk in silence, they approached the bar. It was named The Gate, with ironically an effigy of a gate hanging above the entrance. The bar was located in a modern building, and situated in the basement. They passed the doorman and headed down a flight of stairs to a set of glass doors at the bottom. The doors slid open and they were welcomed by some sultry music, once inside. They took a slight walk then went through the second set of glass doors which took them into a large dark room. There was a semi-bustling bar with all walks of life having after-work drinks. The lights were low, which gave a sleazy feel, even though it was a new place. There were smoked mirrors behind the bar, dark wooden furniture with wrought iron chandeliers hanging from the ceiling and walls. Satin dark wooden flooring with the odd rug here and there to probably help deaden the noise. Also, there were various pictures of people and caricatures that changed when you approached them from various viewpoints. Pav tried to remember what they were called. He knew that it was old-school technology. Then it came to him: lenticular printing. The pictures all appeared to be of the gentry but then changed to a more hideous picture.

They made their way to the bar and waited for some time to be served. Pav glanced for the staff, but there appeared to only be one bartender. She was in her late forties with long orange hair, jeans and a t-shirt with the name of the bar on it. Finally she came over and asked for their orders.

"What do you want?" There was no chit-chat from her, just a direct question and grimace.

"I'll have a Merlot please. And what do you want, Kimberly?" Pav enquired as he leaned casually on the bar and glanced at her.

"Oh, that sounds nice, I'll have the same please," was the response, then started looking for somewhere to sit.

"Over there, I'll be over there, okay?"

"Yeah, yeah," was the reply she got from Pav who was dealing with the payment of the drinks. A short time later, Pav arrived with the drinks. The normal conversation happened, with bland safe questions from both of them. The wine went down, and the talking became more open as both started to relax. In the background, some slow mellow music was still playing to add to the tone of the place.

"I need to go to the toilet," Pav said, then excused himself.

Kimberly noticed that he wandered around the pub for a bit; he was preoccupied with being lost, she thought.

When he was out of sight she opened her bag, then pulled out her purse. Inside was a wafer-thin silver foiled package. Kimberly popped the contents into Pav's drink, just to help him relax a bit more, then dropped one into hers also.

"Hey man, that chick you're with is hot as, you know?" An Irish-sounding guy announced to Pav as they both stood at the urinals.

"Err, thanks, I wouldn't know, man, and she's a work colleague. We're just having a few drinks, then home."

"Oh man, if that's what your story is, then good on you," was his response, then winked at Pav. He was slightly swaying and was not very successful at hitting the urinal Pav noticed.

"Yes, well, okay. Speak later," Pav advised as he pulled his Zip up then washed his hands. Exiting the toilets, a large male carrying a half-full wine glass barged by Pav to go to the toilet.

On his way back, he passed various groups of people with a mixture of males and females. He then noticed the bouncers running in the direction of the toilets. As Pav got closer, he started to intensely look at Kimberly. She was quite attractive, although the light was not the best, which helped him out also, as he was no model himself. Chuckling to himself at the thought, he sat down.

"What's so funny?" Kimberly inquired as she lifted her drink and looked at Pav. Pav then picked his up also.

"To work friends," Kimberly said, then took a drink; Pav nodded his head slightly and also took a drink.

Pav noticed the bouncers escorting the Irish man and the large guy with the wine glass to the exit. They must have been fighting, they were both covered in blood.

As the night went on past one drink, then two and so on. The conversation covered all sorts of topics, from Mars, strikes, schools and more. They talked about things that they never had thought to ask each other. Their body language relaxed and they both became more friendly and open.

"I'm just off to the toilet, is it over there?" Kimberly asked as she got up, swayed slightly and knocked the drink over onto Pav.

"Oh my god, I'm so sorry, I'm so sorry Pav." Kimberly then put her hands to her face with embarrassment.

"It's okay," was the response from Pav. He then started to dry his trousers off with some napkins that were sat on the table.

"I think we're a bit tipsy, Pav. Err, we haven't eaten yet either. Look, my place is on the way home to yours. I can cook something quick and wash and dry your trousers. It's the least I can do. What do you say?"

"Well, I could just drop you off and go home, to be honest."

"Come on Pav, let me do the right thing, I insist," Kimberly begged him. She made a slight tilt of the head to emphasise her plea.

"Okay, we'll do that as my dryer's broken."

"Are you off to the toilet, then?" Pav asked, although Kimberly was ordering a Goober.

"No, I'll wait. It will be here in three minutes. Come on, drink up."

Pav finished his wine and they made their way past various people towards the door. On their way, Pav noticed Davis in the far corner – *who's that he's with?* Pav knew it wasn't Davis's Wife; he did recognise the female but could not place where from or a name.

"Hey look over there!" Pav said.

"Oh my god, that's Villi," was the response from Kimberly.

"Check out the name box," Pav stated, then glanced at her.

They both stopped in their tracks. Then Davis kissed Villi.

"She's married and works in recruitment."

"He's also married," Pav replied, then they both started walking again whilst glancing at the couple. By the time they had got to the top of the stairs there, the Goober was waiting for them with its doors open.

The night was starting to become chilly; Pav noticed that the stars were out. He always looked for the brightest and remembered his mum who was no longer with him. A smile crossed his face when he thought of her. He missed her so much.

They both climbed into the vehicle and an electronic voice came on. "Where to?" The electronic voice asked.

Kimberly shunted to the other side of the seat "District 9/6329," Kimberly said as she unexpectedly snuggled into Pav.

"I'm freezing. Can we have the heating up, please." She then added. Kimberly had said the drive was not long as she lived relatively close to work.

Pav was slightly uncomfortable in his wine-soaked trousers and kept fidgeting around in the seat. When they arrived at the destination, the Goober stopped but the doors did not open.

"Excuse me, but I noticed that you have wine on your trousers. If we deem that you had marked the seating area, we will have to charge you. Do you agree?" the electronic voice asked. Pav looked at Kimberly then frowned.

"Mmm, yes I do," he stated then smiled at her. The doors opened.

"Thank you we will advise you if credits need to be taken from your account. Have a nice night." They both climbed out of the Goober and the doors made a whined sound as they closed, although it drove away in near silence.

"Well, this is me!" Kimberly announced, then made her way up three steps. She held her right hand to the reader. It recognised that it was Kimberly and the door opened. She entered the foyer with Pav following. A bland area with black marble tiles and the standard white wall came into view.

"You will notice there's not even some crap art on the wall, and I pay a fortune to live here! This way." She turned right then stopped at the first door. It clicked open, and she entered. The lights came on automatically and straight into the kitchen. Kimberly put her bag down. Pav followed, noticing that her apartment was small and also featureless and very sparse. The room had no wall art, no family pictures. Not even a picture of her having a good time or even a photo of a cute animal.

"Over through that door is the bedroom. Take your trousers off, then throw them out and I'll wash them and dry them, okay? I'm sorry I don't have any other clothes for you to use while I'm washing them. Err, you could wrap a towel around yourself maybe?" She gestured towards the door.

"Yeah, thanks." Pav followed the instructions. Once inside the bedroom, he looked around. It was a typical bedroom with soft cushions, and a teddy among other things, very feminine. Pav went into the bathroom. He went through a few cupboards looking for a towel. Finally, he found a white towel that was neatly folded on a pile of towels. He took his trousers and underwear off, as they were damp also, then wrapped the towel around him. Then he made his way out with the trousers and passed them to Kimberly.

"Okay, thanks." Taking them off him, she made her way to the laundry and put them in to wash.

"It should only take around twenty minutes to be washed and dried, and you can be on your way. Fancy a roadie?"

"Yes please, do you have a Scotch or Bourbon?" Pav requested as he sat on the cream leather couch, crossed-legged to cover his modesty. Kimberly went to the kitchen and started making two scotch on the rocks, then brought them over to him.

"Just off to the toilet. Lights lower, music on," she requested as she put her drink down and made her way to the bedroom and onto the bathroom. Around five minutes later, Kimberly reappeared.

"Oh, you've changed?" Pav blurted out, as Kimberly appeared in a dark blue dressing gown.

"Yes, I had been in them clothes all day and wanted something slightly comfier." She made her way over to the couch and then sat down, slightly angled towards Pav. She crossed her legs, although the dressing gown slid off her silky-skinned legs. She grabbed parts of it to marginally cover herself once again. Then leaned slightly forward to pick up her drink, and Pav could see down the front of the robe. He averted his eyes slightly as Kimberly's slender neck and arms were now on show, but he could feel himself getting aroused from under the towel that was wrapped around him.

"How's your drink going?"

"Err, good. Do you think my trousers are ready yet?" Pav enquired. Then took a big swig of Scotch to try and calm himself down. The scent of the drink infused his taste buds and completed the job momentarily.

"Why is there a rush? When it is finished, we will hear the buzzer go off, it's all cool." Kimberly responded by shuffling on the couch and slowly moved closer to Pav. The skin on her arms, legs and hips were now touching and her lips were so close. A sense of anticipation was in the air. Kimberly licked her lips and Pav could see the saliva glistening in the dim lighting. He could feel her breathing on his skin. Slowly, she moved her face towards him. Initially, Pav pulled his head back to a point where he could not move any further.

Was it the drinks from earlier or had she spiked his drink... or was it sex? Pav made his move and gently kissed her, which quickly got intense. She pulled back his towel and then in one manoeuvre mounted Pav. Quick rough sex happened with both parties enjoying several minutes of pleasure.

The bell on the dryer pinged just around the time it had finished for both of them.

"Oh Pav, you are a naughty boy, aren't you," Kimberly said, slightly out of breath.

"I'm sorry I don't know how that happened, I'm sorry!" Pav picked up the towel and stood up as if he was going to leave, although he was completely naked from the waist down. He wrapped the towel around him and tied it off to cover his modesty.

"It's okay, I think your trousers are ready, and hey; we are both adults. I won't say anything to Pia. Promise!" Kimberly stated, just to put a slight bit of pressure on him. She got up and retied her dressing gown. Pav swiftly made his way to the dryer, took his pants and trousers out and quickly put them on, then his socks and shoes. He made his way into the living room and noticed that Kimberly was sitting on the couch again.

"I'll get a Goober and be off, okay?" he announced as he ordered one.

"Yes, not a problem. I will see you on Monday," she replied and smiled at Pav.

"Yes, see you Monday, I'll wait outside, okay?" Smiling in the general direction of Kimberly, he made his way out to the front of the building, then jumped in the waiting Goober.

Kimberly got up, then had a quick shower to clean herself up, and dried herself. Pondering on the feeling, she liked the idea of a towel rather than a dryer as it was less clinical. She glanced at the clock in the bathroom. She had around forty-five minutes before her date arrived. Putting her dressing gown on again then made her way out to the kitchen.

She made her way over to the security system and pressed the screen at various places and finally hit the playback button, then a larger smile crossed her face as she watched the video of her and Pav's performance. She glanced at the clock again, then realised that she needed to get a move on for her date. Saving the recording and also sent it to her work email and then to another secure address.

"This sucker was worth a few credits!" Then smiled.

CHAPTER 29

R oman?" Sage asked. They both started to lift their guns in anticipation of
what they were going to do. The man smiled; dropped the coffee then
slowly stepped away. The door started to automatically close and consequently
protect him. Both shot off a round that impacted the door but did not penetrate
through, due to it being a fire door.

They moved quickly to the door and opened it, faintly hearing the patter of
footsteps running down the corridor.

Roman now knew that someone was on to them, and their plan. He had seen
the body of Basher on the floor. He needed to get away!

In the room was Basher now lying motionless, but still alive, whimpering.
His brain was releasing endorphins to reduce the shock, and pain of what his
body was enduring.

Sage glanced back at the man on the floor and thought about shooting him,
she knew what he was going to do, or would have done if they hadn't stepped
in. He was a bad man! A strange moral dilemma was playing itself out in her
overloaded mind with emotions and adrenaline. At the same time, she was
trying to cope with all this chasing and being chased. When this was all over,
she needed to get some counselling or some type of treatment for what she was

212

mentally carrying – not baggage, but probably a full-size ship of trauma, mental pain, anguish the lot.

At least he will get what he deserved. She pulled the trigger. *Their innocent lives saved,* she thought. Sage considered the two dead terrorists in the room. Lots of lives were saved today.

She then turned and started to chase after Jack, and the murderer who was getting away from them. Sliding the backpack on, it was light and durable but it had taken some hammering. Initially, she could feel it on her back, but she knew that after a few minutes she would forget about it and adapt her running style.

Jack was about fifteen to twenty meters behind the man. The terrorists glanced back then turned the corner, through the fire door and started running down the stairs, two steps at a time. Jack picked his pace up, as he followed through the fire door in pursuit. He started his descent except he decided to do one step at a time and then jump the last four steps.

Flight after flight, the pursuit continued, adrenaline was filling the man's veins now, and escape was his goal. Minutes earlier he was thinking about if he had put sugar in the cup of coffees? Basher moaned if his coffee had no sugar in it. Not trying a door on several floors, he kept his pace up and went down another two flights of stairs then through the final door that brought him out into the hotel foyer. People glanced in his direction at the commotion he created when he burst into sight through the fire doors. After a brief stop to think, he started running again, then barged a woman off her feet who unceremoniously fell straight on her ass. He had no time to apologise because he was pursuing his only goal of escape! Then he approached a baggage cart and stopped. He pulled it over, scattering luggage on the floor to slow this stranger who, for some reason, was holding a gun at him when he brought his coffees to the room. *What were the two of them doing there? Who were they? Did they know their plans? How?* Darting left and right, he manoeuvred himself past the obstacles called people. Roman glanced back and he could see his pursuer jumping over suet cases and bags. A smirk shimmered on his face as he knew that he would be able to outrun and outsmart this fool following him.

Going out of the main hotel doors and down the steps then right was his plan, as Roman had premeditated his escape before this, just in case. He always liked a get-out plan. Then right again and into the underground car park, he

213

headed down the ramp and past the gate that controlled the cars going in. The smell of car fumes and the heat of the car park hit him, and he upped his pace slightly as he ran down the ramp, with one more glance over his shoulder. He knew he could outrun this man chasing him, but Roman was not in a position to take him out at this point. No, he would savour that delight of killing him for later. When he had him where he wanted him, begging for mercy! Dodging out of the way of a black car nearly hitting him; he then jumped and slid over the bonnet of a stationary car.

Jack was starting to very slowly fall away in this chase, although he knew that people's lives depended on him not losing this guy. He tried to pick his pace up, to keep up with the man as he followed him down the ramp, passing the barrier. This was hard work, running and killing, why wasn't he at work being boring doing his electrical work?

A black Audi A4 pulled out in front of Roman, he jumped up and onto the bonnet then jumped off it keeping his pace up. The driver just looked on at what he witnessed, a man running across the bonnet of his car. Then, seconds later, Jack ran around the front of the car and glanced at the dint in the bonnet the size of a terrorist's footprint. The driver was an old man with curly grey hair, just looking at Jack as he made his way past the car. Music could be heard from the Audi – now, what was he playing? The bass was thumping from inside the car body and soon faded out of earshot.

Roman sprinted, took in two or three deep breaths; then went through the door at the end of the car park. Down a flight of stairs to a lower level, then through the doors.

Jack was starting to catch this guy up, he had quickened the pace for around thirty seconds or so. Gasping for the vital air to plenish his lungs and body, yes he did jog but this is a higher rate than he normally ran at. Jack was hoping that the terrorist didn't jog at this pace! If he did, he would lose him. Consequently, if the terrorist decided to do his own thing people's lives would be lost. Ever so briefly stopping in the stairwell, Jack decided what to do next, up or down? Jack heard a door click – that was the cue – and the chase was again on. Jack went down the flight of stairs and out of the door, then he stopped; *which way?* He looked intensely left and right for the man he was pursuing, then something caught his eye. There was movement from behind a car. Surprisingly, Jack instinctively moved for cover as a shot was fired in his direction. The sound echoed around the car park as the bullet embedded itself in the wall where Jack had been standing moments earlier. Another shot rang out, then there were footsteps. Jack popped his head out from behind the safety of the car to see if he could locate the man. He controlled his breathing, raised his gun, leaning it on the car bonnet, and squeezed the trigger. The shot resonated, and the terrorist went down!

"Wow, what a bloody shot!" Jack said out loud, out of sheer disbelief at his shooting. He stood up from behind a silver BMW. Then the man got up and started running. Jack stood in awe, his great shot was not as great as he had thought. He started to chase after the man once again. It was very humid, sweaty and hot in this underground maze of a car park.

Sage heard shots coming from the stairwell and knew instinctively who that was. She ran down the stairs to a random level, pushed her head through a doorway, looked and listen for signs of Jack or the Roman. A second shot rang out. Sage knew she had to go up a level! Does she use the fast way and the stairs or the long way where the cars go? Which way should she go? A decision had to be made. She started running the way the cars would go, in the hopes that she would bump into Mr Terrorist. Sage ran as fast as she could toward the ramp, then a figure appeared. He raised his arm and let off a round that ricocheted about three meters in front of Sage. She ducked behind a car for protection as more footsteps arrived. Jack was now in sight.

"He's hiding, Jack," Sage shouted. She could see that Jack was standing in full view of her and was a clear target for the terrorist. Realising this, he ducked behind a car, then there was silence in the car park. The three of them were now deciding who was going to make the next move. There were footsteps to Sage's right, but was it Jack or the terrorist? This was going to be a shit-show, Sage raised her gun and slowly moved in the direction of what she was hoping was the terrorist. There was a shot, then the side window of the car that she was hiding behind exploded. It covered Sage in glass, just like snow blowing off a tree.

"Is that you, Jack?" Sage shouted, knowing she was giving away her position – but she would find out who it was if no reply came back.

The screeching of tyres took over being the number one noise in the car park. Moments later, a second set of screeching tyres joined in. Two cars came into view. With the squealing of tyres on concrete, a Black Audi TT made its

215

move, with the driver being Roman. There was more screaming of tyres, then a Red Alfa Romeo Giulia quadrifoglio appeared in front of her. The driver's door flew open and there was Jack smiling at her.

"Get the fuck over," Sage shouted, getting up from her place of hiding. Jack was starting to move his legs out of the way and Sage got in the driver's seat. She engaged drive and decked the gas pedal – a screech came from the rear tyres, then the traction control kicked in and the Alpha veered forward. There was a slight kick to one side as one tyre grabbed some traction and then the other tyres came to the party, once again in pursuit of their man.

"Seatbelt! We don't know how this is going to end!" Sage shouted out. That was the cue for Jack to reach over and put Sage's seatbelt on, which was not an easy task as they were in a chase. The car pitched and swayed, then came to a straight bit and the belt was on. Jack put his seatbelt on and grabbed anything he could to stop him from being thrown around.

The Audi was on a straight path now, then braked heavily. Then it screeched around another corner of the car park. The Audi went up a ramp to the top, then momentarily lightened its suspension. Then bottomed out, causing dust and dirt to be scattered from under the car.

In the Alfa, Sage and Jack went up the ramp. Their car wasn't as dainty as the Audi in its landing, with the heavy power unit at the front, but the suspension soaked it up.

There was an acceleration, then the screech of breaks. The Audi needed to decrease speed before taking the corner, which it did – just!

Next was the Alfa–even though it was a slightly larger and heavier car, Sage managed to throw it into the corner. The traction control worked overtime getting it around the turn, with the remnants of black tyre marks on the concrete floor.

Roman gunned the Audi through the manual gearbox, then brakes, and the car smashed through the barrier of the car park, which cracked the windscreen with the impact. People jumped out of the way as Roman sounded his horn. He was quite happy to kill them all, but at this point in time he did not want the car damaged for his getaway. He took the corner wide and applied the power. Various cars stopped and crashed into each other as they tried to avoid the Audi.

The horn of the Alpha then it appeared. Luckily, the traffic had stopped and bystanders were watching in awe at the car control. Sage took the same line as the Audi had which saved her some time.

The Alpha was starting to gain on the Audi because it had one major advantage: Sage. Training in vehicles like this was what she did when she used to work for the organisation as an agent. A training class would be, that she would have to break into a car and drive the hell out of it to see how far she could take it. It was fun and dangerous, and normally she would use nearly new cars as they were harder to steal.

The traffic fell well for the Audi as it weaved in and out of cars, trucks and the odd cyclist. It left a trail of destruction behind – of panicked drivers and crashed vehicles. Sage had to steer through the traffic with her horn blaring out so that the drivers realised that yet another speeding car was on its way through.

"This is so bloody exciting, look – he's locked the back wheels... he's turning," Jack shouted as Sage was moving the steering wheel left and right to negotiate the cars.

"Yep got it!" She braked heavily and tweaked the steering wheel left and right to unsettle the Alfa and get the back end out to get around the corner. Full power as the traction control worked overtime. This was not a Sunday drive, as Sage wrestled with the car and then the Alfa was now going straight. This part of the road was relatively clear as the Alpha grunt was starting to close on the Audi. Sage glanced down at the driver modes in the Alpha and turned it to Race. She knew that that would give her everything available from the power unit.

"Right, right... he's going right!" Jack screamed out.

"Yep, got it!" was the response back as Sage started to prepare the car to make the same move but faster than the Audi. Just like before, she unsettled the car and powered around the corner, then hit the brakes as hard as she could.

There was a loud screeching noise, then the ABS kicked in. It seemed like slow motion to both of them, although Sage had been in this situation before. She let go of the steering wheel because she knew that at this point she had very little control of the car as it ploughed into the Audi. The Alfa's front end crumpled, then bounced off the Audi, and made its way to the other side of the road. The rear wheels hit the kerb, then physics started to play into the equation. They then started to go into a roll. Airbags burst into action from all sides to protect Jack and Sage. Glass, plastic and other bits of the car started to slowly float by Jack's face as he watched his arms do a strange uncontrolled dance. They were being thrown about in the car as it rolled down the street, finally stopping on its roof. Then quietness was all that Jack could hear. The impact of what had just happened started to compute then hit him. Liquid could be seen dribbling onto the ground out of the front. Steam was also coming off the liquid – *it must be coolant*, Jack thought.

"Sage, Sage, are you okay? Sage?" Jack screamed out as his brain kicked in.

"Yeh, yeh I'm good, I think? How about you?" Sage replied, although the response was slightly subdued.

A sound like a shot whisked through the car.

Chapter 30

Crap, he's still alive. Undo your seatbelt," Jack shouted. Simultaneously they did, and fell onto the roof of the unturned Alfa. Moving the remains of the airbags out of his view, Jack spotted the terrorist.

"Where is he?" Sage yelled.

"There, there," Jack shouted, then started looking for his gun. He remembered it hitting him in the face when the car was rolling. Spotting it next to his right foot, he picked the weapon up and scrambled for cover. Jack let off some shots in the general direction to let Roman know they would shoot back.

Bystanders started to edge closer but changed their minds when the shots were fired, and they immediately ran away screaming and scrambling for cover. Sage and Jack started to crawl out of their car as fast as they could; through where the windscreens used to be. Shards of glass were everywhere, crunching under their weight and piercing their palms. Once out, they moved to safety (hopefully).

"There, there... he's over there behind the Audi," Jack declared loudly.

"Oh yeah, got him. I'll go round the back to try and flank him, okay?" Sage announced as she got up and started to make her move.

"What are you..." Jack started to reply, then watched Sage go out of sight.

Police sirens could now be heard in the distance, not too far away. This needed to be sorted and sorted fast.

The Police would be coming down on all three of them soon. A terrorist and two-time travellers. *They probably would be more interested in the time travellers than the terrorist.* Jack thought, then sniggered. In all honesty, technically he hasn't done anything yet, whereas Sage and Jack have killed two would-be terrorists and left them lying in a hotel bedroom. *Some poor cleaning attendant would find them in the morning when they enters the room to clean it. Two bodies covered in bullet wounds, with blood everywhere. The poor cleaner will be traumatised for some time after that sight.* Jack thought about it all, and tried to bring himself into the moment to stay alive. What was Sage doing? Flanking him? It was all too technical for him. Two shots rang out, Jack had no idea who from. Jack went the same way that Sage had gone and soon found her hiding behind a wall.

"Sage, Sage, it's me," he said, ensuing he didn't get shot by her. She glanced at him, and nodded to let him know that she was aware that he was approaching.

"We need to get out of here… the police are on their way."

"Yes, I know, Jack, but we can't just let him go to kill innocent people now, can we?" was her response.

"We're going to have to force his move," she said as she shot another round in his direction with the hope that it would connect. Then footsteps could be heard.

"He's on the run, come on." She started to run, with Jack following behind. Roman ran down the street with Sage and Jack following.

Jack made an observation. "He's bleeding, Sage, we've hit him. Look, I can see a trail of blood."

"Yeah, I had noticed that."

Roman ran straight across the road. Cars swerved and screeched to a halt to avoid hitting him. He made his way through some arched doors and out of sight.

"For God's sake!" Sage let out, as they approached the building.

"What?" Jack blurted back at her.

"Oh no, it's a school; he's running into a bloody school…"

220

"Oh, no that's not good!" was all that Jack could muster; this was all starting to where him down. They entered through the archway, then through some glass doors into a large room with stairs at the end. There was a reception desk to the right with an irate female shouting in the direction of the stairs. That's the way to go, Sage thought. She passed the female who was now shouting at them in French to stop. Unfortunately, Sage and Jack had more pressing things on their minds rather than signing the visitors book.

A slight trail of blood could be seen on the white marble floor, a clue to how badly their man was hurt. *It's a trail, but probably a superficial wound*, Sage thought. They ran up the marble stairs with paintings of various men and women along the side. Sage thought they must be of old principles of the school or affluent people. They reached the top of the stairs then onto the landing that went both ways. Left or right?

"The trail of blood suggested right... This way," Sage stated. She took her time as she hoped not to run into a bullet. The blood trail went through a doorway. Sage approached it and glanced through the window of the white wooden door. Darkness! Why was it dark in the room? It was light outside, which was puzzling to her.

Jack was behind, waiting to make the move. Sage thought. He is a good partner, eager to go forward with this quest of staying alive. But at times a bit too zealous, and not thinking ahead to what the consequences could be! He will end up dead if he doesn't just take a moment now and then to stop and think. But when all was said and done, it was her job to keep him alive. After all, he's a pawn in the big game of chess that goes through time.

Sage pushed the handle down and slowly opened the door, trying to keep her body from the shooting area. Glancing back, she noticed Jack standing there waiting to be shot. He had not taken cover again!

"Get back, Jack, you're in full view again," she whispered and indicated with her right hand. Jack complied; he always did. *Very obedient... he will make someone a good husband one day,* Sage thought and internally smiled at the thought.

She moved into the room, then crouched down behind a table, with Jack following her lead. She looked around – it was dark, but not as dark as she had originally imagined. The windows were blacked out for some reason, a sign of what the room might be used for. She noticed pieces of paper hanging – *this*

221

must be the photo room, Sage thought. Slowly and systematically, she made her way through the room, then noticed a door.

Shit, he must have gone through there? God, he could be miles away by now? she thought. Then made her way to the door and slowly pushed down the handle. Sage opened the door gently and light flooded in from the other room. A creak came from the hinges, then a gunshot hit the door, but luckily they must have been fire doors, as it didn't go all the way through. Sage recoiled and took a breath to give herself a moment to calm her nerves. This was not that bad, at least she knew he was nearby. The door was still slightly open. Sage could see a safe hiding place behind what looked like kitchen counters.

Quickly throwing the door open, she dashed to the safe place, she had spotted. Sage thought what would be her next move?

Jack was now pushing the door slowly open, but there was no response from the person that was trying to kill them. He opened the door to a size that he could fit through. He leapt through the gap then dashed across the floor next to Sage. She popped her head out to see the lay of the room. It only took her a split second to figure out what she was up against.

"I think he's over there?" Sage whispered, then also gestured in the direction.

"Come out; let me send you to hell," a voice rang out in the silence.

"It's you that's off to hell, shitface," Jack yelled back.

Laughter could be heard in the room from the antagonist.

Then Sage got a whiff of something that she couldn't place, but her gut feeling was not good. Then, realisation dawned, regarding what it was.

Chapter 31

Quick, follow me – gas – gas!" she shouted, leaping through the still open door with Jack following her as a gunshot rang out.

Then there was a deep roaring sound like a huge lion's roar as the gas ignited in the room. A fireball started to envelop the area that they had just been in. The walls started to swell and crack with the power of expansion putting pressure on them. Just like a balloon being pumped up too much. The room shook like there was an earthquake and the shock wave took over. Items that had once been just sitting minding their own business were grabbed by the shock wave and thrown around. Now becoming missiles to destroy whatever got in their way. The windows' glass blew out with a high-pitched shattering sound, falling to the ground like hailstones on a winter's night. Then the noise followed, to let Paris know what had just happened. Dust and smoke started to appear and the expansions of the explosion started to diminish. What seemed like minutes were in fact seconds. There was a high-pitched sound, and force from the shockwave that hit Sage and Jack's ears. The fire alarm started to sound and the sprinkler system kicked in to try and put out any fires. The water started to fall on them both, like spring rain to bring them back to reality.

"Are you OK?" Sage shouted the best she could, then started to cough. All she got back was silence from Jack. Blood could be seen from various points on his body.

"Jack, Jack, are you OK?" Sage shouted again. She moved in what seemed like slow motion, over to where Jack's lifeless body was lying. Panic was starting to join her along with disorientation and confusion.

"Jack, Jack," Sage shouted again, shaking him vigorously the best she could. A sense of doom started to flood her thoughts.

"Errr yeh, yeah, I think so," the blurted response came back.

Joy then replaced the fear she had. She wiped her face and glanced at the back of her hand. Blood was smeared over it. A glance at herself confirmed the same – she had bloodstains on her clothes.

"Come on, come on," Sage barked at him. She slowly got up, then stumbled towards the doorway that they had initially come in through. Sage had to move obstacles that now scattered the room, as well as negotiate that slippery floor with the sprinklers still raining water down on them.

"He must have gone out of the other exit further up the corridor," Sage shouted at Jack and glanced to see him starting to get up.

"Bloody hell!" she then whispered under her breath. Teenagers and staff were running around like headless chickens, screaming, to add a bit of spice to the plot. Sage then spotted Roman in the crowd running down the corridor. He seemed to have a pronounced limp now. Sage started screaming at the people to get out of the way so she could have a shot, but to no avail – she could not be heard over the ear-piercing noise of the pupils, teachers, sprinklers and alarms. Chaos was now playing its part in helping the terrorist, as it always did when a terrorist was at work.

"Jack come on, come on!" shouted Sage, then she took a glance to make sure he was with her. She exited the room to follow Roman down the corridor. She took tentative steps at first, then slowly got faster, although the backpack, slippery conditions and crowds of people were hindering her rhythm. Then clumsily dashed down a flight of stairs. She weaved around students and teachers to make headway. Sage could sense that she was slowly catching him up. She glanced back to check Jack's stumbling progression.

Roman ran out of the fire escape door with the crowd. Most people stopped once outside, but he carried on across the road and then turned left. Sage followed, knowing that she was catching him now. He glanced back, then went down a narrow street. When Sage got to the turning she also glimpsed back – good, Jack was following. She made her way down the street, then after about twenty metres he went into an alley. Sage followed, then abruptly stopped. Roman appeared in front of her, metres away from a doorway, gun raised, straight at her face.

"No, no, no, it's okay. Put it down Roman." Sage acknowledged the situation by putting her hands in the air. She could feel fear – is this how she was going to die? Was this the end? There was a sickening feeling in her stomach and a wave of emotions flooded her brain, including sadness. After all she had been through, was this how it was going to end?

"Ha, you do-gooder people make me sick, just let us make our protest," Roman said. He moved closer to Sage, up to the point that the gun barrel touched Sage's forehead, then he moved his head towards her ear.

"I'm going to kill you, bitch, then your mate's going to get it!" Roman stated.

"Hey," a voice came from behind Sage. Roman grabbed Sage and pulled her close to him as a shield whilst still pointing the gun at her head.

"Jack, no! No!"

"Hey man, let her go and I'll give you a start… Just let her go."

"Piss off!" Roman said with a sneered tone in his voice and pulled the trigger. A click was all that happened. Sage elbowed Roman in the ribs. In pain, he let her go, and one shot echoed in the alley. There was a thud and Roman lay there, lifeless. A female at the end of the alley started screaming, with what she had just witnessed. Sage did think about putting a bullet in her head to shut her up, but on second thought, maybe that was a bit of an extreme reaction. After all, the woman may have just been shopping for the day, in her little perfect world. Then Roman and Sage had woken her up to reality, and she didn't like it. Sage took a deep breath, turned, smiled at the screaming female, then was joined by Jack who stood next to her.

"Let's get the hell out of here, Jack."

"Good call Sage, god my heads buzzing! But first we need to clean ourselves up slightly. We look as though we are the terrorists that have escaped."

Sage took a quick look around and spotted a water tap on the wall. Noticing that the dead body had a scarf on, she removed it. She ran the tap to wet it.

"Quick, let's clean you up!" Jack complied and let Sage use the scarf and cold water to clean up his face, hands and arms.

"Okay, you're good. Now do me!"

Jack rinsed the blood-stained material and then did the same to Sage.

"There, you don't look like a terrorist now, you just look rough." He then started to snigger.

"Look who's talking, tramp!"

"Come on, let's go." Police and fire engines could be heard arriving at the school. They both hastily retreated up the street onto the main road again. Both tried not to look too conspicuous, although they did look like they had been in an explosion and a fight. To add to that they were dripping wet. They passed the school that was now on fire. Then making their exit against the flow of people who wanted to see what had happened, regardless of their own safety. Onwards to the nearest Metro station that was bustling with people. Sage got the tickets. Walking towards the escalator and descended to their appropriate level in silence. Glances from people, as they looked like two down and outs trying to keep undercover in the bowels of the Metro. Finally stopping on the platform to wait for the train. Luckily they didn't have to wait long, then the train pulled into the station. They climbed on with the other patrons, and sat down in silence. The train set off and after a few moments Sage rested her head on Jack's shoulder. The adrenaline was starting to wear off and the fatigue was starting to take over.

"We'd best stay awake or we will end up missing our stop!" Sage said, then snuggled in even more to Jack, who then put his arm around her for comfort. Moments later, the train stopped at a station. Jack decided that they would stay on to give themselves distance from the chaos of the school. The general public exchanged places as people got off and on.

Then he prodded Sage. Noticing two gendarmes entered the carriage from the far end of the train. Clearly, they were looking for something with the way they were moving around the carriage. Jack prayed under their breath that the gendarmes would go the other way, which they did. Jack let out a breath of relief and glanced at Sage who was starting to wake up.

"What? What?" Sage blurted out with a fright. Then spotted the two gendarmes walking away.

"Finally, a bit of luck has gone our way," Jack announced and smiled at Sage.

A few seconds later, the gendarmes stopped and double-backed on themselves. They slowly started to make their way toward Sage and Jack.

"When's our stop? What do we do?"

"The next one!" Sage said as she kept her head on Jack's shoulder, to try and throw off any suspicion that they were both starting to panic about the gendarmes slowly getting closer. The gendarmes started talking to a passenger further down the carriage who appeared not to have a ticket or for some reason.

"Do we get off and run, walk, or start shooting?" Jack asked calmly.

"Errr, I think we will take it as it goes, although I'm nearly out anyway, and honestly, I don't want to be shooting at them. They are the good guys."

The train started to slow down, they both got up and started to move to a door that was away from the gendarmes. The train stopped for what seemed like an eternity; the doors finally hissed open and they both exited the train. Trying not to look too suspicious, Sage glanced back.

"They've got off and are following us."

"Shit!" was all that Jack said. He could feel his hands beginning to sweat as fear started to take control of his body. He didn't want to get into a shoot-out with the police of all people. He just wanted to get back to their room, then go to sleep and maybe wake up in his time in his own bed. Maybe he had hit his head on something in the house he was working in. Maybe he was on the floor unconscious and this was all a dream. Although deep down, he knew that this whole situation wasn't a dream, it was all real. They picked their pace slightly up and mingled in with the crowd.

All this running, driving, and shooting really takes it out of you, mentally and physically, Jack thought. They both mixed in with the crowd that had also alighted from the train and then got on the escalator. They slowly moved past the people that had graciously moved to one side of the escalator and reached the surface. At the top, Sage sharply moved left, up some marble steps, and then the daylight started to hit her eyes. At the top, she headed out to the left-hand side. Jack just stayed with her as always. And – as always – he had no idea what Sage's plan was until she told him or it happened. Sage glanced at the windows on the opposite side of the road for the reflection of the gendarmes.

"Don't look back, they're still following us, although they don't seem to be making any attempt to catch up. Maybe they have been told to hang back until they get back up to deal with us. Or maybe it's just a coincidence," Sage announced, then stopped in her tracks. Jack carried on for a few steps, then also stopped and turned to look at Sage.

"What are you doing?" Sage screamed at Jack, then slapped him across the face; she slowly moved her position to see if the gendarmes were still there. Unaware of what was happening, Jack just stood there with a blank look on his face.

"Err, I errr," Jack responded, then he noticed Sage winking at him. He then realised that this was one of the moments that he had just been let in on the plan.

"Oh you too, bitch." He started walking away from Sage in the direction that they were originally going, with Sage running after him for once.

"What did they do then?" Jack inquired.

"They stopped!"

"So they are after us then Sage?" Slowly once again, they started to increase their walking pace.

"Over there, we'll get on another train and try and lose them in the Metro," Sage warily announced as she nodded in the direction of the station. They moved to the edge of the curb, took a look left then right, and a gap came in the traffic. They made a quick sprint across the road, down the stairs and out of sight into the station. Jack was caught a bit unawares and reacted slowly to Sage's impulse of crossing the road. He made his move carefully after her and caused a car to jump on its brakes. A horn from the car let Jack know how pissed off the female driver was. There were some lip movements from the driver that Jack could not hear or understand. Jack glanced at her and blew her a kiss. A smile crossed the female's face. She was probably in her late 30s with shoulder-length dark red hair and the longest eyelashes that he had ever seen. Then the female blew a kiss back, her anger had gone! He glanced up at the gendarmes, who were now trying to also find a break in the traffic. Jack moved the pace up as he started to make his way down the stairs at a half-hearted jog to catch up with Sage. At the bottom, he briefly stopped to glance around to find her – bingo! Sage was getting tickets for both of them, hopefully! They were at the machine and Sage passed Jack a ticket. She slid hers into the machine to open the gate and then Jack followed. They started to make their way down deeper into the system and then to a platform.

Observing the people who were standing waiting for the train, Jack noticed that one of them was the female in the leopard skin dress that was sitting in the café when the terrorist attack had happened. What were the chances that he would see her before the event that would now not happen? They had stopped her from being murdered. Hopefully, she would have a long and happy life now. He looked around and noticed that the gendarmes had come through the entrance and were in the process of looking for both of them. He mumbled to Sage, "down!" Then grabbed her sleeve and pulled it down to indicate to her what to do. Complying, they both bent their knees slightly to lower their heads out of sight. A businessman standing to the side of Jack looked at them curiously doing this unusual act, then he looked in the direction of the gendarmes; then he looked back and smiled.

The breeze of the train coming through the tunnel started to be felt, then there was the noise of the wheels on the rails. Then the train came out of the tunnel and started to slow down to a stop. The hissing doors opened and people alighted.

"Do we get on or not?" Jack asked as the crowd started to move to the doors, and the platform started to empty.

"Can you see them?" Jack asked. Sage rose to see where they were.

"Yeah, there at the door, one facing one way, the other facing the opposite way. God, I don't know what to do. Look, if we stop on this platform, it will empty and they will see us. If we get on, we might be able to lose them."

"Okay, then we'll get on!" Jack started to move towards the door, crouching down, as did Sage. The businessman looked at them both in an increasingly concerned way.

"Bad back, mate!" Jack said to the businessman, pulling a face as though he had pain and gesturing with his left hand towards his back, then he climbed onto the train. The businessman slightly nodded as though he had grasped why Jack was stooping like that. Once on the train, Sage and Jack sat down behind the businessman and a woman with a green beret on.

"So, do we have a plan?" Jack inquired, trying to see if the gendarmes had climbed on the train or not. The doors shut, then opened again. More time passed – it seemed to take forever but it was probably only seconds.

"Look Jack, believe it or not, I'm making this up as we go. We have been so lucky so far, this isn't my nine-to-five job, you know. I got into this by accident, remember?" Sage barked at Jack who just sat there staring at her with a blank face.

"For god's sake, Sage! Don't you remember, you're the person that visited me completely randomly at work, and said, *Oh you need to come with me or you will be killed*? We went for a coffee and yes someone tried to kill us. Guess what? I'm not a time traveller like you. I don't know how to shoot guns or things like that. So forgive me if I'm too needy. Oh, by the way, I'm an electrician not a sodding time travelling dude." Silence consumed both of them as the train started to finally move.

Jack took this opportunity to ponder on what was going to happen. So the gendarme would find them and arrest them. When they did, would he tell them? If he told them everything, would they believe him? If they did, they would either throw the book at him, send him to prison and toss the key away. Glancing around the carriage, he could see people sitting and standing, doing their small things in their small world. If only they knew who was sitting on the train. Two-time travellers. For all Jack knew, there were more time travellers on the train that he didn't know of – maybe even space travellers in disguise. He smiled at the thought and brought himself into the present.

The train rattled and rocked through the tunnels, going left and right, with the normal swaying and jerking that you get. Jack decided to start people-watching to try and calm himself down. So in front of him was the businessman and next to him on the outside was a heavy woman. Mmmmm, what does she do? Maybe a teacher or something like that. She didn't look dressed up enough to be a businesswoman, but you never know, she could be the director of a massive conglomerate and it was her day off.

Two guys were standing up, both eating chewing gum to the point that you could see it in their mouths. They seemed unable to chew with their mouths shut. They were dressed in black with a wannabe punk look, except they were about three decades too late. Arrrrgh, punk! Not Jack's favourite genre, although he did like some of the stuff – obviously The Sex Pistols, The

Ramones and one or two others. The genres that came from punk were his favourites, new wave and indie. Such bands as Blondie, Siouxsie and the Banshees, Ian Dury and the Blockheads, and The Buzzcocks, although some people classed those bands as Punk, but he never did. Then later The Smiths and even New Order, although they were technically different genres and a different era. Jack remembered that his dad had seen some of the bands when he was younger. That's how he got into that style of music. The new stuff of the day was good, although a bit commercial. They have the soul of good music and some cracking songs. Green Day, British India and Amyl and the Sniffers. Oh, jeez, Oasis – how could he forget them. The thing about all this music Jack liked was that the musicians played their instruments. They spent years learning and practising to perfect their talent. But the radio stations of today love their throwaway music. *Will the music of today be played in fifty years or so on the radio, just like the Beatles, Rolling Stones, Doors or Pink Floyd are now? Even the later groups like Blondie and Oasis will be played in years to come,* Jack thought (slightly ranting in his head). He was shook out of his daydream by an elbow into his ribs from Sage.

"Are you OK? You look a bit vacant! Wait here." She then got up and started talking to the two punks.

Jack was so over all this. He knew his concentration was shot and started looking around the carriage at people again. A mother (presumably) dressed in grey with a baby hanging from her front and looking at her phone, a workman in a yellow hi - vis shirt, black trousers, toe cap boots and wearing a hard hat. Two females that looked like they should be in a nightclub, with matching outfits on. Green tops, combed-back hair and sparkly silver skirts. Three females in compression skins that hugged every curve on their bodies, a male with them who also had the skins on, except it hugged his balls and dick to the point that you could see them. They all had jumpers on with a symbol of some organisation. Another workman with no hi-vis except his Hard Hat was placed on his knee. He sat barley keeping awake, as his eyes kept shutting. *Been there done that*, Jack thought then smirked to himself. Other random people that were all looking at their phones. Two old ladies with hats on, chatting away, oblivious to everyone else. *How sweet*, Jack thought.

Sage came back and sat down again.

"Okay, I have something for you! I've had a chat with the two guys."

231

"Which guys?"

"The punks!" They're going to walk in front of us, and if the gendarmes start to close in on us, they are going to start arguing and making a commotion to try and distract them, okay?"

"Brilliant, Sage, How did you do that?"

"Errr, I promised them a date. Both at the same time. Um, you could say a threesome!" was the unexpected reply from Sage.

"What?!"

"Yeah, the one on the left was looking at me and winked. Guys are so gullible at any age, I took advantage of it. I'm meeting them later on tonight after I've dumped you. Oh, and by the way, no, I'm not meeting up with them," she responded, then started smiling at Jack as a red complexion came across his face with embarrassment.

"Errr, I'm sorry about what I said earlier on Sage, but I'm sick of all this," Jack said in a low tone of voice that was just about audible above the noise of the train.

"Yeah, me too, but I get what you are saying, and I get why you look to me for answers. You're right, I am the one that's had training and I did get you into this. Believe me, I'm working on a way to get us out of this as well, okay?" Sage smiled at Jack again to confirm this piece of information. The train started to slow down at the station.

"Well, this is it!" Sage announced. They both got up from their seats and looked in the direction of the two gendarmes standing watching them both intensely. The two punks winked in their direction, quite clearly not at Jack due to the promise later on. Jack and Sage started to get close to the punks for shielding. The doors opened, then there was a bustle of people as everyone started to exit the train carriage at once. There was the normal squeeze through the door gap, then onto the platform. The four of them were heading towards the gendarmes; unfortunately, that was the direction of the exit. As predicted, the gendarmes started to intercept the four of them.

"Excusez-moi, Madame. Excusez-moi Madame... Madame!" The nearest gendarmes attempted to get their attention. Then the officers lurched forward to grab Sage, but Sage ducked out of the way and the two punks jumped into action. They started to scuffle in front of the gendarmes to distract them. The two guys started throwing punches at each other, then one or two at the

232

gendarmes to add to the effect. Sage and Jack upped their pace then dashed around a corner and headed to the escalator and the open air.

"Oh Noooo, look, there's two cop cars waiting for us over there... Quick, this way and get down." They both mingled in with the mass crowd exiting the station.

They started to pick the pace up again, making their way down a side street and out of sight, then down an ally to the left.

"We need to get out of this time, Sage."

"Yeah, agreed. It's getting too close for comfort in this city." She opened a side door to a random building.

"Hey, qu'est-ce que tu fais, putain?" a roundish bald man said. He looked as though he was a security man or something.

"Errr, sorry, we're lost, we don't speak French. I, errr, need the toilet," Sage announced as she pretended she didn't understand.

"I said, hey what are you doing? You're not doing drugs, are you?" He then started to look at these two bedraggled humans.

"No, just need the toilet that's all." Then Sage smiled at him.

"Errr, okay, there's a toilet down there. Hey, you're not going to do anything stupid, are you?" was the response from the man as he gestured towards a white door.

"No, thank you," was Jack's response as they both headed towards the door then pushed it open to reveal a long corridor. About halfway down, there was a sign with a picture of a man and a woman on it.

"Okay, we'll go in here, lock the door and do a jump back to 2019," Sage explained, then pushed the toilet door open and they both entered. Jack locked the door to make the small square room as safe as he could.

"Get the Transphone out." Sage turned to help him.

Jack did as he was told and passed it to Sage. She put in the date, time, and year and noticed that the charge was low.

"We should be okay for this jump but we need to charge it when we get back, okay?"

"Yeah, let's get out of here!" That was all Jack could come up with as an answer.

Sage grabbed Jack's hand, smiled and pressed the button. A humming started and then things started to go black – and then there was a voice!

"Hey, you two, what are you doing in there?" Then there was darkness and the voice diminished into the distance of time as the journey started.

Chapter 32

It started to get brighter as they arrived in 2019. Jack immediately puked.
"You're not very good at this time travel jumping are you, Jack!"

He gradually straightened up to try and compose himself, then wiped his mouth and glanced around, straightaway noticing the strangeness of the location they were in.

"We're back near the Café, aren't we?"

Sage glanced around. "Yeah, we have something to chat about, okay?"

"What are you on about? What do we have to chat about? Have you seen the state we're in? Honestly, why didn't you transport us into a car? Anyone could have seen us appear from nowhere!" Jack fired the questions at Sage.

Ignoring him, Sage started to move. She glanced back, "Come on, let's get a coffee or tea and maybe a cake, shall we?" was the response Jack got, regardless of his question. Sage made her way to the front of the little café.

Opening the door and once again the bell above it rang. As before, she made her way over to the counter. Jack followed, shoulders slumped; he momentarily stopped to ponder over what had happened to him since the last time he had been sitting by the window. He glanced at the chair and remembered what this random female had told him. Strange, unbelievable things that had happened in the past – in his past. Things that occurred in movies and books, not in real life. He remembered being in disbelief at what Sage had told him – body parts, time travel? *What a load of bollocks!* he recalled thinking at the time. Since that fateful day, he had been chased, shot at, in a car chase and killed people. Some skills he had learnt were how to shoot a gun, oh, and how to bloody run like your life depended on it, which it did. They had been to Paris, Johannesburg and London. Yes, quite a little adventure for him, and now he was waiting for Sage to drop some information or something on him. What it was, he had no idea, but he would find out soon. *I wonder if she's going to leave me? Or maybe she's going to turn me in? No, she wouldn't do that, would she?* He thought as he glanced at Sage.

Sage placed the order. The woman behind the counter looked her up and down and a slight twitch of her nose indicated an unusual aroma that had wafted in with Sage. Sage smiled politely, placed the order, then moved to the same table that they had sat at the last time. Except this time Sage sat on the opposite side. Making his way over, Jack sat, but at a right angle to Sage, and leaned his back against the window.

"You know sat in front of the window, someone could pick us off with a couple of good shots." He glanced at Sage. Then moved his glance to his finger nails.

"So what do you want to talk to me about then? Personal hygiene?" quipped Jack.

"Err, maybe later, but let's get our coffee first!" was the response he got back. It wasn't what he wanted, but he couldn't pull a gun out and threaten her with it, to make her tell him. To be honest, even if he did, she would probably get the gun off him and possibly end up pointing it at his face.

Their coffees arrived and Sage smiled at the man that delivered them to their table.

"Okay, Jack, it's like this… You know how we have been chased most of the time? Well, there has been a slight change in the way that they are trying to kill us both."

"Like what?" Jack responded as he took a drink, then made a face as it burnt his mouth.

"Well, they have your friend Conner."

Silence was all that Jack responded with, for a few seconds.

"Conner?"

"Yes, Conner!"

"This is not funny, Sage!"

"It's not a joke, Jack. They have him!"

"Where?" was Jack's next question.

"I'm not sure; I presume it's his place. I got an email from this person, an agent called Abbie. She has him. We have to go and see her, obviously; she will want to kill us both. That's no doubt the reason, she has him as a hostage." Sage then started to snigger at the thought, that was all everyone wanted to do; kill both of them.

"Shit, shit, shit, Conner. Why Conner? What are you laughing at? It's not funny, you know!"

"Sorry, I was thinking that's what everyone wants to do. Kill us!"

"Mmm, so what's the plan; if I dare ask? We have to pop this bitch off? I want to pull the trigger, okay?" Jack announced quite aggressively towards Sage. He then took another drink of his coffee and pulled a face again.

"Why do you keep pulling faces?"

"Because I keep burning my mouth, that's why," Jack responded, and then he took another drink to prove the point.

"Okay, well, as normal, just play it as it goes. We'll run our luck as always," Sage responded, then placed her left hand on his hand as if to say *calm down, it will be ok*ay.

"Really, you really think it will be okay? Not much of a plan, is it?" Jack responded. He picked his coffee cup up, looked at it, and then put it down, he knew it was too hot to drink.

"No, but it's how we seem to do things. And we are both still alive and kicking, aren't we?" she responded, and then it was her turn to have a drink.

"We'll finish our drinks then take a walk to Conner's place, okay? We could jump but the Transphone's nearly flat, so it needs a charge up first."

"No, we won't! We will get an Uber to my place, have something to eat, take a shower, put the Transphone on a charge, clean the guns, then go and get Conner," Jack decided for both of them.

"Okay, that's the plan we are running with. Let's order the Uber and get to your place."

"Err, do we have enough charge to order an Uber on the Transphone?" Jack asked. Sage, realised he didn't have a mobile on him.

"Yes, I'll do it." She got the Transphone out and started to order the Uber. After a minute or so she got up, picked her backpack up, then started walking to the door.

"It's here!" she announced, and opened the door. Jack gulped down his semi-hot coffee and chased after her.

Just as Jack caught Sage up, a black Volkswagen Passat stopped in front of her. She opened the back door and they both climbed in.

"Hey, how are you guys doing? I'm Palo," was the driver's opening line, then he glanced over his shoulder at the two passengers. Jet black hair with a white shirt on, and a dark green silk scarf around his neck.

"Lovely scarf," Sage replied to his initial question.

"Thanks, I got it a year or so ago as a birthday present."

"What a nice present, is it silk?" Sage responded, then smiled at him in the mirror. His dark brown eyes were looking at her intensely.

"I think it is, although I'm not sure. Do you want a feel?" He then smiled in the mirror quite obviously at Sage.

"No, no, no thanks, I'll take your word on it."

"All good, it's cool," was the response. He checked his mirrors, indicated, then set off.

The ride didn't take much time. Jack just sat with his head fixed to the window, looking out as though he hadn't been to this area for years. Palo and Sage were chatting away but he was thinking about Conner. The ticking of the indicator then slowed down to where Jack's apartment was.

"Thanks," Jack said, oblivious to what connection was happening between Palo and Sage. He got out of the car, then made his way toward his apartment's main entrance.

"Hey, here's my card, if you want to give me a call?" Palo smiled, then handed the card over to Sage. As he did this, he ever so softly touched Sage's fingers. Enough for her to realise the connection which sent a shiver down her spine. It quickly registered that she was turned on. This was not like her at all. She was starting to get all gooey and soft inside. Realising this, she pulled herself together.

"Yeah, yes, errr, if I want to see you I now have your number Palo, thank you." Sage mentally shook her head to snap out of this dreamland she was in. Then she took a deep breath of the pungent smell in the car and realised how this was happening.

"Is that Christian Dior El Savage?" Sage bluntly asked.

"Busted," Palo replied, he intensely looked Sage up and down and smiled.

"Yeah, my uncle wears that, to be honest, he's a bit of a chick magnet." Then she burst out laughing at what she had just said.

"Hey, you're making me sound bad," The response came from Palo as he watched Sage climbing out of the car.

"Oh well, I'll be seeing you around them?" she responded. She decided to give herself one last view of Palo, then smiled.

"You never know, you never know." These were the last words Palo could get in before Sage shut the door and started making her way to Jack's apartment.

Mmmm, maybe a bit grubby, nice ass, though! A good seven out of ten, Palo thought to himself. He watched her stroll away from the Uber.

"Oh well, maybe the next passenger." Then he chuckled to himself. He pushed the shaft into Drive, indicated, then accelerated away.

The Uber sped into the distance and Sage knew that she would have quite easily slept with him. She didn't know why but did remember that her uncle Callum had once said, whether true or not, that aftershave had some pheromones in it that females just couldn't resist. Sage briefly thought about that fact – maybe it has something going for it.

Jack had left the main entrance door open for Sage. She went through then up the stairs to the flat. Jack was already in his flat and had left the doors open for her. Sage still had a tingling feeling inside as she once again thought of Palo.

By the time she was in the door he had cracked a beer open and was guzzling it down like it was going out of fashion.

"Is there one for me?" she inquired. He pointed to one sitting on the table open and waiting for someone to pick it up. Obliging, Sage started to drink, then strangely also started gulping it down. Must be the amount of stress that they had been through over the past week or so. After they had both finished their appropriate cans of beer, they glanced at each other; they erupted into

238

laughter at what a ridiculous situation they were in, and had been in for some time now. No doubt they would be entering another strange situation soon in the rescue of Conner.

"I'm off for a shower. If you want anything, just look for it," Jack proclaimed as he made his way to the bathroom.

Sage took her backpack off and took out the Transphone, plugging it in to charge. She moved over to the window and looked out. She started thinking about what they had been through recently. She tried not to, but the moments of silence made it hard. She ruminated about what happened in Johannesburg with Mason and running through the ghetto at night – gosh that was scary!

Hearing the shower in the background brought Sage out of her daydream and back into reality. Palo briefly flashed into her mind, which started to turn her on again. God, did she have something wrong with her head? One minute she is thinking about their situation, then, moments later, thoughts of shagging a stranger. What was wrong with her? Was it that she just wanted company? A stable relationship? Sage knew she was a wonderful person, looked nice on the eyes and did all the duties in bed that any man would want. She wasn't one of these females that lay there as if it was a duty to humanity, whilst thinking of shopping.

"Your turn, if you want a shower, smelly!" was Jack's line as he came out of the bathroom with only a burgundy towel around his lower half. He wasn't Mr Universe, although he did have a defined body shape. Any female in any time-line would have won, if they managed to get a ring on this guy's finger. Loyal, thoughtful, not that bad looking, funny. The list just went on regarding Jack, and here she is thinking all sorts. Was he the guy that had been thrown at her by fate?

"Errr, thanks," was the spluttered response. She made her way to the shower, stripped and climbed in. The water was hot as it covered her and slightly washed away the thoughts that she was having. Feeling clean was nice, feeling something was good – something Sage felt she had not had for a few days now. As she washed her face and breasts and continued down, once again she had thoughts of Palo and Jack. How messed up was her head? She knew that when this was all over she would need to get some professional help – if she would ever able to talk about it all. To come to terms with what's happened and the consequential ending of it. Maybe she could get the whole of the last week wiped. Except that would include Jack and Mason and all the interactions that she'd had, good or bad. Sighing and closing her eyes, she let the water run over her face and down her body.

Chapter 33

A bbie knew they would be on their way as she stood by the window, gun in hand, waiting for them. She was hoping that she would get a good shot at one of them to even the odds a bit. The radio was on playing background music, what it was she didn't know and at times thanked God that she lived in the future and didn't have to listen with rap. *God, why do people listen to that? Yes, it has rhymes, but really!* She was struggling to understand what they were saying and what the message of the rap was. Drugs, prostitution, school, getting your hair cut, Abbie had no idea all. She glanced over to Conner who was strapped to the chair. Was he dead or asleep? She watched for signs of breathing, but the snoring gave it away instead. She hoped he wouldn't get killed in the crossfire, but Abbie had a job to do and those two jokers were the reason he was in this position. Abbie moved over to Conner with slight concern for her hostage.

"Conner, do you want a drink of water? Conner, Conner do you want a drink of water?" She asked as life started to come to his face. He nodded at her and grunted.

"If you try anything, you will be a dead man, do you understand?" Then she showed him the gun, to underline the fact. He confirmed with a nod, then she moved around the back and undid the gag.

"Yeh, can I have a glass of water, lassie, please? Oh, and I need to shake the python."

Abbie presumed he wanted to go to the toilet. She moved to the sink and picked up a grubby cup and filled it with clean water, rinsed it out, then once again filled it, this time for him to drink.

"Here you are, your water, but don't try anything when I untie you, okay?"

"Oh no, no, no, I'll not try anything. I remember the ass-kicking you gave me, I don't want that again. Do you know how fucking embarrassing that is? To be a Scottish man and get your ass handed to you by a female. If I was in Glasgow now and my mates knew about it, I wouldn't be able to show my face for days."

Abbie stood looking at him and a smirk came across her face. She started to ponder what he had said. After a moment or two, she concluded that she actually could get to like this guy. Yes, he was a dickhead, with the dickhead traits of a male, but likable. Maybe she could teach him or perhaps she would get to appreciate the qualities. After all, females just cheat on her, so why not try a man for a bit?

She untied him and immediately took a step back, as if he was a wild animal that she had just let loose and she was scared that he would attack.

Conner started manipulated his wrists to get life back into them, and then he did the same with his feet. He was unsure if he could walk on them or not. Would he get pins and needles, then start laughing with the tingling sensation? He remembered being a kid and trying to give himself a dead leg to get the affect, although it was never as good as when you just got pins and needles. Slowly he stood up with a slight waver in his balance, then struggled to walk. With the weird sensation of tingling, and trying not to enjoy the feeling. He slowly made his way to the bathroom.

Abbie was watching him, making sure that he didn't try to pick anything up on the way that could be used as a weapon or something to escape.

He opened the door, looked back and announced that he was going for a crap. Abbie decided that she was not going to stand by the door watching him crouched down over the pot – although he was going to have to leave the door

241

open as she did have a feeling that he would probably try and get away somehow.

"Errr, leave the door open please."

"Eha lassie, are you a bloody fart-smelling perv?" was the response she received back. Conner turned and smiled. He knew deep in his soul that she was embarrassed and was trying to hide it.

"Yeah, I am, do you have a problem with that? It's all the rage from where I'm from. The fruitier the better," she barked back at him. Abbie could now hear him lowering his trousers and squatting down on the cold seat with a few choice words. After about five seconds, the first of many various sounds of him breaking wind, farting, trumping, whatever you called it, but it was not the nicest thing she had heard that day. Abbie tried to listen to the music on the radio but unfortunately, she could not drown out the sounds that were coming out of the bathroom. The main thing was if there was noise coming out then that meant he was still in the bathroom. Then silence for a few seconds.

"The sod was trying to escape," Abbie mumbled to herself. She rushed into the bathroom and caught Conner standing over the toilet. Conner stopped what he was doing and looked at Abbie, slightly embarrassed.

"Do you mind?" was all Conner said. Abby smiled out of politeness and lifted her hand to cover her eyes from this embarrassing situation. She slowly exited the bathroom without a word. About twenty seconds later, the tap ran and Abbie presumed he was washing his hands. Then silence again and he emerged from the bathroom.

"Do I need to apologise?" Abbie inquired, but knew what should be said.

"Aye, you do, lassie."

"I'm so, so sorry for running in on you like that, I thought you were trying to escape."

"Well that may be, lassie, but firstly, have you seen the size of the window in there? And secondly, we are on the second floor, with only one way in and out. That's providing you don't want to jump anyway. But I accept your apology." Conner announced then gradually made his way over to the chair, stopped, looked at it, then looked at Abbie and sighed.

"You're going to tie me up again, aren't you?" Then a stare of contentment into her soul. His right arm started to move, then a glimpse of something shiny caught Abbie's attention. She stepped back and manoeuvred out of the way of

Conner's flailing arm and a weapon that was being held. She raised the gun to Conner's face, which immediately stopped the attack.

"If you do anything like that again, I'll kill you. Do you understand?"

"Aye, aye, I do. I had to try though, didn't I!" Then he threw the pair of scissors on the floor and sat down on the chair that was waiting for him.

"Well, I'll kill you if you try it again, do you understand?"

"Well, you're going to kill me and my mate, anyway? He's a good guy, you know! And to be honest, I'm not that bad."

Abbie said nothing as she tied his hands to the chair, then his feet. She briefly stopped. The gag? She was rethinking this part of the plan. After a second or two, she put the gag on him again. There was silence, apart from mumbling and the radio in the background, which was now playing a song! Abbie still had no idea who they were but lyrically it was it was catchy. When she got back to 2098, she would make a point of listening to more 70s, 80s and 90s music.

She stepped back then intensely looked at Conner sitting tied to the chair, and there was a slight tug on her heart. She could not stop thinking about a life with him. He had no idea what she was thinking. What would he be like as a partner? The mental tick sheet was not good for Abbie. He was male, from the wrong time zone, and had just tried to kill her. Although she did get that one. Abbie glanced around his flat, he was messy, the grubbiness and grime. He had very little etiquette, although he did have a presence and slight charisma. He gave off the impression that he could be a better person with a bit of training, more like the type of a partner she wanted. Abbie internally laughed at what she had just said. *To train him! He's not a dog to be trained up, although could he be loyal? Maybe, maybe not! But who knows who's going to be loyal? Loyalty is a subjective word, will he fuck around? Maybe, maybe not, but he couldn't be worse than my last partner.*

Abbie moved to the window to take her place on guard once again. She then glanced at Conner and again a strange feeling came over her. *Let him go, and let's go on an exciting journey together!* What the hell was she thinking? What was wrong with her head or heart? Why was it so random? Was she dehydrated, or maybe she needed food? She didn't feel hot, no temperature! She confirmed this by lifting her hand and placing the back of it on her forehead. No, she wasn't hot, she didn't have anything. She was just having a slight

243

moment of affection, warmth – maybe even fondness. Briefly sniggering to herself, she once again looked out of the window to see if they were out there.

Then she went over to her Transphone and checked the telemetry. She could see that they were at the right time, although there was a slight delay in their movements and in her receiving the information. They were only a few kilometres away, so they could arrive at any time. Abbie knew that they were forming a plan to rescue Conner – well, that was what she was hoping they were doing. She would be waiting for them, to kill them; and maybe let Conner go. Although she would see what she was going to do with Conner when the time came. Then back to 2098, get her pay, party for a few days and see how she felt. Yes, that was a good plan. She may even try men again. *Mmmmm, maybe one of each, as they both have their good and bad points or maybe stay single; less trouble that way.*

A loud noise filled the room. Wood splintered from the doorframe. Probably only a few shots at it. Quickly thinking, Abbie grabbed her Transphone and backpack, then ran over to crouch behind Conner as a shield. Checking her gun to make sure it was loaded, she waited crouched down behind her protector.

Chapter 34

This was not how Abbie had imagined it going down. No, she was going to have the advantage, a pop at them arriving. Maybe take one out to make it a more level fight, then end it and go home. End of job!

Abbie fired a few shots at the door on the off-chance that they were stupid enough to be standing in front of it. Panicked, Abbie pushed her gun into the backpack, grabbed Conner's hand and pushed the home button on the Transphone. Screams started to come from Conner's gagged mouth. A humming started and Abbie knew she was getting out of this situation.

The door burst open. Standing in the doorway were a female and a male. Abbie heard one shot, then it went dark.

After a few seconds in time, although years, in reality, it started to get lighter. Abbie was back in 2098 with Conner. She smiled to herself with getting out of that shit with the quick getaway, but knew that she had panicked and was annoyed at herself.

She was sure that they wouldn't try and sneak up on her, to try and catch her out – which is exactly what they did. How stupid of her not to think they would transport outside the door and do what they did, what a fool she was. Her brain must have been somewhere else. She shook her head at the absurdity of it, then glanced at Conner. A stinging sensation started up in her heart. She noticed blood running down Conner's head. She moved to a position where she could have a better look.

"Oh shit, shit, shit, he's dead!" Abbie blurted out. She checked for his pulse, although she knew what the answer was due to a hole in his face. Was it the one shot that they got away before they jumped time? It must have hit him. Probably killed him instantly. Her eyes started to swell up with tears – he did not deserve this at all! He was a nice man – although she had not pulled the trigger, she wasn't to blame. She shouldn't have hidden behind him, although they shouldn't have randomly shot with Conner in the way. What was she going to do with the body? Get rid of it in 2098 or take it back to 2019?

The hairs on the back of her neck started to stand on end, as if there was a static charge.

Dread struck Abbie. She spotted two people appear, then in an instant disappear again. They were also in the building. Abbie could hear them – the humming of their Transphone gave them away – and then it stopped.

"Fuck, Fuck, Fuck!" Abbie uttered to herself. She then went into full panic mode. She took a moment to think, then pulled out her gun from the backpack and put the Transphone in. Putting the backpack on and ran out of the room, leaving the body behind. She went through the doorway and down a corridor, took a left then went through some more doors and out into the brisk morning air with the sun shining down.

Sage and Jack ran for cover as soon as they could. Sage had done a trick she knew to get a glance at the layout of the rooms on the Transphone. Then she quickly moved to a spot that was near the door. She took the two guns out of the backpack and passed one to Jack. Sage looked at Jack, who was taking in deep breaths just like her. Clearly they were both slightly apprehensive.

"They're over there through the double doors," Sage uttered as she got up and started to move in the direction that she had just indicated.

Jack followed as always, he hoped she knew what she was doing. She took a glance through the doorway, then pulled her head back; just in case someone was waiting. She then took another deep breath in, opened the door and went into the room. Jack followed, gun raised. He spotted the person that they were after. A smile slipped across his face. There was no one in sight apart from

246

Conner, who seemed to be asleep or knocked out. The room appeared to be clear and both breathed out a sigh of relief, glancing at each other.

"Phew, that was a bit intense, matey!" Jack announced as he started to move over to Conner from the back.

"Hey wake up, you fucker!"

Jack bent down and undid Conner's wrists. The body that used to be Conner slumped forward and fell to the floor. Jack stood motionless looking at Conner. Then he moved closer to him, and bent down to shake him.

"Conner, hey, stop messing around... Conner, Conner!" Sage rushed over to stand next to Jack as he sluggishly got up. Jack was slowly realising what had happened. Blood was slowly oozing out of the wound in Conner's head. Only gravity now played a part with Conner's body. No life, no heartbeat to pump blood around his body. Just an empty shell of what used to be Conner.

"She bloody shot him! The bitch has fucking shot him!" Jack crashed down next to Conner's body which was lying motionless. He grabbed hold of Conner's face and turned it. Shock hit Jack as flesh, blood, and brains covered Jack's hands. With the realisation of the sight, Jack dropped Conner's head, which hit the concrete floor with a thud!

"Fuck, fuck," Jack screamed out loud. Sage wanted to tell Jack to quieten down. For all they know this was all part of Abbie's plan. A few shots of her gun and they could both be dead. Sage felt very vulnerable in this situation and started scanning for any signs of movement. Jack was now a quivering piece of jelly, he needed to be taken to a place of safety, at least for the next few hours, to pull himself together and let it sink in.

It wasn't the ideal time or place but Sage took her backpack off and rummaged around in one of the pockets. Pulling out a small object, Jack looked on as tears rolled down his face. Then the offer of potential relief as Sage held out her hand. An offering of a tablet.

"What's this?"

"It's something that will take the edge off of what you have just seen, it's a post-trauma tablet. I had one after Johannesburg!" Sage responded. Jack took the white tablet out of her hand and looked at it.

"Jack, we need to get out of here. Jack, do you hear me?" she said in the sternest voice, she could muster.

"Yeah, Yeah," was the response.

247

"Down it!" she ordered, and she bent down on one knee and put some co-ordinates into the Transphone.

"Give me your hand," Sage commanded. Jack nearly always obeyed, but this time nothing. Sage looked at him. He was staring at Conner's motionless body.

"Jack, Jack your hand!" Sage stated again, as she looked at him intensely.

"But what about Conner?"

"We'll sort something out for him but we have to get out of here. We are compromised, it's not safe for us."

Jack held out his hand and grabbed Sage tightly. She pressed the button, then as always the humming, darkness and then a different location appeared.

Chapter 35

B lackness started to clear for both of them.

"How are you feeling this time?" Sage enquired, then moved away from Jack, just in case he threw up on her.

"Errrr, I suppose I'm feeling a bit better," was his response. He glanced around a garden. The pungent smell of flowers struck his nose. The next item he noticed was a one-storey house to the side of him.

"Where are we?" enquired Jack. He seemed to have some sort of recollection of the place, but didn't know why. Sage started to move around to the side of the building, with Jack trailing. Seconds later, they arrived at the front of an old single-storey run-down building.

"Who's is this? Is it yours?" Jack said with disappointment in his voice.

"No, god no. It's my uncle Callum's place. Remember, you met him when I first brought you to the future."

"Oh yes, he was the guy holding the gun at my face!"

"Yes, that's him, the slightly eccentric man, but it's safe to stay for a bit. He'll help us out, I hope! Oh and remember you may have some Deja-vu, as I think you came here before the timeline change." Sage started to walk up the path to the wooden front door, then pressed the doorbell. It started to chime Greensleeves.

"Wow Greensleeves… my mum and dad had a similar chime at our house when I was a kid," Jack stated as recollections of his childhood were triggered. Jack recalled that he would run to the front door to open it. Especially if his Gran B was coming over. She would be standing there with her white permed hair and a handbag. Then seemed to remember thinking a similar thing, but could not remember when.

The door opened to a slightly overweight man with a small beer belly and grey blond hair; he was wearing jogging pants and a black AC/DC T-shirt.

"Hello, can I help you? the man said as he stood waiting for a reply. Sage just walked by him.

"It's lovely to see you, Sage," was his first response. Then Sage stopped and turned to look at the man in the doorway. She smiled and moved closer, then they cuddled.

"Hi, can we stop the night?"

"Sage, there's a guy out here – I think he's a bit shifty, maybe a policeman?" he whispered out loud.

"No, he's cool, he's called Jack. Remember, you held a gun to his head," was the response from Sage. Then she moved into the house. Jack stood at the front door, waiting to be invited in.

"Hi Jack, we meet again under slightly different circumstances. I don't know if you remember me, but I'm Callum. It's nice to meet you again, please come in." He slightly moved away from the door to make room for Jack to enter.

"Hi again, yes, it's slightly different. But we're still in trouble."

"Yes, I know, it's the only time I see Sage. She only comes around when she wants something," was Callum's sarcastic response, then he started to laugh.

Jack followed Callum through the doorway and closed the dark hardwood door behind him. Jack could not remember much of his first visit to the future. His brain was overloaded with the fact that he was time travelling.

Jack was surprised that the house wasn't all teched out like he imagined it would be. All the fittings on the door were of a bygone age. Ironically, that past age was probably the time that he was from. Jack sniggered to himself; Callum glanced back at Jack. Music was oozing down a narrow beige hallway with a door to the left and right.

Oh, what was this song? It was familiar, but he could not put his figure on it. Then the chores came on and said it all. It was *Run to the Hills* by Iron Maiden. Jack started to rack his brain to think of the album but nothing popped up in his head. Maybe later, he thought. Jack followed Callum down the hallway.

Jack briefly remembered his record collection, then Conner... Sadness filled his heart. His best mate, his friend was now dead, and that bitch had done it. Then the good times popped up and filled his head. Yes, he had had lots of them with Conner. The pubs and clubs that they went to, and the females that they tried to pick up. Well Jack tried, although Conner was always good at chatting with the girls. His accent was a winner for him and also if he went out in his bloody kilt, of course. Oh yes, yet another talking point. Although in reality they only wanted to know if he had any underwear on! His line was, *well come back to my place pet; you can have a look there!* That worked so many times... so Conner said anyway. Jack remembered a time they went into a pub in Glasgow with two females; both Scottish. A few Glaswegians didn't like the fact that Jack was in the pub with a Scottish female. They both got chased out of the pub and left their two dates. That was so funny. He remembered them running down the road trying to avoid getting beaten up. Although in reality, it was only him they wanted to beat up. Jack had to phone them and arrange a place to meet up with them later that night. That was a good night, they had both gone to his hotel room. A smile appeared on Jacks face as he remembered what a good night it was – one he would never forget. Then he thought of Mandy, the night that started all this off, back in his life. God if he had not accepted that ticket, he wouldn't be here now; and Conner would no doubt be alive. Although he seemed to remember that something bad would have happened to him. But what, he couldn't remember. But that was the reason Mandy wanted to take him to the future.

His mind then shifted to the music playing. How old would this be? Jack pondered momentarily and shook his head to get the idea out. *Stop it, I didn't want to start with that crap again, thinking about my past life. I need to start thinking of the present and focus on the future.* Jack thought. His eyes started to well up with tears at the situation he was in. Sadness hung heavy in the deps of his stomach. He continued to meander behind Callum.

251

Jack entered a bright room with large long windows at the end. Then briefly stopped and began to absorb the information available. *Wow, this house is in the wrong era*, he thought whilst slowly stroking his chin as a comforter.

Sage and Callum were chatting away. Jack looked around the room in awe. To his right was the kitchen with a grey countertop. It all looked familiar, and he knew he had been here before, but that was a blur. He could not remember anything at all, which slightly uneased Jack. Was he losing his memory with all this time-jumping? *If that's likely to happen, then Sage would have said something*, he thought.

Jack noticed various mugs with pictures of Batman, Star Wars and one with the USS Enterprise. He remembered that his dad once had one with a Klingon spaceship on his mug, and when you put hot tea in the mug the spaceship would disappear as if it was cloaked. Jack chuckled again, *what's wrong with me*, he thought. *Probably anxiety or just nerves.*

This must be deja' vu that Sage was on about, Jack thought, then moved over to the shelf of mugs. He was going to pick them up but thought maybe not – after all, he was a guest.

Jack moved around the room. He looked at all the trinkets and pop culture that was on display. Now playing was a song – Jack thought he knew the voice but not the song.

"Who this?" Jack blurted out. Sage and Callum stopped talking. They both turned to look at him standing there on his own.

"Oh bless, look at his confused face," Sage stated, then smiled at him as her heart bled for him and his confusion.

"It's Ed Sheeran. I think it's called *Bad Habits*. I think he released it in 2022. No, it was 2021… Mmmmm I can't remember, sorry," Callum stated.

"So that was two years or so from the first time I met you? This is so messed up."

"Yep. Welcome to my world," Sage said then started laughing.

Then Jack leaned on the back of the chair to support his weight. His head slumped while he tried to take in the situation once again.

"Ed Sheeran's *Bad Habits* video," Callum requested. A picture appeared on one of the walls with the video playing. Underneath, the text stated the song, year and title.

"One to me," Callum victoriously shouted out, as he had got it right.

"Jack, come over here," Sage gestured to him. Complying. Jack made his way to them.

"Okay, Jack, I'm going to get a Goober and go and see what Kimberly has got for me!" Sage announced, then started to order one on the Transphone.

"A what? A Goober? Who's Kimberly?" Jack poetically rebuffed back at Sage. Then a noise came from her Transphone, to confirm the order and give her an ETA.

"Okay, fifteen minutes. Remember, we went in one just after we had broken you out from prison. It's like a taxi.

"Are you staying here or coming with me?" Sage asked Jack, who was quite clearly still in shock. Jack had taken the anti-trauma tablet, and Sage hoped that he was feeling good about things. She knew that they had both been through a lot, but she had the training to help her out, whereas Jack had no training to help him.

"How do you feel, Jack?" She was checking in to see if it kicked in yet.

"What's a Goober?" Jack inquired again, as he avoided the question being asked.

"Can't you remember, it's a taxi, that's all! Do you not remember going in one when we first brought you to the future?"

"Oh yes, I remember now, you had a gun pointed at me!" Jack finally replied. Sage could see the cogs ticking away on his face.

"So are you coming with me or staying here with Callum?"

"Err, yeah, I'll come with you, if that's okay? Who's Kimberly?" Jack just about managed to get out.

"A friend. She's cool."

Sage took her backpack off, and took out her gun and some shells, and loaded it. Then she loaded Jack's gun and gave it to him. Finally, she put her backpack on.

"Okay, we're off now, Callum. We'll be back later. I'll let you know when, okay? Callum smiled at Sage who just nodded back. They both made their way to the front door and outside. They walked to the road and a black Goober arrived.

Jack just stood in silence; he looked at the vehicle standing there now with its doors open and hovering off the ground. The penny dropped and he knew that he had been to the future before and he'd been in a Goober, but it was all vague. Sage looked at Jack standing in silence and had a hunch he would be asking lots of questions soon.

Jack slowly moved over to the vehicle, bent down to look at the mag-plates under it. It was amazing that they were keeping the vehicle hovering just like in *Star Wars* or *Back to the Future*.

"Wow!" was all that came out of Jack's mouth. Sage climbed into the car.

"Are you getting in?"

"Yeah, yeah," the response came back at Sage. Jack had a little boy's face of wonderment on now as he climbed into the car.

"You don't seem to remember – wait until you see what the future looks like, Jack. Err, have you got the address?" Sage said out loud, then the door hissed closed and they started to move off.

"Yes, Sage, District 9/6329. Is that correct?" The electronic voice stated.

"Yes, that's it," Sage responded, then looked at Jack and smiled.

The car made its journey along a road that looked like any normal road in 2019. The trees started to clear, although the site was not of 2019 but 2098.

The car made its way up a spiralling road into the sky, then attached itself to the skyway where it started to accelerate at a ridiculous rate. Sage and Jack were both pushed back in their seats as if an invisible entity was pushing them. The noise of the electric mag-plates filled the cockpit, although once at the desired speed, the noise started to disappear. Then only wind noise was all that came from the car. Sage glanced at Jack again who was gawking out of the window and veraciously looked at the future in awe.

After about twenty minutes, the Goober left the skyway, making its way down to the lower levels and into a tunnel. It emerged in what appeared to be a car park, then it slowly pulled up to a set of stainless steel doors and stopped. The doors opened and the car slowly went into what appeared to be a small room. It hovered above the floor of the room, which Jack thought was a funny sensation. The doors closed behind them and an upwards feeling could be felt.

It must be a lift, Jack thought. The elevator stopped, then the set of stainless steel doors at the other side of the lift opened. The car slowly moved forward and stopped outside an entrance. The Goober's doors whispered open. The electronic voice thanked them and told them of the charge. Jack thanked the voice and it replied, which he thought was amusing.

They both climbed out of the car, then a normal-sized stainless steel door opened up in front of them. Leaving the car behind, they walk down a long grey corridor with no distinguishing features to it. Jack glanced back at the door they had just come through. It had closed.

"Where are we going?" Jack enquired.

"Oh, you'll see soon enough, Jack," was the response he got from Sage, as she stopped at a yellow door. To the side were the numbers 6329 in white with a black outline to them. After knocking and waiting then pressing the bell, a face appeared on the screen to the side of the door.

"Hi, can I help you? Sage, Sage, Sage. On my way!" An excited voice stated. Then the face vanished from the screen and was replaced with the numbers again as they slid over the screen. The door clicked open and a female – who appeared to be wearing very little – rushed out and started hugging Sage.

"Oh my god, it's been so, so long since we've seen each other. I was so, so happy when you got in touch. You should have done it sooner," the female near enough screamed at Sage. Then she started jumping up and down on the spot with excitement. Jack just stood watching the circus performance. He briefly thought, *if this is what they wear in the future? I'll be moving to here.*

"Come in, come in," the overexcited female requested as she led the way. Sage glanced at Jack then smiled. Followed their sparsely-clad host into the apartment. They walked in, then immediately turned right and down a corridor with a glass roof. It opened up into a large area that had windows on two sides of it.

Jack stood motionless as he took in the sight. The furniture was everywhere, to the point of it being chaotic. The walls were an off-white grey colour, spotlights randomly placed in the ceiling, in sets of three or four. Strange types of blinds were hanging from each window, some up, some down. Jack moved over to them and touched one of them – they felt strange, different. He heard the word *dark!* and they instantly went black. Looking around the room they all had turned black. Jack stood there in awe at what had just happened. Then their host said the word *light!* and they became transparent. *Wow that's cool,* was all that Jack could think about what he had just witnessed. A long gaze at the backdrop of the future. Sky scrapers of all sorts of various sizes, contractions, and colour's, lights, enormous video screens the size of football pitches showing adverts on the sides of the buildings. Roads like the one he had just come on, except they were all spiralling in different directions. If this was the future, he liked the look of it. Then he decided to explore more of this apartment. A set of five cream silk cushions were strategically placed on the brown leather sofa. Its back faced the outside of the building, a brown wooden coffee table, a leather Chaise-longue. *There's crap everywhere; this is not minimal design at all*, Jack thought as he followed the two females down towards the eight-seated light wooden table. The kitchen was to his left; with a set of stairs to what Jack presumed would be a second floor and the bedrooms, and bathroom. He stopped in his tracks as the full force of 2098 hit him head-on once again. The buildings, cars flying, all the things that you would see in the movies. Then he glanced back to the other window view which was quite tame compared to the new view. Although initially he thought that it was amazing. A snigger at that thought.

"Like what you see?" Sage asked, as she and their semi-clad host stood in his line of sight. In reality, he was looking through them both and out of the windows.

"Errr yesss, it's errr, well, I don't know what to say." Jack had no idea why he said them words or what they meant. He just stood looking at the wonder in front of him.

"Oh hi, my name's Kimberly," the female said as she moved closer to stand in front of Jack. She put out her hand to welcome him. Jack intensely looked at her, as he came out of his trance. He tried not to look or stare at the female that appeared to be popping out of the bra that she was wearing. *The good thing is that she was not jumping around anymore*. He thought.

"Oh hi, I'm Jack, nice to meet you."

"Yes, I know, Sage has mentioned you to me. You're from the past, aren't you?" Kimberly asked, appearing all excited about their meeting.

"Errrr yes, I'm from 2019."

"Well, you look good for your age," she responded, then she raised her left hand and stroked him on the shoulder.

"Okay, okay, Kimberly, he's not going to fuck you!" Sage butted in. Jack glanced at her with disapproval at her statement.

"Sorry, what did you say Sage?" Jack could not help himself from saying a response. Both females started laughing as if he'd told a joke. There was no response in return, apart from a disapproving look.

"What do we need to do to get a drink around here?" Sage blurted out in the direction of Kimberly.

"I'm not going to answer that. I'll just get you both a drink. What do you want? Scotch, bourbon, beer?"

"Errr, I'll have a beer please," Sage responded, then glanced at Jack with a look of slight embarrassment.

"Yeah, me too," Jack added on as he slowly made his way around the furniture towards the window. He still could not believe how much it looked like a movie set. Clearly, the movies of the twenty-first century had had a massive impact on the design of the buildings and transportation of the future. It just looked so bloody cool. There was no other word for it!

"Errr, can I use your toilet?" Jack asked as the two females chatted away, oblivious to him and his question.

"Excuse me; can I use your toilet please?" Jack asked again in a louder voice.

"Yeah, it's up the stairs," Kimberly replied without breaking eye contact or conversation with Sage. Jack made his way up the white steel spiral stairs to a landing with a rectangular skylight and full-length mirrors on every wall. A few closed doors were randomly scattered along the mirrored walls. He opened the first door and walked in; *this must be Kimberly's bedroom*, he thought. There was a massive king-sized bed in the middle of the room with white pillows and silk sheets covering it. Jack sniggered to himself as he looked at the immaculately made bed. Then glanced around the room; thick plush cream carpets up to the point that you sank into them. His curiosity took control. He could not stop himself investigating the room more. A door opening to the far end of the bedroom wall invited him in to have a look. *Maybe that was the toilet?* he jokingly thought, convincing himself he was not being nosy. He entered a plush white wardrobe that was full of clothes, shoes, bags and mirrors. He pondered for a moment and his conscience about being curious tapped him on the shoulder.

He quickly made his way out of the bedroom and then tried the next door along. This one had a set of stairs in it. At the end of the short staircase was a glass door. Jack could see that it probably went to the roof or somewhere like that, as he could see the sky. He made another hasty exit and went back into the white corridor.

257

He tried another door, Bingo the bathroom. It had a blue tint to it, Like it was a dreamy, murky state. He completed his task and faced the embarrassment of the toilet telling him his deficiency of vitamins and other minerals. Then there was the ordeal of trying to wash his hands in a sink he had to talk to. He felt a sense of relief in more ways than one, as he left the bathroom; the only ordeal in 2019 was running out of toilet paper. A smile crossed his face at that thought.

He made his way back downstairs to find the two females still chatting away.

Moments later, a cool beer was offered to him by the still scantily clad Kimberly. *Why didn't she put some clothes on? Has she no modesty?* Jack wondered as he took the scantily clad sight in. Then he glanced at Sage, whose eyes said it all as they penetrated him as if to tell him to stop ogling. He tried to stop, but Kimberly was wandering around in knickers and a bra. *It wasn't his fault was it*, he pondered. But at least she appeared to have calmed down; *well, she isn't jumping about as though she's on drugs or something. Maybe she was; they seemed to have a drug or potion for everything.*

"Do you want to see the video?" Kimberly asked Sage.

Looking at Jack, Sage was a little concerned about his response to what he might see, but thought *to Hell with it.*

"Yep, let's see what you got up to!" Sage started to make her way to the sofa that was the centrepiece of the room.

Jack had no idea or interest in what they were watching. A shopping channel or whatever they were on about. His attention was focused on the windows and trying to take the sights in, trying to comprehend the timeline he was in.

The sound in the background caught his attention as he glanced in the direction of the picture that was being shown on the white wall. His focus then was set on the images of two people that appeared to be having sex. Then the penny dropped. He glanced at Kimberly and back at the screen and then back at her.

"I'm sorry but I have to ask – is that what I think it is?"

"Yep," was Kimberly's response as she glanced at him and smirked.

"Oh," was all Jack could muster as he started to intensely watch the show.

"Kimberly is a professional, Jack."

"A professional what?" Jack inquired. He could not take his eyes off the images and what they were getting up to.

"A con artist. Her speciality is getting married men into compromising positions and blackmailing them."

"Yeah, and to add to it, I get sex a lot," Kimberley blurted, as she watched herself perform. "Sorry, it's not in surround sound, only mono." Kimberly added.

"It's perfect, you can switch it off now," Sage said, then glanced at Jack who had a smirk on his face.

"Can you do us a copy please. I'll get in touch with him and see if we can stop this whole thing. Then I can get my life back, and you can also get on with yours, Jack."

Jack was still watching the performance on the screen, oblivious to what Sage was saying to him.

"Yeah, yeah," was all he said.

"Jack, Jack, did you hear what I said?" Sage shouted.

The performance stopped and Jack returned to reality. He took a sip of his beer to calm himself down.

"Oh yes… What am I going to do?" he asked, unsure of what was going to happen shortly, never mind the distant future.

"You can stay here if you want with Kimberly. If you're cool with that?" Sage said, then glared at Jack again.

"Yep, all cool," was the response. Then Kimberly passed Sage what looked like a memory stick? Sage got out her Transphone and held it next to it.

"Is that a memory stick?" Jack asked as he came over to look at what she was doing.

"Yes, except it's a bit bigger than the ones you use in your time. It's like Bluetooth, its fifty petabytes. Not a big one, but it will do for what we need." After a few seconds, she gave it back to Kimberly.

"Okay, I know where he lives; I'll use your car, if that's okay?" Sage bluntly asked.

"Why not get a boober?" Jack asked.

Sage and Kimberly looked at each other and broke into laughter. "A Boober? I think you have boobs on your mind after that video. It's Goober, and

Kimberly's car's bulletproof. It also has false plates on it so she cannot be tracked."

Walking to the door, Sage smiled at Jack and shook her head in disbelief at his comment.

"I'll leave the backpack hear ok. Look after her, I won't be long. Just chill, Jack, and enjoy the future."

She turned her back and walked down the hallway and out of sight. The door clicked and she was gone on her mission.

Chapter 36

After leaving Conner's dead body in 2098, Abbie had to calm herself down before she could do anything. *Slow breathing, that's it, in out in, out,* she thought to herself as it started to work. Then she vomited on the grass.

"Bollocks! It's on my shoes now, although I'm alive," she mumbled to herself. Then she took a few more minutes to compose herself. Whilst composing herself, she decided to check in with the Manager, to keep him in the loop. She dialled him up on the Transphone, and also deciding to make it a voice-only conversation.

"Hi, have you completed your task, Abbie?"

"Err, well, no, I just thought I would let you know what's happening."

"They're still bloody alive, aren't they? For fuck's sake; can anyone kill these two? I get that she's trained, but he's a fucking nobody. Surely one of you can kill him at least?" he yelled at her. She could sense that he was probably red in the face by now. Maybe the veins in the side of his neck were raised with excessive blood pressure.

"Look, Abbie, it's simple, kill them or don't bother coming back. I'll tell you what, kill him, and I'll put someone else on to finish it off for you, okay?" The Transphone went dead. He had hung up on her before she could answer.

God, what was she going to do? She stood glancing at the Transphone, she could not believe it. They were about four kilometres away. *What a stroke of luck. Yes, she could go there, kill them and that would be it.* She though. A smile slowly crossed her face at the idea. She then got out her Transphone to order a Goober straight away. Abbie didn't know the area but she had to do this – it was her job after all.

About seventeen minutes later, a dirty green Goober arrived. It parked next to her. Abbie waited for the door to open but nothing happened. She grabbed the handle to open the door the old school way and she glanced at the dirty light green seats with god knows what on them. Climbing in, the smell of smoke along with other unknown smells hit her nostrils. Smoke was triggering for her. She remembered when she used to smoke, but didn't anymore; well not often. There was a strange ticking noise. Abbie realised that this was going to be a bit of a rough ride. Slowly moving off, the noise did not represent the speed at which they were moving. It sounded like they were going at a million Ks an hour, although she thought she could run faster. After a brief time on the skyway, she decided that it was not a pleasant experience as everyone was going fast, apart from them. You could say they were nearly a mobile chicane; cars passed on both sides with angry passengers in them. Abbie decided a good tack was to slump out of sight. They started to come to their destination. Abbie advised that the Goober slowed down – in reality, it stayed the same speed, slow! Then she started to direct the AI unit where to go, as she looked at her transphone intensely.

"Enter through the stainless steel doors." The voice confirmed this and did as it was told. The lift started to go up probably faster than the Goober had gone on their short but scary journey to this location.

"Stop at the next floor, I'll walk from there," she commanded and the Goober did as it was told.

"Your fare will be deducted. Do you want to tip for the ride?"

"God, no!" was all Abbie said to that question. Finally, she opened the vehicle's door after two attempts with the clumsy plastic handle, then accidentally banged the door on the wall as she got out.

"All damage will be deducted from your account," the Goober announced.

"You try it, you piece of shit," Abbie grunted under her breath, then glanced back at the imaginary person, but in reality, she'd just given a speaker the evil eye. Closing the door behind her, a noise started and the excuse of a vehicle slowly moved away and out of sight.

She took a moment to straighten her clothes and get her bearings by glancing at the Transphone. One floor higher would be the destination of the journey. She headed through a doorway. She stopped then pulled the gun from the back of her trousers that was covered under her jacket. She pulled the slide back to check her baby was loaded and ready to go. Then took a glance left and right, and once again tucked the weapon back in her jeans. Making her way up the flight of stairs to a door, then stopped to check the Transphone. It confirmed the address, 6329, then she went through the doorway and into a corridor of doors, left and right. A glance at a sign directed her which way she should go. Right was what the sign said, so Abbie obeyed and started to make her way down the corridor, glancing at the doors to find the one she wanted. A female came out of one of the rooms and started walking away, in the same direction Abbie was heading. All she could see was the back of the female. Slim, about 162 to 165cm tall, with red/brown hair just below her shoulders. Stopping a few seconds later, she glanced at the door and then at the female who was waiting for the lift. Abbie watched her go into the lift and out of sight. Putting two and two together, she realised that she had just missed one of her targets. She smiled to herself over this bit of luck. Hopefully this meant that the guy was in the apartment on his own! *Easy picking* she thought, *on several levels... After all he wasn't expecting her because if they were she wouldn't have left him on his own. Or was this a trap? Maybe she's being paranoid?*

"For god sake Abbie sharpen up, Oh well, it's what it is!" she mumbled to herself, then pressed the doorbell, and moved out of the way of the camera. With a bit of luck, he would answer and she would be in. Pop his ass, then leave and it was one down, then the Manager would get someone onto Sage's ass and Abbie would go home a happy bunny and maybe break even with the credits.

A female voice came over the speaker.

"Hi, who is it? I can't see you, sorry."

"A delivery for you!" Abbie said with her hand over her mouth to mumble the words. *A female voice! maybe they are both in the apartment?* Abbie thought, and hoping this trick would create a certain amount of curiosity for someone to open the door. All being well, they were not expecting Abbie anyway.

"I'm sorry, who did you say you are? It's a bad connection. I cannot hear or see you!"

"It's a delivery for you, I'm sorry but I'm not that tall, I'm shouting as loud as I can to let you hear me." Abbie once again muffled her voice but made the part about her height loud enough to hear. Then she sniggered to herself. The door lock clicked. Taking a deep breath, Abbie moved into the centre of the door so that whoever appeared could be seen and a clear shot could be taken.

The door slowly opened, and appearing in front of Abbie was a pretty female with blue eyes and shoulder-length hair. Abbie pulled the trigger and the female's head and body were pushed back with the impact of the bullet into the front of her forehead. The back of her head exploded with a mist of red over the wall. The noise sounded quite loud in the hallway as it echoed through the building level. Abbie knew that the other person would now be looking for their weapon and be ready for her. Abbie had to shoot – for all she knew, the female had a gun herself and Abbie would now be dead. She mentally justified the blind shot to herself.

Jack heard the noise; although he was no expert, he knew it was a gunshot. After all, he had been in enough shootouts in recent times to know what a gunshot sounded like. A few days ago, he would have run in the direction of the sound, but now he moved swiftly to a place of hiding, got the gun from the back of his trousers and pulled the slide back with anticipation of what was going to happen.

Abbie slowly moved in through the entrance and stopped, she did not want to go bursting into an unknown situation. Then she once again glanced down at the body of the female slumped on the floor. Briefly feeling sorry for the female that she had just killed. Abbie always wondered what the victims did for a living. She concluded that this one was probably in admin or something like that; her hair and nails were too well-groomed to do heavy work for a living. She probably looked quite pretty, although the hole in her head did not do anything to her appearance. The lack of clothing was a puzzle, although she was a little skinny for Abbie. She liked a more robust body, but she knew that she would have had a good time throwing her around the bedroom.

Daydreaming over, she would have to have time for someone else to fuck!

Abbie always had an issue with what she did next, as she moved the body's legs and closed the door behind her; which stopped people entering to try and kill her but also stopped her from escaping in a hurry. She remembered the advice of her instructor, Turner H, when she was at training. He always sat on the fence with doing this to a body, because of the entry and exit reasons.

Then slowly she moved down the intensely lit corridor to the end as it slowly opened up. The adrenalin was now pumping and she felt energised, scared, empowered and all the good and bad feelings you get in this situation. Briefly bobbing her head around the corner of the door frame to reveal a room.

Jack was slowing his breathing down; it seemed to take forever for anything to happen. His palms were starting to sweat. He knew that he was becoming anxious about what was going to happen. Would he survive or die in this place away from everyone he ever knew? No one to help him, this was all on him now. More deep breaths to calm himself down.

Abbie stopped. She took another glance in the room, except slightly longer this time. The first thing that struck Abbie was that it looked cluttered. With a leather sofa, table and bric-a-brac. Windows lined two sides and it was a nice view indeed. After another slow glance around the room, the other person could be behind the sofa, although Abbie scanned into the glass and could see no one in the reflection of the window. That meant that they were at the other end of the room? Although they may be waiting in a bedroom, bathroom or behind the units in the kitchen. A quick run and a squat behind the couch. She slowly moved down the back of it to obtain a different view of the apartment.

Jack knew it was the person after them, shit, *where's Sage?* Kimberly was probably dead. There was no screaming, shouting – nothing. He finally started to control his breathing again – after all, he didn't want to pass out from hyperventilating.

Jack thought, *right, your options are, to shoot out in the kitchen, move to the second floor and have a shootout up there or maybe go to the roof. Maybe there is a pod or something in case of a fire?* But for all he knew, that was a dead-end. Thinking, he made the move and quickly ran for the stairs. A shot was let go and the bullet hit the wall in front of him. Fragments of plaster covered him. He took the stairs two at a time and quickly arrived at the landing. He stopped briefly, he knew the layout of the place. He decided on the bedroom and opened the first door and closed it behind him. Then he moved to the doorway to the closet but stopped. He was thinking, *would behind the bed be a better position to get a shot off or not?* He thought. Indecisively he chose.

Abbie cursed herself, she knew that she should have got him with the shot. Getting up from her position, she moved to the doorway and placed her back against the wall to give herself a few seconds for the adrenaline to calm down. She took a deep breath – in, out, and in. It smelt so fresh and clean in the room, like being at the beach on a brisk cold day. She gazed around the room and out of the window. *I need to get a new job that's less risky,* was the momentary decision she made. She took another deep breath and then she poked her head around the edge of the doorway – *no one waiting to blow my head off, good!* She slowly moved up the stairs and tried to look in every direction at once.

Chapter 37

At the top there were mirrors everywhere, internally sneering to herself Abbie could have put credits on this type of decor. She imagined the female that was now dead, would have probably viewed herself for hours; no doubt before going out into society for the world to see just how beautiful she was on the outside.

At the top of the stairs, Abbie wondered which white door would he have gone through. She glanced at the plush carpet to see if there were any tell-tale signs about which door would lead to which room. The first door's threshold seemed slightly more worn. In general, this meant it was the bathroom or the master bedroom. Abbie knew the target didn't have any training; he probably would have gone into this room. She put her hand on the door handle and waited for a few seconds to gain her composure. Then stood to the side and pushed the door open. Two shots came from the room and smashed the mirror opposite her. She could see that he was hiding in a doorway. He could see her, so she waved to him! The target then waved back, surprisingly – *how strange,* Abbie thought. *Normally they'd freak out rather than have a bit of a laugh before they got killed.* Abbie let off two shots and thought that this was going to be drawn out into a stalemate. *If she went in, he would get her and he was not going to give up his position. Fuck, what was she going to do? Then what if Sage came back?* Abbie pondered.

"Hey, you have nowhere to go to. Just come out and let's get it over with." Abbie shouted.

"Did you kill Conner?" was the reply.

"No, it was one of you two that shot him, but it was an accident," Abbie responded as another shot came through the doorway. Abbie thought he was getting angry and frustration which was starting to show. Frustration on his part at her response to Conner's death.

"Look, it's like this, your friend isn't here to bail you out. You've had a good run and it's now come to the end. Let's just get it over with." Abbie tried to reason with him. Another shot came out of the doorway.

At this rate, he'll run out of bullets and I can just walk in and take him out, Abbie thought, then glanced down the hallway. She was also starting to get irritated internally. In reality, his mate Sage could come back at any time and get a jump on her. This was now playing on Abbie's mind. She needed to get this done.

"I'm going to fucking kill you. He was my mate you know," Jack screamed at her.

A plan popped into Jack's head. He wasn't sure if it would work but it was a plan at least. His current plan was to try and sit it out until Sage came back to help him. He knew that his ammo was low; he had been stupidly letting them off. He dropped the magazine out of his Remington and cleared the chamber as quietly as he could. He placed the bullet into the magazine and then took a deep breath.

"You fucker!" Jack pulled the trigger and all that happened was a clicking sound —once, twice, three times. Nothing no shot, just the clicking sound of an empty gun.

"Fuck, fuck," Jack screamed out then put the magazine back in the gun and pulled the slide to get a round in the chamber. He quickly moved to the rear of the wardrobe, crouching down to reduce the target area, and waited.

Abbie could not believe her luck as she heard the sound of an empty gun. She gradually started to move forward to get her prey but instinct tapped her on the shoulder to let her know that this could also be a trap. Yes, he was inexperienced, but what a bit of luck. She lifted her Colt Defender, just in case

268

it was a trick. Moving ever so slowly into the room, Abbie also knew that she had a bit of ammo left so she could go in shooting to get him, just in case it was a trap. Finally, at closet doorway, with the gun still lifted. She didn't want to let him know she was outside. *Keep him guessing*, she thought to herself. She took some deep breaths, in and out, in, out, to calm herself down again. Standing outside of the doorway, she took a glance around the bedroom to help calm herself. She quickly poked her head around the corner, then out of sight again – nothing from her adversary. *He's out,* she thought, then smiled. Momentarily leaning up against the wall she felt the cold soak through her clothes and onto her back.

"One, two, three," she mumbled then went around the corner. One shot, then another, but nothing… Her gun jammed. She was confused with what had happened as she momentarily glanced at it. In response, Jack fired back, then was out of rounds. Abbie stood there with a gun in her hand that was jammed, pulling the trigger but nothing happened. Jack could not believe he missed her, out of frustration, threw his gun at Abbie. She deflected it with her left hand, although it threw her off balance slightly.

Jack got to his feet, then ran as fast as he could, screaming. Getting his body low, he rugby-tackled Abbie. This was not the way that Abbie had imagined it going, she became a passenger in the tackle. The impact took Abbie off her feet and she landed on her back, with this man on top of her. The gun got dislodged from her hand when she hit the ground. Abbie was winded by the incident and briefly saw stars floating around, confusion then she felt pain. She felt an impact to her left cheekbone then to her right. Abbie could sense she was starting to loose conciseness. Jack started to let loose with the punches. Anger, rage… a red mist took over him.

Abbie was taken aback by this; she pulled her arms up to slow the impacts and punches down. She mentally and emotionally regrouped and the stars started to go. More punches rained down on her head and then to her torso. She spotted her chance as Jack was in attack mode but not defending himself as fury had taken over.

Abbie took a right and left – her target was so intent on hurting her he had no defence up. The shock of the impacts on his face stunned him into stopping his assault on Abbie. The wild man lost balance, twisted, and fell off of her. Abbie had her chance now and looked around for the gun that hopefully would have un-jammed itself when it was knocked out of her hand. Spotting the gun and a bullet was lying next to it. Abbie made a quick move towards the weapon.

Jack jumped on the Abbie's back. He put his arm around her face and pulled her head back. Abbie screamed, and in return, she bit his arm. Jack instantly let go and screeched with the intense pain. Abbie kept squirming and Jack lost his balance yet again and ended up on the floor. Then Abbie pounced on him and put the weight of her right forearm onto his face. She fisted him in the stomach with her left arm, trying to wind him. The punches got lower and lower but stopped as she could not keep the pressure on his face or control him. Jacks legs were randomly kicking, acting like pendulums as Abbie's position weakened. He started to slip out of what she was doing. Abbie moved her weight and started to fist him in the balls as hard as she could. Then Jack winced at this and grabbed her hair and yanked it, which pulled her head and body back. A scream again from Abbie. A fist hit the side of her face and once again Abbie started to see stars briefly.

Jack spotted a gun and scrambled for it on all fours like a raved animal. Grasping, finally he got hold of it. Immense pain came from his balls due to Abbie kicking him as hard as she could. Pulling his knees up to instinctively protect his chance of procreation and turned on his back with his knees close to himself. He felt another excruciating amount of pain as another full force kick impacted on his balls. Abbie was now standing over Jack in a dominant position. Jack pulled the trigger of the gun and a shot went off. Abbie jumped on Jack and grabbed his arm as she tried to take control of the gun. Jack head-butted Abbie, then her grip weakened briefly. Jack twisted his wrist and pulled the trigger as Abbie's head partially erupted with a red vapour from the right side of it. Abbie stopped fighting, then trying to comprehend what had happened. She felt weak. A sense of euphoria came over her, Abbie knew what had happened although it couldn't have; she was trained and he wasn't. Darkness started to come from the sides, she briefly thought of Philippa. Abbie knew she loved her and would never see her again, she knew this was the end as a tear appeared. Then the darkness enveloped her.

Slowly Abbie fell forward on top of Jack. He pushed her off and moved back as fast as he could point the gun at the female. He shot off another two rounds into her body to make sure she was dead. The bullets hit her body which twitched slightly with the impact. Jack knew she was dead, but wanted to make sure. A tear formed in his eye, then he started to shake at what he had just had to do. The shock was now starting to set in yet again, just like it had so many times over the past days. He looked at the gun in his hand, then tossed it away so that it wasn't part of him anymore, as if to try and disown what he had just done. Jack knew it had been him or her, and he was so regretful at what he had done. He sat looking at the female who only moments earlier had wanted to kill him. He was grateful that it was not him lying dead on the floor. The adrenaline and shock were taking care of the pain from his balls to an extent. The first thing he did was to undo his fly and grab them both, to cradle them in his hand as if to say you're safe now boys! He shook his head and more tears came down his face for his fallen friend Conner.

"I did this for you, Conner," Jack announced, then he glanced up to look in the direction of the heavens.

Chapter 38

The Goober stopped outside the house. Sage sat in the car, preparing herself, thinking about what she was going to say, and how she was going to present the evidence. She took a deep breath, and moved towards the vehicle door. She noticed that it had started raining again.

There was a whoosh as the door opened. Sage froze, contemplating all the different outcomes that could happen. Paranoia was tapping her on the shoulder, as it had done so many times recently. Her stomach was churning like she had eaten a bad meal. She hoped that common sense would prevail with what was going to transpire. She finally climbed out of the vehicle. Then it happened! Her last meal arrived to greet her shoes as she wrenched with fear.

Sage stood in the rain with puke on her shoes. She stared at the house, where she was hoping she would be able to come to some sort of agreement in stopping this nightmare. The Goober had now gone. Sage was alone. Slowly she made her way up the path towards the house. The lights were on and she could see flickering through the windows. Clearly, they did not have blackouts on their windows.

She thought of what had happened to her over the past few days and weeks; she could not remember how long it was. It was just a bloody blur. She arrived at the door and once again paused. Lifting her hand slowly, as if to put off what she had to do. Then she pressed the bell and waited for what seemed a very long time. The Manager's face appeared on the screen to the right of the door. A bemused look flashed across it, as he recognised who it was at his front door.

"What the fuck do you want?" was his blunt response. Then he bristled up, as rage crossed his face.

"I'm here to make a deal," the reply came as Sage tried to out-stare him.

"A deal? What sort of deal?"

"I'd rather not talk over the intercom in the bloody rain," came the blunt response. "I'm getting bloody wet. Do you want to talk or am I leaving?"

The door clicked and then opened. The Manager was standing in front of her with a gun pointing at her.

"Nice to see you, Sage!"

Sage grunted. "You won't need that, I have something to show you," she said. The Manager gestured with the gun for her to enter the house and get out of the rain. They moved slowly, with the Manager moving backwards down a green hallway. The gun was always pointing at Sage.

"First door on the left," he ordered. Sage obliged as she opened the door and the light came on. The room was not large, with white walls and a desk to one side. The noise of the rain hitting the glass made the room seem cold.

"So it's the bitch that has been causing me so much pain in my ass. She has come to make a deal with me! As if I'm going to make a fucking deal with you! I should fucking kill you here and now. But it will stain my carpet, and of course, then there's the explanation I need to come up with – why you're dead in my house. And I'm not going out in the sodding rain. So what's the deal then, Sage?" he sneeringly said to Sage, his eyes not blinking, just staring at her.

"It's simple, Manager, or can I call you Pav?"

Silence came back.

"You see, I have footage of you fucking your secretary, oh, what's she called? Kimberly isn't it?"

"You fucking bitch!" Pav shouted as anger crossed his face along with a flaming red glow. The gun was raised. Sage noticed a slight movement in his trigger finger as he was trying to control himself from pulling it.

"Your wife will get it unless you call it all off. So best not shoot, Pav!" Sage declared in a soft calming tone. She was watching the gun pointed at her, with a slight shake to the end of the barrel.

"What? What do you mean fucking my secretary? No, Noooo, it's not me! How do you know?"

"Mmmmm, that's strange. It's not you? But how do I know?" she rebuffed.

Silence was all she got in return as the Manager moved from his left foot to his right, and back again. Repeating the process to ease the situation.

"Well, she was doing me a favour, Pav. She did some filming of you, well, fucking her. Oh, she said she enjoyed it, by the way," Sage advised the Manager, who stood in front of her trying to comprehend what she had just told him. She could tell that he was trying not to lose his composure as the gun was starting to shake even more.

"Errr, can you point that gun somewhere else please? I don't want to get shot and your wife doesn't want the video, does she?"

"You're bluffing! You're fucking bluffing, I want to see it."

"You wish that I'm bluffing," she replied, then smiled at him knowing internally that he was cracking. She took the stick out and pushed it into the nearest computer port situated on the desk. After a few seconds, the system fired up, and the footage of him and Kimberly screwing came on the screen.

"Okay, okay, that's enough, turn it off," was his response as he lowered the gun, knowing that he was beaten this time.

"So, errr, I'll call it all off. And you'll let me have the footage, no tricks, no copies?"

"Look, you're just going to have to trust me that I won't let everyone see it. I obviously will keep a copy in case you change your mind. Like all good blackmailers. If anything happens to me that even looks remotely suspicious, then it goes out into the public – after your wife of course. Do you understand?"

Silence was all that came from The Manager.

"Okay, Okay, agreed!" he begrudgingly stated. He was already thinking of how he could get hold of the copies and set someone on her ass again, to finally kill them both off.

"Okay, call it in, then I'll give you the copy I have on me now, okay? Oh, and I want transcripts of the conversation you're going to have. Then I'll know you have done it."

The Manager stood silent and still. He had a knot in his stomach with anger at Sage and himself for being such a fool. He pondered his next move. Should he take care of this bitch now, and try and play it out? Or just bend over and take it from behind? He went over to a phone that was on his desk. He placed the gun down and picked the phone up, finally acknowledging to himself that he had been outwitted this time. After a brief conversation with someone and a big sigh from the Manager, he hung up.

"Okay, all sorted, your ass and your boyfriend's ass are off the hook."

"Transcript?" Sage requested, holding out her hand.

"Yeah, yeah, it's over here!" he made his way over to the printer and grabbed the piece of paper that had just printed.

"Thanks, Pav." Knowing that her and Jack had made it to the end, and were still alive. She started reading the paperwork to make sure it was true.

"What's B45 mean?" she asked the manager.

"Oh that's just a code for cancelling an order, that's all. So are you happy now?" Pav responded.

"Yes it seems ok." A smile crossed her face as the full reality of what she had managed to negotiate for them both became clear. A sense of elation started to fill her emotions. Sage knew that there was one thing left to do.

"I just want to thank you for putting me and Jack through this ordeal." She pulled her gun from the back of her jeans, pointed it, then pulled the trigger. The Manager had no time to react. All he could do was open his mouth in disbelief. The bullet entered his chest and went through the heart. He dropped to his knees, fear starting to come over his face as he realised that he was going to die in a few seconds.

"Why?" was all he could say before a second shot to his heart meant lights out. A thudding sounded and the dreadlocked Manager was lying dead in a pool of blood. Sage made her way over to the corpse of The Manager and looked at him lying there. No emotions at all. She had known him for a long time and yet nothing. Only relief that it was all over. Sage went over to the desk and picked his gun up and the data stick and put the gun down the back of her trousers. A quick clean of everything she had touched. It was exit time, and she swiftly made her way to the door. She opened it, took a deep breath in of relief, then left the house.

There was a noise to her left, and before she could react, something hit her head. She started to become lightheaded. Everything went black.

Chapter 39

A pounding headache, nausea and disorientation greeted Sage when she woke up. She felt as though the room was spinning, with a woozy sensation, that made her stomach churn; like she was going to throw up. There was bleariness in her eyes as she tried to focus on what was around her. Where was she? What had happened? She tried to move, but was unable to! She blinked her eyes, and things started to clear from the cloudiness of her eyesight. She was in a white room, one light and one window Sage thought. How did she get here? Her arms could not move, stuck together like being in a vice. She glanced down, blinking several times in dismay at what appeared to be a straightjacket! Same question, same answer. How did she get here? What was she doing here? A noise, a click to her right then silence. The light grey door in the small room opened and in walked the Manager! It looked like he was in a uniform of some sort.

"You're dead! How? What the fuck have you done to me? Where am I? Your wife will be getting the footage of you shagging. Get me the fuck out of this. Help, Help, Help."

"Okay, okay, it's a waste of time, but it is story time for you; my sweet one," he announced, then manhandled her into a wheelchair that he had just pushed in. Sage tried to struggle free but was bound.

"What are you doing, you fucker! Why aren't you dead? I killed you!" she screamed out. She struggled all she could, but Sage's energy was almost gone. Her head was not in the best place, maybe biding her time was a plan she could go for.

"Come on, let's go," the manager stated, then laughed.

He slowly manoeuvred the wheelchair out of the small room and into the corridor. A clinical clean white corridor greeted her.

Noises filled her head, as well as the corridor. It sounded like she was in a zoo, screaming, grunting all sorts of strange mixture of sounds. The smell of piss and disinfectant violated her nostrils, as they tweaked with her scenes. Her head was slowly starting to become more normal, as was her eyesight.

Being pushed unceremoniously down the corridor, she took a glance to the left, then the right. Vague images of people in dark rooms looking at her with deadness in their eyes. After a slow and laborious journey in different directions and a brief ride in an elevator. Finally, they arrived at two large dark wood doors.

The Manager stopped, put the wheelchair brake on, then opened one of the doors. Sage struggled and her wish happened: the wheelchair fell over. She tried to escape but was unable to because of the bounds.

"You look like a worm," he said, then laughed. He slowly walked over to Sage, and towered in front of her in a pose of control. He had the power over her, he was free! Grabbing Sage roughly, he picked her up and dumped her in the chair. Glaring at him as if to say stop it! Then he moved behind Sage and released the brake. Leisurely, she was pushed through the doorway.

Once again, she started to struggle but stopped, as it was to no avail. In the room was a bald man with a moustache and beard. He looked strange, even curious in the clothes that he was wearing. The end of her trip was in front of the man's desk. The Manager systematically put the brake back on, said nothing and left the room, closing the door behind him with a solid low bang.

Sage had a quick look around the room. It had high ceilings, a modern chandelier, a dark red carpet and long matching curtains.

277

"Morning Sage, how are we doing?" announced the man who looked familiar, but Sage could not place his face.

"So yesterday, you told me about what has happened to you recently. To be honest I'm intrigued indeed, to hear what happens next..."

"Where am I? What the fuck are you doing with me? Let me go! Help, help, help." She shouted, then once again struggled in her straightjacket to try and escape but it was pointless and she knew it.

"Sage, Sage please stop that, you will hurt yourself. You know you cannot get out and even if you did where are you going to go to?" he said in a soft warm treacle voice, that had a touch of concern in it.

"Who are you? What do you want?" Sage shouted at the man.

"Oh, Sage, can you not remember from yesterday? I'm Doctor Forsyth, your doctor."

"Forsyth?"

"Yes, Doctor Conner Forsyth," he replied, then smiled softly in her direction.

Then it clicked who he was.

"Conner, Conner... you're Jack's mate, Conner. You're not dead?" Sage excitedly replied.

"You're Jack's mate, so you'll let me go, won't you? Come on, come on, let me go?"

"Where's Jack?"

"Well, Sage, unfortunately I'm not Jack's friend; and I cannot let you go. That's not how it works," he replied, then stood up out of his chair and slowly made his way around to stand in front of Sage. He kept about a metre's distance from her, just in case.

"Now who's Conner, Sage? You were telling me about him yesterday. You and Jack were travelling through time. It was a most interesting story. Do you want to carry on with your story, or have you realized that it was all a delusion?" In a calm and soothing voice, he explained what had happened.

"No, no, no. Where am I? What year is it?" Sage screamed out at the man in front of her.

"Interesting, Sage, that's not what you want to be doing. You're in a hospital, remember? It's February 2019. You have been in this facility for around three weeks. You got picked up by the police and taken to hospital after having a drug-induced psychotic episode. Do you remember attacking that female in the streets?"

"What the hell are you on about?" Sage yelled back at him as the veins in her neck stood out with the rage that was consuming her.

"Why don't you tell me more about your story? What happens next, Sage?" the doctor asked then slowly moved back around his desk and sat back down in his black plush leather chair. He placed both elbows on the table and gazed at Sage in anticipation of what was going to be said.

"Why do I have to tell you? Errr, if you let me out of this jacket, I will tell you everything! Why am I in this jacket anyway?"

"Well, Sage, as I said, you were picked up a few weeks ago with a knife in your hand, trying to stab people. The police were called and they ended up tasering you," he replied, then warmly smiled.

"Piss off, I don't believe you." Sage rebuffed, at the suggestion that she would do that.

"Well, you were pretty high on drugs when you came into the hospital, and then you were moved here. Well, Sage, if you don't want to talk, you may as well go back to your room. I will also review your medication!" he replied, got up from his chair and turned to look out of the window, as though it was an insult towards Sage.

"You know, Sage, you are not doing anyone any favours, especially yourself. You have to come to terms with the fact that you cannot travel through time! That you are not a retired hit woman who came back and takes people to the future, to chop them up for body parts. All whilst being chased by your old friend Mandy who stole your boyfriend. Oh yes, to add to that, stopping terrorist attacks in Paris." He glanced back at Sage over his left shoulder. The glance turned into a long stare. Then he turned back to look out of the window.

Silence came from Sage as she pondered the situation. *Maybe he was right? Maybe she had imagined it all? Jack, Mandy, even Conner and The Manager, were they all a delusion?* She looked around the room again, finally focusing on a photo on the doctor's deck. Strangely it had Jack and Doctor Conner Forsyth. Both wearing a black gown and a square academic cap.

The doctor noticed Sage looking at the picture. "That's when I received my first degree, ahhhh good times." Then smiled at Sage.

That was the point that she realised the she was not delusional at all. This was a game. Someone was playing a sadistic game with her.

She hadn't dreamt it all? She was a time traveller? What about her uncle Callum, was he in her head also? No! It was all real. The running, shooting, when she jumped in the river with Jack. Mandy, their friendship, growing up together. Sage was confused by this conversation. It all seemed so real, and it was. Deep down, she knew it was.

Sage heard a brief noise, which she thought was a snigger, escape from the doctors lips.

"Were you laughing?"

"No, why would I? That would be unprofessional, I'm concerned about you Sage."

Silence came back from Sage, she was confused. "I want to go back to my room, cell, or whatever you want to call it?" Sage demanded.

The doctor turned and smiled, and made a brief phone call. About thirty seconds later, the same man that had brought Sage into the room came and started to move Sage out of the office. She was leaving the office with her mind confused and in turmoil at what had been presented to her. The idea that she had been drugged up and was running around with a knife, trying to kill people. She thought about what he had said, that she had got to the point where Mandy had been killed, jumping back in time and the terrorists in Paris! It was all so confusing. But it was all real, wasn't it?

The noises of the zoo or wherever it was, was deafening. Sage was distraught. Her heart was heavy with sadness. Had she lost her freedom? She had a life; well she thought she had one outside. But it seemed that it was all a dream, delusion, well most of it was, she suspected. But she had no evidence to state otherwise.

The journey was a blur to Sage. They went down various corridors, although this time they did not use the lift. Finally they came to a door that was open. She was pushed in, and the Manager man-handled onto the bed. He came close and kissed Sage on the cheek.

"I will be back with some Rohypnol, to relax you again. Then we can have some fun together." He slowly got up with a grin from ear to ear. Sage had a bad feeling and deep down knew what was going to happen. Once again, she started to struggle but realised that it was a waste of time.

"Just wait there for me!" he jokingly said, then left. How long for? She did not know. Alarm bells were ringing in her head; she needed to get out of this place before he assaulted her. She looked around the cell for something that she could use to get herself out or as a weapon, but there was nothing.

Moments later, the door opened and the man walked back in carrying a newspaper. Sage looked at him with disdain and started to prepare herself mentally for what was going to happen. He looked at her and smiled, then brought both hands up and rolled his eyes.

"Sorry I forgot the pills, silly me!" Turning he threw the newspaper to the bottom of the bed, then left the room and closed the door behind him.

She kicked her legs over the side of the bed, struggling to sit up; she took a moment. She remembered that once she was at a party and there was a discussion about how to escape from a straightjacket. *Wow, it would have been a good idea to listen to that conversation,* she thought. But she was too busy enjoying herself at the time. She closed her eyes and tried to mentally transport herself back to the event. It was vague at first with bits missing, but it started to slowly come back and fall in place.

She remembered that the first thing to do was to create some space inside the straitjacket for your arms, when it's been tied up, although she did not do that part as she was unconscious. Sage decided that rather than randomly struggling, she tried to move around it in a controlled way. She breathed in as much as she could to expand her body and pushed with her arms. Then she breathed out to relax her core, and noticed that the fabric was much looser now. Then she slowly started to lift her elbows up, which appeared to be working. After some twisting and wiggling, she got one arm to her shoulder; then with some neck pain over her head. *Freedom!* she thought, then brought the first buckle to her mouth and started to loosen her arms. Now her hands were free. Then it was the back of the jacket, starting to fumble with the various buckles. Finally, it was loose enough for her to once again start wiggling, contorting herself in all types of positions. It started to slowly fall to the floor. "Three, two, one and liberty." A mumble came out of her mouth.

She glanced at the door, then grabbing the newspaper she rolled it up and bent it in half, kicked the straitjacket to the hinge side of the door. She moved to the blind side of the door and backed up, waiting for the man to come in.

A fumble started as the key was put in the door, then a click. It opened and he walked in. Sage swung her arm and weapon around to strike the man's face, dazing him. He brought his arms up to protect himself. Shock sank in, as he started to realise what was happening. Instinctively, he pressed the button on his panic alarm. *Good, help is on the way*, he thought, whilst protecting himself from the barrage of blows to his head and body.

When Sage realised that the panic alarm had gone off, she stopped. What was she going to do now? She had not thought that far into the future. If she was honest, this was going too easy.

The Manager let his guard down, Sage noticed this and gave a swift uppercut to the left side of his face and sealed the deal. Her guard-come-rapist was out for the count. Taking his radio and a set of keys, she exited the room.

Once again, she was in the corridor and on the run, free of the straitjacket, if not physically free of the building. She took a right then stopped, second-guessing herself, then turned back down the corridor. She passed various cells with all sorts of people in them. She got to the end and a white steel door with a square wire mesh glassed window in it. She peered through it – nothing. Deciding that that is the way she was going to go. She tried one, two, and three keys then the lock clicked. She pushed the steel handle down and then another alarm went off. *This is not good at all,* she thought, when she had gone through the door opening. She was now in a large room with windows at the top of the wall. No light, just darkness could be seen through them. There was a noise to her left; she stopped, then looked. A giant of a man or monster sat looking at her. Instinctively she slowly moved back. Then the thing started to rise to its feet. She looked at it in awe. It must be around 220 centimetres tall. Her speed picked up as she exited the room, and the thing quickly made its way towards the door. There was a click and she was outside with the steel door between her and whatever it was. The alarm had stopped now that the door was locked, except whatever it was, was banging on the door in anger.

She came up with a new plan; she started making her way back towards her cell. Then her cell door flung open, and out walked the male nurse, Manager or whatever he was. He looked unsteady on his feet but clearly wanted a piece of Sage. He raised his fists and took a deep breath in preparation for a fight. She started to run towards the man then jumped in the air with both feet first. The impact to the man's chest was epic and Sage felt it through her legs. The man went backwards and ploughed into the wall. They both ended up on the ground but only Sage stirred. She moved away from the man as a protective strategy, then got up on her feet. Momentarily, she stopped as she noticed blood coming out from under the body.

Should I check he's okay? No fuck him, she thought. She quickly moved down the corridor to a dead end! *Left or right?* She took a guess and went left and to some stairs. Down one, two flights and out into another corridor. The alarm was going but why was there no guards?

Quickly making her way down the corridor to what looked like the doors she had been taken through to see Doctor Forsyth earlier on. Sage grabbed the handle and momentarily stopped. Was this the right move... revenge to give him a piece of her mind, to make him pay? Valid reasons to confront him, but the clock was ticking; and she knew deep down that it was the wrong thing to do. Escape was the option she should be taking. But she had to see him. She just had to do this. Sage slowly opened the door and entered. Her heart was pounding. What was she going to find? Silence and anticipation hit her. Panic and paranoia were also playing games with her mind and emotions. She paused and slowly scanned the room. *What's he doing here?* She thought unable to say anything. Stopping in her tracks. "Jack, Jack what are you doing? Are you in on this? Why are you sat in that chair?"

Both elbows were lent on the table. Then he pushed himself off and started to spin in the swivel chair "I'm here to help you Sage. Oh god that makes me feel sick," Then stopped himself from spinning and smiled at Sage.

Silence was all Sage could return. Confusion, apprehension then a cold feeling started to envelop her. She glanced back at the open door she had just come in through. *Shall I run or stay?* She thought whilst slowly moved to close it and give them some privacy. This also gave Sage time to consider what was happening.

"So Jack what are you doing here?"

"It's a long story Sage," he responded, then gazed at the vague look of shock on her face. Jack smiled at Sage, as he bent down to get something from a black backpack...

Manufactured by Amazon.com.au
Sydney, New South Wales, Australia

13875438R00176